THE
FORGOTTEN LEGION

Ben Kane was born in Kenya and raised there and in Ireland. He studied veterinary medicine at University College Dublin but after that he travelled the world extensively, indulging his passion for ancient history. He now lives in North Somerset with his family. For more information visit www.benkane.net.

Praise for Ben Kane

'Bloody, fast-paced, thrilling . . . a masterful debut that should not be missed' James Rollins, author of *The Last Oracle*

'I thoroughly enjoyed *The Forgotten Legion* – so much so that I stayed up until 2 a.m. to finish it' Manda Scott, author of the 'Boudica' novels

'The Forgotten Legion marches again . . . *The Silver Eagle* is an utterly engrossing combination of historical fact and believable fiction that draws the reader in and holds his interest to the last page' Douglas Jackson, author of *Caligula*

THE
FORGOTTEN LEGION

BEN KANE

arrow books

Reissued by Arrow Books 2011

4 6 8 10 9 7 5 3

First published in Great Britain in 2008 by Preface Publishing
This paperback edition first published in 2009
Arrow Books
20 Vauxhall Bridge Road,
London SW1V 2SV

www.randomhouse.co.uk

Addresses for companies within The Random House Group Limited can be
found at:
www.randomhouse.co.uk/offices.htm

The Random House Group Limited Reg. No. 954009

A CIP catalogue record for this book is available from the British Library

ISBN 978 0 09955 6282

The Random House Group Limited supports The Forest Stewardship
Council (FSC). the leading international forest certification organisation. All
our titles that are printed on Greenpeace approved FSC certified paper carry
the FSC logo. Our paper procurement policy can be found at
www.randomhouse.co.uk/environment

Mixed Sources
Product group from well-managed
forests and other controlled sources
www.fsc.org Cert no. TT-COC-002139
© 1996 Forest Stewardship Council
FSC

Typeset in Fournier MT by Palimpsest Book Production Limited,
Grangemouth, Stirlingshire

Printed in the UK by CPI Bookmarque, Croydon, CR0 4TD

To C.V. and P.v.G., with thanks.

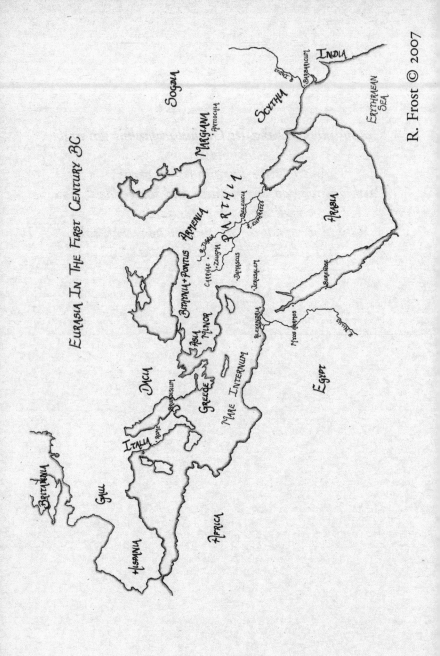

EURASIA IN THE FIRST CENTURY BC

R. Frost © 2007

BRITANNIA

GAUL

HISPANIA

ITALIA
Rome
Brundisium

DACIA

GREECE

MARE INTERNUM

AFRICA

ASIA MINOR

BITHYNIA + PONTUS

ARMENIA

Caesarea
Zeugma

Damascus
Jerusalem
Alexandria

EGYPT

Nile R.

Myos Hormos
Berenice

MARGIANA

SOGDIA

Antiochia

PARTHIA

EUPHRATES
Seleucia

SCYTHIA

Indus R.

INDIA
Barygaza

ARABIA

ERYTHRAEAN
SEA

Crassus at the Euphrates lost his eagles, his son and
his soldiers,
And was the last himself to perish.
'Parthian, why do you rejoice?' said the goddess. 'You
shall return the standards,
While there shall be an avenger who shall take
vengeance for the death of Crassus.'

Ovid, *Fasti*

In his *Natural History* narrative, Pliny the Elder described how Roman survivors of the battle of Carrhae in 53 BC were sent to Margiana.

Situated in modern-day Turkmenistan, this area is more than fifteen hundred miles from where the men were taken captive. Used as border guards, the ten thousand legionaries would have journeyed farther east than most Romans in history.

But their story does not end there.

In 36 BC, the Chinese historian Ban Gu recorded that soldiers in the army of Jzh-jzh, a Hun warlord and ruler of a city on the Silk Road, fought in a 'fish-scale formation'. The term used to describe their formation is unique in Chinese literature and many historians assert that it refers to a shield wall. At that time only the Macedonians and Romans fought in such a way. Greek military training would need to have endured in the area for more than a century to influence those men. Interestingly this battle took place only seventeen years after Carrhae and less than five hundred miles from the border of Margiana.

Further to the east, in China, lies the modern settlement of Liqian. The origins of its name are uncertain, but scholars consider it to have been founded between 79 BC and AD 5 under the name of Li-jien, meaning 'Rome' in ancient Chinese. An unusually large number of its present-day inhabitants have Caucasian features - blond hair, hooked *noses and green eyes. DNA samples are currently being studied by a local university to see if these people are the descendants of the ten thousand legionaries who marched east from Carrhae and into history.*

The Forgotten Legion.

Prologue

Rome, 70 BC

It was *hora undecima*, the eleventh hour, and the sprawling city was bathed by the red glow of sunset. A rare breeze moved air between the densely packed buildings, passing relief from the stifling summer heat. Men emerged from their houses and flats to finish the day's business, chat outside shops and stand drinking at open-fronted street taverns. The eager cries of merchants competed for the attention of passers-by while children played on doorsteps under the watchful eyes of their mothers. From somewhere in the centre, near the Forum, came the rhythmic sound of chanting in a temple.

This was a sociable and safe hour, but shade was already lengthening in the alleyways and small court-yards. Sunlight fell away from the tall stone columns and statues of the gods, returning the streets to a darker and less friendly grey colour. The seven hills that formed Rome's heart would be the last parts to remain lit, until darkness claimed the capital once more.

Despite the time, the Forum Romanum was still thronged with people. Flanked by temples and the Senate, the *basilicae*, the huge covered markets, were filled with shopkeepers, soothsayers, lawyers and scribes plying their trade from little stalls. It was late in the day, but someone might want a will drawn up, a prophecy made, a writ issued against an enemy. Mobile vendors made circuits of the area, trying to sell fruit juices that had been warm for hours. Politicians who had been working late in the Senate hurried outside, only stopping to talk if an ally's eyes could not be avoided. Seeing their masters, groups of slaves jumped up from board games scratched on to the steps. Trying to avoid the blisters on their sunburnt shoulders, they swiftly lifted their litters and moved off.

A handful of determined beggars remained on the temple steps, hoping for alms. Several were crippled but proud veterans of the legions, the invincible army which had provided the Republic's wealth and status. They wore tattered remnants of uniform – mail shirts more rust than rings of iron, brown tunics held together by patches. For a copper coin they would recount their martial stories – the blood shed, limbs lost, comrades buried in foreign lands.

All for the glory of Rome.

Despite dwindling light, the Forum Boarium, where beasts were traded, was also full of citizens. Unsold cattle bellowed with thirst after a day in constant sunshine. Sheep and goats huddled together, terrified by the smell of blood from the butchers' blocks only a few steps away. Their owners, small farmers from the surrounding countryside, prepared to drive them to night pasture beyond the walls. On the Forum Olitorium too, stalls selling foodstuffs were bustling with customers. Ripe melons, peaches and plums added their aromas to spices from the Orient, fresh fish and what remained of the day's bread. Keen to sell all their fruit and vegetables, vendors offered bargains to anyone who caught their eye. Plebeian women gossiped as they finished their shopping and went into shrines to offer a swift prayer. Slaves who had been sent to buy ingredients for last-minute feasts cursed as the light disappeared from the sky.

But away from these open spaces, anyone who was still out scuttled faster to reach the safety of their houses. No decent Roman wanted to be outside after sunset, especially in the dismal alleyways between the *insulae*, the cramped blocks of flats in which most citizens lived. By night the unlit streets were populated by thieves and murderers.

Chapter I: Tarquinius

Northern Italy, 70 BC

The raven hopped on to the dead lamb's head and stared at Tarquinius. He was still more than fifty paces away. It croaked scornfully and pecked at the staring eyeball with its powerful beak. The lamb was no more than three days old, its meagre flesh already devoured by mountain wolves.

Tarquinius stooped, picked up a small rock and fitted it to his sling. A slight figure with blond hair, he wore a loose thigh-length tunic, belted at the waist. Sturdy sandals clad his feet.

'Spare the bird. He did not kill the lamb.' Olenus Aesar adjusted his worn leather hat, flattening the blunt peak. 'Corvus is only taking what remains.'

'I don't like it eating the eyes.' Preparing to release, Tarquinius swung the hide strap in a slow circle.

The old man fell silent, shielding his eyes from the sun. He spent a long time gazing at the broad wingtips of buzzards hanging on the warm thermals and the clouds further above.

Tarquinius watched intently, holding back the stone. Since the soothsayer had picked him as a student years before, the young Etruscan had learned to pay attention to everything he said and did.

Olenus shrugged bony shoulders under his rough woollen cloak. 'Not a good day to kill a sacred bird.'

'Why not?' With a sigh, he let the sling drop to his side. 'What is it now?'

'Go right ahead, boy.' Olenus smiled, infuriating Tarquinius. 'Do what you want.' He waved expansively at the raven. 'Your path is your own.'

'I am not a boy.' Tarquinius scowled and let the rock fall. 'I'm twenty-five!'

He scowled briefly, then let out a piercing whistle and gestured with one arm. A black and white dog lying close by sprinted off in a wide arc up the steep hillside, eyes fixed on a group of sheep and goats nibbling short grass far above. They spotted him immediately and began moving further up.

The raven finished its meal and flapped off.

Tarquinius gazed after it balefully. 'Why shouldn't I have killed that damn bird?'

'We are standing above what was the temple of Tinia. The most powerful of our gods . . .' Olenus paused for effect.

Looking down, Tarquinius noticed a red clay tile protruding from the soil.

'And the number of buzzards above is twelve.'

Tarquinius' eyes searched the sky, counting. 'Why do you always speak in riddles?'

Olenus tapped his *lituus*, a small crooked staff, on the broken tile. 'Not the first time today, is it?'

'I know twelve is our people's sacred number, but . . .' Tarquinius watched the dog, which had begun herding the flock towards them as he wished. 'What has that got to do with the raven?'

'That lamb was the twelfth this morning.'

Tarquinius did a quick calculation. 'But I didn't tell you about the one in the gully earlier,' he said with amazement.

'And Corvus wanted to feed right where sacrifices used to take place,' the haruspex added enigmatically. 'Best leave him in peace, eh?'

Tarquinius frowned, frustrated that he had not noticed the buzzards first and made the link with the location. He had been too busy thinking about killing wolves.

It was time to hunt some down. Rufus Caelius, his evil-tempered master, tolerated these excursions only because he could question Tarquinius afterwards about Olenus and the state of his flocks. The noble would be displeased to hear about further losses and Tarquinius was already dreading his return to the *latifundium*, Caelius' huge estate at the foot of the mountain.

'How did you know about the lamb in the gully?'

'What have I spent all these years teaching you? Observe everything!' Olenus turned around, seeing what was no longer there. 'This was the centre of the mighty city of Falerii. Tarchun, the founder of Etruria, marked out its sacred borders with a bronze plough, over a mile from here. Four hundred years ago, where we are standing would have been thronged with Etruscan people going about their daily business.'

Tarquinius tried to imagine the scene as the haruspex had described it so many times – the magnificent buildings and temples dedicated to the Vestal Virgins, the wide streets paved with lava blocks. He pictured the cheering crowds at boxing contests, racing and gladiator fights. Nobles presenting wreaths to victorious contestants, presiding over banquets in great feasting halls.

His eyes cleared. All that remained of Falerii, one of the jewels of Etruria, were a few fallen pillars and innumerable pieces of broken tile. The depth of its decline was brought home to him all over again. Long association with the haruspex meant that his people's history was ever-painful. 'They took our whole way of life, didn't they?' Tarquinius spat angrily. 'Roman civilisation has completely copied the Etruscan.'

'Right down to the trumpets announcing the start of ceremonies and battle manoeuvres,' Olenus added wryly. 'They stole it all. After destroying us.'

'Sons of whores! What gives them the right?'

'It was pre-ordained in the heavens, Tarquinius. You know all this.' Olenus stared at the young man before taking in the view that fell away to the east and south. A lake at the bottom of the mountain glistened, reflecting the sun's rays with blinding intensity. 'Here we are in the heartland of ancient Etruria.' Olenus smiled. 'Lake Vadimon at our feet, the foundations of the sacred city below.'

'We are almost the last pure-bred Etruscans on earth,' said Tarquinius bitterly. Defeated and then assimilated by the Romans, few families had continued to marry only others of their kind. His had. And generation after generation, the ancient secrets and rituals had been handed from one haruspex to another. Olenus was one of a long line stretching back to the heyday of Etruscan power.

'It was our destiny to be conquered,' Olenus replied. 'Remember that when the foundation stone of the temple was laid many centuries ago . . .'

'A bleeding head was found in the soil.'

'My predecessor, Calenus Olenus Aesar, stated it foretold that the people would rule all of Italy.'

'And he was wrong. Look at us now!' cried Tarquinius. 'Little better than slaves.' There were almost no Etruscans left with any political power or influence. Instead they were poor farmers, or like Tarquinius and his family, workers on large estates.

'Calenus was the best haruspex in our history. He could read the liver like no other!' Olenus waved his gnarled hands excitedly. 'That man knew what the Etruscans could not – or would not – understand at the time. Our cities never unified and so when Rome grew powerful enough, they were defeated one by one. Although it took over a hundred and fifty years, Calenus' prediction proved correct.'

'He meant those who crushed us.'

Olenus nodded.

'Bastard Romans.' Tarquinius flung a stone after the raven, now long gone.

Little did he know the haruspex secretly admired his speed and power. The rock flew fast enough to kill any man it struck.

'A hard thing to accept, even for me,' sighed Olenus.

'Especially the way they lord over us.' The young Etruscan swigged from a leather water bag and passed it to his mentor. 'Where is the cave from here?'

'Not far.' The haruspex drank deeply. 'Today is not the day, however.'

'You've dragged me all the way up here for nothing? I thought you were going to show me the liver and sword!'

'I was,' replied Olenus mildly. The old man turned and began to walk downhill, humming as he used the *lituus* to steady himself. 'But the omens are not good today. It would be best if you return to the *latifundium*.'

It had been eight years since he first heard of the *gladius* of Tarquin, the last Etruscan king of Rome and the bronze liver, one of only a few such templates for soothsayers to learn their art. Tarquinius was chafing to see the ancient metal artefact. It had been the subject of so many lessons, but he knew better than to argue with Olenus and a few more days would make little difference. He hitched his pack higher, checking that all the sheep and goats had come down.

'I need a trip up here with my bow anyway. Spend a few days killing wolves.' Tarquinius affected a nonchalant tone. 'You can't let the bastards think that they can get away with it.'

Olenus grunted in reply.

Tarquinius rolled his eyes with frustration. He wouldn't get to see the liver until the haruspex was good and ready. Whistling the dog to heel, he followed Olenus down the narrow track.

Tarquinius left the haruspex sleeping in the little hut halfway down the mountain, the dog curled up by his feet, wood crackling gently in the fireplace. Even though it was a balmy summer night, Olenus' bones had felt the chill.

The young man picked his way along well-used paths through the sprawling fields, olive groves and vineyards that surrounded Caelius' enormous villa. When he finally reached it, the thick limestone walls were still warm from the sun.

The slaves' miserable shacks and the simple farm buildings housing indentured workers were situated to the rear of the main complex. He reached these quarters without seeing a soul. Most people rose at dawn and went to bed by sunset, making escape and return in darkness relatively easy.

Tarquinius paused at the entrance to the small courtyard and peered into the gloom, seeing nothing.

A voice broke the silence.

'Where have you been all day?'

'Who's there?' Tarquinius hissed.

'Lucky the foreman's asleep. You'd get a beating otherwise!'

He relaxed. 'Olenus was teaching me about our ancestors, Father. That's far more important than digging in the fields.'

'Why bother?' A short, fat man wove into view, clutching an amphora. 'We Etruscans are finished. The butcher Sulla made sure of that.'

Tarquinius sighed. This was an old argument. Sensing their chance to regain some autonomy, many of the remaining Etruscan families and clans had joined Marius' forces in the civil war nearly two decades previously. It had been a calculated gamble that had gone spectacularly wrong. Thousands of their people had died. 'Marius lost. So did we,' he whispered. 'It doesn't mean that the ancient ways need to be forgotten.'

'It was the last opportunity for us to rise up and reclaim ancient glory!'

'You're drunk. Again.'

'At least I did a full day's work,' his father replied. 'You just follow that eccentric fool, listening to ramblings and lies.'

Tarquinius lowered his voice. 'They're not lies! Olenus teaches me secret rituals and knowledge. Someone has to remember. Before it is all forgotten.'

'Do what you will. The Republic cannot be stopped now.' Sergius noisily slurped some wine. 'Nothing can stop its damned legions.'

'Go back to bed.'

His father stared at the shrine in the far corner of the courtyard. It was where he spent his sober moments. All its oil lamps had gone out. 'Even our gods have abandoned us,' he muttered.

Tarquinius pushed the unresisting figure towards the family's small, damp cell. Wine had reduced the once proud warrior to a lonely, morose drunkard. Just a few years previously his father had been secretly teaching him to use weapons. Tarquinius was now equally proficient with a *gladius* or an Etruscan battleaxe.

With a groan, Sergius collapsed on to the straw mattress he shared with Fulvia, Tarquinius' mother.

11

Instantly he began to snore. The young man lay down on the other side of the room and listened to the loud noise. Tarquinius was worried about his father: at the rate Sergius was drinking, he would not live for more than a few years.

It was a long time before Tarquinius slept, and then he dreamt vividly.

He was watching Olenus sacrifice a lamb in an unfamiliar cave, cutting its belly open to read the entrails. Looking round the dark space, he could see no sign of the bronze liver or sword that Olenus had spoken about so many times.

The old man's face changed as he scanned the animal's organs. Tarquinius called out, but could not get Olenus' attention. His mentor seemed totally unaware of him, instead fearfully watching the mouth of the cave.

It was impossible to see what was scaring Olenus so much. The haruspex had placed the dark red liver on a slab of basalt and was studying it intently. Every so often he would pause and gaze outside, his fear apparently lessening each time. After what seemed an age, Olenus nodded happily and sat back against the wall, waiting.

Despite his mentor's apparent contentment, Tarquinius now felt a strong sense of impending dread which intensified until it was unbearable.

He ran to the entrance.

Peering down a steep mountain slope, he saw Caelius ascending with ten legionaries, each face fixed and grim. All the men held drawn swords. In front of them ran a pack of large hunting dogs.

'Run, Olenus! Run!' Tarquinius cried.

At last the soothsayer turned with a look of recognition. 'Run?' He cackled. 'I'd break my neck out there.'

'Soldiers are coming to kill you! Caelius is guiding them.'

Olenus' eyes held no trace of fear.

'You must flee. Now!'

'It is my time, Tarquinius. I am going to join our ancestors. You are the last haruspex.'

'Me?' Tarquinius was shocked. Through all the years of teaching, it had never occurred to him that he was being groomed to succeed the old man.

Olenus nodded gravely.

'The liver and sword?'

'You have them both already.'

'No! I don't!' Tarquinius gesticulated frantically.

Again Olenus seemed not to hear. He stood up and began walking towards the figures at the mouth of the cave.

Tarquinius felt somebody grab his arm. The cave receded slowly from view as he swam into consciousness. He was desperate to know what had happened to Olenus, but could see no more. The young Etruscan woke with a start. His mother was standing over the bed, looking concerned.

'Tarquinius?'

'It was nothing,' he muttered, his heart racing. 'Go back to sleep, Mother. You need to rest.'

'Your shouts woke me,' she answered reproachfully. 'Father would have woken too, if he wasn't drunk.'

Tarquinius' stomach clenched. Olenus had always said never to mention anything he taught. 'What was I saying?'

'Hard to make out. Something about Olenus and a bronze liver. The last of those was lost years ago.' Fulvia frowned. 'Has the old rascal laid hands on one?'

'He's not said a thing,' Tarquinius replied smoothly. 'Go back to bed. You have to be up at dawn.'

He helped Fulvia across the room, wincing at her stooped back and at how much effort it took to climb into the low cot. Long years of hard labour had crippled his mother's body.

'My strong, clever Arun.' Fulvia used the sacred term for youngest son. 'You are destined for greatness. I feel it in my bones.'

'Hush now.' Tarquinius glanced around uneasily. Caelius did not like ancient, non-Roman terms being used. 'Get some sleep.'

But Fulvia was undeterred. 'I've known it since I first saw your birthmark – the same one Tarchun bore. We could not have given you any other name but Tarquinius.'

He rubbed self-consciously at the red triangular shape on the side of his neck. It was something he had only seen occasionally in the reflection of a pool and the haruspex often commented on it.

'It was no surprise to me when Olenus took an interest in you. Teaching sacred rituals, pushing you to learn languages from the foreign slaves.' She swelled with pride. 'I kept telling your father. Once upon a time he listened. But since your brother was killed fighting Sulla, he is only interested in his next jug of wine.'

Tarquinius considered the sleeping figure sadly. 'He was once proud to be a warrior of the Rasenna.'

'Deep down he'll always be an Etruscan,' his mother whispered. 'Like you.'

'There are still many reasons to be proud of our race.' He kissed Fulvia's brow and she smiled, closing tired eyes.

The art of haruspicy is alive, Mother. The Etruscans will not be forgotten. But he did not say it out loud. While Sergius talked to no one, Fulvia was prone to gossiping. It was vital that Caelius did not know the truth about his trips to see Olenus.

Tarquinius clambered into his own bed. By the time he fell asleep, the sky was beginning to pale.

There was little chance to hunt wolves or visit Olenus in the days that followed. It was nearly harvest time, the estate's busiest time of year. The workload for slaves and indentured families like those of Tarquinius had increased fourfold.

Rufus Caelius had returned from Rome to supervise the important task. Most had supposed his trip had been to raise capital to bolster his ailing finances. The redhead was a typical example of the Roman noble class: good at warfare, poor at commerce. Ten years earlier, when the price of grain had begun to plummet due to a large increase in imports from Sicily and Egypt, Caelius had failed to spot the trend. While shrewder neighbours converted entire *latifundia* to growing more lucrative grapes and olives, the bullish ex-staff officer had persisted with wheat. In only a decade, the profitable estate had been brought to the edge of ruin.

It had not taken long for the cheap foreign crops to bankrupt thousands of small farmers throughout Italy,

Tarquinius' family among them. Big landowners capitalised on the opportunity, increasing their properties' sizes at others' expense. New workers were required quickly and the gap was filled by thousands of slaves, the human prizes of Rome's conquests.

Although they were citizens, Sergius and his family were fortunate enough to get low-paid contract work from Caelius. At least they were paid. Thanks to the slave population, others were not so lucky and cities swelled immeasurably from the influx of starving peasants. Even more grain was thus required for the *congiaria*, the free distributions to the poor.

If Caelius had been to see moneylenders in the capital, it seemed he had been successful. The noble was in excellent humour organising work parties in the courtyard each morning. Tarquinius was picked for the harvest, as he had been every summer since arriving on the estate eight years previously.

Huge areas of ripe oats and wheat had to be cut and stacked. It was a backbreaking task, lasting from dawn till dusk for a week or more. Already tanned from days on the mountainside, Tarquinius' skin was burnt a deep mahogany colour. To the delight of some female slaves, his long hair grew even blonder. Its length helped conceal the birthmark.

Fulvia was now too infirm for physical labour and ferried food and drink to the fields with the older women. Caelius had tried before to make the men toil all day without pause, but too many had collapsed from dehydration in the hot summer two years before. One had even died. The noble realised a short daily break was cheaper than dead labourers.

By the fourth day, the sun was beating down with a malicious intensity. Fulvia's arrival in the early afternoon with a mule-drawn cart full of water, bread and root vegetables was most welcome. She parked it in the shade of a large tree and everyone crowded round.

'I've got a bit of cheese here,' Fulvia whispered, patting a cloth-covered package by her side.

Tarquinius winked in reply.

The whole group was stripped down to loincloths and sandals, short-handled scythes shoved into the leather belts that Caelius provided. To prevent attempts at escape, the slaves among them wore heavy iron manacles round their ankles. Like any big landowner's, Caelius' workers were from all over the Mediterranean. Judaeans, Spaniards and Greeks sweated beside Nubians and Egyptians. Conversation was limited as the famished men ate, and soon each basket of food was empty. Only a few crumbs had fallen for the sparrows pecking hopefully round their feet.

Maurus, one of the Greek slaves, chewed the last of his bread wistfully. 'What I'd give for a piece of meat! Maybe we'll get some at the Vinalia Rustica.'

'Caelius is too stingy! And he's got real money worries at the moment,' snorted Dexter, the *vilicus*, a tough ex-legionary from the south. 'But I'd say Olenus eats plenty, eh?'

The others glanced curiously at Tarquinius, whose trips to see the old man were common knowledge.

'Bet that sorcerer feeds him lamb all the time!' said one.

'Is that why you go up there?' There was an envious tinge to Maurus' dark-skinned features.

17

'No. It's so I can't hear your whining.'

There was a burst of laughter, scaring the birds into flight.

The foreman squinted at Tarquinius, a strange look in his eyes. 'You do spend a lot of time on the mountain. What's the attraction?'

'He wants to escape this damn heat!' remarked Sulinus, a thickset slave.

There was a general murmur of agreement. It was fearsomely hot. The uncut wheat shimmered and swayed, baking in the sun.

Tarquinius remained silent, letting the drone of cicadas fill the air.

'So?' Dexter rubbed absentmindedly at an old scar.

'So what?' Alarmed at the foreman's sudden interest, Tarquinius feigned surprise.

'Does that crazy soothsayer eat meat every day?'

'Only if he finds a dead lamb or kid.' Tarquinius' mouth watered. He had eaten freshly roasted meat with Olenus countless times. 'Not otherwise. The master wouldn't allow it.'

'The master!' Dexter scoffed. 'Caelius hasn't a bloody clue how many sheep and goats are up there. He's often said that eight lambs for every ten ewes per year is enough.'

'That's a poor return,' added Maurus spitefully.

'Olenus is the only one who will herd on the peak.' Sulinus made the sign against evil. 'Too many spirits and wild beasts around those cities of the dead.'

Fear filled the men's eyes.

Streets of tombs in the graveyards near the ruins of

Falerii were a powerful reminder of the area's history and few on the *latifundium* dared go near them, even in daylight. The whole mountain had a name for freak storms, packs of wolves and harsh weather, a place where the Etruscan gods still lingered.

'That's why Caelius leaves him be.' Tarquinius wanted to change the focus of conversation, the night-mare fresh in his mind. 'This section is nearly finished.' He pointed at the field. 'We could have it stacked by sunset.'

Dexter was surprised. Normally it took threats to get the men moving after a break. He sank another beaker of water. 'Back to work, boys. Don't make me use this,' he growled, tapping the whip on his belt.

The workers trudged across short stubble towards the remaining wheat, some casting resentful glances at Tarquinius. But none dared to resist the overseer's iron will. Or his whip. Dexter had been hired to keep every-one in line and he did so with brutal force.

Fulvia waited until the others had walked some distance before she handed over the cloth bundle with a sly smile.

'My thanks, Mother.' He planted a kiss on her brow.

'The gods bless you,' Fulvia said proudly.

'Dexter?' The moment his mother had turned the cart, Tarquinius hurried after the burly *vilicus*. 'Some tasty goat's cheese for you.'

'Show it here!' Dexter reached out with eager hands. He tasted a piece and smiled. 'My compliments to Fulvia. Where did she get this?'

'She has her ways.' Everyone knew kitchen workers

were able to obtain foods that others could only dream of. 'I was hoping . . .'

'To finish early today?' Dexter guffawed. 'That'd take more than a lump of cheese. Caelius would have my balls if he caught you skiving again.'

'It's not that.' Tarquinius was risking a beating by speaking out of turn, but the look he had seen on Dexter's face was worrying him. 'I was hoping you might tell me if the master was planning anything. For Olenus.'

Dexter's eyes narrowed.

The haruspex had long existed on the periphery of estate life, tolerated only because of his skills with animals and his isolated lifestyle. Like most Romans, Caelius strongly disapproved of anyone practising ancient Etruscan rituals and Dexter was no different.

Tarquinius sensed the foreman knew something.

Neither spoke for several moments.

'Get me some meat and I'll consider it,' Dexter replied. 'Now get back to work.'

Tarquinius did as he was told. As soon as the wheat was harvested, he would offer to hunt some wolves. Knowing that predators had been decimating flocks on the lower slopes this summer, Caelius might just let him off before the olives and grapes were taken in.

And once up the mountain, he could easily kill a lamb for Dexter. It was a gamble whether the overseer would keep his side of the bargain, but he had no other way of discovering what Caelius might have planned. After years of Olenus' tutoring, Tarquinius' senses were extremely sharp. His dream had been followed by

Dexter's interrogation and he felt sure something was about to happen to the haruspex.

'Put some energy into it!' Dexter cracked his whip. 'You're the one who wanted to get back to work early.'

Tarquinius took hold of a bundle of wheat in his left hand, holding it steady for the scythe. In one smooth movement, he stooped and cut the ripe stalks close to the ground, placed them behind him, turned back and grabbed another bunch. On either side, the men were performing the same rhythmic movement, moving steadily forward into the crop. It was a task Etruscans had been doing here at harvest time for hundreds of years and the knowledge calmed Tarquinius as he worked, imagining his ancestors before the Roman invaders had come.

Chapter II: Velvinna

Rome, 70 BC

Not far from the Forum, seven young nobles picked their way along a dusty side street. Expensive white togas were stained with wine, the result of a prolonged drinking bout. Half the taverns across the seven hills had been visited that day. The men talked in loud, arrogant tones, uncaring who might hear. Slaves armed with cudgels and knives paced behind, torches in hand.

There was a muted curse as a burly figure at the rear stumbled and fell against the wall of a house. He doubled over and was sick, narrowly missing his leather sandals.

'Come on!' A thin, clean-shaven man with an aquiline nose and short haircut barked with amusement. 'We have hours more drinking to do!'

A shutter banged open above. 'Do that somewhere else, you bastard!'

Wiping vomit from his lips, the big noble stared up into the darkness. 'I am an equestrian of the Republic.

Puke where I want. Now piss off unless you want a good beating!'

Intimidated by the speaker's rank and his bodyguards, the householder quickly withdrew.

There were roars of laughter from the drunken men.

It was a foolish person who took on a group of the nobility. All citizens were supposedly equal, but Rome was really ruled by an elite of senators, equestrians or *equites*, and the richest landowners. Together the families that made up the aristocracy formed a clique that was virtually impossible to join, except with great wealth. A few individuals from this small class controlled the Republic's fate.

The burly man retched again. 'Bloody plebeians,' he said, placing a meaty hand on his companion's shoulder. 'Take it easy, old friend. My legs aren't working too well.'

'Plebs are good for little,' agreed his companion. 'Except manual labour and the army.'

Most of his companions smiled, but the stocky redhead at the front spoke impatiently. 'Get a move on! Still got to reach the Lupanar!'

The nobles perked up at the mention of Rome's most famous brothel. Its specialities were known throughout Italy. Even the drunkest ones looked interested.

'Never happy unless you have a screw, eh Caelius?' the lean man replied, a slight edge to his voice.

'Best whorehouse in the city. You should try it some time.' Caelius rubbed his hands together in anticipation. 'Nowhere better for beautiful women after a skinful.'

'Just had a new delivery of slaves from Germania, apparently.' The big noble cleared his throat. 'But I need more wine first!'

'Then the whorehouse!' Caelius clapped him on the arm.

'If I can still get it up!'

'And me!' The oldest of the group, who was forty-five, laughed.

'Coming? Or does your wife need you at home?'

The lean man smiled without rancour. He'd heard the taunt many times before. It stemmed partly from jealousy of his wife's proud lineage and partly from his devotion to her. But no drunken comment could come close to upsetting him. The whole group knew the noble for his restraint and composure and he wasn't about to spoil that impression.

'If the women are really so good looking, I might be tempted. But they're more likely to be pox-ridden hags!'

The others laughed, eager to please their powerful friend. This was a politician who had survived the bloody purges by Sulla, the successor to the first co-dictators of Rome, Cinna and Marius. Despite many threats, he had refused to divorce his wife, the daughter of an enemy of Sulla's. After months of pleading by the lean man's family and its supporters, Sulla had reversed his death sentence. The dictator's prediction that Rome's nobility would eventually be overthrown by him had been forgotten, and the ambitious equestrian was now one of the most prominent young men in the public eye.

'Bugger one of the boys then,' Caelius snapped. 'Leave the women to us.'

The noble rubbed his aquiline nose. 'Thought they were all at your house.'

Caelius' fists clenched.

'Leave it, you two. We are all friends here,' said Aufidius, his normally jovial face serious. A stout figure, he was popular with everyone for his good nature.

Always the politician, the lean man shrugged. 'I have no wish to quarrel further.'

'What do you say, Caelius? Shall we leave this bad feeling behind?'

Biting his lip with fury, the redhead nodded. 'Very well.'

The tone was insincere, but it was enough for Aufidius, who turned to the group. 'Where's the nearest hostelry?'

'Opposite side of the Forum. Behind the temple of Castor.' The burly equestrian weaved to the front. 'Follow me.'

A short time later they were all seated at a table in a stone-walled tavern, its air reeking of cheap wine and sweat. Rush torches guttered from brackets, blackening the walls and casting long, dancing shadows. The inn was typical, with one room on the ground floor and three- or four-storey tenement flats above. Loud conversation filled the air. On some tables games of dice were being played, at others men arm-wrestled for money.

Despite their retinue of bodyguards, most of the newcomers felt uneasy. This was a far cry from their usual watering holes. Unused to mixing with nobles, many customers were also casting wary glances in their direction.

'What are you staring at?' Caelius snarled.

The nearest drinkers quickly looked away.

With a malicious smile, Caelius jerked his head and the biggest slaves instantly moved to stand behind the curious citizens. When he nodded again, they hauled two outside while the remainder stood guard by the entrance. The men's friends sat helplessly as screams carried inside. Even the huge doorman kept his mouth shut.

'You'll win no friends like that, Caelius,' commented the lean man.

'Who needs scum as friends?'

'Beat plebs when necessary.' He glanced at the door. 'Otherwise let them be.'

'Always know best, don't you?'

'These people are not slaves.'

'Equestrians can do as they wish.'

'If you want them to support you for a position in the Senate, keep behaving like that.'

Caelius curled his lip, but had no reply.

'We *equites* are the most powerful people in the strongest state in the world. Those men knew that already, Caelius. Rule them through respect, not fear.'

There were nods of agreement but the redhead scowled.

'Is there nowhere better round here?' Aufidius lowered his voice slightly. 'This place is a shithole.'

Most turned to Caelius, the self-elected expert on brothels.

'I've had better horse piss and the clientele are low class too. But it's only a short walk to the Lupanar,' said Caelius, satisfied to be the centre of attention again. He drained his beaker. 'Let's have a few here. Then we can give some blonde whores a good seeing to!'

Everyone nodded, with the exception of the lean man.

'I'll be going home after this.'

'What? Fading on us?' The burly equestrian refilled his friend's cup and shoved it along the table, spilling wine.

'I have to prepare for a debate in the Senate tomorrow.'

'Genius flows better after a night in the saddle!' Aufidius made an obscene gesture to gales of laughter.

'I want to be a quaestor next year, my friend. Such positions don't just fall into one's lap.' As an assistant to the senior magistrates, the lean man would have the opportunity to learn much about the intricacies of the Republic's legal system, perhaps even to manage some of the public finances. It would be valuable political experience, preparing him for the rank above, the praetorship.

'Jupiter's balls, will you lighten up?' sneered Caelius, aware that without a powerful sponsor, he had no chance of election to such a post.

'The man has a point,' admitted Aufidius. 'Once in the magistracy, nights like this won't happen too often.'

'I'm aware of that.'

'Then stay out with us!'

'I would rather decide the path of the Republic. You can all screw the night away.'

'You're not the only one with an important job.'

'Forgive me,' he said quickly. 'I meant no insult.'

'Did you not?' Caelius gripped the edge of the table so hard his knuckles went white. 'Not a quaestor yet. You're still an equestrian, like us! Arrogant prick!'

The lean man's stare became icy and the pair locked eyes.

'Come now, Caelius,' Aufidius interjected. 'Sooner a whore soothes your brow, the better!'

The redhead forced a smile.

The other's eyes remained stony.

'It's Caelius' balls need soothing more than anything!'

Most laughed at the joke.

The *equites* continued drinking and talking, but the convivial air had been lost. Eventually conversation petered out altogether. In the tavern's din, it was noticeable only to those at the table.

'Who's for the Lupanar?' Aufidius drained his cup to a chorus of approval.

Following Caelius, the group weaved out on to the rutted surface of the street. Two prone bodies lay in the dirt a few steps from the door.

Caelius kicked the nearest in the belly. 'Won't forget us in a hurry.'

The lean man pursed his lips in disapproval.

They had not gone far when Caelius collided with a young girl hurrying through the semi-darkness. She was knocked to the ground and a basket of meat and vegetables went flying.

Recognising a slave by the light wrist chains, Caelius backhanded her across the face as she got up. 'Watch where you're going! Clumsy bitch!'

The girl fell back into the dried mud with a cry, her worn shift riding up slim, shapely legs.

'She meant no harm, Caelius,' said Aufidius, helping her up.

The young woman was about seventeen, very pretty,

with dark hair and blue eyes. Uneasy in the presence of nobles, she bobbed her head in thanks.

'Sorry, Master,' she mumbled, turning to leave.

Caelius was having none of it. He had seen how attractive she was. Grabbing the front of the light woollen shift, he ripped it to the waist, revealing a pert pair of breasts. The girl cried out in terror and embarrassment, but Caelius' blood was up. He tore the dress completely off her shoulders.

She backed away and was instantly blocked by two of the others. Aware they could not help, the bodyguards moved discreetly into the shadows. There was no one else around to help a lone slave. From dusk to dawn, Rome's streets were the province of the lawless. Only the foolhardy ventured out without guards. Or a slave sent on an errand.

'Please, Master.' The girl's voice trembled. 'I meant no harm.'

Caelius grabbed her arm. 'This won't take long.'

There was a murmur of agreement. Only the lean man and Aufidius remained silent.

The girl moaned with fear.

'Let her go.'

'What did you say?' said Caelius incredulously.

'You heard me.'

'Rot in Hades!' Shaking with anger, Caelius took a step forward. 'She's only a damn slave.'

The lean man plucked a long-bladed dagger from inside his toga. 'I am sick of you.' He held it nonchalantly by the tip. 'Do as I say.'

Caelius' eyes darted to the bodyguards.

Instantly the knife was poised to throw. 'I can put this through your heart before they come five paces.'

'Calm yourself, my friend,' said Aufidius, looking worried. 'No point anyone getting hurt.'

He smiled. 'That depends on Caelius.'

The rest watched the argument unfold. It had been brewing for months, and none of them wanted to oppose the powerful and ambitious noble.

Scowling furiously, Caelius released the girl.

The lean man beckoned her over. 'Enjoy the Lupanar,' he said, gesturing commandingly down the street.

'He disapproves of two lowlife citizens getting a beating, then stops an equestrian screwing a slave?' spat Caelius in an undertone. 'The prick is going soft. Or mad.'

'Neither.' Aufidius shook his head. 'He is far too shrewd.'

'What then?'

Aufidius ignored the question, clapping the redhead jovially on the back. 'It's time for more wine!'

Caelius let himself be led away and the others followed meekly, glad the argument had been settled without bloodshed.

It would not always be so.

'See you in the Senate tomorrow,' the lean man called after them.

He stood in silence, holding the slave until the group was some distance away. Two personal bodyguards waited in the shadows. The girl peered at him nervously, hoping to be released, but when the noble's piercing gaze turned back, it was filled with lust. Tightening his grip, he dragged her towards an alleyway.

She whimpered with fear. It was obvious what was about to happen. Only the rapist had changed.

'Be quiet, or I'll hurt you.'

Glancing up from his latest pile of vomit, the burly equestrian saw the pair disappear. 'Probably planned it all, so he could have her to himself,' he muttered. 'That man will not stop at quaestor.'

'He'll be a consul before long,' complained Caelius. The redhead had not seen the girl's fate.

For centuries, Rome had been governed each year by two elected consuls, supported by military tribunes, judges and the Senate. It was a system that worked well if the participants complied with the law. Historically, the pair of officials, effective rulers of Rome, had changed every twelve months. This ancient statute had been passed to stop individuals from holding on to power. But since a civil war over enfranchisement thirty years before, Rome's democracy had been slipping into decline and the important positions had changed hands less than a dozen times in a generation. Ambitious nobles such as Marius, Cinna and Sulla had begun the trend, forcing a weakened Senate to let them retain the consulship long term. Now only a favoured few ever succeeded to the posts, which were jealously guarded by the richest and most powerful families in Italy. It took incredible drive to become a consul by sheer merit.

'The prick will make a mistake eventually,' snarled Caelius. 'Everyone does.' Still seething with anger, the redhead knew he was too drunk to outwit his enemy. Dragging his companion away, he staggered towards the Lupanar.

The lean man strode into the darkness, the girl held firmly by one arm. Waste and broken pottery discarded by the inhabitants of nearby houses littered the alley. Finding a suitable spot at last, he ripped her light shift off and shoved the slave to the ground. She fell awkwardly, exposing a triangle of dark hair at the base of her belly. Adjusting his toga, he swept open both legs with a foot and lowered himself to his knees. The girl cried out in terror. With a shove, he entered her, sighing with pleasure.

The lean man thrust in and out eagerly. His wife had not been well for some time and his physical needs had been neglected. Caught up with furthering an ambitious political career, he had gone for months without sex.

The girl's eyes were wide with fear.

'Look at me again and I'll cut your throat!'

Hastily she obeyed, jamming a hand in her mouth to keep silent. Tears rolled silently from between closed lids. This was the lot of a slave.

With a loud moan, he climaxed, pushing deep inside.

She did not open her eyes as he got up, rearranging his toga.

The lean man stared down with a satisfied smile. Even with a swollen, tearstained face, the girl was a real beauty. Lust sated, he could return home. He had to finish the speech on public spending for the next day. If it was well received, his chances of election as quaestor would be greatly enhanced. Having served in the priesthood of Jupiter and as a military staff officer, he was determined to proceed along the noble's career path – the *cursus honorum* – as fast as possible.

He was sure his father would have been proud to see how far an only son had risen. Though patrician, the family had not been wealthy. His father had worked hard in the Senate for many years to achieve the rank of praetor, just below that of consul, shortly before he died.

Initially the young man's own career had been helped by the family's connections, which opened many doors that would have remained shut otherwise. Long years of listening to his father's conversations with political allies, watching debates in the Forum and attending society banquets had also paid off. He had become a consummate politician and a suitable marriage had cemented his social position. The union of an aunt to a powerful consul had brought him into the public eye, but when his uncle had died during a period of civil war, his progress had faltered somewhat. Sulla's bloody reign had been dangerous for anyone with different ideas. The first general ever to march soldiers into Rome, Sulla had executed virtually everyone who got in his way. It had earned him the nickname of 'the butcher'.

Only the lean man's intelligence and will to survive had carried him through that time. Through sheer hard work, he had built up a network of friends among the rich and powerful and was now a rising star of the Roman political world. People like Cato and Pompey Magnus were starting to notice him. Marcus Licinius Crassus, one of the most prominent figures in Rome, had lent him huge financial backing, but the young politician needed smaller men's support too. It had been a good opportunity to show who led the group.

By cowing Caelius into submission, the lean man had

strengthened his dominance over more lowly equestrian friends. On the road to power, he needed obedient allies for a smooth passage. The capital was full of those who wanted to rule, but that position was really only open to a few. By playing his hand right, he too would be one of them one day.

He came back to the present. 'Go home. Before someone less merciful finds you.'

Disbelief flitted across the slave's face, but it was instantly hidden. 'Thank you, Master.' She had seen the dagger and knew how easily he could have used it.

'Be swift, or you'll end up in the Tiber.' The idea of killing the girl did not appeal – he wasn't a cold-blooded murderer. He turned and was gone.

The girl waited until all sounds had disappeared into the night. Gripping her torn shift tightly, she fled through the dark streets towards her master's house. Returning late and without her basket of food, the reception from Gemellus would be even worse than what she had just endured. But there was nowhere else for her to go.

Nine months later . . .

The merchant opened the door without knocking and entered the small room, his face dripping with sweat. He stared down at the sleeping baby in the cot.

Velvinna, who was nursing the other twin, gazed at her owner with a mixture of terror and hate.

'More mouths to feed! At least this is a girl,' Gemellus

said, scowling. 'If I'm lucky, she'll have your looks. Sell her to a whorehouse in a few years.'

He turned to Velvinna. The young mother's face crumpled with anticipation.

'I want you back in the kitchen tomorrow. Two days' rest is more than enough!'

Velvinna had no choice but to obey. Although exhausted from a long labour, she would have to fire the oven and clean the floors. The other slaves would help as much as they could.

'Keep up with your work,' Gemellus said threateningly, 'or I'll leave both of them on the midden.'

Only the poorest citizens left new babies to die on communal dung heaps. Velvinna clutched the infant closely to her. 'I will, Master!'

'Good.' Gemellus bent over and squeezed her breast. 'I will visit tonight,' he grunted. 'Those brats had better not cry either.'

She bit her lip until it bled, stifling her instinctive protest.

The merchant leered at Velvinna from the doorway and was gone.

She gazed down at the male baby. 'Feed, my little Romulus,' she whispered. There would be no golden *bullae* charms for her twins, no naming ceremonies at nine days of age. Like her, they were slaves, not citizens. Her milk was the only thing she had to give him. 'Grow strong and healthy.'

One day you can kill Gemellus.
And the lean one.

Chapter III: Olenus

Northern Italy, 70 BC

The Vinalia Rustica had been and gone and still no opportunity had arisen for Tarquinius to get away from the *latifundium* and visit Olenus. Normally he enjoyed the annual festival celebrating the harvest, a riotous affair that lasted several days. This year had been different in more ways than one. Large amounts of wine and food had been consumed but Caelius had ensured celebrations did not get out of hand. Just as Dexter had predicted, there had been no meat for the workers. The nobleman never wasted a single *sestertius* if he could avoid it. And Tarquinius was growing impatient. He desperately needed to talk to the haruspex about his vision, which had now recurred a number of times. But he dared not leave without permission because the *vilicus* knew about his wish to climb the mountain. Dexter's speciality lay in punishing the workers who had disobeyed Caelius' rules. It was not uncommon for men to die of the injuries he inflicted.

About two weeks after talking to the foreman, the young Etruscan was summoned to Caelius' stone-flagged office early one morning. Tarquinius was delighted. Events were beginning to move again. Yet it was still intimidating to be in the hard-faced Roman's presence. Tarquinius strongly disliked the estate's owner – he could not have explained why – and his dream had only strengthened this feeling.

Studying a parchment on his desk, Caelius ignored him for some time. Tarquinius waited, staring curiously at mementoes throughout the large, square room. Greek statues of the gods sat either side of a low altar. A bust of a man with a beaked nose and piercing gaze sat in an alcove, displayed so everyone who entered could see it. Shields and swords of different types hung from nails, trophies from Caelius' time in the army. The weapons, evidence of a world outside the *latifundium*, sparked Tarquinius' imagination. He had learned much from Olenus, but most of it was theory. These objects were real.

The noble looked up at last. He had not noticed Tarquinius' interest. 'Too many animals have been killed recently,' he said, tapping a fingernail against his teeth. 'I'm giving you three days. I want half a dozen wolf pelts on the wall by then.'

'Three days?' Tarquinius was stunned by the timing. 'Six wolves?'

Why now? He had told Caelius about the losses a month earlier.

'Correct.' Caelius' tone was icy. 'Unless someone else could do it better? Plenty of men would jump at the chance to avoid harvest work.'

'I can do it, Master,' Tarquinius said hurriedly. It would give him the chance to get meat for Dexter.

Caelius waved a hand in dismissal.

Tarquinius had reached the door when the redhead spoke again.

'Return late and I'll have you crucified.'

'Master?' Shocked, he stared at Caelius blankly. The threat sounded genuine.

'You heard me,' the redhead replied. His eyes were dark slits.

Tarquinius bobbed his head and closed the door behind him. Alarmed by the cryptic remark, he went to the family's room and gathered up a few belongings, together with a bow and quiver. The thought of time with Olenus soon lifted his spirits. Grinning broadly, he kissed his mother goodbye and left the estate buildings behind.

The small groves on slopes above the villa were full of slaves bringing in the olive harvest. The original trees had been brought from Greece hundreds of years before. Green olives and their valuable oil provided a huge part of Rome's wealth. Tarquinius wondered again why Caelius had not planted more of them to help with his financial problems.

'Don't forget our deal,' the *vilicus* yelled when he saw Tarquinius. 'Otherwise I'll put you to work in the mill.' Grinding flour was even more backbreaking than cutting wheat, and a common punishment. 'It's good you're going up there,' Dexter added ominously.

'What do you mean?'

'Crassus has an interest in the old man. Gods alone know why.'

Tarquinius opened his mouth to ask more, but the foreman had already turned away, shouting orders.

What interest could Marcus Licinius Crassus have in Olenus?

The immensely wealthy noble had defeated Spartacus the year before, ending the slave rebellion which had almost brought Rome to its knees. It was now common knowledge that the victory had been cleverly claimed by Pompey Magnus, his main rival. The lie had won him a full triumph from the Senate while Crassus had to be satisfied with a mere parade on foot. For months afterwards, the enraged Crassus had continually failed to regain the political advantage.

But recently he had skilfully manoeuvred to become joint consul with Pompey, and in an initial show of unity, the pair had restored the tribunate, which had been abolished by Sulla. Only plebeians could serve in these posts. With their rights to veto bills in the Senate and to convene public assemblies to pass laws of their own, the tribunes were immensely popular with the Roman public. The reform had been a clever move and Crassus had immediately used his new-found recognition to stir up resentment against Pompey in the Senate. At only thirty-six, his co-consul was legally too young to serve in the post. In addition, he had never even served as a senator. Pompey had quickly heard about Crassus' tactics and soon the pair were publicly disagreeing with each other. Instead of working together as they were supposed to, their rivalry had become more bitter than ever.

Tarquinius shivered.

There could be only one reason for Crassus' interest.

The bronze liver. Tarquin's sword. Caelius was planning to sell the sacred items to a man who wanted – needed – signs of divine approval.

He walked on, mind racing. Time was suddenly of the essence.

'Skiving again?' His leg manacles still in place, Maurus looked at Tarquinius sourly from his position halfway up a tree. In one hand the brown-skinned slave held a small, sharp knife to cut olives from the branches; he gripped the trunk with his other. A wicker basket hung from his back. 'The master know about this?'

'He's sent me to kill some wolves. Half a dozen in three days. Want to help?'

Maurus' face paled at the idea of physical danger.

Tarquinius mimed pulling back his bowstring and loosing an arrow. 'Keep picking, then.'

The gnarled trunks and busy workers were soon left behind as he climbed above the tree line to see the surrounding countryside that he knew and loved so well. Lake Vadimon sparkled in the sunlight and he drank in the view, momentarily putting aside his worries at Caelius' and Dexter's comments.

The powerful aroma of wild herbs filled Tarquinius' nostrils and he breathed deeply. Breaking off a small branch of rosemary from the nearest bush, he stuffed it into his pack to use later. The young man kept his eyes peeled for wolves, though it was unlikely he would see any in daytime. The predators lived in woods much higher on the mountain and came down to hunt only at dusk or dawn. He found traces of their passage here and there, in the form of spoor. There was even the carcass of an adult sheep near the track, bones picked clean of flesh by the birds. Only a jackal remained, sucking the marrow from a cracked femur. It darted away before he could string his bow.

Tarquinius worked his way to Olenus' hut, continuously scanning the sky and slopes for unusual signs. The first thing the old man would ask was what there had been to see on the climb. He counted eight buzzards hanging on thermals that swirled over the peak. Pleased there weren't twelve and that the clouds appeared innocuous in shape and number, Tarquinius clambered surefootedly up the light scree covering the mountainside.

Spotting Olenus' tiny dwelling, his pace quickened. Despite the altitude, the temperature had been rising and he was looking forward to a rest. The makeshift hut where his mentor lived was built into the edge of a clearing, with commanding views south to the lake and beyond. It was one of Tarquinius' favourite places, full of good memories.

'Finally you grace me with your presence.'

He spun round to find Olenus standing on the track behind.

'How did you get there?' Tarquinius was so relieved to find the haruspex alive that he nearly hugged him.

Olenus smiled and adjusted his leather hat. 'I have my ways. Good to see you, boy. Notice anything on the way up?'

'Nothing much. A jackal. Eight buzzards.' Tarquinius made an apologetic gesture. 'I'd have come before, but the harvest took an age to bring in.'

'No matter. You are here now.' Olenus moved past

smoothly. 'We have much to talk about and time is short.'

'I can't stay long.' Tarquinius tapped the bow hanging from his left shoulder. 'I've only got three days to hunt six wolves.'

'Just as well I have killed some then, eh?'

Olenus pointed at the drying racks outside the hut. Five distinctive grey pelts were stretched across their timbers.

'One wolf in three days? That'll be easy,' grinned Tarquinius. 'What's going on? You normally leave the hunting to me.'

The haruspex shrugged. 'A man gets bored talking to sheep all day.'

'You knew how many Caelius would demand?'

Olenus beckoned to him. 'Come and rest in the shade. You must be thirsty after the climb.'

Delighted by the revelation, Tarquinius followed Olenus to a log under the trees. The pair took their ease in silence, contemplating the view. The sun beat down, creating a haze that would eventually obscure the panorama below. Tarquinius drank and passed the leather water carrier to the haruspex.

'Any vivid dreams recently?'

Tarquinius half choked on the liquid in his mouth. 'What?'

'You heard.'

'I had one about you. In a cave. Maybe the one where the liver is kept.' He wrinkled his nose at the smell from the pelts. 'So I've seen it at last!'

'What else?'

'Nothing.' Tarquinius stared down at the impossible brightness of the lake.

'You make a terrible liar, boy.' Olenus chuckled. 'Scared to tell me that I will die soon?'

'I didn't see that.' A shiver ran down Tarquinius' spine at the haruspex' ability to read his mind. 'But Caelius and some soldiers were nearing the cave. It looked like they meant business.'

'He has sold knowledge of my presence to someone in Rome.'

'Crassus!' The name escaped Tarquinius' lips before he could stop it.

Olenus was unsurprised. 'He's got enough money to run the *latifundium* for a year.' His gaze was piercing. 'Not bad for an old man, eh?'

Tarquinius struggled briefly with the concept. 'I thought he wanted the liver.'

'The bronze is of huge importance. Although it is Etruscan, the Romans would revere it highly,' agreed Olenus. 'With it, Crassus can use pet augurs to predict what he likes.' His contempt was obvious. 'And I am sure an aspiring general would love Tarquin's sword. Anything to become more popular than Pompey.'

'Why kill you?'

'Cleans everything up. After all, I'm an Etruscan haruspex,' Olenus cackled. 'And Romans don't like me. Too much of a reminder of the past.'

'How does he know about the artefacts?'

'Caelius suspects, but isn't sure.'

'So why hasn't he tortured you before now?'

'He was too scared. I have always made sure the slaves

43

on the estate knew my predictions over the years. Crop failure, floods, disease. Caelius would have heard them too.'

Tarquinius nodded, remembering stories from his childhood about the haruspex who knew where lightning would strike, which cows would prove barren.

'But Caelius' financial worries have conquered his fear. He has sent you to make sure I am still here when the soldiers arrive.' Olenus twisted the *lituus* between withered hands, the golden bull's head on its top rotating gently. 'Doesn't leave much time to complete your studies.'

'No! You must flee,' Tarquinius said urgently. 'I'll come too. It'd be at least three days before we are missed. Caelius will never find us!'

'I cannot outrun destiny.' His voice was calm. 'It was so obvious on the liver in your dream. Those soldiers *will* kill me.'

'When?'

'Four days.'

Tarquinius' heart pounded in his chest. 'I'll finish Caelius myself,' he threatened.

'The legionaries will still come from Rome.'

'Then I'll stay here and fight them.'

'And die needlessly. You have many years of life and a great journey to make, Arun.'

It was pointless arguing. Tarquinius had never changed the old man's mind about anything. 'What journey?' he asked. 'You never mentioned that before.'

Olenus got up, wincing as his back straightened. 'Let us go to the cave. Take your bow and pack. You can pick up those pelts and kill the last wolf on the way home.' He walked over and grabbed the lamb tied up by the hut.

The animal bleated plaintively as the rope was fastened around both its back legs and it was dangled over Olenus' shoulder.

Tarquinius followed the haruspex along the same track they had been on a few weeks before. They climbed in silence, until only the scrubby grass beloved by sheep and goats remained to cover the stony ground. The weather was much calmer than usual on the mountain and a few clouds sat unmoving overhead.

An eagle appeared over the crest of the ridge above, bringing a smile to Tarquinius' face. It was always a good omen to see the most regal of birds.

They were still picking their way up the steep slopes by early afternoon. A cool breeze kept temperatures bearable, but in the fields far below it would be a different matter.

Olenus came to a halt, a fine covering of sweat on his wrinkled forehead.

'You're in good shape, old man.' Glad of the rest, Tarquinius took a pull from his water bag.

'Sixty years living on this mountain.' Olenus scanned the harsh environment of rocks and the occasional bush which had survived the extremes of weather. It was desolate but beautiful. The sky had emptied of clouds, the only sign of life the bird of prey drifting on thermals. 'It's been a good place to live and it will be a good place to die.'

'Please stop talking like that!'

'Better get used to it, Arun. Haruspices have lived and died here since time immemorial.'

Tarquinius quickly changed the subject. 'Where is this cave?'

'Up there.' Olenus waved his *lituus* at the winding path. 'Another hundred paces.'

Teacher and pupil walked the last few steps to the entrance, hidden until they had virtually fallen into it. The narrow opening was barely wide enough for two men to stand abreast.

The young Etruscan gaped. He must have been past the aperture countless times searching for sheep, but nobody would ever find it unless they knew where to look. Then he smiled. The long years of waiting were nearly over.

'Mind your head.' The haruspex paused, muttering a prayer. 'The ceiling is quite low.'

Tarquinius followed Olenus, squinting as his eyes adjusted from the light outside. It was the cave in the dream, the interior just as plain as he remembered. The only evidence of human presence was a small ring fireplace in the centre of the floor.

Olenus put down the lamb, tying the rope round a large rock. He paced deeper inside, studying the wall. About thirty paces from the entrance, he stopped. With a grunt of effort, the old man reached up into a crevice with both hands, searching.

Tarquinius watched with fascination as the soothsayer pulled out a heavy oblong object wrapped in cloth. Olenus brushed off a thick layer of dust and turned to him.

'Still here!'

'The sacred liver?'

'The first one ever made by a haruspex,' replied Olenus solemnly. 'Bring the lamb.'

He led the way outside, stopping by a slab of black basalt that Tarquinius had noticed on the way in. Olenus set down the *lituus* and pulled a long dagger from his belt, laying it on the edge of the flat rock.

'That is just like the altar I saw in my dream!'

'There is another one, deep inside the cave.' Olenus unwrapped the bronze liver, placing it reverently beside the knife. 'But today's divination must be performed in sunlight.'

Tarquinius peered at the smooth lump of metal, coloured green with age. It was shaped exactly like the purple organ he had seen cut from butchered cattle and sheep. Bulging more on the right, the bronze had two triangular pieces protruding from its inner aspect, like different lobes of a real liver. The uppermost surface was covered in lines, dividing it into multiple areas. Spidery, cryptic symbols had been etched on each part. Having studied diagrams of the liver over and over again, Tarquinius found he could understand the inscribed words.

'It names the gods and stellar constellations!'

'All that time studying wasn't in vain, then.' Olenus took the rope from him. 'You read the whole *Disciplina Etrusca* twice, so you should know most of what I'm going to do.'

Tarquinius had spent countless hours poring over cracked parchments that Olenus kept in his hut. He had digested dozens of volumes, constantly encouraged by the old man leaning over him, indicating relevant paragraphs with long yellow fingernails. There had been three sets of books – the first, the *Libri Haruspicini*, was dedicated to divination from animal organs; the second, the *Libri Fulgurates*, dealt with interpretation of thunder and lightning. The last, the *Libri Rituales*, concerned Etruscan rituals and consecrations for cities, temples and armies.

'Gently, little one,' Olenus whispered.

The lamb pulled the rope taut, an alarmed look in its dark brown eyes.

Speaking reassuringly, the haruspex placed the animal on the centre of the basalt. 'We thank you for your life, which will help us understand the future.'

Tarquinius moved closer. He had seen Olenus perform sacrifices before, but not for some months. The haruspex had never used the bronze liver alongside a fresh offering. And although Tarquinius had tried divining many times after he had been hunting, they had only been practice runs, predicting things like weather and harvest yields.

'It is time.' Olenus picked up the dagger. 'Observe how a fresh liver may be read. Hold him properly.'

Tarquinius gripped the lamb's head and extended the neck towards Olenus. With a swift slash of the blade, the old man cut its throat. Dark red venous blood gushed on to the altar in a thick stream, spattering them in droplets.

'See how it flows to the east?' Olenus cried with glee as the liquid ran away. 'The omens will be auspicious!'

Tarquinius gazed eastward, to the sea. It was from across the water, from Lydia, that the Etruscans had come many centuries ago. According to ritual, the gods most favourably disposed towards humans also dwelt in that direction. Not for the first time, he felt a strong urge to journey to the ancestral homelands of his people.

Olenus laid the dead lamb on its back, exposing the belly. With deft movements, he sliced open skin and muscle from groin to ribcage. Shiny loops of gut spilled out, glistening in the sunlight.

Olenus pointed with the dagger. 'Mark the pattern as large and small intestine emerge to sit on the stone. Both should be a healthy pinkish-grey colour, like these. If they are not, it is likely the reading will be bad when you reach the animal's liver.'

'What else can you see?'

'The wave movement in the intestines is still strong, which is good.'

Tarquinius watched the regular pulses in the small bowel, moving along digested material in a futile attempt to stay alive. 'Anything else?'

The haruspex leaned closer. 'No. When I was a boy, old men used to claim they could interpret much from the bowel and the four stomachs. They were charlatans.'

Olenus reached inside the abdomen with both hands, using his knife to free the liver from its position against the diaphragm. A few swift cuts severed the large vessels anchoring it in place. Forearms covered in blood, he withdrew the organ, balancing its rounded surface on his left hand.

'O great Tinia! Give us good omens for the future of

this Arun.' He raised his eyes to the heavens, searching for the eagle that had accompanied them earlier.

'What are you doing?' asked Tarquinius.

'Reading your life in the liver, boy,' Olenus cackled. 'What better way to complete your learning?'

Tarquinius held his breath for a long time, unsure. Then, as if compelled, he found himself taking in the words. It had been too many years to hold back now, even when it was his own future being predicted.

'Most of what you can discern is on the inner surface. Mark the dog star, Sirius. This is the large bear, Ursa Major.'

He peered at the points indicated, his book learning beginning to make real sense. The haruspex spoke at length about interpretations to be made from the colour, shape and consistency of the glistening organ. To Tarquinius' astonishment, Olenus brought up many details of his childhood that he could not possibly have known. The old man recounted Tarquinius' whole life, pausing every so often to allow his pupil time to interpret.

'The gall bladder.' He poked a tear-shaped sac protruding from the liver's centre. 'Represents what is hidden. Sometimes it can be read, sometimes not.'

Tarquinius touched the warm bag of fluid. 'Is much visible?' It was the hardest part of the divination to perform and he had never made any sense from the livers he had practised on.

Olenus was silent for a few moments.

Heart racing, Tarquinius studied the haruspex' face. There was something there. He could feel it.

'I see you join the army and travel to Asia Minor. I see many battles.'

'When?'

'Soon.'

Tarquinius knew that the eastern region of Asia Minor had been a hotbed of rebellion and conflict for some time. A generation before, Sulla had soundly defeated Mithridates, the warlike king of Pontus, but his concerns about the uncertain political situation in Rome had made him pull back without delivering the final blow. Mithridates had bided his time, until four years previously when his armies had surged into Pergamum, the Roman province in the area. Lucullus, the general sent by the Senate, had achieved impressive victories since, but the war was still going on.

Amused by the idea of fighting for the Romans, Tarquinius felt a sharp nudge. 'Pay attention!' barked the old man. 'Years of travelling, learning. But eventually Rome draws you back. A desire for revenge.'

'On whom?'

'A fight.' Olenus seemed to be in a trance. 'Someone of high rank is killed.'

'By me?' Tarquinius asked suspiciously. 'Why?'

The answer came to him.

'A voyage to Lydia by ship. There two gladiators become your friends. Both brave men. You will become a teacher, like me.'

The dagger tip swept from gall bladder to other points on the purple organ. The haruspex began muttering rapidly. Tarquinius found he could only pick out occasional words. He gazed at the liver, delighted that he could also see what Olenus was reading.

'A huge battle, which the Romans lose. Slavery. A long march into the east. The Lion of Macedon's path.'

Tarquinius smiled. Some said the Rasenna – the name the Etruscans called themselves – had come from further afield than Lydia. Perhaps he would learn something from the travels of Alexander.

'Margiana. A journey by river, then another by sea.' Olenus' expression grew troubled. 'Egypt? The mother of terror?'

'What is it?' Tarquinius tried to see what had alarmed his mentor.

'Nothing! I saw nothing.' The old man threw the lamb's liver down, taking a few steps backwards. 'I must be mistaken.'

Tarquinius stepped closer. The gall bladder had begun to leak a thin, greenish fluid onto the stone. Concentrating hard, he still found it difficult to interpret. Then his vision cleared. 'Egypt! The city of Alexander!'

'It is not.' Sounding angry and scared, Olenus pushed Tarquinius out of the way, turning the liver over so he could no longer see the underside. 'Time to see the sword of Tarquin.'

'Why? What have you seen?'

'Many things, Arun.' Olenus' eyes darkened. 'It is sometimes best not to say.'

'I have a right to know my own fate.' Tarquinius squared his shoulders. 'You saw yours.'

Olenus' face sagged. 'True enough.' He gestured with the blade. 'Look, then.'

Tarquinius held back, considering the options. He had learned how to read the liver thoroughly at last and would have plenty of opportunity to do so in years to come. His mentor had seen a fascinating future. But there had also been something quite unexpected.

Tarquinius had little desire to know everything that would happen to him.

'It will be revealed in time,' he said calmly.

Relieved, Olenus picked up the *lituus* and pointed back into the cave. 'We must find the sword. You are ready.' He patted Tarquinius affectionately.

Before they entered the dark interior, Olenus produced a handful of rushes, their ends dipped in wax. Using two pieces of flint, he lit a pair of torches. 'Take one.'

Making sure the burning wax did not run down his arm, Tarquinius followed the old man inside. The cave opened out as they went deeper, running straight into the rock for a good three hundred paces. The air was cool but dry.

He jumped as the torchlight revealed richly coloured paintings on the walls.

'This place has been sacred for many centuries.' Olenus pointed out the figure of a haruspex, obvious with his blunt-peaked hat and *lituus*. 'See how he holds the liver in his left hand and looks at the sky?'

'This must be Tinia.' Tarquinius bowed before an unusually large image, depicting a figure identical to the little terracotta statue kept on a shrine in Olenus' hut. The deity had staring, almond-shaped eyes and a straight nose, framed by tight curls and a short, pointed beard.

'The Romans call him Jupiter.'

53

Olenus scowled. 'They even took our most important god.'

The soothsayer beckoned Tarquinius deeper into the gloom, past more paintings of ancient rituals and feasts. Musicians played lyres and the *auletos*, the Etruscan double flute. Graceful dark women in colourful, flowing robes danced with fat, naked men as satyrs leered from nearby rocks. Mighty Etruscan warriors in full armour guarded one scene, and a naked male figure with wings and a lion's head hovered overhead. The intensity in the beast's eyes stirred something deep in him.

'Gods above!' Tarquinius swelled with pride, imagining Etruria in its glory days. 'These are better than anything in Caelius' house!'

'Or most villas in Rome.' The old man came to a halt by the entrance to a side chamber. Raising his torch, Olenus moved a few steps towards a large shape on the floor.

'What is it?'

The haruspex did not answer and Tarquinius dragged his gaze away from the murals. It was a moment before he took in the ornate bronze panels, metal-clad wheels and square fighting platform of an Etruscan battle chariot. He gasped.

'Achilles is receiving his armour from Thetis, his mother.' Olenus pointed at the depiction on the chariot's front section.

Chunks of ivory, amber and semiprecious stones had been carved to colour the scene. The central tongue and twin neckpieces for horses were similarly covered with tiny pictures of the gods. Even the nine-spoked wheels had sacred symbols etched on their sides.

Full of awe, Tarquinius ran his fingers over the wood and bronze, soaking up the details and dislodging a thick layer of dust. 'How old is it?'

'It belonged to Priscus, the last to call himself king of the Etruscans,' replied Olenus solemnly. 'And it was over three centuries ago that he ruled Falerii. They say he led more than a hundred of these into battle.'

The young man shivered with delight, picturing the impressive sight of the king dressed in plates of bronze armour, standing with a drawn bow behind his charioteer. Following in a vast wedge would have been the rest of the chariots and then the massed ranks of infantry.

'The testudo formations could withstand their charges though,' sighed Olenus. 'Simply closed up and weathered the arrow storms.'

Tarquinius nodded sadly, familiar with the story of Falerii's end. Somehow it had endured for more than seventy years after Rome had crushed all of its neighbours. When it did arrive, the fate of Falerii – last of the proud city states – had been decided in a few short hours. The Roman legionaries had massacred the less disciplined Etruscan foot soldiers and cut down many of the charioteers with well-thrown javelins. His army in tatters, the mortally wounded Priscus had fled the field. 'Is he buried in here?' he asked, staring into the corners.

Olenus shook his head. 'The king's final wish was that his body should be burned. The surviving warriors followed his orders, carrying the chariot here, away from the pillage of the city.'

'Wouldn't they have burned it too?'

There was a shrug. 'Perhaps they hoped Etruria would rise again one day.'

Tarquinius scowled. 'None of them was a haruspex then.'

'You cannot fight our people's destiny, Tarquinius,' said Olenus, patting his arm. 'Our time is nearly over.'

'I know.' He closed his eyes, offering a prayer to the faithful followers who had sweated to bring the magnificent chariot all the way up the mountain, hoping that one day it would reclaim its former glory. It wouldn't. Etruria's glory was gone for ever. He knew that. It was time he accepted it once and for all.

Olenus was watching him, his eyes inscrutable. 'Come.' The old man beckoned, leading him back into the main chamber.

They walked further into the cave, coming to a halt before a low stone altar with a strange picture on the wall above it.

'This is Charon. Demon of death.' Olenus bowed. 'He guards Tarquin's sword. Here it has lain for over three hundred years.'

Tarquinius stared with revulsion and a little fear at the squat blue creature with red hair. It had feathered wings sprouting from its back and a snarling mouth of sharp teeth. Charon held a large hammer poised above his head, ready to crush anyone who approached.

On the flat slab below lay a short straight-edged sword with a gold pommel. Torchlight winked off polished metal. Olenus bowed again before reverently handing the weapon to him.

Tarquinius balanced the intricately wired hilt across one palm, then swung the sword through the air in a gentle arc. 'Perfectly weighted. Handles well too.'

'Of course! It was forged for a king. Priscus was the last to wield it.' The haruspex gestured and Tarquinius quickly handed the *gladius* back.

Olenus pointed to an enormous ruby embedded in the base of the hilt. 'This is worth a huge fortune. It will attract a lot of attention, so keep it safe. Might come in useful one day.'

Tarquinius' eyes widened at the beautifully cut gemstone, far larger than any he had seen.

'That's enough for one day.' Olenus suddenly seemed drained, the lines deep on his face. 'Let's cook that lamb.'

Tarquinius did not protest. All his expectations for the journey had been exceeded. He had much to think about.

Silently they walked back to the entrance.

Before it got dark, Tarquinius went to find some firewood, and to check for any signs of movement, animal or human. To his relief, all he could find were wolf tracks. Returning with laden arms, he found that Olenus had started a small fire with some twigs. It did not take long to build up the blaze.

The two men sat side by side on a blanket, enjoying the heat and watching their dinner cook. Globules of fat dripped into the flames, flaring as they fell.

As if wanting to lighten the atmosphere, Olenus began talking about a great feasting hall in the city that had once existed below the cave.

'It was a magnificent long room with high couches arranged around dinner tables.' Olenus closed his eyes, leaning towards the fire. 'The tables were marble topped, quite low, with exquisitely worked legs inlaid with plaques of embossed gold. Musicians played while every type of food was served. And both men and women attended the banquets.'

'Really?' Roman nobility usually kept women away from official dinners. Tarquinius turned the lamb slightly on its spit. 'You're sure?'

Olenus nodded, beady eyes fixed on the cooking meat.

'From the paintings?'

'The oldest surviving haruspex told me when I was a boy.' He waved derisively at the guttering rush torch. 'Nothing cheap for our ancestors! They had great bronze tripods with lion's claw feet, topped with silver candelabras.'

Tarquinius' sole experience of luxury was occasionally seeing the simple banqueting hall in Caelius' villa. Its statues and paintings were drab in comparison. His master did not waste money on frivolity.

'The Rasenna were a wealthy people,' Olenus continued. 'In our heyday we ruled the Mediterranean Sea, trading jewellery, bronze figures and amphorae with every civilisation that existed.'

'What did our forebears look like?'

'Wealthy ladies dressed elegantly in fine robes, with beautiful necklaces, arm rings and bracelets of silver and gold. Some wore long hair loose over their shoulders. Others had tresses to the side of the face.'

'Good company for dinner!'

'Not sure they would feel the same way. Here we are – an old haruspex and a young man with only a bow and arrow to his name!' Both laughed at the image of two Etruscans in a cave, celebrating the wealth of a race who had crumbled into dust generations before.

The lamb was very tender, flesh tearing off the bone with ease. As Tarquinius watched the haruspex devour more than half the roasted meat, an image of Dexter came to him. Tarquinius pushed the burly foreman from his mind. He was determined to enjoy the meal, the last days with Olenus.

When they had finished, the two men curled up by the warm embers. Tarquinius could not shake off his sadness and Olenus seemed content to remain silent.

He watched the sleeping soothsayer for a long time. A faint smile occasionally played on his wrinkled features. Olenus was at peace.

It was many hours before Tarquinius' eyes closed.

When he awoke, Olenus had produced bundles of manuscripts, leaving them in dusty piles on the basalt altar. He made Tarquinius study for hours, continually asking him questions about their content. There was a real sense of urgency in the haruspex' manner and Tarquinius concentrated hard, memorising every last detail.

Olenus also handed him a map, unfolding the cracked leather with enormous care.

'You've never shown me this before.'

'Didn't see a need to,' smiled the old man slyly.

'Who drew it?'

'One of our ancestors. A soldier in Alexander's army perhaps.' He shrugged. 'Who knows? The *Periplus* was ancient before I was born.'

Tarquinius pored over the parchment. He had seen none of it yet, but the world outside Etruria was totally fascinating to him.

Olenus indicated the centre of the drawing. 'This is the Mediterranean Sea. Ever since they destroyed Carthage, the Romans have called it *Mare Nostrum*. Our sea.'

'Arrogant bastards.'

'Pay attention!' Olenus' voice was sharp. 'Italy and Greece you know. Here is Lydia in the southwest of Asia Minor. Following the coastline, Syria, Judaea and Egypt.'

'And this?' Tarquinius pointed east of where Olenus' finger had indicated.

'That is Parthia and beyond it lies Margiana.' A strange look flitted across Olenus' face, but he did not elaborate. 'Tarchun came from Resen, a city on the great River Tigris. The land was called Assyria well before the Parthians conquered it.'

'Tarchun!' Tarquinius spoke the name aloud with pride.

'He was a giant to bring our people through so many perils without harm.' Olenus tapped the faded leather again, near the right-hand margin, above Margiana. 'This is Sogdia. Its people have yellow skin and long black hair. They are expert horsemen who fight with bows. To the southeast is Scythia, where Alexander of Macedon finally came to grief.'

Tarquinius was intrigued. The places were further away than he could imagine. 'Did the Rasenna come from Parthia?'

'Who knows?' Olenus lifted a bushy eyebrow. 'Find out for yourself.'

The haruspex' reading came back in a flash. It was beyond Tarquinius' wildest dreams to think of following the route travelled by the first Etruscans.

'A journey back to our origins.' Olenus surveyed the mountainside where he had spent his whole life. 'I would have liked to do the same myself,' he said quietly.

'I will think of you everywhere!'

'That would please me, Arun.'

Awareness of Olenus' impending death never left Tarquinius but he consoled himself by relishing every moment of their time together. To his dismay, the old man announced on the second evening that Tarquinius would have to leave next morning.

'Take it all!' he said. 'Liver, sword, *lituus*, the map. Everything.'

'We need at least one more day,' pleaded Tarquinius. 'There is so much to learn!'

'I've taught you everything, Arun.' The haruspex had taken to using the ancient term all the time. 'And you know it. You still have to kill that sixth wolf, remember?'

'I don't care!' Tarquinius picked up the *gladius*, stabbing an imaginary Caelius. 'I'll gut that bastard!'

'Not now.'

He looked at Olenus keenly. 'What do you mean?'

'Destiny cannot be avoided. Caelius will come in three days.'

Tarquinius clenched his fists.

'Tomorrow morning you will leave and I will spend the day with the ancestors, preparing myself for the end.'

61

Tarquinius sighed. The last few hours together might as well be happy ones. 'Talk me through the points on the liver one more time.'

With a smile, the haruspex obeyed.

'I'll bury it with the *lituus* near the estate buildings. It will be safe there.'

'No!' Olenus said sharply. 'The bronze can be hidden as you say, but everything else must go with you.'

'Why? They'll be there when I get back.'

The wrinkled face was impenetrable.

Tarquinius shivered. 'I won't be returning?'

There was real sadness in Olenus' eyes. He shook his head once in reply.

'May my travels last many years then!'

'They will, Arun. More than two decades.' He touched the map gently. 'The *Periplus* will be of enormous use. Write down all that you see. Complete the knowledge of our ancestors and take it to the city of Alexander.'

Tarquinius tried to take in the scale of the task before him.

'The *lituus* must be there at the end.' Olenus' voice was sombre. 'And burned with your body.'

For once, Tarquinius himself did not acknowledge the comment. 'And when the soldiers have killed you?'

'The birds can pick my bones clean,' said Olenus calmly. 'It does not matter.'

'I *will* come back,' vowed Tarquinius. 'I will build a pyre. Perform the rituals.'

Olenus seemed pleased. 'Be sure Caelius has gone. I don't want all my hard work going to waste.'

A lump formed in Tarquinius' throat.

'We Etruscans will live on through the Romans. Even without the liver, their ambition and the information in the *libri* will help them conquer the world.' Olenus saw Tarquinius glance towards the cave and its huge pile of manuscripts. 'Those I will burn. But the Romans already possess many copies taken from our cities. The most important set is already locked away inside the temple of Jupiter in Rome.' He laughed. 'The superstitious fools only consult it in times of great danger.'

Tarquinius was filled with sadness. He had to make himself look the old man in the eye. 'And our people will just wither into dust?'

'You will pass on much information,' replied Olenus enigmatically.

'To whom? There are few pure-bred Etruscans left in the world.'

Olenus removed a small gold ring from his left forefinger. 'Take this.' Finely decorated with a scarab beetle, it had been on the old man's hand as long as Tarquinius had known him. 'Give this to your adopted son at the end. Although Roman, he will be known as a friend of the Rasenna. Some will always remember.'

'Adopted son?'

'All will become clear, Arun.'

Tarquinius waited, hoping for more.

Suddenly Olenus grabbed his arm. 'Caesar must remember he is mortal,' he hissed. 'Do not forget. Your son must tell him that.'

'What?' Tarquinius had no idea what Olenus meant.

'One day a divination will explain everything.' The haruspex turned away and would no longer respond to questions. He shrank into himself, deep in a trance that lasted till the next morning. It was as if Olenus had been drained of all energy, leaving nothing but an empty husk.

Tarquinius' heart was heavy as he filed away Olenus' words at the back of his mind. Gently he laid out the old man in a comfortable position by the fire and for what remained of the night, sat by him, keeping vigil. He had accepted that everything was pre-ordained, but had never imagined having to accept the death of some-one so close. Waves of grief washed over him and the sky was paling before Tarquinius had reconciled himself to the fate of someone dearer than his own father. He was now the last haruspex and only his efforts would prevent the ancient knowledge being forgotten for ever. Except by the Romans. Olenus' years of love and effort must not be wasted. It was a heavy burden, but his burning pride in his ancestry gave the young Etruscan a huge sense of purpose.

Next morning was chilly and full of bright sunlight. Thanks to the cave's altitude, temperatures dropped much lower than in the valley. Silence filled the crisp air and the sky was clear of birds. No living creatures were visible on the bare slopes, but Tarquinius knew from experience it was a good time to hunt. The tracks he had seen the night before would lead him to the wolves.

Neither spoke as Tarquinius filled his pack and ate a piece of dry bread. The haruspex sat on a rock by the entrance, watching quietly, a satisfied look on his face.

'Thank you. For everything.' Tarquinius swallowed hard. 'I will always remember you.'

'And I will never forget.'

They grasped forearms. Olenus seemed to have aged even more overnight, but his grip was still strong.

'Go safely, Arun. We will meet in the afterlife.' The old man was calm and serene, at one with his destiny.

Tarquinius lifted his pack; it was heavier now with the liver, staff and sword inside. The map was tucked safely against his chest in a small pouch. He tried to find words.

'There is nothing more to say.' As always, the haruspex had read his mind. 'Go now and be blessed.'

Tarquinius turned and strode down the track, an arrow notched to the bowstring.

He did not look back.

Chapter IV: Brennus

Nine years pass . . .
Transalpine Gaul, 61 BC

'Loose, before it sees us!'
'Long shot.' The Gaulish warrior looked at his younger cousin and grinned. 'It's at least a hundred paces,' he whispered.

'You can do it.' Brac held the two hunting dogs close, stroking them softly to stop any whining.

Brennus pulled a face, eyes returning to the deer standing between the trees. His powerful bow was already half drawn in preparation, goose-feathered arrow fitted to the string. They had crept the last distance on hands and knees, coming to rest behind a huge fallen trunk. Thanks to the brisk wind blowing away from it, the animal was totally unaware of the men's presence.

The pair had been following the tracks all morning, the dogs' noses guiding them through dense summer undergrowth. The deer had moved without concern, nibbling on leaves from the lower branches and it had paused to drink some rainwater pooled in the gnarled roots of an old oak.

Belenus guide my arrow, thought Brennus.

Drawing the gut string to full stretch, he closed one eye and took aim. It took immense strength to hold the bow at full draw, but the barbed arrow tip remained steady as a rock. Exhaling, the Gaul loosed the shaft. It flew straight and true, driving deep into the deer's chest with a soft thump.

The quarry toppled to the ground.

Brac clapped Brennus on the shoulder. 'A heart shot! Saved us a long chase.'

The two men loped through the trees, almost unseen in their brown fabric shirts and green trousers. Brac was tall and strong limbed, but his cousin towered over him. The big man's face was broad and cheerful, dominated by a battered apology of a nose. After the fashion of their tribe, the Allobroges, they wore their blond hair in pigtails tied with cloth bands. Both warriors were armed with bows and long spears for hunting. Daggers hung from hide belts.

The deer's eyes had already begun to glaze over. With a few precise cuts of his knife, Brennus freed the arrow, cleaning off the tip on some nearby moss. Shoving it back into the quiver, he muttered another prayer to Belenus, his favourite deity.

'This won't get back to camp on its own. Cut down that sapling.'

They tied the legs to a sturdy branch with strips of leather Brennus carried in his pouch. With a heave of effort, the pair picked up the dead beast. Its head bobbed up and down with the movement. The dogs growled with excitement, licking at blood that dripped steadily from the chest wound.

'How many more do we need?'

'One, maybe two. That'll be enough meat for both families.' Brennus shifted the load on his shoulder slightly, smiling at the thought of his wife Liath and baby son. 'More than the fools in the village will have.'

'They have no time to hunt,' said Brac. 'Caradoc says the gods will look after us when the Romans have been defeated.'

'Old fool,' Brennus muttered and instantly regretted the loss of control. Usually he kept his opinions to himself.

Brac was shocked. 'Caradoc is the chieftain!'

'He may be, but my family needs food for the winter now. When they have sufficient, I will join the rebellion. Not before.' Brennus stared hard at Brac, who was barely old enough to shave.

'Tell him, then.'

'Caradoc will find out in his own time.' Two missing at the spear count would be obvious enough. Brennus would have to justify their absence when they returned.

'You should be in charge of the tribe anyway,' said Brac.

Brennus sighed. He had been approached often enough recently. Many warriors were keen for him to challenge the ageing Caradoc, chief for nearly twenty years.

'I don't like leading men, cousin. Except in battle, and that should be avoided if possible. I am no use at negotiating.' He shrugged his broad shoulders. 'I'd rather be out hunting or with my woman than settling arguments.'

'If you had led the fight last year, the Romans would not have returned.' Blind faith shone from Brac's face. 'You would have smashed them completely!'

'Caradoc's no friend of mine,' growled Brennus. 'But he is a good leader. No one could have done better against those bastards.'

Brac fell silent, unwilling to argue further. The youngster hero-worshipped his cousin. It was why he was not in the village, preparing for war.

'Caradoc says none will leave our land alive,' Brac ventured, eyes still eager.

The big man felt bad at his outburst. 'There'll still be plenty left for us,' he said reassuringly. 'The scouts said there were thousands in the next valley.'

'Not too many?'

He laughed. 'Nobody beats the Allobroges. We are the bravest tribe in all Gaul!'

Brac grinned happily.

Brennus knew that his words were hollow. Sick of broken promises, Caradoc had finally led the tribe against its Roman masters the previous summer, protesting at the new, extortionate taxes. His initial efforts to win justice through negotiation had met with abject failure. Rome only understood war. And remarkably, the first campaign had been successful, driving the legions off Allobroges land.

But victory had come at a heavy price.

Fully half the warriors had been killed or maimed. While the Gauls had no way of replacing their dead, the

Romans seemed to have an inexhaustible supply to draw on. Just two months after their defeat, Republican cavalry had begun raiding outlying settlements. A wave of savage reprisals had only been halted by the arrival of bad weather.

Soon Brennus knew his people would be defeated, crushed and enslaved, just like every other tribe who had once lived nearby. There were too few warriors left to repel the imminent Roman attack.

Pomptinus, the governor of Transalpine Gaul, and ambitious politicians like Pompey Magnus were hungry for slaves, wealth and land and would take it by whatever means were necessary. For several years, burnt-down villages and bloody tales from passing traders had been commonplace. New settlers, tough ex-legionaries who deliberately encroached on tribal territory, provided more evidence. Increasing the taxes had been means to an end, a way to goad the Allobroges into rebellion.

Now they stood alone – against Rome.

And Caradoc would not listen to his counsel.

Confident that battle would not be joined for a week or more, the frustrated warrior had decided to gather his winter meat early. Hunting was a vain attempt to forget what was happening in the valleys below.

'I want an eagle standard,' Brac's face was eager. 'Like the one taken last summer.'

'You will have one,' lied Brennus. 'When the Romans have been beaten.'

The young warrior swung his free arm through the air, mimicking a sword thrust. He nearly dropped the end of the branch.

'Steady now!' said Brennus fondly.

The Gauls reached the temporary camp hours later, both men sweating from carrying the deer. Brac gratefully dropped his end of the carcass. A dog darted in to lick the blood and Brennus kicked it away with a curse.

The site had been their home for four days. The big man had led his cousin away from the village at the valley mouth, far from where other warriors usually hunted. They had toiled up wooded mountain slopes for the whole morning, finally reaching a large clearing through which a shallow stream flowed.

Brennus had gestured expansively. 'Water and firewood. Open space so the sun can dry the meat. What more do we need?'

As soon as they had erected the hide tent that would protect them against rain, the hunt had begun. That first afternoon had been unsuccessful, but Brennus returned calmly to the camp and constructed several wooden racks.

He had gazed at the sky and smiled. 'Belenus will guide us tomorrow. I feel it in my bones.'

By the following evening, the dogs had been fighting over the stripped carcasses of two deer, while Brennus and Brac sat by the fire, stomachs bulging. Further hunts had also been fruitful, with a boar and another deer falling to their arrows. The animal they had just killed brought the tally to five.

'We don't need more.' Brac pointed at the drying frames creaking under the weight of meat. 'And the spear count was today. We should get back.'

'Very well,' Brennus sighed. 'Let's eat plenty tonight

and return in the morning. Today's kill can always dry in the village.'

'Won't have missed it, will we?' Brac was chafing to blood himself against the invaders. The impending clash had been the main topic of conversation for weeks. Caradoc was very charismatic, drumming his people into a frenzy of hatred against the legions.

'I doubt it.' Brennus tried to sound casual. 'We had three weeks of skirmishes before the battle last year. Remember?'

'How could I forget?' Brac could still picture warriors returning laden with Roman weapons and supplies, giddy with success.

Transalpine Gaul had been under the Republic's control for over sixty years and large numbers of troops were permanently stationed near its towns. The Allobroges' final victory, thanks to their guerrilla attacks from the safety of the forest, had been most unusual. And it had come at a high price, something few of the men seemed to have considered.

'Perhaps Caradoc can see what will happen,' Brennus muttered. 'Is it better to die free than to flee our lands like cowards?'

'What was that?'

'Nothing, lad. Get the fire going. Got a hunger on me like a bear after winter.'

Brac had so much to learn and as his oldest male relative, it was Brennus' job to teach him. As he began butchering the deer, the big warrior prayed the gods would allow him to complete the task as well as protecting his wife and child, the only people more important to him than Brac and his family. Thoughts of fleeing with them over the mountains before any fighting seemed weak, but, like defeat, flight was inevitable. In Brennus' mind, certain death awaited any who stayed to fight the Romans. Caradoc had persuaded the warriors otherwise. Concerned and frustrated, Brennus had approached the tribe's druid for help some time before, but Ultan would not get involved. And as expected, Caradoc had refused even to consider leading his people to safety. 'The Allobroges do not run like dogs!' he had roared. 'We will crush the legions. Teach Rome a lesson it will not forget!' Brennus had persisted and a threatening look had entered the old chieftain's eyes. Wary of Caradoc's evil temper, he had sworn his loyalty and not spoken of the matter in public again, even to his friends. Only talk of fighting the Romans was permitted.

The stand-off with Caradoc had made Brennus' decision easier. Using the hunt as a practice run, he would gather the two families upon his return and leave immediately. Liath and Brac's mother knew of the plan, but Brennus had decided not to tell his cousin until the very last moment. Still naïve, Brac might inadvertently reveal the plan to another warrior.

The men worked in silence, gutting the deer, slicing meat into thin strips and hanging it from the racks. One leg was fixed to a spit and suspended over the fire. Soon after the sun had set, the clearing was full of the smell of roasting flesh. The dogs sat close by, knowing they would eventually get something.

By the time the pair had eaten, the moon had risen. Mountain air began to cool fast. They huddled closer, wrapped in blankets, dogs chewing bones at their feet.

'Second-best place in the world up here.' Brennus waved a hand at the panorama, belching contentedly. The moon hung above nearby mountains, casting a beautiful light on the snowy peaks. Only the reassuring crackle of burning logs broke the silence. 'Good day's hunting, then a belly full of meat by a warm fire.'

'Where's the best place to be?' Brac asked curiously.

'Under the blankets with your woman of course!'

Brac blushed and changed the subject. 'Tell me a story about the time before the Romans came.'

Brennus was happy to oblige. Recounting long tales about hunting or cattle raids was one of his favourite pastimes and popular with everyone in the village. He launched straight into the story of the biggest wolf ever killed by an Allobroge.

Brac's face lit up.

'The winter of ten years ago was one of the hardest in living memory,' began Brennus. 'The heavy blizzards drove packs of starving wolves down from the forests. With nothing to eat, they began to prey on our penned cattle every night. But none of the warriors dared go out to hunt them.' He shrugged expressively. 'The snow was waist deep and there were rarely less than twenty of the creatures together.'

His cousin looked round the clearing nervously.

'Within a month, dozens of cows had been killed. Then an old man collecting firewood was attacked at the edge of the forest and Conall, your father, had had enough. With my help, he worked for days making large traps.'

'And you caught plenty!' Brac's eyes shone and he rubbed the long canine tooth hanging from a leather thong round his neck.

Brennus nodded. 'Five in as many nights. The wolves quickly became more cautious and people's spirits rose. But it was not long before the pack's alpha male and a few others began to return, killing a beast with each visit. They had become far too clever to take the bait in the cages and men began to say that they were evil spirits.'

'Ultan says they were too scared to help.'

Brennus raised his eyebrows, taking a drink from his water carrier.

'Conall and I talked. There was no question of following the wolves into the woods. Up there the drifts were deeper than a man. So the next night Conall tied an old cow to a stake outside the palisade. There was no moon, just a few stars. He wouldn't let me stay with him. Said I was too young.' Brennus grinned, fondly remembering the man who had taught him everything he knew about weaponry. His own father had died when he was only an infant. 'So I sat on the walkway with my bow and a hidden torch.'

'Where was Father?' Brac had heard the story a thousand times but always asked.

'Wrapped in a fur cloak and deep in a snowdrift, close by the ox. It was a long, cold wait.'

'Half the night, he said.'

The big warrior nodded. 'Of course the cow smelt the wolves first and began bellowing like mad. Conall stayed calm and waited, as a good hunter always does. I could see nothing at all from my position.' Brennus lifted a hand to his eyes, squinting dramatically into the darkness. 'Then suddenly they appeared: seven grey shadows creeping across the ice.'

Brac shivered with delight.

'The alpha male came in fast, going straight for the kill. I quickly planted the torch on the battlements to give me light, but the wolves were so hungry that they didn't even pause.'

'Father said you roared like devils were after you,' laughed Brac.

'Of course I did! They'd have smelt him any moment.' Brennus shuddered. 'One man against that many wolves wouldn't stand a chance.'

'He jumped up and you had already killed three with arrows.'

Brennus shrugged. 'His task was far more dangerous. As I shot the third beast, Conall took the head off a fourth and maimed another, leaving only the leader and his mate. They were savaging the poor cow. I killed the female and managed to draw a bead on the male just as he turned to face Conall. They were only twenty paces apart, far enough for me to loose safely. But your father yelled at me to hold. "The bastard's mine!" he said.'

There was silence for a moment.

Brennus stared at Brac. 'He was the bravest man I have ever known. That wolf was as big as a bear and Conall had no shield and no armour. Just his sword and a hunting knife.'

Brac rocked to and fro, barely able to contain his excitement.

'The wolf kept darting in, trying to knock him over,

but Conall kept it at bay with ease, waiting for a chance. Then he slipped on the snow and fell flat on his back, losing his sword. Before I could react, the alpha male leapt into the air.' Brennus' voice dropped. 'It was going to rip his throat out.'

He paused and Brac's grip on the tooth tightened.

'Somehow Conall drew his dagger and turned it upwards with both hands. The blade went straight through the wolf's heart as it landed.'

'You thought he was dead!'

'Seemed that way until he pushed the body off,' replied Brennus with a smile. 'I've never been so relieved.'

'Father always said he could never have done it without you. The only one who would help.'

'It was nothing,' Brennus muttered awkwardly.

'It meant a lot to him. And me.'

Brennus quickly looked away.

'Tell me another,' said Brac, trying to lighten the atmosphere, but it was the wrong thing to say.

'Not tonight.' Brennus poked a stick at the blaze, releasing a stream of sparks into the night sky. 'Another time, perhaps.' He gazed sombrely into the flames, mood changed. Conall's death the previous summer still affected him deeply. At the end of a major skirmish against the Romans, Brennus had been swept away from the main body of warriors and surrounded by dozens of legionaries. As the big man had watched his fellow Allobroges run for the safety of the trees, he had asked the gods for a swift death. But instead of fleeing like the rest, Conall had led several men on a suicidal counter-attack, saving his nephew but losing his own life. Guilt had weighed heavily on Brennus since, and Brac knew better than to persist.

'Get some rest. It will be tough tomorrow carrying all that meat.'

The younger warrior obediently curled up in his blanket, secure in the knowledge that he was being watched over.

Brennus stayed awake for some time, brooding about Conall and remembering Ultan's last words.

The tribe's druid had been an old man when Brennus' father was a boy. No one could explain how Ultan had lived for so long, but he was feared and respected by all and his blessings and predictions were an integral part of tribal life. If a child or beast was sick, Ultan was called for. No one could draw an arrow from a wound or treat a fever like the druid. Even Caradoc consulted him before making any important decisions.

Brennus had been weaned on Ultan's amazing tales, told by the fire in the meeting house on cold winter nights. He looked up to the druid like no other and in turn Ultan had a soft spot for the man who had grown into one of the mightiest Allobroge warriors ever seen.

Before he and Brac left to go hunting, Brennus had asked Ultan for a blessing. Frustrated that the druid would not intervene on his behalf with Caradoc, he had not lingered to chat in Ultan's ramshackle hut on the edge of the village. Prayer completed satisfactorily, Brennus had reached the door when the old man spoke.

'You are always one for long trips.'

Peering into the dim interior, Brennus had been unable to make out the druid's features. Bunches of herbs and mistletoe hung from nails beside the dried carcasses of birds and rabbits. Brennus had shivered. It was said that Ultan could brew a potion to charm the gods themselves. 'Will it be a difficult hunt, then?'

'More than that,' Ultan had muttered. 'A journey beyond where any Allobroge has gone. Or will ever go. Your destiny cannot be avoided, Brennus.'

He had steeled himself. 'I will die in the forest?'

Brennus had thought he saw a trace of sadness in the old man's eyes. In the poor light, he had not been sure.

'Not you. Many others. *You* will take a path of great discovery.'

Despite the fire's heat, a shiver ran down the big man's spine. Typically, Ultan had refused to explain further. Unsettled, Brennus was worried enough to offer more prayers to Belenus than normal as they had climbed the wooded slopes. The hunt had gone well so far, but he knew the druid's predictions tended to be accurate. Would his family be safe? Would Brac's? Although it was early summer, the journey over the mountains was not without peril. Snow, ice, swiftly flowing rivers and dangerous paths awaited them.

Or had Ultan meant something else altogether?

He stared round the quiet clearing. The normally alert dogs twitched happily as they dreamt of chasing deer. Nothing. Closing his eyes with a sigh, Brennus pulled the blanket closer and lay protectively beside Brac. He slept well, without dreaming.

It was the last peaceful rest Brennus would have for many years.

When the younger warrior awoke, the sun's rays were

already lighting up the mountains on the other side of the valley, turning the snow on the sharp peaks pink, then orange. He threw off his blanket and stood up, shivering in the early morning air.

'Had enough sleep?' Brennus laughed, over by the drying racks.

Brac flushed with guilt when he saw the packs were ready. All that was left to do was roll up the bedding and fill their leather water carriers from the stream. 'How long was I asleep?' he muttered, hurrying.

'As long as you needed.' Brennus' tone was kindly. 'Feeling rested?'

'Yes.'

'Good! Try this on.'

Staggering under the weight of one pack, Brennus gestured at the other beside him. With help, Brac managed to fit the bulging bag on his back. He noted with shame that it was much lighter than his cousin's.

'Let me take the heavier one.'

'I'm bigger and stronger. That's all there is to it. Yours is heavy enough.' Brennus clapped him on the arm reassuringly. 'It's more than most could carry.'

Brennus led the way, using a hunting spear to steady himself on uneven ground. Brac and the dogs followed close behind. The little party made steady progress through the forest and by mid-morning they had covered just over half the distance back to the settlement.

'Time for another rest.' Gratefully Brennus lowered his pack by a large beech tree.

'I can go further.'

'Sit down.' He patted the moss, thinking it was a good

time to tell Brac about his plan. 'Let's eat. Leave less to carry afterwards.'

They both laughed.

The pair sat beside each other, leaning against the broad trunk. In companionable silence, they drank water and chewed on dried meat.

'Is that smoke?' Brac pointed to the south.

There was a thick grey plume rising over the nearest treetops.

Brennus' fist clenched on his spear. 'Get up! That's from the village.'

'But how . . .?' Brac looked confused.

'Leave your pack and blanket. Take only weapons.'

The young warrior quickly obeyed and moments later they were running full pelt downhill, dogs at their heels. Brennus ran as if the gods were giving him strength and it wasn't long before Brac began to fall behind. He was fit and healthy, but there were few men who could match his cousin's physical prowess. When the big Gaul noticed Brac struggling, he stopped.

'What's going on?' Brac asked, chest heaving.

Brennus was a hopeless liar. 'I don't know, lad. A cooking fire out of control, perhaps?' He stared at the ground, Ultan's words echoing in his head.

Not you. Many others.

'Don't shield things from me,' said Brac. 'I'm a man, not a child.'

Brennus' eyebrows rose. Brac wasn't as naïve as he appeared. 'All right. Our warriors must have been defeated.' He sighed heavily. 'The bastards obviously didn't wait for us to offer battle.'

Brac's face paled. 'And the smoke?'

'You know what happens. The village is being put to the torch.' Brennus closed his eyes. Liath. Their newborn baby. What had he been thinking to leave his family at such a time?

'Why have we stopped?' Brac pushed past roughly, feet sure on the narrow path.

They ran for a long time, guilt and rage giving them strength. Neither spoke, and they stopped to rest only occasionally. A short distance from the settlement, Brennus at last slowed down and came to a halt. Even the dogs seemed glad of an opportunity to rest. But his cousin kept running.

'Brac, stop!'

'Why? They might still be fighting!'

'And arrive completely winded? What damn use would that be?' Brennus breathed deeply, calming himself. 'Always go into combat prepared.'

Reluctantly Brac walked back to where the big man was standing, feeling the edge on a spear tip.

'This is good enough for a boar,' said Brennus, baring his teeth savagely. 'Should kill a bastard Roman or two.'

Brac spat on the ground in agreement, checking every arrow tip was well attached. Then he looked up. 'Ready, cousin?'

Brennus nodded proudly. It was at times like this that a warrior knew who would stand by him. But a knot of fear was forming in his stomach. Terrified for his family's safety, Brennus also wanted to protect Brac from danger. As Conall had done for him.

They moved off at a slow trot, concentrating on their

surroundings, wary of possible ambush. Following paths familiar to both, they soon reached the edge of the trees. Already it was obvious something was wrong. Summer was a busy time of the year, yet there was nobody out hunting or picking fallen wood, no children playing in the shade.

The sight that greeted Brennus would haunt him for ever. Past strips of cultivated land running up to the forest, his village was in flames. Thick spirals of smoke billowed upwards from thatched roofs. Screams carried through the air.

Thousands of legionaries surrounded the defensive wooden palisade that had always served the Allobroges well. The invaders were clad in chain mail and russet-brown thigh-length tunics. They had heavy, elongated oval shields with metal bosses, viciously barbed *pila* and short stabbing swords. Their rounded bronze helmets had protected ear flaps and neck guards. Some were plain, others were decorated with simple horsehair crests. Brennus knew and hated every distinctive part of the Roman soldier's garb.

Behind the close-ranked cohorts stood the *ballistae,* massive wooden catapults that had fired flaming missiles over the walls. Trumpeters at the rear followed orders from red-cloaked senior officers, blowing staccato bursts from their *bucinae* to direct the attack. Every man knew his task, every sequence was planned and there would be only one outcome.

So unlike the brave, disorganised chaos of a Gaulish battle charge.

The deep moat round the stockade had already been filled with wood in numerous places. Long ladders were in place against the walls, allowing attackers to swarm up. More legionaries were heaving a battering ram to and fro against the main gates. Here and there an occasional figure fired arrows from the walkway, but the battlements were almost bare.

'There's no resistance!'

'The warriors won't have run,' said Brac, face pale.

Brennus shook his head, a shiver running down his spine.

The lack of opposition meant only one thing: Caradoc and the men had been beaten, leaving the village defended only by women and the old.

There was no chance of saving Liath and the baby. Nausea washed over Brennus and he bit his lip until he felt the salty taste of blood. The pain focused his thoughts, preventing him from blindly charging forward. *Not you. Many others.*

Ultan had foreseen the attack and sent him hunting anyway.

'Come on!' Brac was also ready to leave the trees' protection.

A giant hand gripped his arm. 'It is too late.' Brennus frowned, staring at the sky. 'We came back a day early. The gods meant us to be up the mountain, not here. Ultan warned me.'

'The druid? He's crazy. We can't just stand here and watch!'

'They are all good as dead.'

'But your wife, Brennus!'

He clenched his teeth. 'Liath will take her own life and the child's before a single Roman touches them.'

Brac looked at him with total disbelief. 'Coward.'

Brennus slapped him hard across the face. 'Two of us against thousands of Romans?'

Brac fell silent, tears running down his cheeks.

The big man stood, trying to think. 'Listen if you want to live.'

Brac gazed at the burning settlement. 'Why live after that?' he asked dully.

Brennus saw the anguish in his cousin's face. The same distorted his own. Brac's mother and sisters were also doomed and he shuddered, trying to thrust their fate from his mind. After Liath and the baby, they were the only family he had in the world. Somehow he conjured up Ultan's expression that last day. Had it been sad? He couldn't be sure. What was now certain was that the Allobroges were taking a voyage to the other side. But that was not *his* path, according to the druid.

Why had Ultan refused to talk to Caradoc and kept silent about this attack? There could be only one answer. The druid's message must have come from the gods. He had to believe that, or his sanity would be lost.

'We go back to the meat. Take enough for a month. Then cross the mountains, join the Helvetii. They are a strong tribe and no friends of Rome.'

'But our people . . .' Brac began weakly.

'The Allobroges are finished!' said Brennus, hardening his heart. He had never imagined it would come to this. 'Ultan told me I was to go on a great journey, one never taken before.' There were only a few moments to convince Brac before they were seen. 'This *must* be what he meant.'

Wiping his eyes, Brac gulped and surveyed the village

once more. As they watched, the roof of the meeting house fell with a great shower of sparks and flames. Cheers rose from legionaries outside the walls.

The end was near.

Brac nodded, trust in his cousin implicit.

Brennus shoved the younger man in the back. 'Let's go. This way the Allobroges will live on.'

The warriors turned to leave, dogs close behind. They had gone only a few paces when Brac stopped.

'What is it?' hissed Brennus. 'There's no time to waste.'

Brac looked stunned. A thin stream of blood ran from his mouth and he pitched forward on to both knees. Protruding from the middle of his back was a Roman javelin.

'No!' The big man darted to Brac's side, cursing as he glimpsed the legionaries who had crept within missile range unseen. There were at least twenty – far more than he could hope to kill on his own.

Grief filled him. There would be no more running.

'Sorry.' Brac gasped with the effort of speaking.

'For what?' Brennus snapped the *pilum* in two, lying Brac carefully on one side.

'Not running fast as you. Not listening enough.' The boy's face was ashen. He did not have long.

'Nothing to be sorry for, my brave cousin,' Brennus said gently, squeezing Brac's hand. 'Rest here a little. I need to kill some Roman bastards after all.'

Brac nodded weakly.

A lump filled Brennus' throat, but anger overtook the grief, surging through every vein. He gripped Brac's arm in farewell and got to his feet.

The druid had been wrong. He too would die today. What reason was there left to live?

There was a rush of air as javelins hummed past him, embedding themselves in trees with dull thudding sounds. One of the dogs collapsed, yelping in pain at the long metal shaft protruding from its belly. Unsure what to do, the second stood with tail firmly between its hind legs.

Many of the legionaries were within twenty paces now, running at full tilt.

'Sons of whores!' Brennus pulled out an arrow and fitted it to the string, drawing to full stretch. He released while hardly looking at the nearest soldier, knowing it would take his target in the throat. The Gaul's next three shafts killed as well. By then the Romans were so close he had to drop the bow and pick up a spear. As his enemies encircled him, curved *scuta* held high, swords ready, Brennus let battle rage engulf him. Any thoughts of a long journey were forgotten.

Because of him, his wife and child had died alone. Because of him, Brac was dead. He had failed everyone, and all Brennus wanted to do now was kill.

'Bastards!' He had learned dog Latin from traders who passed through every year. 'Come on! Who's next?' Without waiting for an answer, he hurled his spear. The heavy shaft punched effortlessly through a shield, driving links of chain mail deep into the soldier's chest cavity. The man collapsed without a sound, blood pouring from his mouth. Brennus stooped quickly and picked up Brac's weapon, repeating the procedure with a second Roman.

'You have only a dagger now, Gaulish scum.' A red-cloaked officer leading the legionaries gestured angrily. 'Take him!'

His men raised their *scuta* in unison, closing ranks, stepping over the bodies.

Brennus bellowed an inarticulate cry of rage and charged. His entire people had just been annihilated in one short, vicious encounter. He was about to die, wanted to die. Anything to end the pain.

Ripping the closest man's shield from his grasp, the warrior turned it on its edge. He swept round in a circle, knocking several enemies from their feet. In the confusion, Brennus jumped to stand over the legionary whose *scutum* he had taken. With a savage blow downwards, he decapitated the man with its metal rim. Blood spurted over his calves as he grabbed an unfamiliar *gladius* from the ground. Its owner would never need a weapon again. Gauging the balance, he swung the straight-edged blade, wishing it was a longsword.

Armed now, Brennus was an even more intimidating prospect. Unwilling to face certain death, the thirteen Romans remaining hung back.

'Seize him, you fools!' the officer screamed, the horse-hair crest on his helmet bobbing indignantly. 'Six months' pay for the man who takes him alive!'

Spurred on by the reward, they closed in, forming a tight circle of locked shields. The Gaul killed another three legionaries when they reached him, but at last a sword hilt connected with the back of his head. He stumbled, stabbing another enemy fatally in the groin as he went down.

A hail of blows followed.

Brennus landed on the bloody ground semi-conscious, his torso covered in minor wounds.

'Thank Jupiter most Gauls are not like this ox!' The officer smiled contemptuously. 'Otherwise you women would never conquer them.'

His men flushed with shame, but none replied. Their superior could inflict dire punishment if they answered back.

Concussed and confused, Brennus was still desperate to fight. He struggled to rise, but the last of his huge strength had been expended. Through a red haze, he heard the centurion speak again.

'Bind his arms and legs. Carry him to the surgeon.'

Fuelled by anger, one of the soldiers found the courage to speak. 'Let us kill the bastard, sir. He's done for eleven of us.'

'Fool! Governor Pomptinus wants as many slaves as possible. This one will be worth plenty as a gladiator in Rome. A lot more than you miserable scum.'

Brennus closed his eyes and let blackness take him.

Chapter V: Romulus and Fabiola

Five years later...
Rome, spring 56 BC

'Curse you, Romulus. Come quickly! Or you'll get another hiding!'

Gemellus paused in his tirade. A short, fat man with a red face, the merchant was prone to terrible bouts of rage. Sweating heavily, he stood in the large, sunlit courtyard of his house, eyes swivelling frantically. He spotted movement near an ornamental statue positioned between the plants and trees and, moving surprisingly fast, he shoved a podgy ringed hand behind the grinning satyr.

Instead of Romulus, Gemellus pulled out a young girl of about thirteen in a torn tunic. The child was covered in grime, her clothes little more than rags, but her extraordinary beauty was still apparent. Long black hair covered finely boned features that would catch any man's eye. She squealed in pain, but Gemellus held tightly on to her ear.

'Where's your brother, vixen?' He looked around, expecting to see Romulus nearby. Normally the twins were like each other's shadow.

'I don't know, Master!' Fabiola struggled even harder.

'You are lying!'

'He's supposed to be in the kitchen, Master.'

'Like you. But the little bastard's not!' replied the merchant triumphantly. 'So where is he?'

This time, the girl did not answer.

Gemellus slapped Fabiola's face. 'Find him, or I'll whip you both.'

She did not cry. No matter what Gemellus did, she always looked defiant.

Infuriated, the merchant swept a meaty paw at Fabiola but lost his grip.

She dodged easily under another wild swing and ran past the open-fronted rooms and banqueting halls forming the sides of the courtyard.

'Tell that useless brat to hurry!' His voice echoed through the house. Angrily, Gemellus eased his bulk on to the edge of a carved marble fountain positioned in the shade against the back wall of the colonnaded garden. A mosaic reservoir decorated its back; the intricate patterns were designed to be seen as visitors entered and gazed across the *atrium*, through the open doors of the *tablinum*.

He trailed a few fingers in the water to wet his brow. Fountains and sanitation were luxuries only the very rich could afford. Gemellus wondered how much longer it would be possible to keep up his extravagant lifestyle. The merchant had no wish to return to his impoverished roots in the *insulae*.

91

A shadow cast by the sundial in the middle of the courtyard told Gemellus that it was nearly *hora quarta*. Noon was still more than two hours off, but the spring air was already as hot as Hades. He cursed loudly, wiping his face with a fold of his grimy tunic. Life was difficult enough without pursuing Velvinna's brats around the villa. Political uncertainty in the Republic and floods of foreign imports had changed the economic climate from bad to worse. Weakened by years of poor leadership and corruption, the Senate had capitulated three years before and allowed Crassus, Pompey and Caesar to form a triumvirate. The move had placed almost complete control of the Republic in the hands of just three men, yet it had done little for stability.

The machinations of an ambitious but disgraced noble by the name of Clodius Pulcher had not helped either. Shunned by the Senate, he had cleverly cultivated popularity in the slums. All Clodius wanted was power, and he would do anything to achieve it. Soon he had a huge base of support amongst the poor, to whom he promised much. Clodius' wily tactics had culminated in his converting from patrician to plebeian, specifically so he could become a tribune.

Recognising a potentially powerful ally, the consul Julius Caesar had allowed Clodius' request to become a plebeian, a man of the people. Duly elected as a tribune, the maverick politician had begun by reforming the *collegia*, the old trade groups which had always existed at every crossroads in Rome. Naturally the heavies he had hired were fiercely loyal to him alone. Within weeks, the streets had belonged to Clodius; he had even turned on Caesar, his former sponsor.

But Caesar had more on his mind than mob politics. His share of the spoils was to be granted consular powers over three of the Republic's provinces. He quickly departed for the most lucrative, determined to make a name for himself as a general. Caesar travelled to Gaul.

Clodius kept on good terms with Crassus, wary of his political ability. But he was scared of nobody else. Pompey had been his next target. Soon the great man had been publicly abused in the Forum Romanum itself, even blockaded inside his own house. In retaliation, Pompey had sponsored Titus Milo, another tribune, who quickly recruited his own groups of thugs, even hiring professional gladiators to make up the numbers.

Fierce gang warfare had now been raging for over a year, affecting trade badly. Gemellus regularly had to bribe both sides to ensure that his merchandise entered and left Rome safely. His profit margins were plummeting. And after decades of unerring success in business, Gemellus' trial investment in Egyptian goods the previous summer had been disastrous. Freak storms had sunk twelve ships transporting the precious cargo of ivory, tortoiseshell and papyrus. The losses had created a huge hole in the merchant's riches, and everything he'd since touched had turned to dust. It was becoming hard not to believe the old superstition that living on the Aventine always brought bad luck.

He had delayed selling Fabiola and Romulus for too long. Even though the twins would fetch much more in a few years, Gemellus needed thousands of *sestertii* immediately. Interest on his debts was extortionate, frightening. He shuddered to think what the brutes working for those Greek moneylenders would do if he didn't keep up the weekly payments. So far, only the size of the arrears had prevented Gemellus from coming to serious harm. He'd be no use floating in the Tiber.

His thoughts turned back to Fabiola. The merchant had been lusting after her for some time, but he'd controlled himself, knowing virgins fetched far higher prices. Instead of an average twelve to fifteen hundred *sestertii* for a slave, Gemellus would get at least three times that for Fabiola in one of the city's brothels. Romulus wouldn't fetch as much, but a gladiator trainer would still pay more than he would get in the slave market.

Wearing only a grubby loincloth, Romulus slipped into the garden, interrupting Gemellus' reverie. He was the spitting image of his sister, but larger and with black hair cut short. An aquiline nose was the most prominent feature of his face. Like Fabiola's, his blue eyes had a subdued, determined look.

'Master?' he said, wishing he were big enough to give Gemellus the thick ear that his sister now had. They were fiercely loyal to each other.

Gemellus was surprised the young slave had appeared so quickly. Despite frequent beatings, it was common for the twins to ignore orders. He would have them both manacled soon, before ideas of escape entered their minds.

'Come over here,' he snapped, noting Romulus' height and strong brown limbs. He was big for his thirteen and a half years. Memor, the grizzled *lanista* at Rome's main gladiator school, would surely pay at least two thousand *sestertii* for him. Or maybe both could be sold to the Lupanar, the high-class brothel where he intended to take Fabiola. The sexual tastes of its clientele were known to be broad.

The merchant gripped Romulus' shoulder. 'I need a note taken to the house of Crassus.'

'The great general?'

'The same.'

The boy's eyes widened.

'Do you know where he lives?'

Like most slaves, Romulus was rarely trusted out alone in case he ran away. But there had been enough occasions for him to learn the city's basic layout and its most important houses. He nodded eagerly.

Life inside these thick walls was one of extreme drudgery. Having worked since the age of seven, Romulus was expert at sweeping the kitchen floor, chopping wood for the ovens, unblocking drains and other menial tasks. But much of the time he was bored. Most of his jobs could be finished in just a few hours. To be ordered to the *domus* of one of Rome's foremost men was a thrilling break in routine.

Gemellus reached into his tunic and pulled out a folded parchment sealed with wax. He frowned, worried that his largest creditor would refuse the plea he had composed.

'Make sure nobody follows you.' The Greeks' thugs had been watching every adult slave for days and they must not discover he owed money to others. 'Understand?'

'Yes, Master.'

'Wait for a reply.' Gemellus dismissed him. 'Be quick!'

Romulus darted into the *tablinum*, skidding across cool mosaic tiles. He paused just long enough to whisper his news to Fabiola, who had returned to peer into the garden.

She grinned as he tore off again, pleased for her brother.

Exiting the imposing reception room at speed, the boy nearly knocked over Quintus, the old slave who was sweeping round the rectangular pool that collected rainwater in the centre of the sunlit *atrium*.

'Sorry!'

Quintus smiled fondly. Aware of Gemellus' cruelty, Romulus often helped him when his chores grew too much. The salt mines awaited any in the house who could not work.

Quickly regaining his balance, Romulus pelted towards the heavy wooden doors that guarded Gemellus' house from the outside world.

Juba, the immense doorman, stood up when he saw Romulus approaching. He wore only a loincloth and his muscular body was covered in old scars. A bald head shone from the covering of grease the Nubian applied daily. Attracted by his size and fighting ability, Gemellus had bought Juba five years before. A man like this would keep trouble from the door and other slaves in check.

The Nubian lifted an eyebrow.

Romulus looked round, making sure nobody was within earshot. 'The master gave me a letter.' He blew out both cheeks and waddled closer, impersonating Gemellus. 'For Crassus, the famous general.'

Juba laughed, revealing the stump of his tongue. Gemellus had ordered it cut out when he had purchased the doorman. It meant the Nubian always had to consult his master or the major-domo when someone was outside. This reduced the chance of thieves entering the *domus*.

Romulus remembered watching with amazement as he walked into the house, still bleeding from the mouth. He was the first black man the boy had seen. And mutilation, poor food and frequent beatings had ensured that Juba hated their owner as much as Romulus did.

Soon after arriving, the Nubian had carved him a wooden sword, delighting the eight-year-old with his first toy. In return Romulus had stolen a loaf of bread from the kitchen. From then on, nightly raids had kept the giant fed. Their friendship had grown from there. Previously, Fabiola had been his only ally. Although the twins were very close, Romulus had unconsciously craved male company, rough and tumble play. He began to seek Juba out every day and, glad of the boy's presence, the Nubian let him share his bare alcove by the door without complaint. Velvinna knew how important the relationship was and did not interfere. Romulus would never have the influence of his father. Or even meet him.

Unless it was to exact revenge.

The rape was something she had always planned to tell Romulus and Fabiola about when they were older. Thanks to his increasing popularity, depictions of a certain noble had recently begun appearing in temples and shrines. Velvinna had seen many examples and was now reasonably sure of the twins' father's identity. She longed to tell them both, especially Romulus. Thirteen years later, the desire for revenge still burned inside her. But it was important that they enjoyed childhood as much as possible – before it was taken away by whatever Gemellus might plan. Mixed feelings filled Velvinna as she saw the merchant gazing speculatively at the children and her prayers to the gods grew more fervent.

Romulus knew none of this. Grinning broadly, he stood before two great portals at the entrance. They were seldom opened, except when important visitors arrived or Gemellus was holding a feast. Instead the inhabitants came and went through a postern gate in the middle of one door.

Throwing back the iron bolt, Juba smiled and held up a stern finger.

'I'll be careful!' Eagerly, Romulus eyed the curved blade shoved into the Nubian's wide leather belt. 'Can we practise again later?'

Juba mimed the cut and thrust of a sword fight.

Grinning broadly, Romulus ducked into the noisy street. A wave of heat hit him, assaulting his senses with its odours. As always in warm weather, the overwhelming smells were of human faeces and urine, fermenting on dung heaps in small dark alleyways.

He wrinkled his nose with disgust.

The narrow unpaved lane was crowded with people going about their business. Rome's working day began at sunrise, especially in summer when the extreme temperatures made life unbearable. The men and women Romulus saw pushing and shoving past were a mixture of every race in the Republic. Italians, Greeks, Spaniards, Nubians, Egyptians, Gauls, Judaeans, even the occasional Goth. Most were ordinary citizens or traders, trying to eke a living in the city designed for, and ruled by, the upper classes.

Many had come here to seek fame and fortune.

Few succeeded.

But their lot was better than those who had arrived as slaves, destined merely to serve as tiny cogs in the huge machine that the Republic had become. Only the rich, born into a heritage stretching back five hundred years, truly enjoyed the splendour of the metropolis and the opportunities it afforded.

A pair of heavily muscled men leaning against a wall opposite stood out, noticeable for their size and stillness. They were watching Gemellus' doorway like hawks. Thick leather wristbands, swords on belts and scarred arms meant only one thing. Trouble.

Juba had pointed them out earlier through a peephole. When Romulus left the villa, one of the heavies hurried after, trying to stay inconspicuous. The boy increased his pace, smirking at how easy it would be to lose his pursuer. Although he hated Gemellus, Romulus felt a loyalty to the household. Delivering the message as ordered was important.

Turning a corner without looking, he was nearly run down by a pair of oxen pulling a cart loaded with pottery.

'Mind where you're going, little bastard!' The drover waved a stick angrily, trying to bring his startled beasts under control. Loud crashes signalled breakages as some of the load came loose.

Guiltily, Romulus disappeared into the throng. Shouts of rage followed but neither carter nor thug had a chance of catching him. During the day all traffic moved at snail's pace through the packed streets. Only the Via Sacra, a paved avenue leading from the Velia's heights to the Forum, was wide enough to take two wagons abreast. Elsewhere, houses were no more than ten paces apart; far less in many places. Sunlight was all but excluded, creating a gloomy warren of narrow lanes.

He ducked down low, using other pedestrians as cover. Romulus was expert at squeezing his boyish frame between people, worming past without anyone noticing. Within a few dozen paces, he would be totally indistinguishable from the crowd.

Gemellus' *domus* lay on the Aventine Hill, a mainly plebeian area just south of the centre. The trader had never seen fit to leave his roots behind, even when he could have moved close to the Forum Romanum itself. As in most parts of Rome, the dwellings of rich and poor were positioned side by side. Large houses with impassive stone walls and monumental gates sat beside *insulae* up to five storeys tall. These buildings contained the tenement flats in which most people lived.

The alleys between paved streets remained as they had been since antiquity – covered with a mixture of mud and human waste. Far from main arteries into the centre, daily life here was a drudgery of using public fountains and toilets. Richer members of society living near larger ways were lucky enough to have household running water and sewage removal. Naturally Gemellus had both.

The note began to burn Romulus' hand as he walked. What did it say? Why were armed men waiting outside the *domus* day and night? He thought of opening it, but there was little point. Romulus longed to read and write but like all the household slaves apart from Servilius, the merchant's bookkeeper, he was illiterate. Gemellus did not spend any money unless it yielded a profit. Romulus sighed. Perhaps he would learn something at his destination.

His evasive move had pushed him along the Via Ostiensis, which led between the Palatine and Caelian Hills to the Via Sacra. This made the journey much longer, and at the next intersection Romulus elected to take the shorter route along the Clivus Publicius. The Servian wall wove in and out of view as the road rose and fell. A massive defensive barrier, it had once enclosed many of the sprawling suburbs, but as the population in these *vici* swelled inexorably, the wall had ceased to define the city's perimeter. Buildings now extended far beyond its protection – on to the edge of the Campus Martius, the plain to the northwest, and the land north of the Quirinal Hill. With Rome's power over the peninsula of Italy absolute for more than a hundred years, few worried about the danger of attack.

At every crossroads stood members of the *collegia*, no longer just traders and artisans, but Clodius' men, armed and dangerous. Romulus knew better than to attract their attention and kept his gaze firmly on the rutted mud beneath his sandals. A few moments later, a funeral procession went past in the opposite direction, the family preceded by a public crier.

'This citizen, Marcus Scaurus, has been surrendered to death,' the official intoned gravely. 'For those who find it convenient, it is now time to attend the funeral. He has been brought from his house and is being taken to the family tomb on the Via Appia.'

Romulus stared at the musicians who followed, playing solemn music to set the tone for mourners. Scaurus' washed body, dressed in a pristine white toga, was being borne on a funeral couch by half a dozen men whose close resemblance meant they must be relations. Slaves carried burning torches, a custom maintained from the time when processions had taken place at night. An attractive woman in her forties walked slowly behind the body, crying. She was well dressed, face painted white with lead. Other family members and friends followed, dressed in grey togas and tunics, the Roman colour of mourning.

Romulus walked on. Death was of no concern to him. Whilst he had no family tomb on the Via Appia, Romulus had no wish to be tossed into the stinking pits on the eastern slopes of the Esquiline Hill where slaves, paupers and criminals were buried with animal carcasses and the excess city waste. Ever since Romulus had become aware of his low status, he had been determined to gain freedom for himself and his family. Gemellus would not always be their master. But he had no idea how to achieve it. Simply having a rebellious spirit was not enough.

Six muscular slaves carrying a litter were preceded by another with a stick, whipping those too slow to get out of the way. Off-duty gang members lounged outside a tavern, drinking wine. It was a sign of changing times.

Historically such lowlife would not have dared appear so near the city centre. Even slaves knew about the recent political unrest and the ruthless manner in which the three nobles who formed the triumvirate had subjugated the Senate. And as the Republic grew weaker, crime and public disorder increased dramatically.

Clad in rough tunics and carrying swords and knives, the thugs whistled and yelled obscenities at any woman, old or young. But as the litter passed, they fell silent, still wary of attracting the attention of the great and noble. Romulus lingered for a moment, studying the hardware on display. Weapons fascinated him. Despite the risk of severe punishment, training with Juba was his favourite pastime.

Shops lining the street had wares stacked on display in front of them, greatly reducing the space for traffic. Potters sat at moving wheels, fashioning tableware. Blacksmiths hammered on their anvils, making iron tools. Amphorae of wine were laid out in rows on beds of straw. A butcher wielded a cleaver while his wife waved a frying pan full of sausages.

Saliva filled Romulus' mouth as he smelt the cooking pork, seldom on the menu for Gemellus' slaves.

'Got an *as* to spare?' cried the woman, recognising him. He had occasionally been sent here to buy meat.

Romulus' gaze dropped. He rarely got to hold a copper coin, let alone possess one.

She glanced sidelong at her husband before handing over half a sausage with a smile.

His eyes lit up at the unexpected kindness.

'Bring me a big order next time,' she said loudly.

Romulus munched happily as he ran past a money-changer sitting cross legged in an alcove. Little piles of coins were laid out in front of him; behind stood a hulking Goth bodyguard. In every available space sat cripples and beggars, their quavering voices competing with shopkeepers' cries.

Romulus had no idea how long the wait at Crassus' house would be. If the errand took too long for Gemellus' liking, he would receive a beating, so the faster it was done, the better. His pace increased.

Soon he reached the temple of the Great Mother, Cybele. It was one of many shrines to gods scattered across the city. The Romans had always welcomed foreign deities, even those of conquered peoples. That way subject nations more easily accepted the Republic's yoke.

Romulus' breath quickened in fear. Gemellus had threatened to sell him to Cybele's devotees many times. The alien goddess, with her strangely garbed priests and their blaring horns and bizarre practices, was held in high regard by most. But he did not care for the Magna Mater.

'To prove total devotion, the priests castrate themselves,' Gemellus had smirked.

That menace had only added to Romulus' hatred of the merchant. For many years, he had dreamt of killing him. Indelible images of the fat man's visits to his mother filled his mind. He would never forgive Gemellus for what he did to her each and every night.

'Close your eyes, children,' Velvinna would hiss when the door inched open.

Terrified, the twins had done their best to obey. But once the loud creaking had begun, it was hard not to look. Over many years, they had never heard their mother make a sound while Gemellus grunted on top of her.

Romulus stared at the enormous building coming into view on the Capitoline Hill. It was dedicated to Jupiter, the most important Roman deity, a god whose auspices were sought before war. The temple gazed down impassively from its vantage point, the most important structure built by the founders of Rome, the Etruscans. The façade's six massive columns were topped by a triangle of decorated terracotta and framed three doors to the *cellae*, sacred rooms dedicated to the triad of Juno, Minerva and Jupiter. Consuls sacrificed oxen here at the beginning of their term of office and the first meeting of the Senate took place inside each year. Triumphal marches always ended on the Capitoline Hill; its importance to the Roman people was immeasurable.

Jupiter, Greatest and Best! Give me one chance to kill Gemellus before I die. It was Romulus' silent daily prayer.

Finally, he reached the imposing stone wall marking the outside of Crassus' mansion. Like all houses of the wealthy, it presented a blank face to the outside world. Only a pair of large doors with sculpted lions' heads either side broke the smooth surface. Romulus stepped up to the entrance and lifted a heavy iron knocker carved in the shape of Jupiter's head. He rapped three times, then stepped smartly back, intimidated by the deep sound.

The door opened abruptly. A doorman as big as Juba, but with intricate tattooed spirals on his tanned face, emerged. 'What is it?' His fierce gaze fixed Romulus to the spot.

He pulled out the note. 'I have a message for Crassus, from my master.'

The slave checked out the street, then jerked his head. 'Inside.'

Romulus stepped across the threshold, into the house of the richest man in Rome. The huge figure slammed the door shut, throwing the bolts. He yanked on a rope hanging from the ceiling then sat back in his alcove, glaring. Clad in a rough tunic, his arms covered in old scars, the pigtailed slave was some kind of Goth.

Romulus stood rigid, not daring to move.

A moment later the slap of sandals came down the tiled corridor. A thin man with a neatly tonsured head appeared, dressed in a clean white toga. He seemed vaguely annoyed. This was not the time of day to be disturbing Rome's ruling class.

'Yes?' The high-pitched voice was imperious.

'A note for Crassus, sir,' said Romulus, handing it over.

The major-domo studied the now greasy parchment with disgust. 'Looks like something picked from the sewer,' he sniffed.

'It got a little dirty on the way, sir.' Romulus stared at the floor, trying to hide a scowl.

'Who is your master?'

'Gemellus the merchant. From the Aventine.'

'Gemellus, you say?'

'Yes, sir.'

The official considered whether to turn the boy away or not. Crassus had dealings with countless people, not least the merchants whose business kept the wheels of industry turning. Practically all of them owed him money. And for those who did not, Crassus would go to any lengths, make himself amenable to anyone he came across, just so long as he obtained what he wanted. There would be some advantage to be had from this.

'Wait here.'

The slave walked away, the note held at arm's length.

'Effeminate fool! Thinks he's so bloody important.' The doorman snorted, shifting angrily on his stool. Behind him lay a sword, spear and wool blanket. It was where he lived and slept, much like Juba.

Relaxing slightly, Romulus looked round with awe. The flagstones leading off on each side, into the house proper, were of solid green marble. Magnificent statues of the gods, better carved than he had ever seen, lined the hallways. It was a clear manifestation of enormous riches. Gemellus was well off, but this put his wealth into the shade.

Crassus' ways of making money were well known. Under Sulla he had profited hugely from the executions of proscribed nobles, buying up their seized properties cheaply. Other methods were similarly unsavoury. As most buildings in Rome were wooden, fires were common and large areas were regularly razed to the ground. Crassus would visit affected quarters with his private fire brigade, refusing to put out the flames unless the owners of burning tenements sold for knockdown prices on the spot. It allowed him to rebuild and sell for huge profits. While other *equites* admired the ruthless practice, citizens despised it. Rumours abounded that the night-time blazes were not accidental, but the proceeds had added to Crassus' incredible wealth. He had only one other purpose in life: to become the Republic's leading citizen. To achieve this, Crassus needed massive public support. Military success was the best method of ensuring that in Rome and so he determined to forcibly expand the state's borders once he became governor of Syria. His only problem was that the more popular Pompey wanted the job too.

The *atrium* walls in front of Romulus had been covered in stucco and then painted. Aware of his low status, he strained to see without moving more than his head. Hunting scenes covered one side of the well-lit room, while the other depicted Crassus leading armies in battle. He jumped as the doorman spoke.

'That's the master defeating Spartacus.'

Everyone knew the story of the Thracian gladiator who had taken up arms against the state. The slave rebellion had been the biggest threat to Rome since Hannibal a hundred and fifty years before.

Romulus opened his mouth to reply, but fell silent as a brown-haired man with an unsmiling round face passed. The stocky noble was in his early thirties, clad in a toga of the finest fabric. He glanced disinterestedly at them.

Romulus waited until the figure had disappeared through a door down the corridor. Slaves knew it did not pay to attract attention.

'Spartacus the Greek?' Since first hearing the story, Romulus had idolised the man who had defied all the rules to throw off his chains. It had given him hope, fuelled his own dream of seizing freedom. It was a dream he had never articulated, except to Juba.

The big doorman sighed. 'Such a leader.'

Romulus gasped. 'You knew Spartacus?'

'Quiet! You'll get me killed.'

Romulus moved closer to the slave, whose tattooed face had turned sad. There was a long silence before he began to whisper.

'I was in Capua the day Spartacus struck down the *lanista*. A gladiator was injured and could not fight. Flaminius began to beat him cruelly, as he often did at such times.'

Romulus was rooted to the spot.

'Spartacus watched for a moment, then walked up to Flaminius without a word. Cut off the bastard's head with one swing of his sword. "Who's with me?" he roared. Crixus was first.' His voice shook with pride. 'Then we all joined in.'

'The rebellion lasted a long time, didn't it?'

'More than two years. And we kicked the shit out of every army Rome sent at us.'

'They say you marched north.'

'We were heading for Gaul.' A wistful smile crossed his face. 'Spartacus wanted to leave Italy. Then Crixus won him over with talk of overthrowing the Republic and things started to go wrong.'

'Crassus drove you south again.' It was common knowledge that the rebels had been pushed down into the narrow heel of the Italian peninsula and a defensive wall built to hold them in.

'They didn't defeat us, though!' retorted the doorman. 'Until Brundisium.' It was there that Crassus had smashed the slave army.

'I thought all those captured were . . .' Romulus paused. The prisoners' fate had been the talk of the city, dashing the hopes of the slave population.

'Crucified.' He nodded sadly, tears glinting in his eyes. 'Poor bastards. On the sides of the Via Appia. All the way from Capua to Rome. Six thousand of them. Just so Crassus could claim back the glory from Pompey Magnus.'

The public had discovered long afterwards that Pompey had only mopped up a few thousand slaves fleeing the main battle. But in a masterly stroke, he had immediately written to the Senate, claiming victory over the whole rebellion. His opportunism had worked and he had been granted a full triumph through Rome. Crassus, apoplectic with rage, had ordered a prisoner crucified along every mile of the Republic's main road in response – gory proof of his success. It was rumoured the vultures had filled the sky above the road for weeks.

As Romulus stared, he noticed a thick scar running down the side of the slave's face on to his neck.

The doorman grimaced, rubbing at the red welt. 'Got that the night before the final battle. Some of us fled when Spartacus gave his blessing, see? But we should have stayed. Died like men.'

'Does Crassus know?'

'What do you think?' he snapped.

'But to end up here?'

There was a sad shrug. 'I went on the run for a year and then killed a citizen in a drunken brawl. Got captured again and sold to a gladiator school in Rome. Crassus bought me after seeing a fight there.'

'At least you're still alive.'

'I might as well be dead.' The doorman's broad shoulders slumped.

Conversation ceased abruptly as the major-domo reappeared. His lip curled knowingly. 'Has Pertinax been telling his stories? Don't believe a word!' He handed Romulus a rolled parchment. 'See what your master says when he receives this!'

'Thank you, sir.'

'Let the boy out.'

Pertinax hastened to obey and Romulus ducked out of the postern door, which promptly slammed shut behind him.

Mind racing, he walked back, the reply clutched tightly in one hand. Who would have thought he would see inside the *domus* of the richest noble in Rome? And meet one of Spartacus' original men? Despite the major-domo's scorn, there had been a ring of truth to Pertinax' words. Romulus couldn't wait to tell Fabiola and Juba. But first he had to get inside Gemellus' gate without the thugs stopping him. He grinned – it was a challenge he would relish.

Near the last crossroads before home, Romulus heard the noise of loud chanting. The street was thronged with even more people than usual and potentially that meant trouble. Keen to get back, he ducked into a narrow alleyway off the main street and worked his way around the junction, the cries of the crowd filling his ears.

'Who wants a trip east?' a man cried.

'Pompey!' came the response.

Romulus paused to listen. It sounded as if Clodius

was up to his usual tricks. The leader of the *collegia* had been on a mission to humiliate Pompey for some time.

'But who should go instead?'

A great roar answered the master rabble-rouser. 'Crassus!'

Romulus kept moving, remembering Gemellus' complaint that tolerating the mobs was just another sign of the Republic's decline.

In the event, distracting the two heavies did not prove at all difficult. Romulus simply waited until a cart was rolling past Gemellus' house. Using it as cover, he crouched down and ran alongside, leaving the men opposite completely unaware until he was by the door. The boy darted forward and rapped hard with his fist; the pair saw him, cursed and lumbered forward, reaching for their swords. But Juba was waiting and instantly emerged into the sunlight, his blade ready.

Few men in their right minds would take on the Nubian.

They skidded to a halt, leaving Romulus to saunter inside with his friend. He did not linger: delivering Crassus' reply was far more urgent than anything else. Smiling his thanks at the big doorman, he went in search of Gemellus.

The sound of voices carried to him through the *tablinum* and instinctively Romulus tiptoed across its mosaic floor. From a statue near the open doors, he could hear every word spoken in the garden. The twins had discovered early on that eavesdropping on Gemellus was most informative. It also taught them plenty about his murky business deals. Although much of what he overheard meant little to him, Romulus took every opportunity to learn more about the world outside the high walls.

The merchant was deep in conversation with his bookkeeper. Servilius was a thin Egyptian with protuberant eyes and receding hair and the only slave Gemellus trusted. Excellent with money, Servilius was despised by the other slaves, who could not understand his unswerving loyalty to his owner.

'Continue.' Gemellus sounded unusually good-humoured.

Servilius cleared his throat. 'My cousin in Alexandria mentioned a possible business venture in his last letter. A very profitable one.' He paused. 'But it would not be without risk, Master.'

'Nothing is these days,' growled the merchant. 'Tell me more.'

'Menes has dealt with a Phoenician *bestiarius* by the name of Hiero,' Servilius began, 'who proposes to lead an expedition into the deep south, near the headwaters of the Nile. There he will capture all manner of beasts for the arena.'

Romulus could sense Gemellus' interest and craned his head, desperate not to miss a word. The job of the *bestiarii* was very dangerous and appealed to him immensely.

'Lions, leopards and elephants,' announced the bookkeeper, warming to his task. 'Antelope and unearthly creatures with long necks and legs. The *bestiarius* even claims he can catch huge armoured monsters with lethal horns on their noses.'

'Is Menes tempted to invest?'

Servilius coughed awkwardly. 'He is providing two-thirds of the financial backing, Master.'

There was no reply for a moment.

'Each one would be worth its weight in gold,' exclaimed Gemellus. The trade in wild animals for gladiatorial contests was fast becoming one of the most lucrative in Rome.

'I thought you might be interested, Master.'

'How much capital is Hiero looking for?'

'For the last third share,' Servilius said, sucking in his breath, 'one hundred and twenty thousand *sestertii*.'

Romulus' mouth opened. It was more than he could even imagine.

'Fortuna's tits!' cursed Gemellus. 'Where will I get credit like that these days? I'm up to my neck in debt already.'

'Crassus, Master?'

Startled by the name and the nature of Gemellus' dilemma, Romulus jumped. He had had no idea that the merchant was in financial difficulties. It was then that he heard the sound of someone coming down the corridor, probably a kitchen slave with a cool drink for their master. He could not risk being caught, so he squared his shoulders and stepped into the garden, making as much noise as possible.

Gemellus' face darkened further when he saw who it was. Servilius immediately busied himself with his ledger, the giant tome that contained all the merchant's financial details.

'What took you so long?' Gemellus peered at the sundial. 'It's been two hours!'

Not daring to reply, Romulus held out the parchment.

Gemellus scanned it silently. The only noise was the bookkeeper's stylus scratching out figures behind him.

Romulus waited, knowing a beating would follow regardless of what Crassus had written.

Closing his eyes, Gemellus crumpled the note and dropped it to the floor. The rate of interest demanded by Crassus for an extension of his loans was completely extortionate. He did not need that hanging over his head as well. Full of anger, the merchant beat Romulus harder than usual, but the boy took the punishment without a sound. The unexpected outing and the conversation with Pertinax had been well worth it.

Fabiola watched from behind a bush, biting her lips to avoid crying out at the sight. It would only have earned Romulus an even worse hiding. Her hatred of Gemellus grew day by day. Not only did he rape her mother every night, he regularly beat her brother black and blue. Only the fear of what would happen to her family prevented Fabiola from trying to kill their master.

It was two days before the bruises began to settle and an opportunity arose to confide in Juba. Every time Romulus went to talk to him, someone happened to be present.

Gemellus was ingratiating himself with every banker and moneylender he knew, trying to raise capital for a proposed business venture. Romulus suspected it was to do with Servilius' suggestion. But word must have spread about his huge debts, because visitors came and went, shaking their heads regretfully. The merchant's temper grew even worse. Household slaves crept about, trying not to be noticed. Eventually Gemellus could take no more and stormed off to the Lupanar, his favourite brothel. The bookkeeper was told he would be gone at least a day.

Hearing the master was gone, Romulus ran immediately to Juba, wooden sword in hand. The Nubian listened intently to the story, nodding approval when Spartacus was mentioned. His eyebrows rose with surprise to hear Pertinax had fought with the rebel Thracian.

'I would have joined Spartacus if I'd been old enough,' said Romulus fiercely. He had not been born until a year after the slave uprising ended.

Juba tapped his chest, signifying agreement.

'Show me more moves! I must learn to fight like a gladiator.'

The Nubian smiled and moved into the hallway. Ensuring Romulus was paying attention, Juba turned sideways to present less of a target, holding his sword out just above the waist, shield at chest level. He indicated that Romulus do the same. They stood side by side, repeating the same actions until Juba was happy.

'Shield up. Thrust. Step back,' the boy muttered. 'Shield up. Thrust. Step back.'

Next Juba handed over the shield. Romulus slipped his left arm into the smooth leather grips, hefting the unfamiliar weight. The Nubian showed him how to protect chest and face, keeping his weapon ready for an opportunity to strike.

After a moment, they began to spar in slow motion, Juba taking care not to strike Romulus' wooden sword too hard with his own of iron. The knocking of blades echoed down the hall, and soon Fabiola arrived to watch.

'What if the master catches you?' Her face was a picture of concern. 'Stop it, Romulus. I'll tell Mother!'

'Go away! I'm learning to fight like Spartacus!'

His sister watched with a mixture of pride and fear. 'It's too dangerous. Please stop!'

Suddenly the idea of holding a real sword to Gemellus' neck came to him. Romulus redoubled the attack on Juba, who fell back, a wide grin splitting his ebony features.

It would be the last time he ever practised with the Nubian. When they had finished, Romulus returned to the family's small cell, bursting with excitement. Images of freeing all the household slaves and killing Gemellus now filled his mind. It terrified and exhilarated him.

Chores over, that night Velvinna listened to her son recount Pertinax' tale yet again.

'Be careful, Romulus,' she said, her voice full of pride. 'Nobody must see you with a sword, especially Servilius. Gemellus will not stand for it.'

'Don't worry, Mother.' Romulus' eyelids drooped with tiredness as Velvinna pulled the blanket over his shoulders. 'Nobody knows.'

Exhaustion brought him sleep at once, and dreams of being a soldier in Spartacus' army.

Romulus was rudely awoken the next morning when cold links of metal fastened around both wrists. Confused, he found they had been bound with a light chain. The boy sat up and gazed round the room, terror replacing the alarm. Fabiola and his mother were motionless in their beds, staring at Gemellus.

The merchant stood in the doorway, flanked by Ancus and Sossius, two burly kitchen slaves. Neither would meet Romulus' eye. Most of the household had known him since he was a baby.

'Try and use a sword under my roof? Little bastard!' Gemellus spat. 'Then stab me in my sleep, no doubt. I've been soft far too long. It's the gladiator school for you. Today.' A smile flickered across his lips. 'Learn how to fight there.'

Romulus knew instantly that his life as a common slave had come to an end.

'No, Master, please.' Velvinna threw herself at Gemellus' feet.

Fabiola sat bolt upright, her face stricken. This was just what she had feared.

'Get up, bitch.' Gemellus hauled Velvinna up by the hair. She cried out in pain, but the merchant backhanded her across the cheek and she fell back on to the cot, sobbing.

'Take him,' Gemellus gestured.

The end of the chain extended far beyond Romulus' wrists. With a powerful yank, Ancus pulled him out of bed and on to the floor.

Tears filled Fabiola's eyes.

'My son!' Velvinna screamed.

'Useless whore. You'll never see him again,' sneered Gemellus. 'I'll be back for his sister later.'

'Don't worry, Mother.' The words rang hollow, but Romulus did not know what else to say.

She wailed and cried even louder. Everyone knew what entering gladiator school meant.

'Let's go. I can't listen to this.' Gemellus turned and led his men out of the room.

'It wasn't me who told on you!' Fabiola's voice was frantic. 'Romulus!'

'Take care of Mother!'

As Romulus opened his mouth to shout again, Gemellus gestured at Sossius, who turned back and slammed the door shut.

More sounds of distress echoed down the hallway as he was marched off, clad only in his loincloth. Romulus knew Fabiola would not lie. They were far too close. One of the others must have seen Juba training him and informed to curry favour. Servilius?

Slaves had no choice in their lives; they could be bought and sold at will. But Romulus had never imagined leaving Gemellus' possession – he had known no other life. He was torn between fear and excitement at what was happening. While the prospect of becoming a fighter was thrilling, he would probably never see his family again. Romulus looked back one last time, Velvinna's sobs tearing at his heart, wishing his weapons practice with Juba had been quieter. But the man holding the chain was twice his size.

Stories were frequently told in the kitchen about famous gladiators who fought barbarians and wild beasts in the arena. Romulus had always enjoyed listening to the tales, but had never been inside a training school and seen the reality. For a moment, his heart began to race, full of romantic ideas about being one of the people's heroes.

119

Sensing something, Gemellus cuffed him across the head. 'A boy like you will be dead inside a month.'

Romulus' heart sank. Of course. What chance would a thirteen-year-old have against professional gladiators?

'You'll need to prove yourself damn quick.'

They had reached the alcove by the front door. Romulus saw with alarm that the Nubian was not in the usual spot.

'Think I'd keep anyone who teaches others to fight?' Gemellus laughed. 'The brute's on his way to the Campus Martius right now.'

He gaped at the merchant, confused.

'To be crucified.'

Romulus lunged at Gemellus, eyes full of murderous rage.

Ancus pulled reluctantly on the chain, stopping the attack before it even started. Romulus stumbled and fell heavily, all too aware he could do nothing to save Juba.

Gemellus kicked him in the belly. 'Born a slave!' Another kick followed. 'Die a slave. Now get up.'

The door creaked open and the merchant led the way outside. No one paid any heed to the little party. It was common practice to shackle slaves outside the home.

Romulus remembered little of the walk. Still winded, he followed numbly, mind awash with grief and guilt at Juba's fate, whose only crime had been teaching him how to use a sword. Now he was responsible for a man's death. For the sale of Fabiola. What would happen to his mother? How long would he last in the savage world of the arena?

All four lives had been turned upside down overnight.

Romulus blinked away tears. *Show the bastard no weakness. Be strong, like Fabiola.* He took a deep breath in, concentrating hard, trying to release the guilt. *Jupiter protect me. Look after my family.*

By the time Gemellus reached a set of iron gates set into an archway, Romulus had regained some control of his emotions. Red-eyed, shoulders broad, he was determined to remain courageous.

A square stone was set into the bricks over the entrance, inscribed with two words. Although he could not read, Romulus knew their meaning. It was the Ludus Magnus, largest of the four gladiator schools in Rome and a supplier of men for Milo's gangs.

The bare-headed guard outside wore a battered chain mail shirt reaching to mid-thigh. Leaning against the wall behind was a long spear. A short stabbing sword was ready on the man's belt; a sturdy oval shield decorated with a strange emblem hung from his left arm.

'State your business.'

'I want to sell this brat to Memor.'

He looked Romulus up and down. 'Bit young, isn't he?'

'What has it to do with you?' Gemellus snapped. 'Let us inside!'

Sullenly the guard pulled open the nearest gate a fraction, just enough space to enter. As soon as they had passed inside, it clanged shut.

Romulus' pulse quickened at the finality of the sound. Many of the inmates were criminals, hence the sentry. For most, entry to the *ludus* was a death sentence, a career that only the very best survived for more than a year or two. His dreams of glory had been ludicrous, but he could not suppress a shiver of excitement.

Gemellus advanced through a short corridor into an open training area. The large two-storey building was built with a hollow square in the centre, providing a whole world within four walls. It was full of gladiators training and sparring with each other.

Romulus watched, fascinated. The two nearest made up the classic pairing of *retiarius* versus *secutor*.

'You will be a fisherman.' Gemellus pointed at the man in a loincloth, armed only with a trident. The *retiarius* was waving a weighted net back and forth, readying himself to throw. The merchant spat in Romulus' face. 'Lowest form of fighter. Good prey for a hunter!'

The *secutor* crouched warily, oval shield held high, a short wooden sword ready in his right hand. Romulus took in the visored helmet, the greave on the left leg and the leather bands protecting the right arm. It all seemed very one-sided. The *secutor* was so heavily armoured compared to his opponent, whose only protection was a fitted piece of hide on the right shoulder.

Suddenly the hunter began weaving from side to side. He lunged forward to the left, then immediately to the right. But the fisherman judged the perfect time to throw the net. The *secutor* went down, limbs flailing in the weighted mesh. In a flash, the *retiarius* was on him, wooden trident touching the throat. The defeated gladiator thrust up a hand, forefinger extended, pleading for mercy. Laughing, the *retiarius* hauled him to his feet and they started the process all over again.

Romulus felt a tiny surge of hope. He saw the merchant scowling at the unexpected turn of events.

Gemellus led the way around the edge of the training area to a thick timber post, against which other gladiators were practising.

'The *palus*,' whispered Ancus. 'If chosen to fight with a sword, that's where you'll spend your days.'

Romulus glanced at the two kitchen slaves. Still neither would meet his eyes, but he felt no anger towards them. If Ancus and Sossius had not followed Gemellus' orders, they would have swiftly followed Juba to the Campus Martius.

On one side of the *palus* was a short, grizzled figure in a richly cut tunic. The long grey hair contrasted with his lined, tanned skin. Alongside him stood a huge man carrying a whip. When he saw Gemellus approach, the *lanista* stopped shouting orders.

'Gemellus. I don't normally see you here.' He studied Romulus.

The merchant propelled him forward. 'What will you give me for this boy?'

'I need men here. Not children.'

The hulk with the whip grinned toothlessly.

'Look at the size of him,' protested Gemellus. 'And he's only thirteen!'

Cold eyes sized Romulus up. 'Can you fight with weapons?'

Romulus stared back. To have any chance of survival, there must be no fear visible. He nodded.

'That's why the little bastard is here,' interjected the merchant.

Memor rubbed the stubble on his chin. 'A thousand *sestertii*.'

Gemellus laughed. 'I'd get more on the slave block! He's worth at least three. Look at those muscles!'

'I'm in a good mood this morning, Gemellus. Fifteen hundred.'

'Twenty-five hundred.'

'Stop wasting my time.'

'Two thousand?' There was still hope in the merchant's eyes.

'Eighteen hundred. Not a *sestertius* more.'

Gemellus had little choice but to accept. It was a better price than Romulus would fetch in the market. 'Very well.'

Memor snapped his fingers.

A scrawny little man with ink-stained fingers and a dirty tunic materialised, money bags in both hands.

The *lanista* counted the coins with care, in the manner of someone proud of his ability to do so. When finished, he handed a pouch to Gemellus.

'Beat him often. It's the only thing he understands.'

'My sister, Master?' Romulus asked pleadingly.

The merchant smiled. 'I'm going to sell the bitch to a whorehouse. Piece of ass like her will fetch a good price. And as for your whore of a mother — we'll see what the mines' overseer offers.'

Romulus glared at his former owner with utter hatred.

One day I will kill you, very slowly.

To the boy's surprise, Gemellus' eyes flickered away and he turned on his heel without another word. But Romulus had no time to savour the minor victory. A vice-like grip took hold of his chin.

'You're mine now.' Crisscrossed with old scars, Memor's face was uncomfortably close. The smell of cheap wine was overpowering. 'In the Ludus Magnus, men learn to be killed. Till the end of your life, the fighters here will be your new *familia*. You eat. You train. You sleep. You shit with them. Clear?'

'Yes.'

'Do what I say quickly and there'll be no beating, like that fat bastard suggested.' Memor's jaw hardened. 'Don't do what I say and, by Hercules, you'll regret it. I know ways of hurting most cannot even imagine.'

Romulus did not let his gaze waver.

'Before everyone present, take the oath of the gladiator!' Memor's bellow had stopped every fighter in the yard. This was a ritual they had all been through.

'Do you swear to endure the whip? The branding iron? And do you swear to endure death by the sword?'

Romulus swallowed, but when he spoke his voice was steady. 'I swear it.'

The circle of hard faces relaxed a little. If nothing else, the new addition was courageous.

'Brand the boy and strike off those chains,' Memor ordered the clerk. 'Find a blanket and a space to sleep. And return him to me swiftly!'

'Come on, lad.' The voice was not unkind. 'The iron won't hurt that badly.'

Carefully, Romulus surveyed the dirt of the training yard and the *ludus'* thick stone walls. Like it or not, this was now home. His survival would be a decision of the gods alone. He followed the thin clerk, his head held high.

Chapter VI: The Ludus Magnus

Forum Boarium, Rome, 56 BC

'Bren-nus! Bren-nus!'

The chanting was deafening.

The Gaul stood over his vanquished opponent, listening to the familiar noise. Over five years, the blond-haired warrior had become one of the mightiest gladiators Rome had ever seen. And the crowd loved him.

Warm afternoon sun lit up the entire circle of sand contained within temporary wooden stands. That morning the grains had been a rich golden colour, raked by slaves into uniform smoothness. But after more than an hour of savage combat, the surface had been kicked into disarray. Bloodstains spread around dead men lying scattered all over the arena. The air was filled with moans and cries of the injured.

It was late spring and the citizens watching were happy. The set piece between two teams had been gripping and all the participants were now dead or maimed – except the prize fighter who had led each side.

The organisers of such fights were *lanistae*, owners of the gladiator schools in Rome who met on a regular basis to arrange spectacles with real mass appeal. When the rich and powerful wanted to stage a contest, they could offer a range of options from basic single combats to tailor-made arrangements. It depended on the depth of the purse of the *editor* – the sponsor – and how impressive a display was required.

The clash between Narcissus and Brennus had been something the public – even the *lanistae* – had craved for a long time. Within months of his arrival in Rome, the huge Gaul had defeated every gladiator of repute. After that, there was no entertainment in watching Brennus cut weaker men to pieces. Fights were supposed to take time, impressing the crowd with skill and endurance. Memor had quickly limited Brennus' appearances even though his popularity demanded ever more exposure.

Today the sponsor wanted real quality and had personally asked for the Gaul. The *lanista* had had to look far and wide for a worthy opponent. Eventually he'd found Narcissus the Greek in Sicily, where the formidable *murmillo* had earned a similar reputation to Brennus.

The fight had seemed perfect. Gaul against Greek. Muscle against skill. Savagery against civilisation.

Not a seat had been left empty in the stands.

Now Narcissus lay on his back, bare chest exposed, sucking air painfully through a twisted visor. The fish crest of his bronze helmet was bent in two, battered into submission. His sword lay ten steps away, kicked beyond reach.

The contest had not lasted long. Brennus had unexpectedly shoulder-charged the *murmillo*, knocking him off balance. A spinning blow from his shield had followed, breaking several ribs and driving Narcissus to his knees, half stunned. Then a savage chop of Brennus' longsword had cut open the Greek's right shoulder above the *manica*, the thick leather bands protecting the arm. Narcissus had dropped his weapon, collapsing on to the baking sand, screaming in pain.

Sure of victory, Brennus had paused. He had no desire to kill yet another opponent. Raising both arms, he let the crowd's approval fill the air. Despite the speed with which he had ended the fight, Rome's citizens still loved Brennus.

But Narcissus had not been defeated. Suddenly he had produced a dagger from under his *manica*, lunging at the Gaul. Brennus had skipped out of reach, then swept in from the side, using the shield's iron rim to smash his opponent's face through the soft metal helmet. The *murmillo's* head had slumped as he lost consciousness.

Brennus looked over to the nobles in their white togas. They were shielded from the sun by the *velarium*, a cloth awning erected by the command of the *editor* of these games. Julius Caesar sat dressed in a pristine purple-edged toga, surrounded by followers and admirers. He gave an almost imperceptible nod and a great cry of anticipation went up.

The Gaul sighed, determined that Narcissus' death would at least be humane. He nudged the *murmillo* with his foot.

Opening his eyes, Narcissus found the strength to raise

his left arm in the air. Slowly he extended a forefinger upwards.

An appeal for mercy.

The audience roared with disapproval, drowning the confined space with their animal noise.

Caesar stood and surveyed the arena, holding up his arms commandingly. As people noticed, the chanting and whistling stopped. A strange silence fell over the Forum Boarium. Wooden stands erected for the occasion were jammed with the poorest plebeians, merchants, and the patricians that Julius Caesar called friends.

All waited, held in the grip of the finest military mind that Rome had seen in an age. Ignoring the rule that prohibited generals with armies from entering the city, Caesar had returned, fresh from his successful campaigns against the Helvetii and Belgae. While these had gained him huge public favour, Caesar was paying a price for being absent from Rome for months on end. Despite the work of his friends and allies, it was proving hard to maintain his influence in the city. This visit was all about showing his face, pressing flesh with politicians and retaining the people's affection.

Traditionally, gladiator fights had only taken place as part of celebrations to honour the death of the rich or famous. But in the previous thirty years, their immense popularity had prompted politicians and those seeking office to stage them at every opportunity. As the contests grew in size and magnificence, the need for a permanent arena became ever greater. Desperate to retain the public's affection, Pompey was currently funding the building of a fixed arena on the Campus Martius, news that had immensely pleased Memor and the other *lanistae*.

'People of Rome! Today a gladiator with more than thirty victories has been vanquished!' Caesar paused with theatrical elegance, and there was a shout of approval. It was clear that his choice of fighter and command over the audience pleased him. 'And Narcissus was beaten by whom?'

'Bren-nus! Bren-nus!' Drums beaten by slaves pounded to the repetitive chant. 'Bren-nus!'

There could only be one outcome.

The *murmillo* gestured weakly with his right hand. 'Make it quick, brother.'

The words were barely distinguishable above the cries and hypnotic drumming.

'I swear it.'

The unspoken bond between gladiators was strong, just as it had been with warriors of Brennus' tribe.

Caesar held up his arms again. 'Shall I show mercy to the loser?' He stared down at the prone figure on the sand, whose finger was still raised.

Baying sounds of anger joined the clamour. Men in the stands nearest the temple of Fortuna gestured downwards with their thumbs and the signal was quickly copied by the entire audience.

A wave of thumbs pointed south.

Caesar turned to his companions. 'The plebs require a reward.' A smile played on thin lips. 'Do you want Narcissus to die?'

The citizens screamed their pleasure.

Caesar surveyed the arena slowly, increasing the

tension. Then he raised his right hand, thumb extended horizontally. For several slow heartbeats it stayed in position.

The crowd held its breath.

Abruptly it turned to point at the ground.

The shouts that went up exceeded all those that had gone before. It was time for the loser to die.

'Get up.'

Narcissus managed to kneel with difficulty. The wound on his right shoulder began to bleed heavily.

'Take off your helmet.' Brennus lowered his voice. 'It will give me a clean swing. Send you straight to Elysium.'

The *murmillo* moaned as the battered metal came off. His nose had been reduced to a bloody pulp, the cheek-bones crushed inwards. It was an agonising wound and there was a loud gasp of shock and pleasure from those watching.

'Aesculapius himself could not fix that,' said Brennus.

Narcissus nodded and looked at Caesar. 'Those who are about to die, salute you,' he mumbled. The Greek smacked his chest with a clenched fist and extended the quivering left arm forward.

The *editor* acknowledged his pledge.

Silence took hold of the Forum.

Quickly Brennus stepped back and gripped the longsword's hilt with both hands. The Gaul's chest and arm muscles stood out as he half turned, swinging from the hip. Narcissus' head was swept clean off his shoulders by the blow. It flew spinning through the air, landing with a wet thump. Blood gushed from the neck; the torso fell twitching to the ground. The sand absorbed the red liquid, leaving a dark stain around the *murmillo*.

The people went wild.

Caesar gestured. 'Let the victor approach.'

Brennus walked slowly towards the nobles, trying to ignore the delighted roars of the crowd. It was hard to resist the adulation. The Gaul was a warrior and enjoyed combat. Coins, pieces of fruit, even a wineskin showered down. He stooped to pick up the bag and took a large mouthful of wine.

Caesar smiled down generously. 'Another great victory, mighty Brennus.'

The Gaul half bowed, sweat-streaked pigtails falling forward on to his bare chest.

Is this the journey you meant, Ultan? To end up as a performing animal for these bastards?

'A worthy prize!' Caesar raised a heavy leather purse and tossed it through the air.

'Thank you, great one.' Brennus bowed more deeply, sweeping up his reward at the same time. He weighed the bag in his bloodstained hand. There was a lot of money in it, which only made him feel worse.

Behind him, the figure dressed as Charon, the ferryman across the River Styx, had entered the arena, clad from head to toe in black leather, a mask concealing his face. A large hammer dangling from one hand, he paced towards Narcissus' head as screams of mock horror went up from the audience. The hammer, visibly encrusted with blood and matted hair, rose high in the air. Swinging it downwards, the ferryman split Narcissus' skull like an egg, proving the *murmillo* was truly dead. It was time for the Greek's journey to Hades.

Brennus turned away. He still believed that brave men went to Elysium, the warriors' paradise. He found the Roman ritual with Charon disgusting and had sworn it would not happen to him. And the option of allowing himself to be slain, ending the torture, went totally against his nature. Deep inside, Brennus clung to a tiny strand of hope. It meant continuing to kill men he had no quarrel with, but the pragmatic warrior had come to regard competitions as defending his own life. Kill or be killed, he thought bitterly. Hunting with Brac, lying with his wife and playing with his child were all distant memories now. They seemed almost unreal.

He tried to bring back an image of Ultan's face, the sound of his voice. The druid had never said anything about journeying to this. After five years, it was hard not to lose faith in the gods. In Belenus, who had guided him since childhood.

Ultan had spoken of the destiny awaiting him as something incredible. This could not be it. Brennus steeled his resolve, ignoring the arena's noise. The Gaul did not know how, but he would escape captivity.

I am the last Allobroge, he thought. I will face death as a free man. With a sword in my hand.

'Put some effort into it!' The trainer knew how to encourage Romulus. 'Imagine it's Gemellus!'

The young man had lived up to the anger and promise shining in his eyes when he'd first been brought in. Cotta had seen many slaves enter the school, wretches whose will broke under the iron discipline. But Romulus held a burning rage inside, fuelled by the guilt about Juba and his family.

Romulus shifted his grip on the hilt and swung hard against the *palus*. The wooden sword and shield were both far heavier than the real thing. His arm juddered as the weapon connected with the thick stake.

'More like it. Now do it again.' Cotta smiled briefly. 'You can rest tonight.' He moved away to watch two other gladiators.

'Shield up. Forward thrust. Step back.' Romulus repeated the words just as he had with Juba, only a few months before. Thoughts of the Nubian came less and less. The *ludus'* harsh regime had driven almost everything other than survival from Romulus' mind. Only the most precious memories of his mother and Fabiola appeared readily now. Those and his guilt about that last fateful day. Life might have been so different if he had not asked Juba to train him with a sword.

The image of Gemellus was burnt indelibly into his soul.

'Wait. Watch. Turn. Backhand slash.' Deftly Romulus spun and hacked the *palus*, imagining the merchant's face crease in agony as the blade struck.

'Good work.'

His trainer was a former mercenary who had been captured by the Romans fifteen years previously. Military training had helped him survive longer than most. Finally granted his freedom, Cotta had stayed on at the Ludus Magnus. Romulus had been awestruck when he heard the story of Cotta's last combat. Overcoming more than six opponents, it had been a trial of extraordinary endurance. The dictator Marius had been so impressed that he had freed the *secutor* on the spot.

A Libyan of average height, Cotta was still fit and lean, although well over forty. His left arm was half paralysed, a legacy of the day he had won the *rudis*, a wooden sword symbolising freedom. He was feared and respected by almost all gladiators in the *ludus*. Even Memor stopped to watch occasionally when the grey-haired veteran was training his men.

'I've liked you ever since the branding,' said Cotta. 'Most scream when the iron hits.'

Romulus looked at the red, puckered marks on his upper right arm, reading 'L M' and marking him as the property of the Ludus Magnus. The pain of the red-hot metal had been almost unbearable, yet somehow he had managed not to cry out, ignoring the agony and the stench of searing flesh. Like his vow of obedience, the process had been a vital test of courage.

'Something told me to pick you,' the old gladiator said approvingly. 'A cut above the usual rabble.'

Romulus was lucky to have Cotta, to be training as a heavily armed *secutor*. He had a much better chance of surviving than a lowly *retiarius*, the most likely choice for a thirteen-year-old. When they arrived in the *ludus*, men were picked for each fighting class by size, strength and skill with weapons. Few would have seen enough potential in Romulus. It took months of hard instruction to produce a trained gladiator, ready for combat. He mouthed a swift prayer of thanks to Jupiter, promising to make an offering later at the shrine in his cell.

'Memor wants you ready in a month. Stand a good

chance by practising like that.' Cotta jerked a thumb at the group of *retiarii* in the far corner of the yard. 'He'll probably put you up against a fisherman. And not a novice either.' He winked. 'That'd be far too easy. More sport for the crowd watching a rookie *secutor* fighting a crafty old *retiarius*.'

Romulus redoubled his efforts with the *palus*, knocking chips off with each blow. He knew the self-educated Libyan spent more time with him than the other new gladiators. Sensing Romulus' thirst for knowledge, Cotta had also been giving him regular lessons in military tactics. It was immensely empowering to learn the details of battles such as Cannae, when Hannibal had annihilated eight Roman legions, and Thermopylae, where three hundred Spartans had held off a million Persians. There were recent tales too, stirring accounts of Caesar's incredible victories against the Gaulish tribes. Romulus now knew the basics of warfare and how great minds could often beat overwhelming odds. While his body was contained within the walls of the *ludus*, his mind, fed by Cotta's classes, roamed far beyond. Now, more than ever, he longed to be free.

'I will be ready, Master Cotta,' he muttered. 'I swear it.'

The old gladiator smiled as he walked away, yelling instructions.

After five months of intensive exercise, Romulus' frame was heavily muscled and his black hair had grown long. A thin leather band held it back, exposing a tanned face. The boy was becoming a handsome young man.

He was already as tall as some of the gladiators, and as fast, even if he lacked combat experience.

When Cotta let him finish at last, Romulus' arms were burning. He let the shield fall wearily to his side and trudged off the dirt practice ground.

All but one side of the square building was given up to cells accommodating the trainers and fighters, while the other contained the baths, kitchens, mortuary and armoury. On the second floor lay the offices, sick bay and Memor's luxurious quarters. Apart from prostitutes and rich clients, few ever set foot inside the *lanista's* domain.

It was only a dozen steps to the tiny room he shared with three other gladiators. There was barely space in it for their beds and a shrine to the gods. Sextus was the most friendly inmate, a short, tough Spaniard who seldom spoke. Lentulus was nearer his own age, a Goth with two years' experience and a fierce temper. The last was Gaius, a broad-shouldered *retiarius* with little brain, whose flatulence was the main topic of conversation in the cell.

Fortunately Romulus' roommates had no taste for young men, and he had slept undisturbed since arriving. From the glances some fighters gave him, Romulus knew that he would be raped if they ever cornered him. He had already had several lucky escapes. He was particularly careful never to go to the toilet area alone and wore a sharp dagger on his belt at all times. Although Memor did not allow swords or larger weapons in the cells, knives were tolerated. The *lanista's* archers had nothing to fear from these.

The walls of the poorly lit room ran with damp. Anyone who slept by them constantly had wet bedding. And as he was the newest inmate, the worst spot belonged to Romulus. He bore his obligation silently, knowing it was part of the ritual of acceptance. Each morning, he dutifully carried his straw mattress outside to dry while the others laughed. Every evening he reversed the performance.

Romulus picked up the heavy load beside the door and paused. Taking a deep breath, he entered.

'Still soft, boy!'

'Too used to the good life!'

Romulus flushed. There was some truth to the jibes. Life in the *ludus* was much harsher than in Gemellus' service. He dropped the bedding back onto the rough slats of his cot.

'Wait till winter comes,' sneered Lentulus. 'Then you'll really know how miserable that corner is!'

Romulus disliked the stocky young Goth, who was always looking for ways to bait him. Angered by the constant comments, Romulus suddenly took a stand. 'I might take your bed instead.'

Gaius opened both eyes warily.

'How are you going to do that?' Lentulus laughed. 'Stick me with that excuse for a sword?'

The *retiarius* sniggered.

Lentulus lay back on his mattress, picking his rotten teeth with a splinter.

Romulus took hold of his dagger. 'I'll teach you a lesson,' he said slowly.

The Goth stiffened, hand reaching for something on

the floor. Iron grated off the stone as he slid out a *gladius* that he had hidden under his bed.

A rush of adrenalin and fear hit Romulus. *Better to pick a fight in the yard, not such a confined space.* And when he had more than a knife or a wooden sword to fight with. His own real one was locked up with all the others in the armoury. Thirty paces and a lifetime away. Maybe it had been a mistake to answer back.

Lentulus began to sit up, pulling the *gladius* on to his lap.

'Peace, Lentulus,' said a familiar voice. 'We are all tired and hungry.'

Romulus looked gratefully at Sextus.

The little Spaniard was one of the *ludus'* most feared gladiators. Wielding his axe with ferocious skill, the *scissores'* speciality was picking off the weak and wounded men in the arena.

Not confident enough to antagonise Sextus, Lentulus fell silent. But it was only a matter of time before things with the malevolent Goth got physical. And the *scissores* wouldn't always be around to defuse the situation. Sooner or later he would have to fight Lentulus. The thought filled Romulus with a mixture of dread and excitement. As well as being five or six years younger, he was a lot shorter than the *secutor*, who had survived half a dozen single combats unscathed, a respectable record for any gladiator.

The dinner gong clanged loudly.

Sextus smiled and got to his feet. 'Time to eat.'

Lentulus made a stabbing motion that was not lost on Romulus.

They glared at each other, both refusing to drop their gaze.

'Time for food,' repeated the *scissores*.

Romulus picked up his bowl and trooped out, keeping Sextus between him and Lentulus. Next time he would be more careful. Stomach growling, he put the matter from his mind.

'Keep rubbing!'

The *unctor* poured more drops of aromatic oil on to the Gaul's vast back, expertly kneading the muscles.

Brennus lay naked on a bare wooden table, luxuriating in the massage. Memor took care of his top gladiators, allowing them favours others only dreamt of. After the *unctor* had finished, he was going to enjoy a long soak in the baths, followed by a meal prepared by Astoria, his woman.

'You killed the *murmillo* too quickly today. That damn contest took months to arrange.'

Brennus opened his eyes to find that Memor had entered the room. 'The crowd seemed to like it,' he replied casually.

'They are fickle,' snapped the *lanista*. 'How many times must I tell you to make the fights last as long as possible?'

The Gaul's habit of dispatching men fast was something that had irritated Memor for years. But despite Brennus' unorthodox *modus operandi*, the people had come to love him, which annoyed the *lanista* even more.

Brennus grunted as the *unctor* found a knot in one shoulder. He wasn't prepared to make men suffer and Memor knew it.

'Pay attention, damn you!'

The Gaul closed his eyes. 'I heard.'

Memor flushed at the disrespect. 'You are still my slave!' He prodded the brand on Brennus' left calf. 'Remember that!'

Brennus looked up. 'Next time I will kill slowly. Happy?'

Nervous, the *unctor* paused.

'Did I say stop?'

Hastily he continued rubbing.

'Just make sure you do.' Memor wasn't going to punish his most skilled fighter severely. The Gaul was worth far too much money. But long years of managing gladiators had made the *lanista* sharp as a blade. 'And no harm will come to that whore of yours,' he added, almost as an afterthought.

The *unctor* gasped in dismay as Brennus jumped from the table, knocking the bottle of oil flying. Pottery shattered on the floor. Stepping over the shards, the big man clenched his fists and stalked naked towards Memor. Five years before there had been no chance to defend his wife. The same would not happen again.

The *lanista* took several urgent steps backwards.

'You piece of Roman shit!' Brennus' face was less than a finger's length away. 'Touch a hair on Astoria's head and you'll eat your own balls. Before I cut out your heart.'

Memor did not flinch. 'You and your friends can't watch Astoria all the time.' He shrugged apologetically. 'She might have a nasty accident. Terribly easy, you know. Wagon out of control on the street. Thief might slip a blade in her down an alleyway.'

Brennus ground his teeth in rage, all too aware that the beautiful Nubian could not be under his constant protection. 'Very well, Master.' The words nearly choked him. 'I will fight better next time. More slowly.'

Memor smiled. 'Where is the purse from Caesar?'

Brennus indicated the pile of clothes by the table. Quickly the *lanista* emptied more than half the coins into a leather bag.

'Plenty left – for a *slave.*' Memor scattered the rest on the floor. He left, satisfied that the Gaul had been brought to heel.

Brennus climbed resignedly back on the bench and gestured for the *unctor* to resume.

Before falling in love with Astoria, life in the *ludus* had been simple. Other than threats of torture or death, there had been few forms of control over him. Brennus was scared of neither and the *lanista* knew it. Thirty lashes soon after his arrival had only made the Gaul laugh in Memor's face. Since the massacre of his whole tribe by the Romans, he had not cared if he lived or died. He felt completely hollow inside. Brac, his wife and child were gone for ever. People Brennus had sworn to protect had died because of his failure. Ultan's predictions had come to nothing.

That left no reason to live.

Initially, Brennus had made countless attempts to seek out death, but it had always evaded him. Nobody could beat the Gaul in combat and dozens of opponents had died beneath his blade. He'd grown rich on the rewards lavished by the *editores*, the prominent men like Julius Caesar who hosted the games that were now becoming a staple of daily life in Rome.

But money and men's lives were not what Brennus wanted. He could have fled the *ludus* and gone on the run; even an existence as an outlaw would have been better than this. What had stopped him was the shocking message that he had been given three years previously by the ancient augur who plied his trade outside the gates of the Ludus Magnus. Memor tolerated the soothsayer's visits to the school, knowing it kept his men happy. But Brennus had watched gladiators paying to hear good omens and then seen them die in the arena too many times to set much store by the old man's prophecies. He was a charlatan.

At length a friendly *murmillo* had paid for Brennus to have a reading. Feeling bored, the Gaul had gone along with the charade. The augur had smiled initially as Brennus had sat down before him. He reached into the basket alongside, produced a hen and quickly slashed its neck. Then, uncharacteristically silent, the old man had stared long and hard at the entrails. The Gaul had waited, surprised that he was not being promised victory over an entire troop of gladiators.

'You have lost everything.'

The melodramatic words had amused Brennus. So had every fighter in the *ludus*. Most were free men who had been enslaved.

Before he could stop him, the augur had spoken again. 'A long journey still awaits you.'

Shaken, Brennus had held his breath.

'A journey longer than any of your people have ever taken.' The old man had seemed as surprised as the Gaul by what he was seeing. But his interpretation had remained the same with every divination thereafter.

It had given Brennus some hope.

He tried to remain solitary but men were drawn to his friendly character. In the *ludus'* harsh atmosphere, the Gaul's willingness to train others and share useful tips on combat was unusual. While his exalted status helped to make some jealous, many gladiators called him friend. And the year before, fuelled by memories of how Conall had saved his life, Brennus had even rescued Sextus, one of the *scissores*, from the depths of an uneven mass combat. After that, Brennus became one of the *ludus'* most popular figures, although he trusted no one.

Things had changed when Astoria had arrived in the *ludus* kitchen a few months before. Brennus had immediately noticed her beauty and poise. He'd had many women since Liath's death, physical needs in the end overtaking his grief. First he had bought prostitutes with his winnings, then enjoyed rich matrons who flocked to the *ludus*. The renown of the best prize fighters attracted noblewomen like moths to a flame. Among the wealthy it was considered normal to seek pleasure from those whom they might watch die. While his comrades revelled in the attention, no female had really interested Brennus until he saw Astoria and was captivated by the curves of her ebony body, barely concealed by a ragged shift.

Brennus had quickly claimed the Nubian for his own and had thus exposed a weakness in his emotional armour. Such was the Gaul's reputation that none dared touch Astoria, confining themselves to lewd comments. But her presence was a source of intense jealousy among a small group of less successful fighters. And now, with

Memor's threats, Brennus feared more for Astoria's safety than he did his own. He grimaced. Maybe a long bath would help him forget the *lanista*'s menaces.

'Enough.'

The *unctor* stepped smartly back.

Brennus refilled the purse, tossed him a coin and walked naked into the *frigidarium*, which held a large, unheated pool. The water was cold enough to make him shiver as he climbed in. With closed eyes, the Gaul ducked his head completely under, knowing it would be refreshing before the heat of the next room.

When he had bathed in the *tepidarium*, the resident body slave oiled his skin, scraping it clean with an iron strigil. Moving on to the *caldarium*, Brennus lingered in its steamy atmosphere, sharing the warmth with the other top gladiators. Conversation was muted as the men relaxed, enjoying the intense heat radiating from hollow bricks in the walls and floor. Continuous currents of hot air from the *hypocaustum*, the nearby underground furnace, ensured the temperature remained constant.

Some time later, Brennus sauntered in better humour from the bathhouse door. Dusk was falling, and across the yard his cell door was ajar. Flickering light shone from candles that Astoria would have lit. He smiled in anticipation, imagining her naked.

A woman's scream pierced the air.

It was immediately cut short.

Brennus sprinted across the yard, his drying cloth falling unnoticed to the ground. He ripped open the door to find four of the men he least liked inside. His fears had been fulfilled. Since Spartacus' rebellion, only champion gladiators were allowed to keep weapons in their rooms. And in Brennus' absence it had been easy for the group to overpower Astoria and help themselves to some of his.

Two now waved swords threateningly at the Gaul while the other pair sat on the bed, mauling Astoria with greedy hands. The Nubian's shift had already been ripped off, and she was vainly trying to cover herself with her hands. As she whimpered, he noticed a thick welt rising on her cheek.

A vein in Brennus' neck pulsed with rage. 'The fancy boys and Lentulus,' he sneered. All his other weapons lay on the far side of the room.

'Don't come any closer!' Titus' voice wavered although the Gaul was unarmed.

The three *murmillones* were inseparable. Titus and Curtius were brothers, thugs who had worked in the *collegia* for Clodius. They had been sold to the *ludus* after a rich matron had been raped by a mob that they were leading. There were still some crimes that the *lictores*, the magistrates, would not tolerate. Flavus was a short, unpleasant man whom the pair had been trained with. Thrown into a group combat in the arena soon after arriving, they'd found it useful to fight as a trio. Since that day, the *murmillones* had lived, trained and slept together, scarcely leaving each other's company. It had earned them a reputation of doing more than sharing beds.

'What are you doing with these scum?' He moved closer to Lentulus, the fourth intruder.

The Goth swallowed hard and stepped back, keeping his sword pointing towards Brennus.

The big Gaul smiled coldly. 'Leave now and I'll be nice. I won't even kill any of you.'

Unsure, Lentulus turned to Titus, the ringleader

'He's full of shit!' retorted the *murmillo*. 'Think of the woman. You can have her next.'

Lentulus glanced at the Nubian's naked body, his eyes full of lust. Curtius nodded in agreement and pushed a hand into Astoria's groin. He sniggered and stuck several fingers in his mouth.

'Tastes sweet, Lentulus.'

'Keep him over there, boys!' Flavus laughed too, an erection visible through his loincloth. 'It won't take long with this bitch.'

Lentulus was still gazing between Astoria's legs with fascination.

There was only a moment to act. Brennus darted forward, swinging a huge fist into the side of Lentulus' head. The Goth collapsed, sword dropping to the floor. Before Brennus had time to pick it up, Titus lunged at him. Desperately the Gaul dodged to one side, but the blade sliced a long, shallow cut on his chest.

As another thrust followed, Brennus caught the sharp iron in his left hand. Ignoring the pain, he gripped the *gladius* so tightly that Titus was unable to pull it away. With his right, the Gaul grabbed the *murmillo* by the windpipe and began to choke him.

Titus' eyes bulged with terror and he let go of the sword, trying frantically to break Brennus' powerful grip. His efforts were futile. Within moments the *murmillo*'s face had gone puce, his tongue protruding from a desperate, gaping mouth. Brennus tightened the hold, grimacing as the cartilage made a cracking sound.

Curtius jumped up when he saw his brother struggling to breathe. 'Hold the girl!' he screamed at Flavus, launching himself across the room, weapon raised.

Half strangling Astoria, the evil-looking *murmillo* quickly obeyed.

Brennus dropped the limp figure to the floor, smoothly turning the sword hilt into his good hand. Blood dripped from the deep cut, but the naked Gaul was now in berserker mode. He moved closer, *gladius* at the ready.

'Four not enough to take me? Limp prick!'

'Bastard!' Distraught with grief, Curtius slashed madly at Brennus, who simply ducked under the blow.

He leaned forward, burying his blade deep in the *murmillo*'s unprotected chest. The Gaul smiled as Curtius' momentum carried him further on to the sword.

The *murmillo*'s eyes opened wide with shock as he died.

Placing a huge hand on Curtius' chest, Brennus shoved him backwards. There was a sucking noise as the razor-sharp metal pulled free, allowing air to rush into the chest cavity. Curtius' body sagged on to the sandy floor, pouring blood.

'Your friend has dirtied my room.' Brennus' tone was almost mild as he stepped towards Flavus.

'Come any closer and I cut the bitch's throat.' Flavus' eyes darted around wildly, but the point of his dagger stayed fixed under Astoria's chin.

Brennus could see the *murmillo* wasn't lying. 'Let her go.'

'So you can kill me too?' Flavus pricked Astoria's skin with the tip. A fat red drop ran down velvet black skin. 'On your feet!'

Brennus let the *murmillo* walk slowly towards him, the girl held in front.

'You first,' Flavus shouted. 'Outside.'

The Gaul stepped backwards, taking care not to lose his footing on the bloody surface.

The darkened yard was full of curious gladiators, drawn by Astoria's screams and the sounds of combat. Their flickering oil lamps illuminated the scene.

Romulus was standing in deep shadows not far from the cell door. Unlike the others, he had an idea who had attacked the Nubian. For some time Lentulus had been training with the *murmillones* and bragging about raping Astoria. He had presumed it was just talk. Now it seemed the Goth really was bad news.

Romulus had seen Brennus many times since his arrival in the *ludus* but had never spoken to him. The big Gaul and Astoria both seemed friendly and they certainly did not inspire the kind of hatred that welled up when he thought of Lentulus. Fists clenched, he prayed they had not been killed.

Relief filled him as Brennus emerged stark naked, blood running from his wounds. He was followed by Flavus, holding Astoria by the throat.

'Help me kill the Gaul!' The *murmillo* peered into the darkness, hoping to see gladiators who would come to his aid. 'We can all have his whore!'

'The first one who comes near gets his throat cut,' Brennus said calmly.

Nobody moved. In the *ludus*' unwritten rules, grudges like this usually had to be settled by those involved.

His voice shaking, Flavus called out to two fighters. 'Figulus! Gallus! Fight with me!' The pair shifted from foot to foot, deeply tempted by the attractive Nubian. It had been months since they had been with a woman, but the sight of Brennus with a bloodied sword arrested further action.

Astoria sobbed quietly.

Romulus' heart pounded in his chest. Despite the noise, there was no sign of Memor yet. Should he get involved? It took only a moment to decide. The invitation to gang-rape the girl had filled him with disgust. Velvinna had never revealed the exact circumstances of their conception, but she had hinted at it. And the merchant had forced himself on her night after night. In Romulus' mind, rape was a crime of the worst order.

He tiptoed towards Flavus' unprotected back, gently easing the dagger from his belt. Nobody spotted him. Rage replaced the disgust as he stole within striking range. Flavus was like those who had raped his mother. An anonymous noble. Gemellus.

Dirty bastards.

The *murmillo* was oblivious, still pleading with Figulus and Gallus to join him.

Romulus took a deep breath, knuckles whitening. He stepped in close, grabbing Flavus' left shoulder tightly and pushed the thin blade through his tunic to break the skin.

'Let the girl go!'

Flavus froze.

'Release her,' he hissed.

'Romulus?' The *murmillo*'s voice was incredulous. 'This has nothing to do with you. Now piss off before this bitch gets herself killed.' He poked Astoria with his knife and she screamed.

Brennus took a step forward.

'Stay where you are!' roared Flavus.

Glowering, the Gaul moved back.

Blood pounded in Romulus' ears as he took in the dramatic sight of Brennus and the circle of gladiators. Every face was watching them. In front of Flavus, Astoria's shoulders shook with fear.

'I'll give you one more chance.'

'This is men's business,' spat Flavus. 'Walk away before you get hurt. Badly hurt.'

Backing off was not an option. He had no choice. *Stab high up under the ribcage.* Cotta's advice echoed in Romulus' mind. *Cut the liver – it is always fatal.*

With a quick shove, Romulus shoved his dagger deep into Flavus' right side, twisting as it went in. The *murmillo* shrieked as he felt the thrust, and his grip on Astoria fell away. She ran sobbing to Brennus. Romulus pulled the blade free and Flavus staggered round, eyes glazed. A large area of his tunic turned bright red, the cloth filling with blood.

Flavus' face held a look of total disbelief.

Silently, Romulus stabbed him once in the chest and stood back as the *murmillo* collapsed, his strength evaporating. He jerked a few times and was still.

Romulus gazed down in fascination at the first man

he had killed. Then his stomach lurched and both legs began to wobble.

'You have my thanks.'

Romulus sensed Brennus looming above him. He nodded, suppressing the urge to vomit.

It was then that Lentulus emerged from the cell, half stunned but still clutching his sword. He saw Romulus standing over Flavus' body and gave an inarticulate cry of rage. Hoisting the weapon with a shaking hand, he weaved towards them.

Instinctively Romulus bent to retrieve his knife.

'Hold!' Memor's voice cut in. 'Next man who moves, dies!'

Everyone froze as the *lanista* pushed his way through to stand before Brennus. He was flanked by six guards with drawn bows.

'Trying to butcher everyone in the damn *ludus*?'

'What was I supposed to do?' Brennus scowled at the Goth, the only survivor. 'The bastards were going to rape Astoria.'

Memor snorted. 'And how many men are dead because of that black bitch?'

'Three.' Lentulus nursed the side of his head, bruised from the Gaul's punch.

'*Three*?' the *lanista* screeched.

'Curtius, Titus and Flavus.'

Memor's mouth opened and closed. The *murmillones* had been prize fighters.

'Anyone who touches my woman dies,' said Brennus.

'Lay a finger on another man and I'll have you crucified.' Memor was incandescent with rage. 'You might be the best gladiator here, but you are still a fucking slave!'

The Gaul's fist bunched around the hilt of his sword.

Memor gestured quickly. The archers drew back, iron-tipped arrows pointing at Brennus' heart.

Astoria screamed.

Brennus' hand dropped to his side. 'I'm not going to commit suicide to satisfy you.'

'You have some brains left, then,' replied Memor, his voice taut with anger. 'I have a good idea.' He pointed at Romulus and Lentulus. 'These two look like they aren't on best terms. They might as well settle that. At dawn tomorrow. A duel to the death. Right here in the yard.'

The pair stared at each other.

Lentulus repeated the stabbing motion. Romulus hawked and spat. The Goth made to launch himself forward, then paused.

'Go right ahead,' said Memor. 'One archer might miss, but at this range, six . . .'

Lentulus grimaced and lowered his sword. Content that he had won the confrontation, Romulus turned away.

The morning might prove different.

'Fucking great ox.' The *lanista* glared at Brennus. 'No excursions into the city till further notice. You're barred from the baths as well.'

The Gaul shrugged. He waited in case there was more.

Memor jerked his head in dismissal. 'Piss off. Before I think of a better punishment.'

Brennus obeyed. He was not worried about Memor and his threats. Astoria was a far greater concern. There had been too many men who seemed interested in Flavus' offer.

Chapter VII: The Lupanar

The Lupanar Brothel, Rome, 56 BC

Fabiola gazed uncertainly at the bare walls. The small cell was where the madam had led her after Gemellus had been thrown on to the street. The huge man who ejected him had smiled toothlessly at the new girl in an effort to seem reassuring.

The attempt had not worked. One violent master appeared to have been replaced by another.

Apart from the low bed she was sitting on, the only furniture was an empty chest and a tiny statue of a naked Aphrodite in the corner. The room smelt musty, but the floor had been washed and the worn woollen bedclothes were clean.

Fabiola hunched up in a ball, hands round her feet, rocking backwards and forwards. The manner in which she and Romulus had been ripped from Velvinna had severely dented her usual confidence, which was not even affected by Gemellus' beatings. Fabiola was terrified to think that she would never see her family again. Romulus was in mortal danger, if not dead already. Gods alone knew what would become of their mother.

For a short time the grief became all consuming. She was alone, sold to a brothel, with no chance of escape and could only imagine what would happen to her now. Silent sobs racked her. Soon complete strangers would be paying to have sex with her. Bile rose in Fabiola's throat. She felt degraded already.

It was all because of Gemellus.

The thought helped the tears disappear and a spark flared deep inside.

No weakness, only strength. No grief, just revenge.

Gemellus.

Women's laughter echoed in the corridor and Fabiola listened intently as they passed by. She might learn something useful.

'. . . told him he was the best lover I had ever been with. The fool swelled with pride!'

'Get a tip?'

'An *aureus*, no less.' There was a loud cackle and the pair passed out of earshot.

Fabiola sat up on the bed, mind racing. There was money to be made here. The *aureus* was more than she'd ever held in her hand. And the Lupanar seemed to be full of beautiful women of every race, clad in robes and dresses that left nothing to the imagination. Flimsy garments, intricate head-dresses and exotic jewellery filled her with wonder. In all Fabiola's years at Gemellus' house, she had never owned more than one threadbare shift. It was a small consolation to have been sold into the best brothel in Rome. But that thought was followed immediately, guiltily, by the memory of the scene when Gemellus had dragged her away, only a short time before. When Velvinna had realised he intended to fulfil his promise of selling Fabiola as well, her distress had partially overcome her fear of the merchant.

'Please, Master. Leave me one child!'

'This little beauty is worth far more than the brat.' Gemellus leered at Fabiola's curves. 'I'd fuck her myself if it didn't halve the value.'

'I'll do anything,' Velvinna wailed. 'Even make noise when you take me.'

'As if I'd bother! Used-up old whore,' Gemellus sneered. 'The salt mines are the only place for you.'

The salt mines? There was a heartbeat's shock. She had nothing left to lose. Velvinna threw both arms around the merchant's legs, weeping hysterically.

'Get off, or I'll sell you today as well!' He viciously pried tight fingers loose, throwing Velvinna to the stone floor.

The slight figure lay prone, sobs racking her body.

Gemellus laughed.

It was Fabiola's last sight of her mother. She had been dragged from the room and hauled away to the Lupanar. More tears flowed. Life seemed cruel beyond belief. But the self-pity did not last very long. Fabiola's spirit burned too fiercely to succumb, and Velvinna's oft-repeated advice rang in her ears: *Make the best of every situation. Always.*

Calming herself, Fabiola clenched her fists into the coarse wool bedclothes and offered a fervent prayer to the gods.

Protect Mother and Romulus.

Just an hour before, Fabiola had been gazing with wide, frightened eyes at the walls in the brothel's lavish reception area. Satyrs, fat cupids, gods and goddesses returned her stare from a brightly coloured landscape covered in rivers, caves and forests. On another surface were numbered depictions of sexual positions that customers might desire. Fabiola had shuddered, imagining Gemellus forcing her to perform the more outlandish ones. In the centre of the mosaic floor was a life-size statue of a naked woman entwined with a swan.

'Eight thousand *sestertii*,' mused Gemellus. 'Not a bad price.'

'That's what we agreed.' Jovina, the old madam, pursed painted lips in disapproval. Beady eyes shone from the powdered whiteness of her face.

Gemellus, well pleased, clutched the leather purse tightly to his chest. 'I know. What a little beauty.' He reached over, allowing himself a good feel of Fabiola's small breasts. She flinched in horror, but did not dare move away.

The merchant's hand dropped lower, searching for the hem of her tunic.

'No touching. She's mine now.'

He removed his hand resentfully.

Fabiola looked at the floor, cheeks burning.

Gemellus smirked. 'A few moments alone might be worth it,' he said, hefting the money bag.

'It will cost. She's a virgin, you know.' Jovina revealed decaying teeth. After many years at the Lupanar, men like Gemellus were easy to spot. She twisted a ring on a thin finger, watching the ruby catch the light. The crone carried a fortune on both hands, presents from satisfied customers. Jovina's services – and her discretion – were famous.

Fabiola shuddered at the memory of the examination that had just been performed to confirm her virginal status. She felt ashamed and violated. The madam's prodding fingers still burned her skin.

'Of course I know!' Gemellus snapped. 'By Jupiter, I resisted the urge to take the vixen for long enough.' He licked moist lips. 'How much for a night?'

Jovina placed a claw-like hand on the girl's head. The slight pressure made Fabiola feel remarkably protected.

'Fifteen thousand *sestertii.*'

'Fifteen *thousand?*' The merchant's eyes bulged. 'Nearly twice what you just paid!'

'Virgins like her are hard to come by,' Jovina replied sarcastically. 'Noble customers pay well for the first time with such a beauty.'

Gemellus was purple with rage.

'Come back in a few weeks and the price will only be three or four thousand.' Jovina's lips twitched. 'Per hour, of course.'

'Old whore!' the merchant yelled, bunching his fists.

'Benignus!'

An enormous slave with thick gold bands round both wrists emerged from a side room. Gemellus took in the bulging muscles and metal-studded club.

'This gentleman is leaving.' Jovina pointed. 'Escort him to the door.'

158

Benignus towered over Gemellus. There was no doubt who was in authority here.

He paused, even now reluctant to obey a slave.

'Master.' The hulk had taken Gemellus' right arm in a grip of iron and he felt himself being propelled towards the entrance. A powerful shove landed the merchant in the dirt outside, at the feet of two of his waiting slaves. Quickly they helped him up, their faces studiously blank.

Benignus loomed over him like a Greek colossus. 'Next time, Madam will require evidence that you have sufficient funds to enter.'

The passers-by laughed at the carefully worded insult. They'd seen many people ejected from the arched doorway for the same reason.

Gemellus angrily brushed away the dirt and stalked off, his leather purse gripped tightly in one hand. It would keep the moneylenders at bay for a while.

Jovina knocked just once as she opened the door, startling Fabiola. The madam took in her reddened eyes at a glance. Many girls like this had entered the brothel. She walked in, still appraising her new purchase.

Fabiola met the look, chin trembling faintly.

'Forget the past, my dear,' Jovina said in a friendly but firm manner. 'Coming here saved you from Gemellus' advances at least. Life here can be good. It's simple. Learn how to work the customers well and satisfy them every time. Many powerful men visit the Lupanar. Senators, magistrates, tribunes. We've even had consuls in here before.'

Fabiola nodded. It was important she learn quickly and make friends with the old woman.

Jovina paused for a moment. 'Is the fat man your father?'

'Gemellus?' Fabiola stared at the floor. 'No, Madam.'

Jovina did not hesitate. 'One of his other slaves then?'

She shook her head. Velvinna had always been adamant about their parentage. 'A woman knows these things,' she would mutter darkly. 'Mother was raped by a noble one evening as she came back from the Forum Olitorium.'

Jovina was unsurprised. 'And did Gemellus often lie with her?'

'Nearly every night.' Fabiola felt anger deep in her belly. Revenge on Gemellus would give a purpose to life in the brothel. That and trying to rescue her mother and Romulus. Best of all would be to discover the rapist's identity.

If it was possible.

Something to plan, while she pleasured men. Something to dilute the horror of her situation.

'See much of what happened?'

'No, though I did see him naked once when he was excited.' She recoiled at the memory of the merchant's erection.

'You've watched dogs in the street mating?'

'Yes.'

'Heard other slaves talking about sex?'

'Many times.'

'It's much the same as with animals, although you must know more positions.' Jovina quickly described those that most men preferred.

Fabiola struggled to control her surprise at the more outlandish ones. Gemellus knew only one.

'Make lots of noise. The customer must always think you are in ecstasy.'

'Yes, Madam,' she replied quickly.

'The first time a man penetrates you, it will really hurt. Probably be a fair amount of blood too. That's normal. After that, it often feels good.' She cackled. 'There is more for you to learn, but the others will instruct you. Make absolutely sure that you can give oral pleasure.'

Fabiola forced a smile, relieved that the lesson seemed to be over.

'The room is yours to do with as you will.' Jovina grinned, and the wrinkles on her whitened face became more pronounced. 'But no men are allowed back here. The chambers where customers are entertained lie at the front of the building. The doormen, Benignus and Vettius, are always nearby. Scream if you need them.'

'When do I start?'

'Tomorrow. I just paid out eight thousand *sestertii* so you've got to start earning. But I'll let you settle in today. Find your way about the place.'

Fabiola kept her voice calm. 'What about food?'

'Some more meat on those bones won't hurt business.' Jovina laughed at her own joke and gestured at the slave who had been standing behind, unseen. 'Docilosa will show you round. The clothes room is worth seeing. It's got a better selection than any bazaar in Rome.'

Fabiola's mouth opened.

'And make sure you dress seductively.'

A smile flitted across Docilosa's face.

'Yes, Madam.'

'Good. You will do well.' Jovina turned and was gone, leaving a strong smell of perfume.

Fabiola glanced at Docilosa, who was a similar age to her mother. Short, plain and clad in a simple smock, she had a kind face.

'Can I have something to eat?'

'Of course,' Docilosa nodded. 'Follow me.'

Soon Fabiola was seated by a rough wooden table in the kitchen, devouring a piece of bread and cheese. The ordeal had given her an enormous appetite, increased by the fabulous selection of foods on the shelves. Gemellus had never given his slaves enough to eat, and her childhood had been dogged by hunger.

Slaves clad only in loincloths looked at the new girl curiously. Docilosa pointed them out one by one.

'That's Catus, the main cook. He's all right, but watch his temper.' Unable to hear what was being said, the balding man chopping meat at a large wooden block smiled.

Fabiola soaked up the information. She wanted to know everyone in the Lupanar.

'The two tending the fire are Nepos and Tancinus. The girl sweeping the floor is Germanilla.'

The men sweating over the hot brick oven glanced over without interest. Though relatively young, both were quite overweight.

'Do they get extra food?'

'Of course not,' said Docilosa. 'They've been castrated.'

Fabiola gasped.

'To make sure they leave the girls alone. You're valuable merchandise and Jovina guards her property closely.'

'What about Catus?'

'Catus only likes men.' Docilosa's tone was scornful. 'And Madam rarely buys any – they're too much trouble.'

'And the doormen?'

'They receive favours from many women and she tolerates that.'

'Why?'

'Some customers get violent.' She made a chopping motion. 'The boys sort them out.'

Fabiola made a mental note to make friends with Benignus and Vettius.

Docilosa filled a plain black and red earthenware jug from a tank in the corner. Like Gemellus' house, the Lupanar had running water and sanitation.

'You'll need this in your room.' She handed over a beaker as well, studying Fabiola closely. 'You remind me of my own daughter.' There was a brief smile before Docilosa gestured towards the door, all business again. 'I'll show you where the clothes are kept.'

Fabiola followed her guide out of the stone-flagged kitchen, down a corridor filled with the smell of burning incense. Alcoves along its length displayed Greek statues.

The room exceeded all Fabiola's expectations. Dozens of richly adorned costumes hung from iron hooks on its painted walls. Large bronze plates on stands acted as mirrors. Tables were covered in glass bowls, bottles and silver hand mirrors. Oblivious to the new arrivals, two women were trying on dresses at the far end.

Docilosa gazed at the display and sighed. 'I'll leave you to it. Get to know some of the others.'

Fabiola could see that both were years older than her. It was intimidating. Trying to remain calm, she walked further into the dressing room.

A buxom Germanic-looking prostitute had already half turned in her direction. She was holding up a mane of long blonde hair, admiring her reflection in the mirror. Fabiola stared, intrigued. The only person she had regularly seen naked was her mother. A scanty red robe barely covered this woman's generous breasts and a flat waist. At the top of creamy white thighs sat a small puff of hair. She was very beautiful.

'Who are you?'

'Fabiola.' She paused, then added unnecessarily, 'I'm new.'

The blonde was displeased. 'How many young ones is Jovina trying to pack in?'

'Ignore her.' The second woman's face was more friendly. 'She's having a bad day. I'm Pompeia and that's Claudia.'

'I've never seen so many types of clothes.' Fabiola's mouth opened as she surveyed the selection.

'Wonderful, isn't it?' Pompeia giggled and Fabiola took an immediate liking to the tall redhead. With green eyes and an alabaster complexion, she was extremely striking. A tight *stola*, slit at the sides to the waist, and then above the belt to the shoulder, revealed tempting expanses of flesh. 'Wear whatever we like, too.'

'Jovina said I must dress seductively.'

'She would,' cackled Claudia.

Pompeia threw her a frown and cocked her head at Fabiola. 'How old are you?'

'Thirteen. Nearly fourteen.'

'Gods above. Still a virgin?'

Fabiola looked at the marble floor.

'Never mind, you're here now.' Pompeia strolled along the wall, trailing her fingers through the garments. 'Come with me.'

Fabiola followed slowly, touching the items with disbelief.

'Mustn't overdo it. The most important thing is that you're a virgin.' She produced a white robe of fine linen with a purple hem. 'Try this.'

Fabiola reached out eagerly. 'It's beautiful.'

'Only the best for Lupanar girls. Put it on.'

Fabiola lifted off her ragged smock and pulled on the crisp fabric. It felt luxurious against her skin, far better than anything she'd ever worn. Fabiola smoothed the dress against her body. 'It's lovely,' she whispered.

Claudia snorted dismissively.

Fabiola found Pompeia appraising her keenly.

'Perfect. You look like a Vestal Virgin.'

'But you can buy this bitch!' said Claudia.

Pompeia spun round. 'It's sad that fool Metellus Celer has just died, but you'll soon find another rich client. Stop taking it out on her.'

'The master used to lie with my mother most nights.' Fabiola's voice was steady. 'I know what to expect.'

'He no longer owns you,' Claudia said unexpectedly. 'Forget him.'

Fabiola smiled at that thought.

'I saw the fat pig through the peephole.' Pompeia screwed up her face. 'Many customers here are far better looking. Play it smart and they'll become regulars.' She turned to Claudia for confirmation. 'Men love giving presents. Taking you out.'

'All you have to do is satisfy their every desire,' said the blonde.

A twitch of apprehension crossed Fabiola's features. Her only knowledge of sex had come from watching her mother, who had loathed Gemellus' visits.

Noticing, Pompeia took her hand. 'We will teach you lots of ways to do that, my girl. Come over here. Take a look in the mirror.'

Fabiola stared at the beaten bronze. Light shimmered from the tiny curves and dents across its surface. With a shock, she saw that the reflection was indeed pretty. Her confidence lifted slightly.

'How many . . . prostitutes work here?' The word still felt disgusting. But that is what she was now.

'Including us? About thirty. Varies a bit.' Pompeia dipped a brush into a bowl of ochre and applied a little to her cheeks. 'According to how many get sold or gain manumission.'

Fabiola's ears pricked up. 'Sold?'

'Sometimes a customer likes a girl so much that he buys her. Mostly they go off to a life of luxury. Villa in Pompeii or the like.' Pompeia looked wistful. 'Unlucky ones are got rid of when they are sick. Or too old.'

'So are those who disobey Jovina,' said the blonde ominously.

'Where to?'

'One of the cheaper brothels. To someone needing cheap labour.'

'Salt mines, *latifundia*, you know.' Claudia scowled. 'Got to remain popular and stay beautiful.'

Fabiola thought of her mother and shuddered.

Mistaking the reaction for one of fear, Pompeia patted her arm. 'Don't worry! Jovina won't be selling a prize catch like you.'

'Do some girls gain their freedom?'

Pompeia smiled. 'Jovina lets us keep a tiny amount of the fees for our services. Regular clients will give you some money too. Save every last *sestertius*. Isn't that right?'

Claudia nodded vigorously, powdering her face with chalk and white lead.

'A little more – that's not pale enough. Don't forget a bit of antimony on your eyebrows.' Pompeia turned back to Fabiola. 'Keep on Jovina's good side. In a few years she might let you buy out of here.'

Claudia snorted. 'The old witch only says that to keep us happy. You know that. Can you name anyone who has bought their manumission since we arrived?'

Pompeia's face dropped, and Fabiola's heart went out to her. Life in the Lupanar was obviously not secure. She would have to work hard to survive.

The redhead saw her staring at the huge array of bottles and jars on the table. 'It's makeup. Lotions.'

'Can I try some on?'

'You're far too beautiful.'

'But you're both using it.'

Pompeia laughed. 'We've been here for a long time! Have to keep looking good. You're as fresh as a flower.'

'Not even some ochre?'

'Perhaps a little. On your lips. Nothing else.'

Unsure what men who visited the Lupanar would want, Fabiola gazed into the big mirror.

'The clients will love you.' Pompeia gestured expansively as if talking to an audience. 'You might need some lead in a while, but for now you're the Vestal Virgin.'

'Pompeia's right.' Claudia's tone was slightly more friendly. 'Understatement's better. For you.' She laughed, indicating her own generous curves.

Fabiola smiled.

'We're forgetting ourselves. Must be nearly sundown!' Suddenly Pompeia was all business. 'Have a good soak and an early night. It's time for us to work. Customers will start arriving soon.'

Fabiola threw her new friend a grateful look. 'Thank you.'

'I'll come and fetch you in the morning. We can chat about how to make men groan and beg for more!'

'Or cry out!'

Pompeia rolled her eyes. 'That's Claudia's speciality.'

Fabiola left them to it and walked down the corridor, rubbing the linen fabric with secret pleasure. To her relief, she was the only person in the tiled bathing area apart from an old female slave, who silently provided olive oil and a strigil.

The experience was far better than she had imagined. Gemellus had only allowed slaves to wash in the back courtyard with a bucket of cold water. Being able to lie back in a heated pool, admiring colourful paintings through the steam, seemed like total bliss. Fabiola fantasised about a time when talented craftsmen would paint the walls of her villa with similar depictions of Neptune and mythological marine creatures.

Clean and relaxed, Fabiola retired to her room. She lay on the bedcovers, staring at flickering shadows cast by the torch. The grief at being parted from her family had abated a little with the discovery of a new friend and the Lupanar's soothing luxury. Pompeia would be a good ally, someone she might be able to trust. And she had something to aim for: to become the best prostitute in the brothel. With influential politicians and nobles as customers here, there was real power to be had by being good at her new profession. It gave her strength to know that rich men paying for sex might prove to be at her mercy.

Fabiola stayed awake for some time, trying to imagine what intercourse would be like, but she couldn't. Rest would be better than worrying over something beyond her control. She closed her eyes and fell asleep. There were no nightmares.

Pompeia arrived as promised early the next morning. Hearing the gentle knock, Fabiola threw back the covers and padded to the door, running a hand through her hair.

'Still sleeping? You weren't working half the night!' There were dark rings under Pompeia's eyes, but the vivacious redhead was full of energy. 'Let's go and wash. There's a lot you need to learn.'

Fabiola flushed with embarrassment at that prospect, but picked up a drying sheet and followed Pompeia down the corridor. A waft of warm, moist air accompanied by the noise of talking women met them at the door. It felt decadent.

Suddenly an image of Romulus came to mind. The thought hit hard. Seeing her brother being dragged away was something Fabiola doubted she could ever forget. *All I have to do today is sit in a heated bath and learn how to pleasure a man, while Romulus learns to fight for his life.* Guilt swept over her.

Inside, half a dozen prostitutes were washing and talking animatedly with each other. Conversation stopped when they saw the newcomers.

'This is Fabiola,' Pompeia announced. 'Girl I was telling you about.'

The majority nodded in a friendly enough manner and resumed chatting, glancing over occasionally. Pompeia stripped naked, indicating that Fabiola do the same. The redhead was full-bodied and curvaceous, her breasts larger than any the girl had seen before. Fabiola stared with fascination at Pompeia's bush of auburn pubic hair. Her milk-white skin contrasted sharply with the tall Nubian in the circular bath, who moved over so the two friends could enter and sit down.

Fabiola sat bolt upright in the warm water, smiling nervously.

Pompeia saw how ill at ease she was. 'Relax! We're all family here and we all look out for each other. The only rule is that you never try and steal another woman's regular.'

For a good hour, Fabiola concentrated hard as Pompeia lectured her on the subjects of personal hygiene, the herbs to drink that prevented pregnancy, and how to make interesting conversation with a man. Every so often one of the others would chip in. Pompeia talked completely without embarrassment, and eventually Fabiola began to feel more at ease.

'Some men just want to lie in your arms and fall asleep.'

'Who cares as long as they pay?' interjected the Nubian, to shrieks of amusement.

'And then your twentieth customer arrives,' intoned another. 'A soldier returning from years on campaign. The bastards always want to go at it like Priapus himself!'

The women roared with laughter.

'At the Lupanar, it's rare to see more than two or three men a night,' said Pompeia reassuringly. 'One of the perks of working in an expensive brothel. But you have to learn to be an amazing lover.'

Claudia groaned loudly. 'Performer, more like.'

Pompeia smiled in acknowledgement. 'No man must ever leave unsatisfied, or you'll get a name for being frigid.'

'And Jovina will be at your throat before the customer is out the door,' said a plump, black-haired girl.

There was a chorus of agreement from those listening.

Pompeia began to explain various sexual positions and techniques to Fabiola, and the girl's eyes widened. It seemed that Jovina had only described a small number to her.

'Use my mouth and tongue?' Fabiola screwed up her face. 'Like that?'

'The Lupanar's signature act. Men love it. So get good at it quickly,' replied Pompeia in a serious voice. 'No whores in Rome are as good as we are.'

'Make sure he is clean first,' advised the Nubian with a wink.

'Washing him can be part of your technique.'

'Sounds revolting.'

'Better get used to the idea, my child.' Pompeia took Fabiola's hand. 'Your body is no longer your own. The Lupanar owns us completely.'

Fabiola met the other's gaze with some difficulty. 'It is a lot to take in.' She would have no choice about who paid for her time and someone like Gemellus might be her first customer. Fabiola instantly decided that sex would be her job and nothing else. A way to survive. It was the brutal reality of her new profession. She thought of Romulus training as a gladiator, risking his life with little or no chance of escape. If this new life was a success, she would be able to buy his freedom one day. It was up to her.

'You're clever and beautiful.' Pompeia grinned slyly. 'Learn to pleasure a man well and you could nab a nice old senator.'

'With a house on the Palatine Hill!' added Claudia.

Fabiola nodded firmly.

The redhead smiled and squeezed her hand.

'Tell me everything I need to know.'

Pompeia resumed Fabiola's education with more details of the physical act. This time the thirteen-year-old paid even more attention.

At last Pompeia lay back in the water, luxuriating in the heat. 'That's enough for one morning,' she said, closing her eyes. 'Get cleaned up. Jovina will want you available soon.'

Fabiola's heart quickened, but she did not argue.

Soon after, Pompeia took her to try on the linen robe again. She turned the young girl round in front of a bronze mirror, then wove some flowers through her thick black hair.

'Just need a hint of perfume.' She plucked a tiny glass phial from inside her dress and handed it to Fabiola. 'This will be delicate enough.'

Fabiola lifted the bottle to her nose. 'Lovely.'

'Rose-water. A Greek sells it in the market. I'll take you there soon. Dab some on your neck and hands.'

Fabiola obeyed, enjoying the beautiful smell.

'Worth every last *sestertius*.'

'I'm sorry!' She had applied a large amount without even thinking.

'Don't worry. You can look out for me when I need help,' said Pompeia warmly. 'Time to meet the customers. Jovina will be getting impatient.'

Fabiola took a deep breath. There was little point in prolonging the inevitable. She followed Pompeia down the corridor, head held high.

Chapter VIII: A Close Call

Rome, 56 BC

Tarquinius tossed a copper coin at the stallholder and turned away, tearing at the crust of the small loaf. It was early afternoon and the Etruscan had not eaten since dawn. Although his stomach grumbled for more, the fresh bread would suffice until later. Tarquinius had more on his mind than hunger. *Finding Caelius.* He had only been in the city for a week, and frustratingly there had been no sign of his former master at all. It seemed that nobody knew of a middle-aged, red-haired noble with a bad temper. Tarquinius' daily sacrifices had been equally unhelpful in revealing Caelius' whereabouts. It was the nature of haruspicy to be obscure from time to time and by now he was used to it. Without any guidance, plain footwork through the busy streets would have to do.

The Forum Romanum was as good a place as any to wait and watch. The most important open space in the city, it was thronged with citizens from sunrise until sunset every day. Here was the Senate, the centre of the democracy that had taken control of Italy after crushing the Etruscans' civilisation. Here were row upon row of shops in the *basilicae* where countless lawyers, scribes, merchants and bankers vied for business. The air was filled with shouts and cries as each competed with his neighbours. Limbless cripples held up begging cups, hoping for alms while moneylenders sat at coin-laden tables nearby. Rolls of parchment by their feet detailed the unfortunates who were in their power. Hard-faced, armed men lounged behind them: security against theft and debt collectors rolled into one.

Finishing the loaf, Tarquinius pushed his way through the crowds, working his way towards the steps up to the temple of Castor. It was a good vantage point. His eyes constantly scrutinised the faces of those passing by. The haruspex was an expert at being unobtrusive, which was exactly what he wanted. And if noticed, Tarquinius appeared very unremarkable. A slight figure with long blond hair, he was wearing a typical thigh-length Roman tunic; sturdy sandals clad his dusty feet. Over one shoulder hung his pack, containing a few clothes and the golden-headed *lituus*. A cloak concealed the Etruscan battleaxe hanging on his back. Tarquinius had discovered long ago that it drew attention – of the wrong kind. The small pouch hanging from a leather thong around his neck contained his two most valuable possessions: the ancient map and the ruby. The haruspex reached inside his tunic and rubbed the huge jewel absent-mindedly, a comforting gesture he made when thinking.

At the foot of the imposing carved steps to the shrine was a group of soothsayers wearing distinctive blunt-peaked hats and long robes. Their kind were to be found everywhere in Rome, feeding on people's superstitions and desires. Tarquinius often found himself sitting near such men, partly so he could smile at their fraudulent claims and partly because it comforted him to see an art practised that he himself seldom did in public. If he was near enough, it was possible for him to divine from the fraudsters' sacrifices, a habit that amused Tarquinius greatly.

The Etruscan's mind ranged back to the last time he had seen his mentor, fourteen years before. Incredibly, Olenus had been at peace with his destiny, content that his knowledge had been safely passed on. It had been much more difficult for Tarquinius, who had battled with himself all the way to the *latifundium*, the liver and other artefacts weighing him down. Only his love and respect for Olenus had prevented Tarquinius from climbing back up the mountain to fight Rufus Caelius and the legionaries. But it would have been wrong to have interfered. One of the cornerstones of the old haruspex' teaching had been that each man's fate was his own.

Tarquinius knew now that the whole experience had been part of Olenus' last lesson to him. Returning two days later to prepare a funeral pyre for the man he had loved as a father had changed him for ever. It had made him utterly determined to carry out Olenus' wishes to the letter. He was the last Etruscan haruspex.

On his final, grief-stricken return from the mountain, Tarquinius had prised the ruby from the hilt of the ancient sword and buried the weapon and the liver in a

grove near Caelius' villa. This was because he preferred
to fight with an Etruscan battleaxe but also because the
fine blade would have attracted too much attention. He
was sure that Olenus would have understood. The gem
had been worn against his heart ever since.

In deep gloom, he filled a pack and said goodbye to
his mother, knowing he would never see her again. Fulvia
understood instantly when he mentioned that Olenus
had predicted this road for him; nearby his father was
lying in a drunken stupor. The young man kissed Sergius'
brow and whispered in his ear, 'The Etruscans will not
be forgotten.' The sleeping figure rolled over, smiling
gently. It lifted Tarquinius' spirits as he walked along the
dusty track that led to the nearest road.

A good place to start, Rome had drawn him south.
Tarquinius had never visited the capital before and its
great buildings did not fail to impress him. He was immediately drawn to the great temple of Jupiter, where he
witnessed the priests as they emerged from a reading of
the Etruscan *libri*. The young haruspex burned with rage
while watching the Roman augurs pronounce their interpretation of the winds and clouds that day. And it was
incorrect. The sacred books stolen from Etruscan cities
were in the keeping of charlatans. It crossed his mind to
steal the *libri*, but there was little point. Where would
he take them? Copies had already been made and stored
elsewhere and if he were caught, the *lictores* would sew
Tarquinius in a sack and drop him in the Tiber.

In the event a week in the city had been enough. The
Etruscan had not known anyone there and lodgings were
filthy and expensive. Slightly at a loss, Tarquinius headed

south on the Via Appia. Ten miles from the city, he paused by a roadside well to slake his thirst. A group of legionaries were resting under some trees, their javelins and shields stacked nearby. Soldiers were a common sight on the roads, marching to join their units, being sent on engineering duties or heading to war. Despite his training, Tarquinius still struggled not to hate their very existence and what they stood for. It was such legionaries who had crushed the Etruscans centuries before. But his emotions were well hidden as he leaned back against a thick trunk, chewing on a piece of bread and cheese.

Seeing Tarquinius' wiry build and the axe he had unslung from his back, the centurion strolled up and asked him to enlist. Rome was always on the lookout for men who could fight. With a smile, the Etruscan had complied. It seemed the most natural thing in the world to join the force which had been responsible for the subjugation of his people. He had been expecting it.

After two months of hard training, the legions took Tarquinius to Asia Minor and the third war between Rome and Mithridates, the King of Pontus. There the general Lucullus, a former right-hand man of Sulla's, had been fighting for three years. By the time the haruspex arrived, Lucullus had successfully vanquished Mithridates, forcing the king into neighbouring Armenia, where he licked his wounds under the protection of its ruler, Tigranes. Yet Mithridates was still a free man. And as Rome knew from previous bitter experience, this meant the conflict was not over.

Rebuffing all offers of friendship, Tigranes refused to

hand over Mithridates, which made him fair game in the general's eyes. Without hesitation, Lucullus led Tarquinius and his legions into Armenia. Battle was joined near the capital city of Tigranocerta. Although vastly outnumbered, Lucullus had crushed the Armenian forces, winning one of the most stunning victories in the Republic's history. Tens of thousands of the enemy were killed. Tarquinius fought with great distinction, helping to turn the enemy flank at a crucial stage in the battle. Using the Roman *gladius* when in formation, the young soldier switched to his battleaxe when pursuing the Armenians from the field. Nearby legionaries watched in awe as its iron blades flashed through the air, carving men in two. Tarquinius' reward was a promotion to *tesserarius*, the junior officer in charge of the guard in each century.

He smiled at the memory. Once Tarquinius' centurion had realised that the new *tesserarius* was capable of filling in the complex duty rosters on his own, he had offloaded large amounts of paperwork on to him. Soon Tarquinius was requisitioning supplies, calculating the men's pay and ordering new equipment.

Meanwhile, Mithridates had escaped yet again. Returning to Pontus, he raised new armies and defeated the local Roman forces there. Bogged down in Armenia, where he was now fighting a guerrilla war, Lucullus had been powerless to respond. To make matters worse, mutiny broke out among his own troops, who by now had been on campaign with him for six long years. Like all legionaries, they had endured harsh discipline and constant danger for little pay. During another long, cold winter under canvas, rumours arose about the generous treatment that Pompey's veterans had received. Despite the efforts of Tarquinius and the other officers, they swept through the legions. And fuelling the discontent was an arrogant and disgruntled young patrician called Clodius Pulcher. He was Lucullus' brother-in-law and Tarquinius had disliked him on sight. Sending his troublesome relation packing, Lucullus dragged his mutinous army to Pontus by sheer force of will, but was no longer able to trust it in combat against Mithridates.

While there was little actual resistance left in the area, no complete victory had been obtained. In situations like this, Rome was merciless. Pompey Magnus was immediately dispatched to the rescue with the largest force ever sent to the east. Upon the newcomer's arrival, Tarquinius watched with the rest of the soldiers as Pompey stripped Lucullus of both his command and his legions, reducing him to a private citizen. It was a demeaning end for the able general.

Pompey swiftly mopped up the last pockets of resistance, driving Mithridates into the hills, a broken man. Armenia became a new Roman province, Tigranes a mere client king. Peace was restored to Asia Minor and the wily Pompey took all the credit. By this time, Tarquinius had spent four years in the legions. It had been a surprise to find that military life suited him. The camaraderie, the foreign languages and cultures, even the fighting provided the young Etruscan with much more than his former life on the *latifundium*. Or so he had thought. Since joining up, he had avoided the few chances to perform divinations that had come along, even choosing not to study the weather patterns.

First he had tried to explain it as a way of keeping a low profile, but finally Tarquinius realised that it had all been an attempt to forget his grief, to pretend that Olenus had not gone for ever. This revelation had made the Etruscan desert the army, determined to rediscover himself. Leaving his unit without permission was a crime punishable by death, and had instantly made Tarquinius a fugitive. He was not troubled by this. As long as he did not draw attention to himself, the haruspex knew that he could pass virtually anywhere without being detected. His disappearance would cause little fuss: he had been just another of the rank and file in Rome's legions.

And so Tarquinius visited the temples of nearby Lydia, seeking evidence of links with the Rasenna, his people. He found little more than the occasional shrine to Tinia and a few crumbling tombs. This was enough to prove that the Etruscans had lived there, but not whether they had previously come from somewhere else. Unable to draw himself away from the Mediterranean yet, the young haruspex journeyed to Rhodes and encountered the great philosopher Posidonius, whose opinion on the ascendancy of Rome had interested him greatly. Visits to North Africa and the ruins of Carthage followed, then Hispania and Gaul. Always he took great care to avoid military camps and the men who populated them. Rome sent its soldiers all over the known world, and even in far-flung outposts it was remotely possible he might encounter someone who knew him as a deserter.

It did not matter where Tarquinius laid his head. Every night he was haunted by images of Caelius, his former master.

Eventually Rome draws you back. A desire for revenge.

Olenus had been correct. More than a decade after he had left Italy, Tarquinius returned, bent on one thing. Retribution. A price had to be exacted for the death of his mentor.

Deep in thought, Tarquinius did not hear the loud voice until it was practically upon him.

'Make way!' cried a huge bodyguard stalking in front of an imposing litter borne by four muscular slaves. Liberal strokes of a cane whipped the shoulders of anyone slow to obey him. 'Make way for Crassus, the conqueror of Spartacus!'

'I thought that was Pompey,' quipped a man nearby.

There were roars of amusement from those who heard. Crassus was still famously angry at the manner in which his rival Pompey had stolen the credit for crushing the slave rebellion fifteen years previously.

Drawing his *gladius* with a scowl, the bodyguard swung round to see who had made the insolent remark. Used to shouting insults, the citizen ducked his head, making himself anonymous in the crowd. While they had little say in what went on in their name, the people of Rome were free to make their opinions known. Politicians had to live with such taunts and the graphic, poorly spelt graffiti that was often daubed on the walls of public buildings or their own homes. The perpetrators were rarely caught. Venting his fury, the guard reached out and slapped the flat of his blade across the nearest street urchin's back. The loud yelp this produced brought a sour smile to his face.

Tarquinius watched keenly as the litter came to a halt at the foot of the steps. Inside was the man who had paid Caelius a fortune for the information about the bronze liver and Tarquin's sword. He was therefore indirectly responsible for Olenus' death. Those around the Etruscan also craned their heads to see. Crassus was one of the most prominent nobles in Rome and although less popular than Pompey, he was so rich that everyone at least admired him. Or envied him.

Lifting the cloth of the litter's side, the bodyguard indicated to his master that they had arrived. There was a brief pause and then a short, grey-haired man wearing a fine toga emerged. He stood to acknowledge the crowd for a moment, his piercing gaze judging their mood. Public approval was important to all those who wished to achieve high office. And Crassus did. Everyone knew that. The stranglehold that he, Pompey and Julius Caesar had on the reins of power was growing ever tighter. While the rivalry between the members of the triumvirate remained behind the scenes, the city was constantly awash with rumours. It seemed that each man wanted sole power. At virtually any cost.

'People of Rome,' Crassus began dramatically. 'I have come to the temple of Castor to seek his blessing.'

There was a sigh of anticipation.

'I wish the great horseman himself to give me a sign,' announced Crassus. 'A divine seal of approval.'

He waited.

Tarquinius looked around, seeing the tension rise in

men's faces. Crassus is learning to work the mob, he thought.

'For what, Master?' It was the man who had cracked the joke about Pompey. Even he wanted to know why Crassus had come to pay homage.

Pleased by the question, Crassus rubbed his beaked nose. 'A sign that I will gain great glory for Rome!'

This produced an instant cheer.

'As governor of Syria, I will expand the Republic's borders to the east,' said Crassus boldly. 'Crush the savages who mock us. Who threaten our civilised ways!'

Roars of agreement rose into the air.

This was a common theme. If Rome considered herself in peril, then woe betide those who were perceived to be responsible. The mightiest power on the Mediterranean in an age, Carthage had dared to wage war against the Republic two centuries before. It had taken three long wars, but eventually its cities had been ground into dust by the legions.

Tarquinius had to respect the casual arrogance of even the lowliest citizen. They were scared of nothing. And though most had no understanding of why Crassus craved the leadership of Syria, the idea of military glory appealed to all. It did not matter that there had actually been no insults made, no envoys killed in the east. Romans instinctively respected war. Since deepest antiquity, its people had fought for it every year, returning to their farms each autumn.

'And when I come back,' Crassus continued, 'I will double the distribution of grain!'

This produced an even better response. Thanks to the

precipitous decline in the price of agricultural goods, most of the population were now landless and dependent on *congiaria*, handouts of food and money, for their survival. The current amount of grain allowed was not enough for a family to survive for a year and any promise to increase it would be met with instant approval.

Crassus smiled with satisfaction and mounted the steps to the entrance, the cries sweeping behind him in a great wave of sound. At the top, a grovelling priest waited to usher him inside. The clamour was gradually replaced by excited muttering as the crowd discussed what they had just witnessed.

Tarquinius understood exactly what was going on. The visit to the temple had been completely staged. This was the busiest time of day in the Forum. If Crassus had wished to say his prayers in private, he would only have needed to arrive a few hours earlier or later. The ante was obviously upping in the struggle for dominance. Keen to emulate the military successes of his rivals, Crassus was beginning to reveal his hand. Tarquinius lifted his eyes upwards, squinting in the bright sunshine. A fair breeze. Few clouds. Soon the air would change, bringing rain.

Crassus will travel east with an army, he thought. To Parthia and beyond. And I will go with him.

'Tarquinius!'

He was so unused to hearing his own name that for a moment the haruspex did not react.

'*Tesserarius!*' cried the same voice.

Tarquinius stiffened and his eyes quickly focused on a familiar figure shoving his way through the onlookers.

The unshaven man was about thirty-five, of average height, with hair close cut in the military style. A drink-stained tunic failed to conceal the wiry muscle of his arms and legs, while a belt with a short dagger proved the newcomer was a soldier. The Etruscan spun on his heel, but already his left arm had been taken in a firm grip.

'Forgotten all your old comrades?' sneered the man.

Feigning surprise, Tarquinius turned back. 'Legionary Marcus Gallo,' he said calmly, cursing his decision to remain inconspicuous. It meant that his own knife was out of reach in his pack. 'Finally been thrown out of the army for drunkenness?'

Gallo's lip curled. 'I'm on official leave. Deserter scum,' he hissed. 'Remember what they do to men like you? I'm sure the centurion would be delighted to demonstrate.' He glanced around blearily, clearly looking for his drinking companions.

They were nowhere to be seen – yet. But with so many people in the vicinity, attention had immediately been drawn by the accusation. Tarquinius' pulse quickened. He took a deep breath, asking for the gods' forgiveness. The Etruscan had little choice. Gallo's grip was like a vice on his arm. If he did nothing, he would be hanging on a cross by sunset, an example to all.

'You drunken fool!' Tarquinius cried, smiling broadly. 'Have you forgotten how I saved your miserable life in Pontus?'

The swift, humorous response was exactly what was needed. Frowns were replaced by laughs and most of those nearby looked away. Gallo scowled and opened his mouth to rebut Tarquinius' comment.

Before he could say a word, the haruspex stepped in close and drew the other's dagger with his right hand. Pretending that they were embracing like old friends, Tarquinius shoved the blade between Gallo's ribs, straight into his heart. The legionary's eyes bulged with surprise and his mouth gaped like a fish out of water. Tarquinius kissed him on the cheek as Gallo's grip fell away, allowing him to hold the mortally injured man upright with his left arm. In the close-packed throng, no one saw what was happening.

'I'm sorry,' he whispered, but his words fell on deaf ears.

Gallo's features went slack and a dribble of spit ran from his lips.

The haruspex twisted the dagger to make sure.

There was a burst of laughter from the crowd as an overripe plum flew through the air to hit Crassus' bodyguard in the face. It was followed by a hail of fruit. Intent on revenge, the bruised street urchin had returned with plenty of reinforcements. Wearing little more than rags, the gang of filthy children screamed with glee as they hurled their stolen plums at the guard. He cursed and swept his blade at them, but they easily dodged his half-blinded attempts. Men smiled and pointed, shouting encouragement at both sides. Nobody was paying attention to the two soldiers any longer.

It was the perfect opportunity for Tarquinius. Gently he lowered Gallo to the ground, turning him face down so that the red stain on his chest wasn't visible. Then he plunged into the crowd, taking a direct line towards the nearest street off the Forum. Within two dozen paces, he would no longer be discernible to those on the temple steps. Even if the fools noticed, they wouldn't be able to catch him.

But the chance encounter with Gallo had been a close escape. It must not happen again. Tarquinius stepped into an alleyway and took off his bloody cloak, wrapping it around the axe. He would have to be even more cautious and from now on, the distinctive weapon would stay in his lodgings. No one must suspect who he was and why he was in Rome.

The smell of cooking pork from a nearby stall reached Tarquinius' nostrils and his stomach rumbled in response. Reaching into his purse, the haruspex walked calmly towards the tantalising odour. A smile played across his lips.

Parthia. Olenus had been right yet again.

Chapter IX: Lentulus

Ludus Magnus gladiator school, 56 BC

Romulus did not feel safe climbing into his cot with Lentulus only a few paces away, but he had nowhere else to go. The *ludus* was full of tough men, none of whom had offered him shelter after the fight. Not even Cotta.

He cursed.

Memor was probably hoping the argument would be settled that night with a quiet knife between the ribs for one of them. It was not how Romulus wished to finish the quarrel, but the Goth could not be trusted. Unsure what to do, he lingered in the starlit yard long after other fighters had returned to their cells. The spot where Flavus had died was still obvious, marked by several dark stains on the sand. Romulus shuddered. It had been so easy to stab the *murmillo*, but the enormity of the killing was beginning to sink in.

He was truly a gladiator now.

'First time?'

Romulus turned with a start to see Brennus peering round his door.

'Yes.' He paused before the words came in a rush. 'I gave Flavus a chance. Told him to release Astoria, but he didn't think I was serious.'

'The prick deserved to die. Unlike many you'll meet. You do have to kill them though, or you'll end up dead.'

Romulus eyed the largest bloodstain, imagining lying injured on the sand. Flavus' life had bled away in a few agonising moments. Regret surged through his veins. The *murmillo* had not done anything to him directly. Then he remembered Flavus' offer to the other gladiators.

'They wanted to rape Astoria,' he muttered.

The Gaul frowned. 'Is that why you stabbed him?'

'Partly.' Guilt mixed with anger in the young man's face. I should have told Brennus before all this, he thought.

Brennus looked confused so he explained about Lentulus' boasts.

The big fighter was visibly pleased. 'No one else tried to help, did they?'

Romulus shook his head. 'I wish it had been Gemellus, though.'

'Who?'

'The merchant who sold me. Bastard also sold my sister to a whorehouse. Gods alone know what he's done to Mother.'

Brennus' eyes darkened with old memories. 'Life can be bloody hard.' He stuck out a massive paw. 'I'm glad you finished Flavus off.'

. Romulus took the grip. 'There's just Lentulus to deal with now.'

'Nothing to worry about,' Brennus said conspiratorially. 'Romulus, isn't it?'

'Yes.'

'Good name.'

'Does killing get any easier?' Romulus spoke with a little awe.

'In some ways.' Brennus laughed hollowly. 'I try not to worry about it any more. Fight. Kill fast. Get it over with.'

Romulus found himself liking the Gaul, but he detected real sadness in his voice. Despite his fearsome reputation, Brennus seemed to be an honourable man.

'Need somewhere to sleep?'

He nodded.

'I wouldn't want to close my eyes with that little bastard near me either.' Brennus indicated that Romulus should enter his cell. 'Sleep on the floor in here. It's far from comfortable, but nobody will slit your throat.'

Romulus studied the darkened yard uneasily. He wasn't sure what to do.

'It's the least I can do.' Brennus beckoned. 'You helped save my woman.'

Romulus had no real option apart from returning to his own bed. He shrugged and walked curiously into Brennus' quarters. The floor was clear of bodies; the *murmillones* had been dragged off to the mortuary like so much meat. Astoria was busy with a bucket of water and a cloth, but there was still the occasional splash of blood.

The room was plain, holding little furniture. A decent-sized bed sat at one end, a couple of wool rugs scattered nearby. Bread and meat lay unfinished on a battered wooden table. Two racks at the foot of the cot held more weapons than he thought one man could own. Shields and spears were stacked untidily against the walls and other pieces of equipment filled any remaining spaces. It was the living space of a champion gladiator.

As he entered, Astoria beamed at him. 'Thank you again, Romulus.'

'It was nothing.' Romulus bobbed his head, embarrassed.

'It was more than that. The man had a knife at my throat.'

Romulus grinned, remembering the magnificent sight of Astoria's naked body as much as Flavus' blade.

'It was well done.' Brennus waved a bandaged hand at the thickest carpet. 'Take a seat. We can fix up something more permanent later. I don't think you'll be rushing back to a cell with any other fighters for a while.'

Astoria handed him a piece of bread and a thick slice of beef. Brennus moved to a whetstone in one corner, sharpening a longsword with practised strokes.

Romulus watched. Few other gladiators in the *ludus* used a similar one. 'Why do you use that?'

'It's the blade of my own people.' Brennus proudly raised the long piece of iron. 'And there's no better weapon in the world!' He pointed it at Romulus. 'More reach than those little knives you Romans use. Of course it needs strength to wield properly.'

Romulus stared at the floor, flushing. He was not yet big enough to fight with the sword.

'You haven't fought for real yet, have you?'

'No.'

'I've seen you practising at the *palus*. Not bad.'

Romulus swelled with pride that Brennus had noticed him.

The Gaul's voice hardened. 'But Lentulus will slice you up if you're not careful.'

'So what must I do?' He was all ears.

'I've seen him fight before. That Goth's cocky,' warned Brennus. 'He'll rush you. Try and get in a killer blow with brute strength. You'll have to hold the bastard off long enough to injure him.' He squinted along the blade's edge, looking for imperfections. 'Then Lentulus will give you space. Time to think.'

Romulus chewed thoughtfully on the meat and bread. Cotta was a good teacher, but some in the *ludus* said that he taught old, outdated techniques. While Brennus' size and strength were huge factors in his fighting ability, the Gaul was also expert with weapons. He might learn something that would save his life the next day.

'Keep that pig sticker in your belt. Come in useful if things get up close and nasty.' Brennus mimed a stabbing action. 'You knew to hit Flavus where it hurt.'

'Cotta showed me that.'

'A good man, that Libyan. Remember what he taught you. It's all about not forgetting the basics.'

'The basics?'

'Shield up. Thrust forward. Step back.' Brennus grinned. 'I still remember that every time I fight.'

'But I've seen you turn and slash at an opponent before.'

'Only when I know how he moves.' Brennus tapped his head. 'And thinks. Takes a while to get the measure of an enemy. Until you do, play it safe.'

'I will, Brennus.'

Romulus listened for a long time as the Gaul expounded on fighting technique and showed him new moves. Watching him wield a sword was awe-inspiring.

'In the arena, you're supposed to fight according to the gladiator code.' He stared hard at Romulus. 'That's what Cotta says, right?'

The young fighter nodded.

'Fine if you're talking about an ordinary points contest. But when it's to the death . . .' Brennus paused. 'Do whatever it takes.'

'What do you mean?'

'Kick sand in his face.' The Gaul scuffed a heavy sandal along the floor. 'Headbutt him with the edge of your helmet.'

Romulus' mouth fell open.

'Kick him in the balls if you can.'

'That's not fair.'

Brennus looked at Romulus shrewdly. 'Do you think Lentulus will hang back if you fall on the sand?'

He shook his head.

'Fighting in the arena is not about what is fair or unfair,' said the Gaul regretfully. 'It is about one thing only. Survival. Your life – or his!'

Kill or be killed. It was a stark choice.

'It's time Romulus slept,' Astoria broke in. 'Otherwise he'll be too tired to fight that son of a whore.'

'Always take note of what your woman says.' He kissed Astoria's cheek.

'When do you ever listen to me?' she replied, stroking Brennus' arm.

Romulus was glad to lie back on the carpet, covered by a woollen blanket. The others soon retired to the bed alongside, the Gaul instantly starting to snore. In normal circumstances the noise would have kept Romulus awake for hours, but the nervous tension had drained away, leaving only exhaustion. He closed his eyes and let a dreamless sleep take hold.

In the morning, the gods would decide whether he or Lentulus would die.

Brennus woke Romulus well before dawn. It was still dark outside but Astoria was coaxing the fire in a small brazier.

'It's important to stretch the muscles before a fight.' Brennus led him in a series of exercises for some time before he was satisfied.

Astoria watched them loosen up. When they had finished, she gestured to bowls of steaming porridge. 'Sit down and eat.'

'Thank you, but I'm not hungry.'

'Eat. Even if it's only a few mouthfuls.'

'I'd be sick.'

'There's more than an hour till dawn and you'll be hungry by then.' Brennus sat down and launched into the huge portion that Astoria put in front of him. 'It's not good to fight on an empty stomach either.'

Romulus forced himself to eat the cooked oats. To his surprise, they tasted much better than the slop from the *ludus* kitchens.

'There's honey in it.' Astoria had seen his expression.

There was silence as they ate.

Wiping his mouth, the Gaul walked to the weapon racks and selected a short stabbing sword. 'Try this for size,' he said. 'A little small for me, but should do you well.'

Romulus took the *gladius*, admiring the simple wire design of the hilt and lethal edge on the straight blade. He held it loosely, gauging the balance. 'Feels good.'

'Take this too.' Brennus proffered a handsome round shield covered in dark red leather.

Romulus slipped his left arm into the grips and dropped into a crouch, peering over the iron rim, sword ready. 'These are far better quality than those Cotta lets me use.'

'I paid good money for them. Quality weaponry doesn't let you down.'

'Feels heavier than I expected.'

Brennus flashed a smile. 'Look at the bottom.'

Romulus lifted the shield. 'The metal's sharp as a blade!'

'You can slice a man's arm or leg with it. Or smash open his helmet. Like I did with Narcissus yesterday.'

The story of that fight had already been round the *ludus,* increasing the Gaul's stature even more. Many now said there wasn't a gladiator in Italy who could beat Brennus.

'The fool might still be alive if he hadn't tried to stab me at the end,' the big man said sadly.

'And if I hadn't killed Flavus, Astoria would have died.'

'There is no mercy in the *ludus*,' agreed Brennus. 'So always have a little surprise ready. And never presume the fight's over until you've cut a man's throat. Or Charon cracks his skull open.'

'I will kill Lentulus.' Romulus was surprised how steady his voice was.

Brennus clapped him on the shoulder. 'What about your *manica* and greaves? They'll still be in your cell.'

'No. I can move faster without them.'

Respect flared in Brennus' eyes. 'I knew a man like that once,' he said softly.

Beams of sunlight began to creep through the window, illuminating the floor.

'Let's head outside. Nearly time.'

'May the gods protect you, Romulus,' Astoria blurted.

The Gaul led the way, with Romulus one step behind. The yard was already full of gladiators and a collective sigh went up as the pair emerged into the cool morning air.

Brennus turned quickly. 'Ignore anything they say,' he whispered in Romulus' ear. 'Some will be trying to scare you, others baiting you to get a response. Stay focused. Think only of Lentulus and the fight.'

The combat would take place in the area reserved for training with real weapons. As they walked, Romulus fixed his gaze on Brennus' broad shoulders. Plenty of derogatory comments were hurled.

'Lentulus will gut you like a fish!'

'Time to fight a man fairly – instead of stabbing him in the back.'

'Murderous little bastard!'

A *murmillo* who had been friends with Flavus spat on the ground directly in front. His hand was ready on the hilt of a curved knife. It seemed the man might do more but Sextus stepped forward, axe raised.

'Leave him be. You'll soon see whether Lentulus can extract revenge for the killing.'

Cowed by the *scissores* and his double-headed weapon, the *murmillo* moved back.

It was hard not to feel scared under the baleful glares of so many adult men. Romulus forced himself to inhale slowly, taking the breaths deep into his chest. It was a technique that Juba had taught him. He let the air out gradually and the effect was immediate. Romulus reached the square feeling calmer, following Brennus as he shoved past gladiators pressed up against the ropes. Everyone was eager to witness the duel.

A few fighters muttered encouragement and Romulus' spirits rose. Lentulus was not popular.

His opponent was already in the opposite corner, loosening muscular shoulders. 'I'm going to cut you up. Son of a whore,' he snarled.

Romulus ignored the Goth and continued to breathe deeply. Brennus lifted the rope for him to duck under.

'Let's stop pissing about! The rest of us have important training to do.' Memor stalked into the centre of the freshly raked sand and glared at both young fighters. His archers were ranged close behind, arrows notched in their drawn bows. Sextus moved to stand near the *lanista*, his axe at the ready. Sunlight glinted off razor-sharp metal. Romulus wondered with a thrill of dread what purpose Memor might have in mind for the *scissores*.

'No helmets. I want this over quickly.'

'I've no need.' Romulus smiled at the Goth, who had crammed on as much protection as possible.

Reluctantly Lentulus obeyed, but his right arm was still covered with a *manica*. Bronze greaves were strapped to the Goth's lower legs and his *scutum* was larger than that usually carried by *secutores*. In contrast, Romulus bore only Brennus' shield for defence.

'Remember what I said,' the Gaul muttered. 'Hold him off for a while. Then do what you have to.'

Romulus had just enough time to nod before the *lanista* looked at both. 'Begin!' Memor quickly stepped away to safety.

Just as Brennus had predicted, Lentulus rushed forward. Romulus raised his shield, moving out to avoid being caught on the ropes. But the Goth didn't attack with his sword. Instead he rammed the big *scutum* straight into Romulus' chest. The impact knocked him back on to the hot sand. Air rushed from his lungs. Desperately he swung at the *secutor*'s legs, but the blade swept harmlessly off the greaves.

Lentulus stamped the *gladius* from Romulus' hand, crouching low. 'Stopped me fucking that Nubian bitch.' His eyes were merciless dark pits. 'So now I'm going to gut you.'

'You couldn't have got it up anyway.' Romulus felt for the hilt of his dagger and pulled it free. He would have only one chance.

His enemy drew back to thrust downwards and Romulus acted fast. He lifted the knife and stabbed it into the Goth's foot with all his might, pinning the leather sandal to the ground. Lentulus roared in agony, allowing him to get up safely. The shield was still on his arm, but Brennus' sword lay very close to the *secutor*.

Lentulus had fallen to one knee, still screaming in pain. Romulus paused, wondering what to do. Eventually the Goth dragged the blade free with a groan and hurled it outside the ropes. He stood with difficulty, the wound bleeding freely.

'You have no *gladius*. No dagger.' Lentulus raised his weapon, moving towards Romulus more cautiously. With each step, a trail of blood stained the sand.

Romulus eyed his sword, knowing he'd have to recover it as fast as possible. Otherwise there would be no chance of killing Lentulus.

For a short time, the pair circled each other, loud jeers egging them on. Memor glowered from the side, irritated. Whatever happened, he would lose a gladiator who had cost good money. Brennus watched intently, his jaw clenched.

The Goth was now wary of attacking. Romulus was waiting for a chance to retrieve the *gladius*, but every time he edged towards it, Lentulus stepped in the way.

'Finish it!' Memor was losing patience. 'Or I'll send in Sextus.'

The little *scissores* grinned, lifting his axe.

Lentulus' face hardened and he advanced purposefully. The Spaniard would attack the weaker fighter in the ring. He had to kill fast.

Unsure what to do next, Romulus risked a quick glance at Brennus. The Gaul mimed a movement of his shield arm and he remembered. The young man let Lentulus come closer, bracing himself for the barrage of blows.

'I'll break both arms and both legs,' Lentulus panted, 'before I slice open your belly.'

'How's the foot? Looks painful.'

The Goth hammered his sword towards Romulus' head. The parry was difficult, his arm shaking under the force of the blow. But Brennus' shield held firm. He shuffled back a step, instinctively making Lentulus use the injured foot. The *secutor* cursed and stepped after him, taking a wild sideways slash. Again Romulus held it off, the impact almost numbing his arm.

Abruptly Lentulus changed tactics, stabbing straight at his chest. Romulus had just enough time to deflect the thrust. The wily Goth followed through with a huge shove, knocking him to the ground for the second time. Desperate to finish the fight, Lentulus swung his blade in the air.

Romulus did the only thing he could. He thumped a fist down on the Goth's wounded foot. It wasn't a very hard blow, but it didn't have to be. Lentulus screamed in agony, unable to deliver the *coup de grâce*. Romulus rolled away and stood up, panting.

Tears ran down Lentulus' face as he swayed in front of Romulus. Time was of the essence. He seized the opportunity and ran straight at the Goth, shield raised as if shoulder-charging.

Lentulus braced himself.

At the last moment, and using all his momentum, Romulus swept the sharpened edge down in a scything blow. It took off all five toes on Lentulus' right foot.

The Goth shrieked in agony. Blood spurted on to the sand.

Romulus ran to pick up his *gladius* while Lentulus slumped to one knee, gripping his foot in a futile effort to stop the bleeding. He seemed dazed, staring fixedly at the neat stumps in front of him. The spectators, who had remained silent for some time, began to chant.

'Rom-ulus! Rom-ulus!'

He touched the point of his sword to Lentulus' chin. 'Why did you get involved with those *murmillones*?' he said. Although Romulus didn't like the Goth, it seemed brutal the quarrel should end like this. But Memor had decreed one of them should die, and it was not going to be him.

Lentulus let go of his foot. Fresh blood poured from the gaping wounds. If the surgeon didn't attend to him shortly, the Goth would collapse from shock. 'I cannot stand.' His voice was taut with pain. 'And I'll never be able to fight again.'

'Finish him!' Romulus heard Sextus yell. The cry was taken up by all.

Except Brennus, whose face was proud but sad. Romulus is like Brac, he thought. A natural. And he doesn't want to kill an unarmed man. Brac wouldn't have either. The Gaul closed his eyes.

The *lanista* would allow only one outcome.

Noise filled the enclosed yard, recreating the arena's claustrophobic atmosphere.

Romulus saw Memor nod.

It was time.

Heart pounding, adrenalin coursing through every vein, the young man moved closer. Against the odds, he had won a gladiator battle. Romulus did not want to execute Lentulus, but Brennus' advice echoed in his mind. *Kill or be killed.*

Still he held back, oblivious to the fighters' roars.

As if in a dream, he saw the Goth lunge clumsily at him with a short blade that he'd concealed under the leather *manica*. Romulus was too close to stop the thrust, but managed to deflect it from the groin artery with Brennus' shield.

The action saved his life.

Romulus staggered back, vision blurring, the dagger buried deep in his right thigh. Teeth bared, the *secutor* tried to knock him over, get close enough to finish the job.

It would only be a few moments before shock took over. Slamming the *scutum* downwards, he caught Lentulus' wrist with the sharp edge, drawing blood. The Goth cursed and pulled away.

Romulus waited no longer. He leaned forward and stabbed in one side of Lentulus' throat and out the other, severing the major vessels. Bright red blood gushed over his arm in a warm spray.

Lentulus gurgled as the back of his mouth and throat filled with fluid. Clawing uselessly at the iron, he stared into Romulus' eyes. The Goth seemed more startled than anything. He tried to speak, but could not.

Anguish filled the boy.

'Rom-ulus! Rom-ulus!' He was aware that the chanting had grown louder. Kill or be killed, he thought grimly, twisting the *gladius* as he pulled it free. Lentulus fell face forwards into the sand with a soft thump and did not move again.

The pain was suddenly overwhelming. Romulus staggered, staring at the hilt protruding from his leg. Dropping both sword and shield, he reached towards it.

'Stop!' Brennus was at his side.

Romulus toppled back into the Gaul's arms. Gently the huge gladiator lowered him to the ground.

'I let my concentration slip,' he said, voice tailing away as shock began to set in.

'Get the surgeon!'

The words came as if through a fog. Head swimming, Romulus could no longer focus. Pain surged upwards from his thigh, radiating in agonising waves. It took superhuman effort not to scream. 'Am I going to die?'

'You'll be fine.' Brennus took his hand in a grip of iron. 'Well done, lad.'

Romulus' last memory was hearing his friend roaring again for the Greek surgeon.

When Romulus' eyes opened, the first thing he saw was Astoria's voluptuous figure, bent over the brazier. A rich, aromatic smell reached his nostrils and he stirred restlessly under his blankets.

'I'm hungry.' He managed to sit up on one elbow. 'What time is it?'

'Past noon . . . the following day. You've slept for

almost a day and a half,' Astoria replied. 'How do you feel?'

'I'm alive.' Romulus moved a hand down to his right thigh, finding a heavy bandage. He grimaced. 'My leg aches.'

'It was a deep wound. The Greek gave you mandrake to kill the pain.' Astoria came over to the makeshift bed, a bowl in her hands. 'Time for some more.'

He sipped a little, instantly screwing up his face. 'Tastes awful.'

'It will hurt less afterwards. Drink.'

Romulus drained the bitter liquid obediently. He was too weak to do anything else.

'Now lie back and rest.'

'How bad was it?'

'Lentulus missed the artery by a whisker. The gods were looking after you.' She smiled. 'Dionysus cauterised the bleeding and stitched the muscle.'

'When can I start training again?'

Astoria rolled her eyes.

Romulus tried to speak again, but his tongue already felt thick and useless. The mandrake was starting to take effect.

'In about ten days.' Brennus came stamping into the room, torso covered in sweat. 'Light exercise only!'

Romulus felt his eyelids grow heavy. A few moments later he was asleep.

'Can't leave him in the hospital, that's certain,' said Brennus. 'Figulus or one of the others would cut his throat.'

'Good. You need a friend to watch your back.'

The Gaul sighed. It had been years since he trusted anyone. But Romulus reminded him strongly of Brac. Grief welled up at the memory, which was still raw.

'You haven't got eyes in the back of your head,' she scolded. 'Neither can you kill ten men at once.'

Brennus' face darkened as he pictured the village in flames. Brac's death. Capture. *I killed more than ten legionaries that day. Wasn't enough.* 'Be good to have some-one reliable around,' he mused.

'You said before that Romulus is a good fighter.'

Brennus rubbed his chin thoughtfully. 'And it wasn't universally popular to kill the *murmillones*.'

'Figulus and Gallus have been talking to many of the others.' The Nubian looked uneasy. 'They're probably planning to kill you, my love.'

'Nobody in the *ludus* would dare touch me.' Trying to conceal his worries, Brennus patted her arm.

'No one alone – but working together?' she replied. 'You could be in danger!'

'I know,' the Gaul finally admitted. 'And Romulus seems like a good man. Let's take care of him till he can walk, anyway.'

Relieved, Astoria kissed him.

'Then we'll see if Romulus wants to fight with Brennus.'

The pair were as good as their word. Over the next ten days, Romulus was looked after better than he had been since he was a small child. By the third day, the young fighter was able to swing both legs out of the bed and stand unaided. Two days after that, he was taking short walks outside using a crutch that Brennus had fashioned. The Gaul stood by, encouraging him.

'Don't seem too happy.' Romulus indicated Figulus and Gallus, gazing sourly from the other side of the yard.

Brennus spat in their direction. 'So?'

Romulus did not answer straight away.

The two fighters were fearsome enemies. Figulus was an ox of a man, a veteran Thracian with more than ten single combat victories under his broad leather belt. Gallus was short and stocky with a bad limp, but his skill with net and trident was well known in the *ludus*.

'Have to kill both of them too,' Romulus said with as much bravado as he could muster.

'Fighting talk, my young friend! But you aren't a match for either.' Brennus grinned. 'Yet. Two or three years, maybe.'

'That's a long time if they want to kill me now.'

'It is.' The Gaul paused, thinking. 'So I propose we become allies. Look out for each other.'

'Me look after you?' Romulus' mouth opened and closed. 'But I'm only fourteen.'

'With two kills to your name. And one was in fair combat.' Brennus' eyes were bright. 'You show great promise, lad. You'll be an excellent fighter one day.'

'I'd be honoured.'

'Among my people, such friendship is not made lightly.' A flicker of emotion passed across the Gaul's face. 'Needs be, we fight to the death for each other. Makes us brothers until one or both is dead.' His jaw clenched. 'Are you prepared for that?'

Romulus paused, aware the gesture meant a lot to

Brennus. It did to him as well. Previously Juba had been the only man he had trusted. Taking a deep breath, he nodded.

Brennus held out a muscled arm and the two clasped firmly. Romulus met the other's steady gaze and the Gaul smiled in satisfaction.

'The first lesson will be how to kill quickly. Lentulus nearly got you at the end.'

'I was so excited at winning.'

'Exactly. You didn't stay focused.' Brennus punched him on the chest. 'Always keep in mind what an enemy might do next.'

Romulus glanced over at Figulus and Gallus. Judging by their scowls, they were none too pleased at the clear gesture of friendship.

'We need to watch those two constantly for a start.'

'We'll have to kill them sooner or later,' said Brennus, shrugging. 'Forget the pricks for now. A good soak is what we need!'

The Gaul saw Romulus' questioning look. 'Memor gave in, let me start using the baths again,' he said with a grin. 'Hot water will loosen up that leg. Then the *unctor* can get to work softening the scar tissue.'

Romulus limped across the yard, his arm on Brennus' shoulder. For the first time since losing Juba and his family, the young fighter felt he had a friend he could trust.

With his life.

It was a good feeling.

Chapter X: Brutus

The Lupanar Brothel, Rome, 56 BC

Fabiola trembled as she heard Jovina's summons. Two days had passed in the Lupanar without a customer agreeing to the high price for her virginity. Several old men had lustfully eyed the stunning girl and one had even begun pawing at her breasts until Jovina intervened. To Fabiola's relief, none had been able to come up with the money required.

It was late on the third morning and Fabiola had been waiting nervously in a small anteroom beside reception. She had been there throughout the previous two days too. The walls were covered in pornography. At least half the sexual positions looked physically impossible. Pompeia had taught her the basic techniques of most, but Fabiola's stomach constricted at the thought of actually performing them. She had only ever kissed one of the merchant's other young slaves before.

Stay focused. Become the best. Remember Gemellus. Remember Romulus.

More than half a dozen brightly adorned prostitutes sat on benches lining the room. A powerful smell of perfume filled the air. The women giggled and laughed among themselves – it was just another working day – while Fabiola sat alone in one corner. Although no one had been unkind, Fabiola missed Pompeia keenly. The redhead was engaged with a well-paying regular, a middle-aged senator who liked dressing up in her under-clothes.

When clients arrived and let the madam know their preferences, Jovina called out the names of suitable girls. The chosen prostitutes would walk out to be appraised and then selected by whoever took their fancy.

Fabiola was the only virgin in the Lupanar. Her wait had been a lonely one. But she had managed to remain calm, planning her future.

'Get out here!'

'Be quick,' hissed the Nubian. 'Don't put off the customer or Jovina will get angry.'

'Coming!'

'Good luck! Remember what Pompeia has taught you.'

'Tease him until he begs for more,' said another woman.

Grateful for the encouragement, Fabiola stood, smoothing down her dress. It was the fine white linen one with a purple hem that Pompeia had selected a few days before. Fabiola walked to the open door, out on to the colourful mosaic floor. Her heart was pounding. She forced herself to breathe in calmly as Pompeia had shown her, letting the air out very slowly.

'You look amazing!' Jovina stood waiting, head cocked

to one side. There was an encouraging smile on her painted, wrinkled face.

Beside the madam was a man in his twenties with a tanned, pleasant appearance. Fabiola had never seen him before. He was of average build, clean shaven, with short brown hair. A simple, well-cut tunic was belted at the waist, which marked him as a soldier. The jewelled hilt of a dagger protruded from the narrow belt.

'Closer!'

Fabiola obeyed, gazing demurely at her soft white leather sandals. *At least he's not old.*

'Look at me.' The man's voice was calm and deep.

Fabiola lifted her head and stared into his clear blue eyes.

'Quite a beauty, aren't you?'

She glanced back at the floor, unable to hold his gaze.

'Fifteen thousand *sestertii*?'

'A trifle for the virginity of such a girl.' Jovina's voice was wheedling.

'That's a lot of money.'

'When have my girls ever not been worth the price, Decimus Brutus?'

He smiled. 'Turn around.'

Fabiola revolved slowly under the intense scrutiny. From the corner of her eye, she could see Benignus standing unobtrusively in shadows by the front door. It lent a feeling of safety to the inspection.

'Very well.'

Fabiola felt her stomach turn over. The moment had come.

'If you'll just sign a chit first, Master.' Jovina scuttled

to her desk, deftly unrolling a parchment. She added a few quick details, in the manner of someone who had done the task before.

'You know I am good for it.'

'Of course, Master. But when Fabiola has finished, you will be in no state to even sign your name,' said Jovina with a cackle.

Brutus laughed, taking the stylus. He scrutinised the parchment before adding his signature to the bottom.

The madam immediately picked up a lighted candle, tipping it so a circle of wax pooled beside Brutus' mark.

'Your seal as well?'

'By all the gods! You'd make a great quartermaster in the legions, Jovina. Never happy until the paperwork's complete!' Brutus pressed his signet ring into the hot liquid.

Jovina grinned from ear to ear. 'You know where to go, child.'

Unable to speak, Fabiola nodded. Taking Brutus by the hand, she led him down the dimly lit corridor. The soldier followed but did not speak, which added to her nerves. Torches flickered from brackets in the walls, lighting up alcoves filled with statues of the gods and the small offerings to them. As they passed the figure of Aphrodite, she offered up a prayer.

Fabiola led Brutus into the first bedroom and closed the door. The chamber was tastefully furnished with a wide bed and marble washbasin. Heavy fabric drapes hung from the walls. Small oil burners provided light and a thick smell of incense hung in the air. Tables laden with food and wine stood on one side.

'You never know. He might want to eat between courses,' Pompeia had joked as she explained what to do earlier. Her instructions had been quite clear. 'Make sure the customer's satisfied. That's all that matters!'

Fabiola turned to face Brutus, who was studying her closely.

'Would the master like me to wash him?'

'I've just been to the baths.'

Slightly relieved, Fabiola moved closer, running long fingertips down one muscled arm. Brutus was in good physical shape, making the task much easier. 'Let me undress you,' she said with a confidence that surprised her. She beckoned seductively and led him over to the bed. Rose petals covered the silk embroidered spread. Docilosa was proud of her job.

Fabiola tugged at the belt buckle, undoing it with difficulty. She found herself hurrying but remembered Pompeia's advice to take everything slowly. Soon the belt had opened and she'd lowered it to the floor. Fabiola lifted Brutus' tunic off, pushing him gently backwards until he fell on to the covers.

The noble lay back, enjoying the experience.

She knelt to unlace the leather straps of his *caligae*. The sandals' soles were covered with metal studs – standard military issue, a sure sign Brutus was no reluctant soldier. 'You serve in the army, Master?'

'I am a senior staff officer of Caesar's,' Brutus said proudly. 'Home on leave from Gaul. Two months at least, thank the gods.' He rubbed a hand across his eyes. 'It's good to be back in civilisation.'

Fabiola clambered on to the bed and began caressing

him from head to toe. He sighed with pleasure as tight muscles were kneaded and squeezed into relaxation.

'Close your eyes. Rest, Master.'

Brutus seemed glad to obey.

She changed tempo, moving both hands very slowly in gentle circles around his chest and belly and the tops of his thighs. According to Pompeia, this was one of the most important parts of the seduction. After a while, Fabiola strayed across his *licium*, the linen loincloth all nobles wore. Gradually this was included with every circuit as she continued to rub the officer all over. The ministrations succeeded and soon Brutus' excitement was evident through the *licium*. He moaned as Fabiola began to pay more attention to his stiff member. The young prostitute did not rush. Soon Brutus was writhing around, small sounds escaping his lips.

At last she freed his erection from the underclothes. As she rubbed up and down with one hand, Fabiola looked carefully at Brutus. His eyes were still closed, but by his response, things were going according to plan. Concentrating on Pompeia's advice rather than what she was actually doing, Fabiola took him into her mouth.

She made the experience last a long time, just as the redhead had drummed into her. At the end, unable to take any more teasing, he held Fabiola's head in place, thrusting in a frenzy of lust.

Afterwards Brutus slept deeply and she lay watching his chest rise and fall. The officer was quite handsome in his own way. Fabiola was glad that he wasn't a horrible, fat man like Gemellus. A first sexual experience with someone like that would have been too like the suffering endured by her mother. She was also pleased that Brutus was an associate of Julius Caesar's. Like everyone in Rome, Fabiola knew of the ambitious former consul who had decamped to Gaul, determined to win new territory for the Republic and a name for himself. Ensuring that Brutus became a regular customer might be a good start.

When Brutus awoke, he found Fabiola observing him. 'That was very good, girl.'

'My pleasure, Master.' She stroked his chest.

'I've been without a woman for more than six months.' Brutus guided her hand downwards. 'Why don't you take off that dress?'

Feeling slightly self-conscious, she obeyed. Surprisingly, when Brutus had pushed Fabiola down on the bed, he began to caress her body all over, and when he entered her a few moments later, it was with a gentleness she had not expected. The pain was sharp but bearable and disappeared quickly. Fabiola found it quite easy to hold on to Brutus as he thrust in and out of her eagerly. She moaned loudly, gripping his buttocks with both feet to hold him in.

At the climax, Brutus cried out with ecstasy. Then he relaxed into Fabiola's arms, smiling contentedly.

She lay back, holding the taker of her virginity. The sheet below was stained with blood, vivid evidence. Fabiola had known what life in the Lupanar would entail, but had not truly understood what sex would be like.

It was good the waiting was over.

Later she took Brutus to the baths. Acting as a body slave, Fabiola washed and massaged him, rubbing perfumed oil into his skin. When she had clad the officer in a clean tunic, they went back to the bedroom.

There she aroused Brutus so much he was able to take her again.

'By all the gods, you are insatiable!'

'You make me like this, Master.'

'What a liar!' said Brutus as he got dressed. He touched her cheek. 'Good to hear it, all the same. And a pleasure to see such beauty. Gaulish whores are either hags or crawling with disease.'

'Stay in Rome, Master.' She batted her eyelashes. 'Come and see me every day.'

'Love to,' he replied with a smile. 'But I could not afford it! I will visit when possible. You satisfy me. What was your name again?'

'Fabiola, Master.'

Brutus removed an *aureus* from his purse and placed it on the table. 'This is for you. Don't let the old crone near it.'

Fabiola picked up the gold coin, clutching it tightly. 'I'll be waiting,' she said.

Brutus caressed one of her small breasts before leaving her alone.

A few moments later, Jovina was beaming at the bloody sheet. Her rapid arrival made Fabiola wonder if she had been waiting outside the door. The madam rubbed wrinkled hands with excitement.

'Brutus had the look of a satisfied man! Even said the price had been worth it. Well done, child.'

'You and Pompeia taught me what to do.'

'Teaching's not the same as practising something,'

Jovina replied. 'Keep every customer as satisfied as Brutus and you'll go far.'

Fabiola nodded. There had been no choice about being sold, but she was determined to make the most of her new situation. Becoming the Lupanar's best prostitute would grant the power and influence Fabiola craved. She was not going to be just another whore in a brothel. There were so many things she needed to achieve, and having men in her thrall was the only method available. Freeing her mother from Gemellus was the most urgent task, although well nigh impossible. The merchant would never sell Velvinna if he knew that her daughter was involved. But it might be possible to get a customer to buy another slave, as a favour for Fabiola. And there was Romulus, sold to the death-trap of the arena. A way must be found to rescue her twin before he was injured.

Or killed.

She was brought back to reality by Jovina's voice.

'No point daydreaming about Brutus. One pleased customer doesn't run the Lupanar,' she said briskly. 'Have a wash and be at reception in half an hour, wearing a clean dress.'

Fabiola forced a smile. Clutching the tip, she pulled on her robe and left the madam calling for Docilosa to clean the bed.

The confident manner she had shown with Brutus was needed later. Fabiola's next customer that evening was a perspiring senator with a red face who did not balk at the price for two hours. Her ability to please was proved again as she teased the elderly man to a frenzied orgasm. No further clients appeared and Fabiola finally had the chance to gossip with Pompeia.

'One of Caesar's officers? The gods must be in a good mood. My first one was old and dirty.' The redhead made a face. 'Had to wash him for an age just to get rid of the smell!'

'Brutus gave me an *aureus*.'

Pompeia nodded in approval. 'Will he visit you again?'

'I think so.' A trace of doubt entered Fabiola's mind. 'He's returning to Gaul in two months.'

'Plenty of time!'

'Sure?'

'Make his next visit even more amazing,' Pompeia whispered, 'and he'll be infatuated. Men are like that. Brutus will come running each time he's back in Rome.'

Fabiola listened carefully.

'They say Caesar's star is in the ascendancy. So Brutus' will be also.' Pompeia gave her a sly wink. 'Just remember that.'

'I will,' Fabiola replied, delighted that her hunch had been correct. She resolved to do her utmost to win the young noble's affections if he did return as promised.

Gemellus returned from the Lupanar in the foulest of moods. He had been outwitted by Jovina, wounding his pride. To add to the embarrassment, the merchant had been publicly ejected from the brothel for the second time. The idea of visiting the madam with a gift of jewellery and sweet-talking his way to a percentage of Fabiola's earnings had only seemed fair. After all, the brat was making her a fortune.

The plan had gone spectacularly wrong.

Jovina had accepted the present readily enough, even serving some acceptable wine. They had talked politely about the state of the Republic and the economy before Gemellus had brought up the topic of Fabiola.

Jovina's face had gone cagey the moment the girl was mentioned. A queasy feeling had flared in Gemellus' stomach, unsettling him, and he'd started badly by immediately demanding a cut of Fabiola's earnings. The sharp skills at bargaining which had been honed over two decades seemed to have evaporated overnight. Jovina had refused point blank and Gemellus had lost his temper. Beleaguered now on all sides by creditors, he had not forgiven the madam for duping him out of thousands of *sestertii*.

Gemellus hadn't even had the satisfaction of wrapping his fingers around Jovina's scrawny neck. Before he could lay a hand on her, the enormous doorman had again materialised as if from thin air. Benignus had plucked the merchant bodily from his seat, and carried him to the door. The colossus had held Gemellus' arms while Vettius drove two powerful punches into his solar plexus, winding him completely. A moment later, he flew out the door to land face first in a fresh pile of mule dung.

'Next time I'll tell them to cut your balls off!' Jovina had yelled.

Scandal did not take long to move through the city. It would only be a matter of time before Gemellus' enemies heard the news of his public disgrace. The merchant's poor standing with certain influential members of Rome's financial underworld would be damaged even further. The frantic attempts he'd made to keep his lenders happy were all going wrong. Gemellus had managed to placate Crassus, his biggest creditor, but a number of the Greeks in the Forum had threatened to break his legs if he couldn't meet their extortionate weekly payments.

If he wanted to fund the *bestiarius'* expedition, Gemellus would have to sell the house in the Aventine or even his beloved villa in Pompeii. This realisation darkened an already black mood. He stalked along stone-floored corridors to the room Romulus and Fabiola had shared with their mother. Throwing open the flimsy wooden door, Gemellus found Velvinna on an old cot, sobbing into the pillow.

'Useless bitch. Why aren't you in the kitchen?'

'I am sick, Master.'

Gemellus was filled with disgust. Velvinna's once lustrous hair was matted with dirt. The features he had lusted after were etched with lines of worry and sadness. Although she was only thirty, Velvinna looked ten years older.

'Get up and do some work!'

'My children, Master. Where are my beautiful twins?'

Gemellus pursed his lips. He was sick of Velvinna repeatedly asking the same question. It did not matter how many times she was raped. The merchant stalked over and grabbed her by the hair.

There was not even the satisfaction of a whimper in response.

'With any luck the boy is dead,' he spat. 'I didn't do so well with the little vixen though. She's making her new owner a fortune in the whorehouse.'

Velvinna stared at him dully. It was almost too much to take in. 'Kill me, Master. I have nothing left to live for.'

Gemellus laughed. The idea that she would have a reason to exist was most amusing. She belonged to him – he could sell or even kill her without any legal implications. Whether Velvinna cared about Romulus and Fabiola or not was entirely irrelevant.

'I'll get a few hundred *sestertii* for you instead. The salt mines will take anything that breathes,' he said. 'I should have done it the same day as the brats. Now get back to work.'

'And if I won't?'

The merchant was so shocked that he released his grip on her.

'Everything I held sacred has been taken. My virginity. My body. Even my children. There is nothing left.' For the first time in her life, Velvinna's face showed no fear. 'Sell me to the mines.'

'Be ready at dawn!' Gemellus blustered, unsure what to say to a slave who requested certain death. Severe discipline and an incredibly harsh environment meant even the strongest of men survived only a few years digging salt. Someone as weak as Velvinna would last weeks at most.

He turned to go.

'One day there will be a knock on your door,' she said ominously.

The merchant raised a hand, but something held him back.

'Romulus will stand outside. And may the gods help

221

you when he discovers my fate.'

Memories of Fabiola's defiance and the hatred in Romulus' eyes as he stood in the yard of the Ludus Magnus were vivid in Gemellus' mind. Maybe she was telling the truth. Terror consumed him and he slapped Velvinna so hard that her head snapped back into the wall. She collapsed to the floor, the shallow movements of her ragged dress the only sign of life.

He eyed Velvinna's bare legs and a flicker of desire stirred in his loins. The merchant considered taking her there and then, but the prophecy had shaken him. He closed the door softly and walked away. In the morning, he would take Velvinna to the slave market. She and the twins would be forgotten for ever.

One day there will be a knock on your door.

Chapter XI: Prophecy

Rome, winter 56 BC

Tarquinius was squatting by the steps of the great temple to Jupiter on the Capitoline Hill. He felt at home here, in a place where echoes of the Rasenna were still strong. It was also an excellent spot to watch goings-on; to assess the general mood in the city. The Etruscan had been coming every day for weeks. Built by his people hundreds of years before, this shrine was the most important place of worship in Rome. It was busy from sunrise to sunset. And with political uncertainty now ever-present, business was better than ever. The bitter cold could not keep worshippers away and the complex was crowded and noisy.

Self-important priests stalked past, young acolytes scurrying at their heels; a group of *lictores* sat around, eyeballing anyone foolish enough to look in their direction. Small boys who had climbed the hill without parental permission gaped at the panoramic view of the sprawling metropolis. Ordinary citizens passed inside the doors to mutter their requests, ask for help with their problems, and curse their enemies. Stallholders roared and yelled, trying to sell food, wine and statues of Jupiter, as well as hens and lambs to slaughter as offerings. There were snake charmers, whores, jugglers, pickpockets; even a senator canvassing for votes amongst the wealthier devotees. All were here because of people's constant desire to know the future.

Tarquinius smiled. Judging from the number of tricksters and con-men about, there was little chance of an accurate prediction. It was the same outside every temple in the world. In all his years of travelling, Tarquinius judged that he had encountered perhaps two other genuine soothsayers and augurs. Only one had been from Italy. His lip curled with contempt. The Romans might have smashed every Etruscan city and stolen their entire culture, but they had never completely mastered the art of haruspicy. Unlike Olenus, whose ability to see the future had been uncanny.

Eventually Rome draws you back. A desire for revenge.

But Caelius, the reason for him to linger in the capital, was proving surprisingly hard to find. With the last of his fortune long spent and his *latifundium* seized by moneylenders, the redheaded noble had taken up a new career, hoping to renew his fortune. Tarquinius had been revolted to discover that Caelius was now a slave trader, following in the wake of destruction left by Caesar's army in Gaul. Despite many attempts at divination, the Etruscan had been unable to discover Caelius' exact whereabouts. So he had waited patiently in Rome for nearly twelve months, biding his time. If he kept searching, animal entrails or the weather would eventually reveal something. And they had. The man who had killed Olenus would return to visit the city within the year.

Content with that thought, Tarquinius watched the nearby soothsayers plying their trade. Wearing blunt-peaked leather hats, the men were surrounded by clusters of eager supplicants with open purses. The Etruscan leaned back on his heels, studying the people's faces. There was the barren wife, desperate to conceive a son; alongside stood the worried mother whose legionary son had not written home in an age. The gambler with moneylenders on his trail; the rich plebeian eager to climb the social ladder; the spurned lover eager for revenge. He smiled. They were all transparent to him.

The young lamb he had bought earlier bleated, taking his attention away from the crowds. Barely a month old, it was restrained by a thin cord round its neck that was attached to his wrist. The haruspex looked up, taking in the wind and the clouds above. It was time to see what lay in store for him. For Rome. Tarquinius picked up a short dark blade that he used for sacrifices and close-quarters fighting. Muttering a prayer of thanks for its life, he pulled the lamb closer, holding up its head with his left hand. A swift slash of the razor-sharp metal and the young animal collapsed, blood pouring from the gaping cut in its throat. It kicked a few times and lay still. Flipping the body over on to its back, Tarquinius sliced open the abdomen and let the loops of small intestine slither on to the cold stone. After a moment, seeing nothing of interest, he moved on, expertly cutting free the liver. Balancing it in his left hand, the haruspex raised his eyes to the sky once more. He had performed divinations countless times, yet the ritual still excited him. Not once in fourteen years had the results been the same.

Tarquinius had never tried to divine what had scared Olenus so much in the reading at the cave.

He could guess what it was.

A flock of starlings flew by and his eyes narrowed as he judged their number. *Conflict was coming. In the spring.* Tarquinius waited, counting his heartbeat to estimate the speed of the air moving overhead. The mounds of dark clouds being swept along were huge, promising rain. *It would come across a great river. From Germania. And Caesar would retaliate, to demonstrate that those who struck at Rome never go unpunished.* Far to the north, the youngest member of the triumvirate was burning a bright trail. Determined to outshine both Crassus and Pompey, Julius Caesar had crushed the tribes of Gaul and Belgica, making sure that regular news of his outstanding victories reached the Roman public. It seemed he was not about to rest on his laurels.

When he was satisfied there was nothing more to observe in the air above, Tarquinius bent his head to study the liver closely. What he saw did not surprise him. It was all routine, just as it had been for many months. He could see no signs of Caelius in Rome; the surly landlord who owned his one-room garret above an inn would soon die of food poisoning; thanks to a poor harvest, the price of his favourite wine would climb sharply.

The gall bladder was less full than normal and Tarquinius pushed at it with a finger to check that there was nothing there. He frowned, bending closer. There *was* something . . . a trader of some kind . . .

'How much for a reading?'

Startled, Tarquinius looked up to find a short, fat man in a grease-spotted but expensive tunic standing over him. He was middle-aged, with a red face; an unpleasant expression twisted his lips in a permanent sneer. A plump hen hung by its feet from one hand, a small amphora from the other. As with any citizen who valued his safety in Rome, a knife hung from a long strap over the newcomer's shoulder.

Tarquinius did not answer immediately. Since the episode with Gallo, he had been careful to avoid human contact when at all possible. Had it been a mistake to kill the lamb? He took a quick look at the liver again. No. He relaxed. 'Why not ask one of the others?' Tarquinius indicated the nearby soothsayers.

There was a grunt of derision. 'All bloody liars, aren't they?'

'And I am not?'

'Been watching you. You're making no attempt to do business.' He pointed at the lamb's liver. 'And you're divining for yourself. Means you know what's what.'

'I don't normally sacrifice for strangers.'

'Work for some patrician bastard, eh?' growled the fat man. He spat a curse and turned to go.

'Wait,' said Tarquinius suddenly. 'Are you a merchant?'

'I might be. What's it to you?'

'Five *aurei*.' There was no compromise in Tarquinius' voice.

The merchant blinked. It was an extortionate amount

of money for an augur to charge, but without arguing, he rummaged in a battered purse. 'Here,' he said, passing over five gold coins. 'This better be good.'

The Etruscan palmed the *aurei* and gently took the hen from him. It looked up with a beady eye, unaware that it was about to die. 'What age are you?' he asked.

'Fifty-one.'

'And you reside . . .?'

'On the Aventine.'

Tarquinius pursed his lips. 'Name?'

'Gemellus. Porcius Gemellus.'

'Why are you here?'

The fat man snorted. 'What do you think? To know what the bloody future holds for me.'

Tarquinius moved to one side, away from the dead lamb. Holding the hen down on the cobbles, he intoned a prayer of thanks to Jupiter. Then he slit its throat and watched as the blood drained out, filling little cracks between the stones. It flowed west: the direction where malevolent spirits lived. It was not a good start.

'Well?'

Without answering, the haruspex gutted the bird and laid out its entrails on the ground before them.

Gemellus watched silently, his jaw clenched.

Tarquinius' lips moved as he pondered the meaning of what he was seeing. It was no surprise that the merchant wanted guidance. He took a deep breath and began. 'I see problems in business. Financial worries.'

Gemellus was unsurprised. 'Go on.'

'But you need not worry about your biggest creditor.'

'Crassus?' said the merchant sharply. 'Why not?'

'He will take up a new post in the east,' said Tarquinius. 'And never return.'

'You're sure?'

Tarquinius nodded.

'The prick is going to die in Syria!' cried Gemellus, barely able to conceal his glee. Several people nearby looked over at the mention of the word. It was common knowledge how much Crassus wanted the governorship of Rome's easternmost province.

'That was not what I said,' said the Etruscan mildly. 'I said that Crassus would never come back to Rome.' *It is Parthia where the arrogant fool will meet his fate. And I will witness it.*

'That's good enough.' Gemellus smiled broadly. 'Anything else?'

Tarquinius probed the hen's liver, searching. 'Moving water. Waves? A storm at sea,' he pronounced.

The merchant looked confused.

'Ships full of beasts . . .'

Gemellus froze.

There was a delay as the haruspex peered at the channels of blood between the paving stones. 'Sink as they cross the sea.'

'Not a second time!' whispered Gemellus, his voice trembling. 'It cannot be true.'

Tarquinius shrugged. 'Only telling you what I see.'

'I sold my villa for nothing? For nothing?' Gemellus sagged down, as if the weight of the world had landed on his shoulders. 'There'll be no money to pay those fucking Greeks either.' He took a great swig from his amphora and turned to go.

'Wait.'

The merchant stopped, but did not look back. 'There's more?'

'One day there will be a knock on your door,' said Tarquinius.

Gemellus spun round, his face pinched with terror. 'Who stands outside?'

Tarquinius concentrated for some moments. 'It is unclear. A man. A soldier, perhaps?'

Pulling his dagger, Gemellus shuffled closer. 'If you're lying,' he hissed, 'I'll cut your throat and feed you to the dogs.'

Tarquinius lifted his cloak and laid a hand on an unsheathed *gladius*, lying there for just such an occasion. It was easy to conceal and attracted less attention than the battleaxe. The sight of polished metal was enough. Gemellus spat on the ground and walked away, making the sign against evil.

Tarquinius glanced down at the dead hen, but could not see who it was that had scared the merchant so much. He shrugged again.

Not everything could be predicted accurately.

Chapter XII: Friendship

Nine months pass . . .
The Ludus Magnus, Rome, late summer 55 BC

Romulus spun to one side, hacking at Brennus as he swept past. The Gaul parried the blow with some difficulty. 'Getting better by the day,' he grinned. 'You're strong too.'

Romulus lowered his sword, panting. 'I still can't beat you.'

The big warrior smiled. 'That might take a while yet.'

'I'm a better fighter now,' Romulus said defensively.

'You are. And still not even fifteen.'

'I want to be the best.'

'It takes many years to become a top gladiator,' replied the Gaul. 'You've come a long way, Romulus, and survived a serious injury too. Be patient. You have courage and strength and just need more experience.'

Romulus gazed round the baking hot yard. It was the centre of his world – unlike the Gaul, he was rarely allowed into the city – and claustrophobia was inevitable.

There had to be more to life than weapons training, lifting weights and occasional fights in the arena. Even Cotta's lessons in tactics frustrated Romulus now, tantalising him with information about countries and places that he never saw. And outside the *ludus'* walls, great things were happening. News had reached Rome of Julius Caesar's recent punitive expedition against the barbarians in Germania. Now the rumours were that he had invaded the mystical isle of Britannia. Every fresh piece of information about Caesar's campaigns sparked Romulus' imagination.

He wanted to be free – to throw off the chains of slavery. To discover the world.

Brennus' voice brought him back down to earth. 'Most men haven't got your balls and it shows in the way they fight. But you're like me. Nothing matters except victory!' He thumped his bare chest and laughed. 'Gauls fight with their hearts!'

Romulus scuffed the ground with a dusty foot, glad of the encouragement. For eighteen months, Brennus had been a good friend and teacher to him, building up his confidence and skill with weapons. Although he would never forget Juba, the Gaul had slowly come to take his place in Romulus' heart.

'Use your mind too. Anticipate what your enemy will do. Remember Lentulus.'

He flushed, determined never to be caught out again.

Brennus clouted him affectionately. 'Keep it up and you might end up with a *rudis* one day, like him.' He pointed at Cotta, who was breaking in his latest recruit.

The mention of freedom instantly brought back

thoughts of his mother and Fabiola. 'I still want to show that bastard Gemellus a few tricks.'

'Forget him.' Brennus' voice changed, the laughter gone. 'Unless the gods are truly generous, you will never get the chance for revenge on those who hurt you.'

Romulus could sense real pain in the Gaul. His friend never spoke about the past, but Romulus suspected Brennus had suffered terribly before becoming a gladiator. 'Did something like that happen to you?' he ventured.

Brennus was silent. The candid question stirred memories, unsettling him. *Brac. Liath. My son.* He swept an uncharacteristically wild overhand blow at Romulus.

'Never let anger control you.' Romulus skipped neatly to one side and lunged forward, forcing the Gaul to retreat several steps.

Brennus laughed. 'Trying to teach me? Eat this!' With a sweep of his sandal, he kicked a cloud of sand at Romulus' face.

The young fighter saw the move coming just a fraction too late. Yellow grains filled his vision. He dodged to the left, knowing the big man had bested him.

'Dead meat,' said Brennus, pricking Romulus' throat with the tip of the blade.

He rubbed angrily at reddened eyes, coughing to clear his throat.

'Watch your enemy's expression.' Brennus poked a thick finger at him. 'He'll always give away something. A frown, a sideways glance. Use it to predict what he does.'

'I knew you were going to do that.'

'Doesn't matter this time,' replied the Gaul with a grin. 'It wasn't real.' He sheathed his sword, brushing the sand off. 'That's enough for now. Let's go and wash.'

For once Romulus was glad to relax. He followed Brennus across the yard, determined not to be caught out again. Several men greeted them as they walked by. The duel with Lentulus had earned Romulus considerable respect, which helped preserve the uneasy truce that had been simmering since the fight over Astoria. The majority had not cared about the *murmillones*' deaths, but would not take sides either.

Undeterred, Figulus and Gallus had been busy stirring up discontent among a select few and eventually it had become noticeable. At first it was only small things – vinegar poured in Brennus' wine, a foot stuck out to trip Romulus, straying hands touching Astoria's breasts. Tension had been rising steadily and Romulus had taken to wearing a dagger again at all times. The security he had felt for months after becoming Brennus' friend was being eroded day by day. He fought his worries by pushing himself to new levels of fitness and sparring with the Gaul at every opportunity.

Brennus scratched his thick blond curls. 'I'm surprised Figulus and his cronies haven't made a move before now.'

'They're scared of you.'

'And you!'

Romulus was delighted.

Quickly checking that the *lanista* was not about, Brennus roared at the small group in the far corner of the yard. 'Anyone feel like taking us on today?'

There were plenty of stares, but nobody spoke.

'It won't be an open fight. There aren't enough of the bastards.'

'I know.' Brennus nudged him. 'Still, doesn't do any harm to give them a warning.'

The big man's attitude was heartening and Romulus pushed open the door of the baths with a smile.

All would be well.

A month later it became clear when the showdown would be. Early one morning, Memor ordered all gladiators to gather together in the yard. It was an odd demand.

The air was already warm even though it was not long after sunrise. Rome had been baking in late summer heat for some weeks. Like most, Romulus and Brennus got up before dawn to exercise while it was still cool. There had been time to complete a full set of weights training before the gathering. The men talked eagerly as they waited. No one knew what was going on.

When Memor appeared, he had a strange smile on his face.

'You're probably all wondering why I called you here.' He paused.

'What is it, Memor?' shouted a fighter near the back.

'Milo needs us to keep Clodius in line again!' cried another.

There was a roar of approval. During the previous spring, with bloodshed on the streets escalating, the tribune Milo had been accused by his rival Clodius of using violence. The action showed breathtaking gall and the trial in the Forum Romanum had been abandoned when a full-scale riot had broken out. Milo's men had quelled the trouble, but with great difficulty. More unrest had followed, providing many gladiators with regular periods outside the *ludus*.

There had been further need for their services when the consular elections had taken place only a few months before. As Pompey and Crassus blatantly acted together once more to secure the posts for themselves, public disturbances had soared. The travesty of democracy had not stopped there. Pompey was now the effective ruler of Hispania and Greece; Crassus had his governorship of Syria. Caesar had also done well, being granted consular powers over the provinces of Illyricum and Gaul. The triumvirate's shameless and open criminal behaviour had enraged the people and widespread mayhem had followed.

'No,' Memor snapped dismissively. 'Pompey Magnus has added an extra day of entertainment to his celebratory games.'

'Chariot races!'

'And you have a good tip for us!' added the wit in the crowd.

Everyone laughed.

Even Memor's lined face cracked into a smile. 'Better than that,' he replied. 'An opportunity to show that the Ludus Magnus is truly the best in Rome.' The *lanista* raised his voice. 'General Pompey wants a special contest! Two groups of fifty against each other.'

'We haven't got a hundred gladiators,' said a *murmillo*, looking confused.

'Fool!' snapped Memor. 'Fifty of you versus the same number from the Dacicus school.'

'What a fight!' Brennus bared his teeth expectantly.

'This is not a points contest,' he continued. 'Everyone will fight to the death until one side is victorious.'

There were gasps of shock at the most unusual announcement.

'But every man who survives unhurt will receive a bag of gold.' The *lanista* raised a fist. 'For the Ludus Magnus!'

Faces lit up at the prospect of such wealth, even though many would die in the combat. 'Lu-dus Magnus! Lu-dus Magnus!'

'Look at Figulus,' Romulus whispered. 'The bastards will make their move during it.'

'He does seem very pleased,' agreed Brennus. 'Be a good opportunity too. There'll be bodies everywhere.'

'A hundred gladiators fighting to kill?'

'Pompey must be feeling the need to impress. You know how it is.' Prominent politicians were always trying to outdo their rivals' efforts.

Romulus nodded. Everyone in Rome knew that the struggle for power was intensifying. But politics paled beside the prospect of such a large fight. Romulus felt both excited and anxious. Most of the spectacles he had taken part in had been for points only. He had slain two men in single combat, but this would be very different. 'Will I be picked?'

'Of course! Need you to watch my back.'

Romulus stared at Figulus, who was deep in conversation with Gallus and a small group of fighters. They must be planning something. Too many evil glances were being cast in their direction.

The following two days passed in a blur of activity as

every chosen gladiator prepared for the contest. Virtually all bar those who were injured had been picked. When it was Romulus' turn, Memor did not hesitate before waving him over to those who would take part. In the *lanista's* mind, the boy had already become a man. Swelling with pride, he joined Brennus.

The smithy rang with the sound of hammers as faulty armour and weapons were repaired. Ignoring the extreme heat, men ran circuits of the yard and lifted weights. Using real weapons instead of the normal wooden training pieces, others sparred ceaselessly with each other. The *lanista's* archers supervised from the balcony above, eyes peeled for any sign of trouble. Several fighters were injured when training sessions got overheated and Memor ordered leather covers placed on all blades until the combat.

In contrast to most, Brennus spent the day before the combat relaxing and being massaged by the *unctor*. The cool atmosphere behind the bathhouse walls provided welcome respite from the sun. Feeling unsafe on his own, Romulus joined him.

'You're fit enough. Lie down! Relax.' Brennus groaned with pleasure as his back was pummelled. He indicated the clay jug and beaker on the tiles by the bench. 'Drink some grape juice. It's very good.'

Romulus spun and twisted, lunging back and forth with his sword. 'You don't need to worry about this fight. I do.'

'I choose not to care.' The promise Brennus had made to himself over Narcissus' body was becoming ever harder to keep fresh in his mind. One-sided combats had begun to follow each other with a sickening regularity as the *lanista* sought greater wealth and fame. Brennus had killed many men since the Greek.

'Got to keep practising,' replied Romulus stubbornly.

'It's breaking the rules,' the *unctor* broke in, voice trembling. 'Training inside with a weapon.'

'Leave it, Receptus. Not safe out there for him any more.'

The atmosphere in the *ludus* had deteriorated even more since Memor's announcement, the leers and threats from Figulus and his friends now constant. Everyone knew that the blood shed the next day would not just be by the blades of the enemy. Even the friendly masseur had noticed. Receptus resumed rubbing Brennus' back. It was not for him to tell the champion fighter and his protégé what to do.

'What will happen tomorrow?'

'Figulus and his mates will stick close,' Brennus said confidently. 'They'll try and catch us off guard. Probably strike right in the thick of it.'

'We just wait for an attack? Dacicus fighters in front and those bastards behind? That's madness.'

'Peace, Romulus.' Brennus rolled his eyes at the *unctor*. 'Have a rub-down.'

Romulus reluctantly placed his sword on the floor before climbing on to the other bench. It felt wonderful as Receptus worked the tension from tight muscles, yet he could not unwind completely; he always kept an eye on the door. Brennus in contrast was dozing contentedly, confident in the knowledge that nobody had the courage to attack him face to face.

The afternoon passed without incident and the sun set, allowing temperatures to drop to a more comfortable level. Memor toured the cells, muttering encouraging words. The contest was about more than just victory. It was about reputation.

That evening Astoria prepared a special meal. They sat at the table in Brennus' cell, drinking red wine and enjoying bread, fresh fish and vegetables bought in the market. A warm breeze blew through the open door, bringing with it the smell of food cooking and the murmur of conversation. Everyone in the *ludus* was relaxing, perhaps for the last time.

'Go easy on the wine,' Astoria ordered Romulus. 'One cup is enough. No point having a sore head to fight with.'

'Try a dormouse.' Brennus proffered a large plate. 'A real delicacy.'

He shook his head.

'All the more for me!' The Gaul opened his mouth wide, swallowing one whole. 'Don't normally go for Roman food, but these I like.'

Romulus ate sparingly; his stomach was knotted with tension. All his previous fights had been one on one and the idea of being in the arena with so many gladiators filled him with anxiety. It was no help knowing that Figulus and Gallus would be out for their blood. He tried to block images of losing the combat and being killed by one of them.

'Worrying doesn't help,' said Brennus kindly.

Astoria murmured encouragement.

Romulus pushed a piece of bread around his plate.

'And it's no good being wound up like a spring. Go to bed. Get as much sleep as possible.' Brennus clapped him on the shoulder. 'Tomorrow will be an important day for us both.'

Chapter XIII: Intrigue

The Lupanar, Rome, late summer 55 BC

It was early afternoon and the quietest time of the day. The prostitutes' routine began mid-morning, when they rose to bathe and beautify themselves. Any men who arrived early were entertained first before taking their ease in the baths. There the influential of the Republic could relax, share wine and converse. After this most Roman activity they could get on with daily business.

Fabiola shifted position quietly, keeping an ear against a small hole in the wall. Sitting in the warm pool of the *tepidarium*, none of the clients had any idea they were being overheard. Ever since Pompeia had shown her the tiny space a year before, Fabiola had used every spare moment listening to those who frequented the brothel. There was usually little of interest to be heard. Chariot racing, gladiator fights, the weather, which women were best at what – the subjects rarely changed. But sometimes the pretty girl would catch snippets of information about politics or business that educated her about the outside world.

'Crassus is raising an army, you say?'

'Tired of Pompey and Caesar taking all the glory, Gabinius.'

Fabiola smiled at the sound of Mancinus' voice. She had slept with him on several occasions and had been amused at how fast he became attached. But the old merchant could rarely afford her. Recently he had been forced to satisfy his appetites with cheaper prostitutes but Fabiola did not worry about this. Mancinus was not nearly influential enough. She had only three purposes in life – to free herself and her family, to gain revenge on Gemellus and to destroy the man who had violated her mother. This could be done by maximising her influence over as many rich and powerful men as possible. And so Fabiola pragmatically reserved her charms for more important customers, of which there were several.

Brutus was the most keen. The young noble had become utterly devoted over the previous year. Fabiola had put enormous effort into bringing him completely in her thrall. When he was in Rome, not a week went by without a visit to the Lupanar. Brutus had taken Fabiola on trips to the theatre and his villa on the coast. She hoped it was only a matter of time before he bought her, possibly even granting the coveted manumission. Fabiola burned to be free.

'Caesar's recent victories have been popular. Is Crassus jealous?' Scorn was obvious in the third man's voice.

Gabinius snorted. 'Not forgotten the Senate's refusal of a full triumph after the defeat of Spartacus, has he?'

'Might be fifteen years ago, but it still rankles,' said Mancinus indignantly. 'Crassus crushed the greatest threat to Rome in over a hundred years and all they granted him was some shitty parade on foot!'

'Yet Pompey Magnus managed to procure the full thing,' commented the last speaker. 'Just for cleaning up the crumbs.'

There was a loud chuckle from Gabinius. 'And Crassus has done nothing but complain since. He needs to get off his backside and win another war if he wants to keep up with Pompey and Caesar.'

'What do you mean?' spluttered the merchant.

'Come on! Pompey's list of victories is second to none,' said Gabinius. 'Marian rebels in Africa. The Cilician pirates. Then the armies of Mithridates in Pontus. That's why the Senate granted him ten days of public thanksgiving. Crassus might be the richest noble in Rome, but he hasn't had a military success in a generation.'

Mancinus did not reply.

'Pompey's victories in Asia Minor were thanks to Lucullus anyway,' interjected the third man. 'And the public forget quickly. That's why Caesar is more popular now.'

Fabiola finally recognised the voice of Memor, a new customer of Pompeia's. It amused her how those who visited the brothel could always be placed in one of three camps. The parcelling off of the best political positions in Rome by the triumvirate had divided the public more than ever. Men had come to blows in the pool more than once during heated arguments. Pompey, one of the current consuls, was still enormously popular thanks to his military credentials and generous treatment of the veterans of his legions. Crassus, his co-consul, had been spending vast sums in his efforts to compete with the others. An extremely adept politician, he was not as good at drumming up public support as the others. Caesar, on the other hand, was drawing attention to himself by his recent conquests, all achieved in the name of Rome.

'Julius Caesar is the one to watch,' Memor boasted again. 'Gaul has been vanquished, providing huge resources. That got him fifteen days of public holidays. And the general hasn't earned his money by burning citizens' houses to the ground!'

Gabinius laughed.

'Nobody has ever proved those fires were started deliberately,' blustered Mancinus.

'Anyone who did would end up with a cut throat!' sniped Memor. Crassus' close links with the unsavoury Clodius were well known.

There was another titter from Gabinius.

Fabiola pressed her ear closer to the hole, anxious to learn about Memor. Pompeia had recently revealed that he was *lanista* of the Ludus Magnus. The increase in gladiator fights' popularity had apparently made him very wealthy. While Fabiola had no idea which school her brother had been dragged off to, getting to know Memor would be a start.

For more than a year she had heard nothing about Romulus. Clients only ever talked about the most famous fighters. Fabiola's heart ached at the thought of the only family she had left. An anonymous attempt by Brutus to buy her mother the previous year had been unsuccessful. Gemellus had been true to his word and sold Velvinna at the slave market. Brutus' men had visited many salt mines and bribed every overseer they encountered, but all their efforts had proved fruitless. Frail, heartbroken, Velvinna had disappeared, never to return.

It made finding Romulus all the more urgent.

'Caesar's a good general, I'll give you that,' said Gabinius. Water slapped off tiles as he shifted position.

'He has conquered all of Gaul and Belgica. Britannia is next,' the *lanista* responded. 'While Pompey and Crassus do nothing but talk!'

'Not for much longer,' Mancinus added quickly.

Pompey's supporter was also in full flow. 'Caesar's only chasing victories to pay off his huge debts. Millions of *sestertii*, I heard.'

'He owes much of it to Crassus,' gloated Mancinus. 'Besides, Caesar is never in Rome. The people need to see nobles to follow them.'

Gabinius was not going to give in easily. 'Have you not seen Pompey's new building complex on the Campus Martius? Heard him speak at his ceremonies there?'

Memor snorted. Built to impress the people, Pompey's massive construction had taken years, and cost a fortune, to complete. Typically, the fickle public had not received their gift particularly well. 'That place is so over the top,' he said confidently. 'It's more about showmanship. When he was aedile and in charge of public entertainment, Caesar sponsored a contest with three hundred pairs of gladiators in silver armour. The crowd went wild!' said Memor triumphantly. 'And I should know – it's my line of work.'

There was a sudden silence and Memor sensed he

would get no further. An invisible social barrier had appeared in the room.

The *lanista* was unperturbed. 'Time for some games of my own. That redheaded whore is incredible with her mouth.'

The others laughed and Fabiola heard the *lanista* climbing out of the bath and bidding farewell. She decided to arrange an introduction to him, even though he was fast becoming one of Pompeia's regulars. With some persuasion, her friend might step aside so she could win Memor's affections.

It might be a way of finding Romulus.

If he was still alive.

Fabiola's heart raced with excitement at the thought of seeing her brother again. The conversation seemed to have petered out, but she had learned it was always worth waiting a little longer.

'More wine!'

As the bathing attendant hurried off, Fabiola was sure there was whispering below. Frustratingly, she was unable to hear what was being said. Snippets like 'bastard *lanista*' and 'that big Gaul' wafted up, but she could not make any sense of them. The muttering went on until the slave returned.

'That's me done. I have work to do.'

'Have another cup.'

'Some of us have to work for a living! All right for you equestrians with huge *latifundia*,' Mancinus slurred. 'Merchandise doesn't sell itself.'

'But we hardly see each other these days,' wheedled Gabinius. 'One more.'

The merchant settled back into the warm water, keen for more alcohol in spite of his words. The pair made some small talk, then Fabiola heard Gabinius probing for information. Mancinus seemed to know plenty about Crassus, and the noble was keen to find out. It was so obvious to Fabiola what was going on.

In the previous year, she had learned how to gain information from customers without them even realising; it was amazing what men would reveal while being driven half mad with desire. Pompeia's advice had proved very useful, and by now had made Fabiola one of the most sought after women in the Lupanar.

'Is Crassus going to move his army now he's the governor of Syria?'

'Common knowledge!' Mancinus slurped some wine and lowered his voice. 'While Pompey sits around, he has plans to conquer Jerusalem.'

'Really?'

'And he won't stop there.'

Fabiola heard Gabinius lean over and pour Mancinus another drink.

'Seleucia,' announced the merchant. 'He has his sights set on Seleucia.'

Gabinius sucked in a breath. 'Invade Parthia?'

'Its wealth is said to be incalculable. All that trade from the east.'

'But Rome is at peace with the Parthians.'

'So were thousands of the Gauls whom Caesar massacred! Didn't stop him, did it?'

'Are you sure?'

'They say the Parthian temples are dripping with gold. I'd join Crassus myself if I were younger!'

'He's at least ten years older than you,' needled Gabinius.

'Not all are born to be soldiers,' Mancinus huffed.

'I meant no insult.' Gabinius realised he had gone too far. 'Have another drop.'

Fabiola snorted silently at the crude approach. The offended merchant refused to be drawn again, and she left them to it. She padded down the corridor, robe flowing in the warm summer air that filled the house.

She found Benignus sitting in the kitchen while Germanilla fussed around, loading his plate with bread and vegetables.

The doorman's craggy face split into a grin when he saw her.

Fabiola pulled over a stool and sat down beside the huge slave. 'Busy last night?'

'Not too bad. Only threw out one customer.' Benignus took a mouthful of bread and chewed noisily. 'Silly bastard knocked the new girl Senovara about.'

'Is she all right?' Fabiola asked worriedly.

'Bruised and shaken, but she'll be fine.'

'Who did it?'

'Nobody important. One of Caesar's soldiers wanting to blow all his spoils from Gaul.' Benignus grinned. 'He's nursing a broken arm instead.'

'Glad to hear it.' Fabiola winked at Germanilla.

The serving girl reached under the wooden counter. Producing a large hunk of beef, she placed it on Benignus' plate.

'Is that for me?' The doorman's eyes were eager. 'From you?'

Fabiola nodded from under her long fringe. 'Keep looking after us girls.'

He beamed, revealing rotting stumps. 'Me and Vettius would kill anyone who tried to harm you.' Benignus patted the bone handle of his dagger.

Fabiola watched contentedly as the shaven-headed hulk wolfed down the meat. She had never needed to call for help as Senovara had the previous night. But if the occasion ever arose, she knew both would come running. Winning the doormen over had been simple. Instead of having sex with them, Fabiola had won their hearts by ensuring they always had good food, and that the best surgeon tended to any injuries they incurred.

The beautiful young woman slept only with men who could provide her with money, useful information or the possibility of freedom.

Chapter XIV: Rufus Caelius

Rome, late summer 55 BC

Tarquinius adjusted his position, moving his cloak slightly so it provided more of a cushion. He was sitting with his back against the wall of a house on a narrow street not far from the Forum. On either side of him were beggars and food vendors competing for business from the passers-by. The nearest, a middle-aged army veteran with one arm, was still wearing his russet-brown military tunic. He threw Tarquinius a curious glance, slightly resentful at having to move two paces closer to his neighbour. But the ten *sestertii* in his fist was more than he would earn in a day. Who cared why the blond stranger wanted to sit here? And he had promised the same every morning. The cripple caught Tarquinius returning his stare and quickly dropped his gaze, keen not to upset his new sponsor.

Diagonally opposite their position was a large, arched doorway with an erect stone penis protruding on either side from the wall above. The huge members were painted in bright colours to attract attention and it seemed to work. Many of the men walking past paused to stare through the open door. But few actually entered: instead they stood outside weighing their purses and looking wistful.

The one-armed ex-legionary saw Tarquinius watching. 'Only the rich go in there.' He hawked and spat. 'That's one of the most expensive whorehouses in Rome. The Lupanar girls can drain a man dry!'

'Tried it?'

He laughed sourly. 'In my dreams.'

'Who owns it?'

'An old crone called Jovina,' came the reply. 'She's worth a bloody fortune. And sharp as a blade. Always keeps her customers happy.'

The Etruscan nodded encouragingly.

Happy to have someone to listen, the veteran filled Tarquinius in on the comings and goings from the Lupanar. Soon the haruspex knew which prominent senators and nobles visited regularly, the methods used by the doormen to expel troublesome customers and the fact that few prostitutes ever set a foot outside the premises.

'What's your name, soldier?' said Tarquinius at last.

The cripple was both surprised and pleased. Few ever bothered to ask. 'Secundus,' he replied. 'Gaius Secundus. And yours?'

'Marcus Peregrinus.' Although Secundus seemed honest, there was no question of Tarquinius revealing his identity after the episode with Gallo months before.

'You served in the legions too?'

Tarquinius smiled. 'Not me! I am a trader.'

The explanation was good enough and a cordial silence fell.

Time passed and the two men began to share stories about their experiences – Secundus with the legions in Pontus and Greece, Tarquinius expanding on his visits to Asia Minor, North Africa and Spain. The noise of oxen pulling carts and the conversation of passers-by washed over them. Like all thoroughfares in Rome, the street was constantly busy.

At length, the Etruscan indicated Secundus' right arm. The shiny red stump had been evenly cut across and tiny scars were still visible from where stitches had been placed. It was a sign that it had been amputated by an expert. 'Where did you lose that?'

Secundus frowned, rubbing at the remnant of his arm. 'Tigranocerta.'

'You served with Lucullus?'

There was a proud nod.

'One of the Republic's greatest victories, I've heard.' The haruspex could still picture the scene on the ground before Tigranes' showpiece capital. Deep, intimidating pounding from the Armenian drums. Hot sun beating down on the massed ranks of legionaries. The sheer size of the king's host. It had been immense. *Bucinae* blaring orders from Lucullus' position, officers roaring at their men when they had heard and understood. The gradual advance towards the enemy, swords tight in their fists, sweat running down from under their helmets. Javelin volleys scything into the Armenian infantry. The panic spreading amongst them like wind through the trees. Tarquinius smiled. 'Even though you were vastly outnumbered,' he said.

'Twenty to one! Didn't take long for us to turn the savages, though,' exclaimed Secundus. 'It was nearly over when suddenly a big Armenian broke through the shield wall near me. Cut down four men in the blink of an eye.' The veteran's face creased with anger. 'I managed to hamstring the bastard, but he turned and hacked at me as he went down. Smashed the bone so badly the surgeon had to take the damn thing off.'

Tarquinius clicked his tongue in sympathy. 'That was the end of military service for you.'

'A man can't wield a *gladius* with his left hand.' Secundus sighed. 'And I only had three years left to serve.'

'The gods work in strange ways.'

'If they take any notice of us at all!'

'They do,' answered Tarquinius seriously.

'Seem to have forgotten me, then.' Secundus cynically indicated his clothes, which were little more than rags, and a worn blanket, his only shelter against the weather. 'Even though I still sacrifice to Mars.' The veteran glanced around to make sure no one could hear. 'And Mithras,' he whispered.

Tarquinius' ears pricked up. He was fascinated by the ancient and secretive warrior religion which had been brought to Rome by legionaries returning from the east. Only the initiated were allowed into the Mithraic underground temples, but he had heard many rumours when serving in Asia Minor. Bulls being sacrificed. The study of particular constellations. Ordeals of heat, pain and hunger as rites of passage between stages for devotees.

Central tenets of truth, honour and courage. With luck, he might find out more from Secundus. 'Do not lose faith in the gods,' he said, scanning the narrow band of sky visible between the buildings around them. 'They have not forgotten you.'

Secundus grunted. 'Believe that when I see it.'

Tarquinius' dark eyes glinted.

Opposite them, the brothel's door opened and a huge slave with a shaven head peered out. When satisfied there was nothing going on, he opened the portal fully and emerged, clutching a metal-studded club. A final check up and down the street was enough.

'Fabiola! It's safe.'

Secundus nudged Tarquinius violently. 'If this is who I think it is,' he said with a leer, 'we're in for a real treat.'

The haruspex watched keenly as a black-haired young woman joined the doorman, a cloth-wrapped bundle in her hands. She was extremely beautiful and even a plain robe could not conceal her slim figure and large breasts.

'Hurry up,' the hulk urged. 'You know what Jovina's like.'

'Stop fussing, Benignus,' the prostitute said with a smile. 'You're not an old woman. Yet.'

Benignus grinned adoringly at her and the pair moved off in the direction of the Forum. Heads turned and whistles of appreciation filled the air as men noticed the stunning girl.

Fabiola's gaze glided over them as she passed and Tarquinius caught a glimpse of piercing blue eyes. Quickly he glanced down at the lava paving slabs, anxious to remain inconspicuous. But one look had been enough for the haruspex to detect deep sadness in her. There had also been loss. And a burning desire for revenge.

'A beauty, eh? Like Venus herself,' breathed Secundus. 'What I'd give for an hour with her.'

'How often is she allowed out?'

'About once a month. Always carrying something, too.' Secundus rubbed his grey stubble. 'One of the doormen goes with her every time.'

'She's probably going to deposit money with the bankers in the Forum.'

'Won't be the takings,' said the veteran. 'Jovina hires half a dozen ex-soldiers the days they bring that out.' His eyes lit up. 'It comes out in a bloody great iron-clad chest and gets placed in a litter. One of her bruisers sits on top of it all the way to the bank.'

'Her savings then,' Tarquinius commented. 'She must be one of the more favoured prostitutes.'

'I'll go along with that,' said Secundus wistfully.

'Have you no wife?' asked the Etruscan.

Secundus shook his head. 'She died of the flux five years ago. No one else will have me now.' He waggled his stump bitterly.

'Come now!' cried Tarquinius, clapping him on the back. 'Some wine will help lift your mood.'

The veteran was easily persuaded and Tarquinius led him away, enthusing about the nearby tavern he had discovered only the day before. The pair left their spot and walked in the same direction as the prostitute and her companion. Tarquinius made sure that the hostelry they visited happened to be close to the moneylenders' pitches in the *basilicae* on the Forum.

Any information about the beautiful young girl might be useful.

Something told the haruspex that she was of importance.

Not just to his future, but to that of Rome.

Seeing Fabiola turned out to be the most interesting thing to happen that day. And that week. Tarquinius sat patiently in the same spot from dawn until dusk, talking with Secundus and barely moving unless it was to relieve himself in one of the tiny alleyways that led off the street. Always his gaze was fixed on the arched doorway opposite. Customers came and went; slaves were sent on errands to buy food. Occasionally Jovina sallied forth on some private business. Tarquinius watched the madam surreptitiously, taking in her beady eyes and the large amount of expensive jewellery that adorned her hands and arms. In the male-dominated Roman world, this was clearly a woman of considerable ability. A few questions in the local inns had confirmed this. Thanks to her range of customers and her dedication to satisfying their desires, Jovina was well respected. It seemed she also had influence in many circles. 'Half the Senate has visited the Lupanar!' laughed one innkeeper. 'The girls are incredible there. You should try it some time.' Making polite excuses, Tarquinius had left, his mind working overtime.

Despite its impressive range of clients, nothing had explained why his divinations kept revealing that the Lupanar was important. Every few days, Tarquinius sacrificed a hen at the temple of Jupiter on the Capitoline Hill. And each time the reading was the same: the brothel was crucial to his past. And his future. The Etruscan could see that Rufus Caelius, his former master, had something to do with it. Logically that meant that the redhead would turn up at the Lupanar sooner or later. What he could not interpret was why an expensive whorehouse should impact on his future once he had taken revenge on Caelius.

Unless it had something to do with Fabiola.

'Got any female customers?'

Running a finger across his thick lips, the money-lender eyed Tarquinius speculatively. 'Maybe,' he replied. Short, fat and arrogant, the Greek was obviously amused at the question. 'Anyone in particular?'

'A girl by the name of Fabiola,' the haruspex answered. 'Black-haired. Slim. Very pretty.'

There was another smirk and the Greek leaned back on his stool, glancing at his two bodyguards, a pair of heavily muscled ex-gladiators. 'Do we know anyone like that?'

'I'd remember one like her,' one answered, making an obscene gesture.

The second sniggered.

Tarquinius had been expecting this. 'A man might pay well for such information,' he said quietly.

The Greek's eyes narrowed and he gazed at the haruspex, trying to gauge his reasons for asking. And the depth of his purse.

Around them rose the clamour of business as another day went by for the inhabitants of the huge covered markets in the Forum. Few gave Tarquinius a second glance; just another citizen down on his luck and in need of a loan.

The Etruscan waited. Silence was a powerful weapon.

The moneylender made his play. 'A hundred *sestertii* might jog my memory.'

Tarquinius laughed and turned to go.

'Wait!' He had overestimated. 'Fifty.'

Twelve *denarii* dropped on to the low table between them. It was two *sestertii* less than he had demanded, but the Greek wasn't about to quibble.

The silver coins were swept from sight. 'She's a whore,' he sneered. 'Belongs to that old bitch who runs the Lupanar. Know it?'

Tarquinius nodded. 'What else?'

'Comes here once a month to deposit her tips. Brings along a brainless fool like this pair.' He jerked his head contemptuously at the men behind him.

The two fighters shuffled their feet angrily but did not dare speak. Work like theirs was well paid and hard to come by.

'Ever mention family?' asked the haruspex. 'Friends?'

The Greek's lip curled. 'She's a fucking slave. Who cares?'

Tarquinius leaned in close, his eyes boring into the other's. 'I do.'

The moneylender felt his palms grow sweaty.

'Well?'

The Greek swallowed hard. His men could easily get rid of this troublesome stranger. Break a few bones if he ordered them to. But for reasons he could not explain, it felt like a bad idea.

'She mentioned something once about saving to buy her brother's freedom,' the moneylender admitted grudgingly. 'He got sold to the Ludus Magnus.'

Tarquinius had heard of the largest gladiator school in Rome. He smiled. The link with the Lupanar was not a false trail after all.

Fabiola's brother was a gladiator.

He gave the three men a long, hard stare and was gone.

The Greek threw a muttered curse after the haruspex, and shoved the incident from his mind. He had no wish to remember the brief encounter. There had been a glimpse of Hades in the stranger's eyes.

Tarquinius strode away, his spirits soaring as he remembered Olenus' words. Everything was starting to make sense.

Two gladiators become your friends.

The gods continued to smile on Tarquinius.

A day later, dusk was falling and Secundus was preparing to go in search of some food. Most evenings he would spend his takings on a chunk of roast pork and a few cups of vinegary wine in one of the rough taverns which dotted the city's streets.

'Come with me,' he urged, tapping the only memento of his army career: a bronze *phalera* that always hung from his tunic. 'Still haven't told you the full story of how I won this.'

Tarquinius smiled. The warm breeze was telling him to stay put. 'Where are you going?' he asked.

'The fleapit on the corner one street over. You know the one.' Secundus scowled. 'As long as there aren't too many *collegia* thugs throwing their weight around. Otherwise it'll be the place beside the Forum Olitorium.'

'Keep a seat for me,' the Etruscan said. 'I won't be long.'

The one-armed veteran knew better than to ask why his friend wanted to linger outside the Lupanar. All his tactful enquiries had been met with complete silence. And since the blond trader was still paying him ten *sestertii* a day, Secundus had long since decided that prudence, rather than curiosity, was called for. He nodded, expertly rolling up his blanket with one hand. 'See you later.'

The ex-soldier was quickly gone into the falling light, a hand gripping the sheathed knife that was slung from a strap over his left shoulder. Already the streets were emptying of decent folk, to be replaced by the unsavoury types who favoured the hours of darkness.

Tarquinius was not scared of being on his own. And the local lowlife knew better than to tackle the slightly built stranger. When four of them had jumped him a week previously, there had been a flurry of blows so rapid that afterwards neither of the survivors could explain it. One thug had gone down instantly, blood bubbling from a gaping slash in his throat. While his companions gaped in dismay, the haruspex had opened another's chest with his *gladius*. Then a third had sustained a nasty wound to his left thigh, leaving only one man to escape unscathed. Tarquinius had not even suffered a scratch and now thieves gave him a wide berth when they met him on the street.

The Etruscan leaned back against the wall, pulling closer his *lacerna*, a lightweight open-sided cloak with a hood. He loosened his *gladius* in its scabbard, keeping it close to his right hand. His waiting was nearly over. Tarquinius could feel it.

It was not long before the flicker of torches could be made out through the gloom, followed closely by the noise of drunken voices. Preceded by large slaves armed with clubs and knives, five toga-clad nobles weaved unsteadily towards the Lupanar. It was a common sight. After a day spent in the stuffy atmosphere of the Senate, politicians liked to relax with some wine. And after that, a whore.

Tarquinius pulled up his hood. This was not just another group of senators – Olenus' murderer was amongst them. Old, unfulfilled rage bubbled up from deep inside but the haruspex breathed deeply, keeping himself calm. Now was not the time to lose control. He glanced up occasionally as the party neared his position. The poor light meant that he would not be able to recognise anyone until they were virtually on top of him.

'Come on, you drunkards!' cried one of the nobles. 'I've been wanting to get here all day.'

'This place better be worth it,' growled another.

Recognising the voice, Tarquinius stiffened. Lifting his head carefully, he peered at the figures now only a few steps away. But none of the equestrians was facing in his direction: they were staring lustfully in through the open door of the Lupanar.

'Take a look, Caelius,' said the nearest. 'You won't be disappointed.'

The Etruscan watched as a stocky man, his greying hair still tinged with red, shoved forward to take in the prostitutes who were visible in the brothel's reception area. It was Caelius. Older and slightly fuller at the waist, but the same bastard who had changed the haruspex' life for ever fifteen years before. An involuntary sigh escaped Tarquinius' lips.

At this, one of the slaves gave him a cursory glance. He was not troubled by what he saw. A small shape, wrapped in an old cloak. Probably a leper. Nothing six burly men couldn't handle.

Arguing over who wanted what type of girl and in what way, the nobles passed through the arched door-way and out of sight. The slaves were left to stand outside until such time as their masters' pleasure had been sated. Tarquinius stirred. Inevitably, their attention would be drawn to him, the only beggar left on the street. And there were too many of them for him to attack Caelius anyway. Tarquinius was not troubled by this. Now was not the time.

Scooping up his *gladius* in a fold of his cloak, he stood up awkwardly, affecting a bad limp. No one even watched as he shuffled off into the darkness.

One of the narrow alleyways close by would serve as a hiding place until Caelius and his friends emerged. It would be easy to follow the equestrians home. When Tarquinius knew where the arrogant noble was staying, he and Secundus could keep watch night and day. Pick an opportune time to strike. The haruspex smiled, offer-ing up a prayer of thanks. His long years of waiting and remembering were nearly over.

Olenus would be avenged. Soon.

Chapter XV: The Arena

The Ludus Magnus, Rome, late summer 55 BC

Bright sunlight pouring through the window woke Romulus. Brennus was still asleep. The young fighter got up and started his daily routine of stretching, now second nature. The rest had done him good. He breathed deeply, emptying his mind.

'Time to kill Figulus and Gallus.' The Gaul had woken. He sighed heavily. 'And settle this once and for all.'

Romulus nodded and kept moving. The end of the vendetta would be a relief to him too.

Brennus climbed out of bed naked and went to the table. 'Let's eat,' he said. His heavily muscled body revealed a network of old scars. Romulus had seen the fearsome evidence of Brennus' career before but it still filled him with awe. All he had was a thick purple welt on one thigh. Unusually, Brennus' slave brand was on his left calf, while Romulus' was high on his right arm.

Brennus covered a piece of bread in honey. 'Want some?' he asked, shoving it in his mouth.

'No.'

'By all the gods! Sooner we get you to the arena, the better.' Brennus finished eating and pulled on a loin-cloth. He felt jaded. *Can this really be what Ultan saw for me?*

Once he had warmed up, they donned their armour. Bare-chested, Brennus wore a wide leather belt covering the groin, and a pair of bronze greaves. Romulus had a similar belt and a *manica* for his right arm. A single greave on his left leg completed the attire of a *secutor*.

'Use the same shield you fought Lentulus with.'

'What about you?'

Brennus lifted an elongated oval *scutum* from a pile in the corner and smiled wolfishly. 'Sharp edge on this too.'

Romulus strapped on his *gladius*, eyeing Brennus' longsword enviously. He was still too small to wield it.

'Be careful.' Astoria seemed worried as she kissed the blond warrior. 'Stay together.'

'Stop fussing, woman!' Brennus gently squeezed her backside. 'Cook me more of those mice.'

He swaggered outside without looking back. Romulus nodded nervously at the Nubian and followed.

Most of the gladiators had gathered in the yard to do stretches or sharpen weapons. Fifty men in full armour, ready for battle, was an impressive sight. A dozen *retiarii* stood, tridents and nets ready, beside ten burly Thracians. *Murmillones* with their characteristic fish crest helmets, mailed right shoulders and round shields were there. Wearing plumed helmets, Samnites carried elongated oval *scuta*, their thighs covered by *fasciae* of leather with greaves protecting the lower legs. Sextus and three other *scissores* stood off to one side. A group of *secutores*, dressed similarly to Romulus, completed the tally.

'It should be interesting today,' said the short Spaniard, inclining his head in recognition. He had refrained from joining in the ongoing feud. Such was Sextus' reputation that Romulus' enemies did not make trouble if he was nearby. Only Brennus commanded the same level of respect.

'Figulus and Gallus want blood,' replied Romulus, feeling he could trust Sextus enough to confide in him.

'I heard something along those lines.' Sextus hefted the double-headed axe with a wink. 'Keep an eye out for you.'

'Thank you.'

'You would do the same for me.'

'I would.' Pleased to be recognised as an equal at last, Romulus grinned.

Sextus and his fellows provided a critical part of the *ludus'* fighting capability. Most gladiators were absolutely terrified of the lethal axemen, who could cut down the unwary with ease.

Soon all fighters bar the four trusted *scissores* were forced to have a light chain placed around their necks. Two long files formed up in the yard, held together by iron links. Dressed in a fine belted tunic and carrying a staff topped by a metal hook, Memor led the fighters out through the gate. Extra hired archers patrolled alongside, maintaining a wary distance from the heavily armed men.

The journey to the Forum Boarium began as a real

pleasure for Romulus. Since his arrival there had been few outings from the *ludus*. Even a favourite like Brennus had only been allowed to come and go unsupervised since Memor had the threat of Astoria's safety to hold over him. Romulus stared round him, soaking up every detail. Rome was busy despite the hour, as people got business done before the worst heat. It was a good time to avoid Clodius' and Milo's thugs, who tended not to rise early. Citizens had also been encouraged on to the streets by the bonus of extra games with a large group combat.

Whistles and cries of encouragement filled the air as the procession went by. Ahead of the gladiators groups of acrobats tumbled and rolled, delighting the crowds. Men bearing statues of Mars, Nemesis and Nike, the goddess of victory, took up the rear, flanked by musicians clashing cymbals and pounding drums. Women made lewd comments at their favourite fighters. Everyone supported the Ludus Magnus, the local gladiator school.

The onlookers knew nothing of the ongoing feud.

Suddenly Romulus felt keen to get to the arena. Many would die in the forthcoming contest and if their enemies succeeded, he and Brennus would be among them. Romulus had no wish to shed the blood of Magnus fighters, but he would not let someone slip a knife between his ribs either. The sooner it was over, the better. When the vendetta had been settled, normal life in the *ludus* could resume.

He glanced at the Gaul. Brennus seemed as calm as if he were going to the market.

Romulus took a deep breath and wiped the sweat off his face. 'Quite warm already.'

'It will be like Hades by midday.'

'At least we won't be fighting then.'

'Poor bastard *venatores*,' said Brennus. 'The wild beasts won't be too friendly in these temperatures either.'

Romulus was glad he had never seen an animal hunt before, usually the first performance of the day. Stories were common of hungry lions tearing gladiators limb from limb, and elephants trampling men underfoot like firewood. *Venatores* did not live for long and he had only escaped such a career because of his bravery on the day Gemellus sold him. That, or the intervention of the gods.

Passing through the city gates, they reached the Campus Martius, the plain of Mars. It was the site of elections to the magistracy and the place where citizens were sworn into the army. Pompey's new complex had transformed the huge open space. The most blatant attempt to win popularity ever seen, it contained an ornate people's theatre, a chamber for the Senate, a house for Pompey and a majestic temple to Venus. Every few moments, a great roar rose up from the packed auditorium.

Memor led his fighters towards a small doorway to one side of the main entrance. Four heavily armed slaves stood guard outside.

'State your business,' the largest said arrogantly.

'What does it look like?' snapped Memor. 'Here are fifty of the finest gladiators in Rome.'

'The *lanista* of the Dacicus might disagree.'

Memor whipped up his staff, catching the man off guard.

'I meant no harm, Master,' he stammered, the sharp metal hook pricking the back of his neck.

Memor pulled him closer, drawing blood. 'Like to join the combat today?'

'No, Master.' Beads of sweat sprang out on the guard's brow.

'Then open the fucking door!'

One of his companions swiftly pulled back a heavy iron bolt. Memor released the slave, allowing him to guide them inside. As the fighters passed into the darkness below the stands, the din made by shouts and drumming of spectators' feet filled their ears. It was a sound Romulus had heard before, something that quickened the pulse of even the most hardened gladiator.

Brennus cocked his head and listened. 'The crowd's excited. Something, or someone, is about to die.'

There was a lull in the cacophony. In the momentary silence they heard the distinctive snarl of a large beast.

The hairs on Romulus' neck stood up. 'What's that?'

'A lion. Angry too, by the sound.'

People above reacted with alarm as the big cat roared again. A man started screaming and the audience responded with jeers and boos.

'What happened?'

'He probably missed with his spear or trident.' Brennus grimaced. 'A goner.'

The cries outside intensified, then suddenly fell silent.

'Poor bastard,' said Romulus, even more glad that Cotta had chosen him.

Inured to the suffering, the guard sullenly brought the fighters along a narrow corridor with a dirt floor. Large empty iron cages stood on each side. There was little light apart from what filtered through gaps in the wooden planks around them. Memor stopped by the open door of the cell nearest the arena. It was marginally brighter than those at the back. He gestured at the empty space and laughed. 'Luxury accommodation.'

The gladiators trudged in, followed by the *lanista*'s guards, who struck off the neck chains then beat a hasty retreat.

'We got the best spot!' Memor jerked his head opposite. 'The boys from the Dacicus have been left that one.' The cage across the corridor lay empty, floor covered in bloodstained bandages and damaged armour.

'No one's cleaned it since the last fight,' Brennus said. There was little surprise in his voice. 'Put them on the back foot having to sit in that.'

'When it starts, you know what to do.' Memor's fierce eyes bored into each man. 'Stick together. Fight bravely. Kill every last one of those bastards! And remember – a bag of gold if you survive unhurt!'

'Lu-dus Mag-nus!' A *retiarius* started the shout. Instantly it was taken up by the rest. 'Ludus Magnus! Ludus Magnus!'

The *lanista* grinned, clenching a fist and thumping it off his chest in salute.

Even Brennus responded to the gesture.

'He's sending us out there to be killed!' Romulus hissed as Memor turned and left.

The Gaul was confused. 'That's his job.'

'So why acknowledge him?'

'Memor was a gladiator once,' Brennus replied lamely. 'He deserves respect for that.'

'And now he grows rich while men die.'

Unsettled by the comment, Brennus looked away.

Forget Memor, thought Romulus. Focus on the fight instead. *Survive.*

Most fighters quickly found a spot on the floor to sit and began talking with each other, sharpening weapons or tightening straps on armour. Two Thracians were wrestling, watched idly by a dozen men. A few knelt in one corner, praying to their favourite gods for protection. Anything that whiled away the long hours before combat was a good idea. Figulus and his cronies were deep in conversation and Romulus felt safe enough to wander away from the Gaul.

Beyond the bars were horizontal wooden planks making up the enclosure's main wall. Above were the seats of the rich and famous. Romulus smiled at the possibility of Gemellus' backside being so close to his sword. The merchant was an enthusiastic supporter of gladiatorial contests.

Romulus stared through a gap in the timbers. The lowest rows of benches were only a man's height from the ground and the spectators could almost reach out to touch the fighters and animals on the hot sand. 'Isn't it dangerous?' he asked.

'Look.' Brennus pointed at regularly placed archers with drawn bows round the perimeter. 'They can usually pick off anything that jumps out.'

'Usually?'

'Occasionally someone gets killed,' said Brennus. 'The people love it!'

'Apart from the poor bastard who gets mauled to death.'

'They want to watch the fight . . .'

'So why should we be the only ones to die in there?'

'Exactly,' smiled Brennus.

Romulus nodded, familiar with the citizens' huge thirst for blood. He shivered as he took in the slaughterhouse outside. The fight between man and beast they had heard was nearly over. Bloody corpses were scattered across the sand like rag dolls, limbs at awkward angles. Three lions and two leopards lay dead among the bodies, spears protruding from their chests and bellies.

'Gods above, help me!' The plaintive cry echoed around the open space. 'I have killed one cat. Is that not enough?'

Romulus stared in horror at the hunter who was limping round the arena, pleading with the people above. All his comrades had been slain and he was unarmed, with only a shield as protection. The young man's well-muscled torso was covered in deep, bleeding scratches and his right arm hung uselessly. Jagged shards of bone protruded from the gaping wound in it, clear evidence of the animals' terrible power.

'Behind you!' Spectators above Romulus sniggered as the last remaining lion padded after the injured *venator*.

'Help me!'

'Help yourself, scum!'

'Die like a man! Entertain us!'

Insults and pieces of bread and fruit rained down. He would get nothing from the crowd.

They wanted more blood.

Romulus' knuckles turned white as he gripped the bars, wishing he could do something. Anything.

The *venator's* dilemma was immediate. With the *scutum* on his good arm, he might hold off the lion for some time, but could not hope to injure it. The continuing blood loss from his injuries would eventually allow the lion to overcome him. With a weapon, he might have had a small chance of killing it, but now there would be no protection from the powerful claws that had ripped apart his companions.

Indecision played across the hunter's features. Then the survival instinct surfaced and he trotted to the nearest body, putting a little distance between himself and the lion. Discarding his shield, he picked up a heavy spear lying beside its dead owner.

'Roman savages.' Brennus materialised beside Romulus, watching the drama unfold. 'That's a good move, though. He wouldn't have enough reach with a sword.'

'What about a trident?'

'Too unwieldy. A spear has more length anyway.'

'Now what?'

'Wait until the beast tries to jump. Shove the butt into the sand and let it run on to the tip,' Brennus said softly. 'That's his only chance.'

Closing his eyes, Romulus asked Jupiter to help the wounded fighter.

With morbid fascination, they watched the newly armed *venator* back away. The big cat seemed content to follow, the only sign of impatience its twitching tail. Every so often it would lash out at the spear, but each time the man retreated, biding his time.

Soon the crowd began to grow bored and taunts filled

the air. Coins and clay cups were thrown to encourage an attack. The lion grew noticeably angry, growling and lashing its tail from side to side.

Brennus grinned and pointed. 'He's leading it away from the bodies.'

'Why?'

'To get away from the rubbish being thrown, for a start. Then he'll try and goad the cat into jumping.'

Romulus could hardly watch. 'Got to end it soon or he'll be too weak.'

'He knows that.'

The *venator* had finally reached an area free of corpses. Pushing his spear shaft into the ground with one hand, he lowered the broad-bladed head and glared at the lion.

'There is a man at peace with death!' Brennus thumped the bars excitedly. 'Kill the beast! Go on, kill it!'

The lion padded to within fifteen paces of its prey and paused, sunlight turning the pupils in its amber eyes to slits. It sank down on to the sand, tail tip moving faintly. The *venator* stiffened, crouching low behind his spear. He would only have one chance when it charged.

At last the audience stopped shouting and throwing objects. The tension became palpable.

'Watch the muscles in the back legs. It'll leap any moment.' Brennus gripped Romulus' shoulder. 'Could you stay calm? Your right arm in shreds?'

Romulus swallowed hard, trying to imagine the pain of the gaping wounds. The fighter did not look much older than himself and probably had a similar story. But it appeared he would not give in – life was too precious.

Springing up, the lion flew into the air. There was a

collective intake of breath from the crowd. Refusing to allow fear to take over, the *venator* steadied himself.

The cat came down at speed and impaled itself on the spear.

Its momentum drove the sharp blade through its ribs, ripping heart and lungs to shreds. The hunter was knocked to the ground by the impact.

Silence reigned as the spectators took in the impossible.

Romulus jumped up and down, screaming at the top of his voice and thanking the gods. Laughing, Brennus joined in. Gladiators beat sword hilts off shields in appreciation, making as much noise as possible. It was a Herculean feat to kill a big predator with such severe injuries and inspiring for all of them.

Eventually the *venator* managed to push the dead weight off his lower body and stand. The people had been slowly responding to the din from below but the cheering doubled in volume when he got up.

'Fickle bastards,' said Brennus. 'Abusing him a few moments ago. Bloody Romans.'

Romulus agreed with his friend. The reaction of the audience was hypocritical; all that seemed to matter to them was mutilation and death.

The lesson was about to be reinforced in the most final of ways.

Emboldened by his actions, the *venator* walked to the hoarding near those who had thrown insults earlier. 'That good enough?' He spat in a clear gesture of defiance.

Romulus cheered, but a strange quiet fell over the Forum Boarium. The citizens of Rome did not like being mocked.

The wounded man proudly turned to walk away.

'Not clever,' Brennus said to himself. 'He shouldn't have done that.'

'But he killed the lion.'

'And just insulted someone rich or famous.' The Gaul sucked in his lower lip, peering between the planks. 'Wouldn't be surprised if . . .'

Brennus had not finished speaking when an arrow flashed through the air. With a soft thump, it buried itself in the unsuspecting *venator*'s back. He staggered, screaming with surprise and pain. As he struggled to reach the metal-tipped shaft, two more struck him in the chest and neck.

Roars of laughter rang out.

'You bastards!' Romulus cried.

'Keep quiet,' whispered Brennus, 'unless you want to be executed as well.'

Romulus fell silent, grinding his teeth with rage at the injustice. What glory was there in being a gladiator if one could be killed like this?

The *venator* had fallen to his knees, clawing at the arrows and coughing up blood with each attempt. At last he toppled to the sand, twitched a few times and was still. He was only a few steps from the dead lion.

No living creature, animal or human, remained in the arena.

Tears filled Romulus' eyes. 'No man should die like that.'

'Upset the rich and it might happen to you.' Brennus' tone was dull with resignation. 'We are always at their mercy.'

'His life meant nothing to those scum.'

'And yours is no different. We're slaves, remember!'

Romulus stared at the *venator*'s body, anger pulsing through every vein. Their own situation had been brought home as never before by the utter powerlessness of the brave fighter. He had beaten all the odds, yet still he had not survived. In a short while, Romulus would be risking his own life in the same arena, when the crowd's bloodlust would have to be satisfied once again. Savage injuries and the deaths of dozens of men counted for nothing. Everyone in the cell would be subject to the same caprice, the same brand of harsh justice.

Up till now, Romulus had chosen to see only the glory and fame of gladiatorial life. The veil had lifted momentarily when he'd had to kill Flavus and Lentulus, but seeing a valiant man executed on a whim had ripped it asunder.

Gladiators' lives were simply about fighting and dying for the amusement of the Roman mob. They were paid killers, nothing more.

The realisation was brutal – and total. Stunned, he sank into a deep gloom, slumping to the hard-packed dirt of the cell floor. Brennus tried to cheer him up, but his jokes fell on deaf ears. After a while the Gaul gave up and started sharpening his longsword with a small whetstone. It was his usual way of passing the time.

The slaughter in the arena went on and on, but Romulus did not have the stomach to watch. Bulls and bears that had been chained together tore each other to shreds; hunting dogs were released to prey upon terrified gazelle. Packs of starving wolves were set upon criminals tied to wooden posts. Shrieks and cries of pain from every species filled the air for hours, to roars of approval from the audience. The once golden sand was turned into a thick red morass that stuck underfoot.

Deep in his daze, Romulus thought of his mother and Fabiola. Even if he survived the impending fight, he would probably never see them again anyway. Life would be a succession of rest periods and combat, with only one possible outcome.

Death.

They were slaves to the bloody desires of the Roman public. Waves of anger and sadness washed over him and Romulus' spirits fell further. Never before had he felt like this.

'Time to go soon.' Brennus was looking concerned. 'What is it?'

'We're all going to die out there.'

'Some aren't!' The Gaul flexed huge biceps. 'Stick with me and you'll be fine.'

'What's the point? Why bleed and die for complete strangers?' Romulus' shoulders sagged. 'I'm stuck here and my mother belongs to a sadistic bastard who sold Fabiola to a whorehouse. Life means nothing. I might as well let Figulus kill me.'

Brennus grabbed Romulus' arm. 'You're not the only one with a sad story! Think of that *venator*,' he hissed. 'And every man in this cell has suffered under the Roman yoke. Even bastards like Figulus and Gallus.'

Romulus shook off the Gaul's hand. 'What do I care?' he replied angrily.

There was a long silence before Brennus began to speak again.

'I watched while Roman soldiers burned the village with my wife and baby son inside,' he began. 'Then the cousin I had sworn to protect was killed right in front of me.'

Romulus looked at his friend, his heart filling with sympathy.

'And the memories crowd my head every day.'

'I . . .' Romulus began guiltily, but the Gaul kept talking.

'I spent five years looking for death. But the gods did not allow it. Been saving me for something else. Don't know what it is yet, but first Astoria came along. Then you.' He ruffled Romulus' hair affectionately. His protégé's similarities with Brac were startling.

'What are you saying?'

'Even in the midst of all this,' said Brennus, gesturing at the bloodstained sand, 'life is worth living. Die today if you want, Romulus. But think about when you arrived in the *ludus*. What made Memor buy you? Or Cotta choose a boy of thirteen to train?' He loosened his sword in its scabbard. 'The gods favour courageous men. Remember that.' He gave Romulus a hard stare, then fell silent.

The young fighter pondered what Brennus had said for some time. Perhaps there was more to it than sheer luck. Perhaps Jupiter did have a purpose for him after all. Feeling slightly better, he looked up and caught Gallus' gaze on him. The stocky *retiarius* nudged Figulus, leering as he drew a finger across his throat. Romulus got to his feet. Brennus' words had struck a chord and Gallus' threat had acted as the final impetus. What use was there in dying so easily?

Thoughts of Spartacus came to Romulus, lighting a spark of hope. The gladiator who had shaken Rome to its core. He smiled. Even on the bloody sand of the arena, it was possible to choose one's destiny. There were reasons to live.

Romulus began to roll both shoulders as Cotta had taught, pretending he was warming up for a training session.

'That's the attitude!' said Brennus delightedly.

'The bastards won't kill me without a fight.'

'I'm glad to hear it.'

Together the two friends stretched their muscles, readying themselves for the slaughter.

Chapter XVI: Victory

Early afternoon had passed and the bloody sand had been raked, a clean layer scattered on top. After the distraction of beast hunts, there was an interval before the main attraction. Mobile vendors selling wine, meat and bread clambered between rows of seats, doing a brisk trade with the hungry citizens. Much of the audience had been replaced with those drawn by the prospect of a large group combat. Only the most bloodthirsty remained to watch the entire day's entertainment.

Underneath the stands, the cells opposite the Magnus fighters still lay empty.

'Where are they?' growled a *murmillo*.

Hours had passed. It could not be long until the fight began.

'Scare tactics. The Dacicus *lanista* will send his boys directly into the arena,' said another.

'So there's no chance to size them up beforehand,' added a *retiarius*.

Whispers of unease rippled through the gladiators.

'Who gives a shit?' Brennus said loudly. He stepped forward before the unrest turned to fear.

The fighters looked up, curious. None was used to having a leader.

The Gaul smiled grimly. 'Many of us will die today.' Instantly he had everyone's attention. 'But it doesn't have to be that way.'

'What's your fucking point?' snarled Figulus, moving forward with his friends. A space spontaneously appeared between Brennus and the group.

Romulus tensed, ready to react if they attacked. It was pleasing to see the four *scissores* react in the same way. He and the Gaul were not totally alone.

'We are far better than the Dacicus lot,' cried Brennus. 'You all know that!'

Many men growled acknowledgement. There was fierce rivalry between the different schools.

'If we hit them hard and fast, we can finish this before it's even started.'

Hope appeared in the anxious faces.

'Follow me and fight together! I want the *retiarii* to the front and sides. Everyone else in the centre. We'll take the bastards out with a full frontal attack.' Brennus raised a clenched fist. 'LU-DUS MAG-NUS!'

There was a short silence as the gladiators muttered to each other, taking his words in. A few nodded, shouting the infectious refrain. More gradually began to join in and finally the cell echoed to roars of 'LU-DUS MAG-NUS! LU-DUS MAG-NUS!'

Satisfied, the Gaul stepped back. Figulus scowled at

those nearby, but the moment to respond had been lost. The men would follow Brennus.

Sextus nodded with approval. 'Raised our spirits, and with luck, divided our enemies at the same time.'

'I led warriors into battle long before I was a gladiator.'

'And I pray you lead them again.' The *scissores* pointed at the entrance. 'Still no sign of them. That *murmillo* was right – we'll be going into the arena blind.'

'Soon too.'

'May the gods be with us.'

'And may they guide your axe!' Brennus raised his voice. 'Remember what I said.'

To Romulus' delight, the gladiators responded immediately, forming up in groups.

The Gaul grinned and drew his sword.

'Where do you want my boys?'

'Doing what you do best, Sextus! Pick 'em off around the edges!'

The *scissores* bared his lips at Brennus' double-edged comment.

At that moment, a group of guards clattered down the corridor, spears in hand.

The hoarding between the rows of cages had an exit to the outside cut into it. Some men lifted a heavy locking bar and placed it on the ground, removing planks to open a gap wide enough for two fighters to stand abreast. The remainder closed off the passage to the street.

The slave who had earlier been insolent to Memor opened the padlock with a long key, pulling wide the gate. 'Time to die!' he said, smirking.

A number of fighters lunged at him through the bars with knives and swords. He jumped back in fear. 'Get out there! Don't make us get the archers.'

'Watch your mouth, you son of a whore,' growled Sextus. 'We'll go in our own time.'

Romulus was baffled and angered that a fellow slave should want other slaves to die. If they could only unify and fight together, the foundations of the Republic would crumble beneath the weight of their numbers. Think like Spartacus, he thought. All men should be free.

The guard gestured outside again, but had the wisdom not to speak. These fighters were dangerous, even when behind locked gates. Trumpets blared expectantly and the crowd cheered, eager for the spectacle to begin.

Brennus hefted his shield. 'Time to shed some blood for the good citizens of Rome.'

Romulus swallowed, squaring both shoulders.

Followed by their companions, the pair trotted into bright afternoon sunlight. The gladiators quickly fanned out into a semicircle, occupying half the sand. Shouts of encouragement from Magnus supporters competed with the jeers of those who backed the Dacicus.

Many in the audience were studying them, judging their fighting ability. Comments and insults filled the air and bookmakers ran up and down the steps, offering wildly varying odds. Bags of *sestertii* changed hands as huge bets were laid by eager nobles.

Announcing the arrival of the Dacicus fighters, trumpets rang out again, silencing the crowd.

Romulus held his breath as fifty men emerged from an opening on the opposite side of the arena. Most were similar in appearance to the Magnus gladiators, but there were some he did not recognise.

'See the *dimachaeri*?' Brennus pointed. 'Those with two swords.'

'They have no shields,' said Romulus with amazement.

'Crazy easterners from Dacia. What do you expect?'

'And the ones with lassos?'

'*Laquearii*. They fight in pairs with *murmillones* or Thracians. Rope an enemy so the other can kill him.'

'Dangerous?'

'Some are as good as Gallus is with a net.'

Romulus blew out his cheeks. This is going to be interesting, he thought. Remember the basics.

Beside him, Brennus was shifting excitedly, eyes lit. Battle rage was taking control.

When the Dacicus fighters had formed up opposite, the trumpets blew a last fanfare and fell silent. Nobody spoke as the heavily armed groups faced each other.

Death was in the air.

'People of Rome!' A short, fat man in a white toga addressed the crowd from the boxed area reserved for nobles. 'Before us today are one hundred of the finest gladiators in the city!'

Wild cheering erupted; many of the women screamed and threw flowers.

'We are here because of the generosity of one person . . .' The speaker paused, allowing the noise to build. 'I give you – the conqueror of Mithridates, Lion of Pontus. The victor over the Cilician pirates. The builder of the people's theatre. Today's *editor* – the great general – Pompey Magnus!'

As if ordered to do so, sunlight streamed from a break in the clouds. Roars of approval rose into the air and Romulus realised that the two groups had been encouraged to stand so they formed a corridor. Beams shone from the west across the arena, between the fighters.

Lighting up Pompey, the sponsor.

'Just a big show,' he muttered to Brennus.

'Politics. If the people love the games, they support their sponsors. That gives him power.'

'We are fighting for a damn politician?' Romulus had not thought to question the reason behind fights. The citizens of Rome adored bloodshed, but it was not they who actually held the contests. It was those in power who were responsible – the senators and equestrians. The gladiators were just puppets on strings.

Used to it all, Brennus nodded.

Romulus was outraged. 'Lots of us are about to die. Why?'

'We are slaves, Romulus,' he said simply.

An image of Crassus' doorman came to him. 'Says who?' Romulus countered. 'That prick?' He pointed at the nobles' box.

'Shut up!' Brennus looked over both shoulders. 'Memor would execute you on the spot if he heard that.'

'It's been done before,' argued Romulus passionately. 'Imagine what fifty of us could do to the bastards up there.'

'Rebellion?' The Gaul whispered the word.

'Claiming freedom, more like.'

'Pompey Magnus!' cried the master of ceremonies again.

'Time to fight.' Brennus winked. 'We'll talk later.'

The crowd cheered dutifully while Pompey acknow-ledged their adulation with a languid wave. A middle-aged man with white hair, prominent eyes and a bulbous nose, he surveyed the fighters keenly.

'Salute Pompey Magnus!'

'We who are about to die, salute you!' The gladiator's vow roared from a hundred throats.

Pompey nodded with more respect than he had given the audience.

'At least he is a warrior,' said Brennus. 'Not like that dog Crassus, who never stops telling everyone what a great general he is.'

'Pompey is paying for us to die,' hissed Romulus. 'Fuck him!'

The Gaul seemed startled, but a light Romulus had not seen before stirred in his eyes.

'Die like men!' Pompey addressed the combatants. 'Show courage. Those who survive unhurt will be well rewarded. Begin!'

There was silence for a few moments as the fighters watched each other, bodies stiff with tension.

Romulus was filled with excitement at the Gaul's response to his comment. But everything would have to wait until the combat was over. If they survived. He turned round. Figulus and Gallus were some distance away, pretending not to look in their direction.

'Stay close. Watch your backs!' Brennus shouted, grip-ping his sword in a huge fist. 'Move it! Don't let them come to us!' he yelled at the *retiarii*.

The fishermen shuffled forwards, holding their

weighted nets low, ready to throw. Dacicus fighters fanned out in response, beginning to advance. Romulus stood three steps to Brennus' right, shield high, dagger in hand. The standoff with the guards had given him an idea.

'Once the *retiarii* are occupied, I want a charge through the centre.' Brennus spoke in a low voice so that only those nearby could hear. 'Ignore normal combat rules. Kill quickly and move on.'

'We're with you, Brennus,' said a Thracian.

The others muttered agreement. Brennus looked at each of them, nodding grimly.

Moments later, the fight began as Magnus *retiarii* reached the first Dacicus gladiators. Nets twirled and spun through the air, men dodged and cursed, skidding on the hot sand. Romulus saw a trident piercing an enemy's throat, tearing flesh apart in a crimson spray of blood. Fighters circled each other, weaving and thrusting in lethal, mesmerising dances.

The main body of the enemy had been unprepared for the sudden attack. Apparently leaderless, the intimidated Dacicus gladiators were at a loss how to respond.

The moment was ripe.

'On me!' Brennus roared, lifting his longsword and loping through the individual combats in front.

Thirty men followed, weapons at the ready.

Romulus kept pace with the Gaul, eyes peeled. As he passed a fight between a Magnus fisherman and a Samnite, he took a chance. The heavily armed warrior had lowered his oblong shield for a moment, watching the *retiarius* balance the net to throw. Romulus leaned forward on one foot, cocking his right arm back. Taking aim, he swung forward, releasing the knife. It flew straight and true, cutting deep into the unsuspecting Samnite's throat, below the visored helmet. The man made a choking noise and dropped both sword and *scutum*. Blood poured around his clutching fingers as he slumped to the sand.

The *retiarius* turned to see who had felled his opponent.

With surprise, Romulus recognised Gallus.

'Bastard!' The *retiarius*' face twisted with anger. 'You're dead meat.'

Gallus' violent reaction shocked him and proved that the threat from the disgruntled fighters was very real. But his enemy had no time to react as a heavily built *secutor* lunged in for the kill.

'Got one already!' Romulus pulled his sword free as he raced to catch the Gaul.

'How?'

'With my dagger!'

'Good work! Pick up another if possible. Never know when you might need it!' Brennus smiled and increased his speed, outstripping the others.

Brennus' charge was awe-inspiring. With a roar that simply froze the first Dacicus fighter on the spot, the Gaul smashed down on to his bronze helmet with the longsword, crushing the skull.

The Thracian crashed to the ground.

Brennus stepped over the body, swept the next gladiator's shield out of the way with his own and stabbed him in the chest from close range. He roared a deafening battle-cry that echoed round the enclosure.

A few moments passed. Unsure what to do, the Dacicus fighters stood transfixed by the fearsome apparition.

The Gaul dispatched a *secutor* with ease.

'Come on!' Romulus shouted as he ran forward, pressing home the advantage. '*Ludus Magnus!*'

An inarticulate bellow of pent-up rage and fear answered. With a crash of swords on shields, the Magnus gladiators ran at their bewildered enemies.

Romulus found himself facing a *murmillo* only slightly larger than he. His opponent swung a heavy overhand blow, trying to hammer through with sheer force. Romulus parried with relative ease, keeping the shield high. He drove forward under the other's *gladius*, staring at his enemy as he drew within range. The gladiator's mouth opened, knowing what was about to happen.

Romulus plunged his sword into the man's exposed midriff.

The *murmillo* screamed and folded over in agony. Swiftly Romulus withdrew the blade, letting him fall to the sand. A huge blow downwards with the shield's sharp edge sliced open his neck. Sure the fighter was critically injured, Romulus stepped away.

Cotta had taught him the old-fashioned methods of gladiator combat. In this way, formal fights could last for hours, impressing the crowd with the skill and swordsmanship of the participants. But in the situation Romulus was in right now, there was no point in showing off. Although more brutal, it was better to follow Brennus' method by incapacitating or killing as fast as possible.

Brennus was ten steps away to the left, hacking a Thracian to pieces while fending off a second with side-sweeps of his longsword. On the right, Magnus men were head to head with enemy *murmillones* and *dimachaeri*. One figure with two swords was particularly skilled. Romulus watched in amazement as he spun like a dancer, maiming and killing at leisure. The end came when a Magnus *retiarius* smothered him from behind in his net. As the *dimachaerus* tried to struggle free, several gladiators swarmed in, spitting him like a wild boar.

Already a dozen enemy were prone on the sand. More were injured and no longer fighting. Helped largely by Brennus, the combat was going the way of the Ludus Magnus. The Gaul's value to his side was incalculable. Everyone he faced was quaking with fear before a blow had even landed.

Quite suddenly Romulus came under attack from a *laquearius* and a Thracian. He dodged one throw of the lasso with ease, but barely managed to ward off the lightning quick thrust from the man's partner that followed. Romulus spun away, almost putting his foot into the loop of rope that the wily *laquearius* had placed on the ground. Heart pounding, he cut and slashed back at the Thracian, desperately keeping his eyes on the other.

He could not win this fight alone.

Between sword thrusts, he tried to see who was near enough to help. Brennus was now busy with two *murmillones* and a *secutor*. There was no sign of Sextus. Romulus swore bitterly, chopping at the rope that came hissing through the air. He nearly lost the *gladius* as the lasso whipped backwards just a moment too soon. If he did not kill one in a matter of moments, his life would be over.

Romulus took a deep breath, kicking a shower of sand at the *laquearius'* face. He turned and shoulder-charged the Thracian, muttering a prayer to Jupiter and expecting to feel the noose land round his neck with every step. To Romulus' relief, the *laquearius* uttered a strangled cry as his eyes filled with burning grit. He reached the armoured fighter with ease, driving him back several steps.

Romulus used the momentum he had gained to stab at the Thracian's face. His enemy lifted a large shield in response. Instantly, Romulus swung his own down on to the man's right knee. Slicing deep into muscle, it severed the attachment to the kneecap. The Thracian's leg buckled, unable to take the weight.

Roaring with pain, the Dacicus fighter fell. Blood spurted from the wound as Romulus risked a glance behind for the *laquearius*. He was falling in slow motion, face contorted in agony, Sextus' axe planted deep in his spine.

'You looked hard pressed.'

'Thanks!' Remembering Lentulus' last act, Romulus spun round, thrusting his sword through the Thracian's throat. The man choked on blood and toppled to one side, eyes wide with shock. Quickly Romulus grabbed a bone-handled dagger from the dead gladiator's belt. Two weapons were always better than one.

When he looked back, Sextus was gone.

'Well fought!' Brennus walked over, breathing heavily. He was covered from head to foot in blood.

Romulus glanced round for enemy fighters. Seeing none nearby, he relaxed slightly. 'The fight's nearly over,' he said with satisfaction. 'Thanks to you.'

Brennus nodded in acknowledgement. 'Kill or be killed,' he muttered to himself.

Romulus did a quick head count: fewer than twenty Dacicus gladiators were still standing. 'It won't take long now.'

'Let's hope the fools surrender soon,' sighed the Gaul. 'They have no chance of winning.'

It was then that a net came flying through the air and landed over Brennus' head, weighted folds falling to the sand. The big man struggled to free himself, but his sword tip was caught in the heavy mesh. A vicious trident thrust followed and Brennus barely managed to avoid being gutted.

Instinctively Romulus slashed down with his *gladius*, severing the attacker's arm at the elbow. Shocked to recognise one of the Magnus *retiarii*, he did not pause. A swift kick to the groin knocked the maimed gladiator to the sand.

'Look out!' Brennus dropped his longsword and grabbed at strands of the net to lift it off.

Romulus saw movement from the corner of his eye. Alarmed, he turned to face Gallus, who was flanked by Figulus and two other grim-faced fighters, a Thracian and a Samnite. Bloody weapons were in their hands.

'On your own now, scum!' The *retiarius* lunged with his trident.

'I should have knifed you instead of the Dacicus gladiator,' replied Romulus, dodging to one side.

'Missed your chance,' sneered Gallus.

Keeping himself between Brennus and the attackers, Romulus shuffled backwards. The *retiarius* laughed, thinking Romulus was trying to get away.

Without thinking, Romulus stabbed his sword into the sand, drew the new knife and flung it.

The gladiators paused, surprised.

Gallus stopped abruptly, making a strange gurgling sound. A bone handle protruded from his throat. With a faintly startled expression, the stocky fighter dropped to the ground, killed the same way as his first opponent.

Freeing himself, Brennus moved to stand alongside Romulus. 'Three against two. Good enough odds, I reckon!'

'Vulcan's prick! You said Gallus would net the big bastard!' The Samnite on Figulus' left shuffled his feet nervously in the sand.

'Why didn't you gut him when he was down, idiot?' The Thracian licked dry lips, but did not back away. 'Let's end this!'

'Finished squabbling?' Brennus smiled grimly and charged.

Romulus was only a step behind.

The Samnite took one look and turned to run. As he did, Sextus appeared from nowhere. With a huge swing of his axe, he cut the man's head clean off. A fountain of blood sprayed into the air from the headless torso, which fell twitching on to Gallus' body.

The sand all around was stained crimson with the

blood of countless Dacicus gladiators. And now those who were supposed to be on his side. Gallus. The Samnite. Men are dying in droves. For what? thought Romulus.

Figulus threw his shield at Brennus and sprinted to safety, leaving the last of his cronies alone. The man paled as the three friends advanced.

'I surrender!' Dropping his weapon, the *murmillo* fell to his knees.

'Try to kill one of your own, eh?' Brennus raised the longsword high and brought it down on the man's left shoulder, breaking the clavicle.

The *murmillo* let out a high-pitched scream, the sound echoing loudly. Romulus realised the arena had gone quiet. All the fighting was over. The entire audience was now watching them.

'Let him live, Brennus.' Sextus had noticed too. 'It's over. He has asked for mercy.' The *scissores* stood back, planting his bloody axe on the sand. 'Memor will be observing.'

'This piece of shit is a traitor to our *familia*!' spat the Gaul. 'Loyalty is everything. Without it we are nothing.'

'It's not worth it,' Romulus said tiredly. He was revolted by the number of bodies, scattered like discarded puppets. 'Enough men have died.'

There was a long pause. Brennus was trembling with rage.

'Brennus!'

At last the Gaul seemed to hear and the fire in his blue eyes subsided.

The *murmillo* quickly raised a forefinger, but the

crowd jeered at the appeal for mercy. This was not what they had come to see.

Romulus was disgusted. No one cared that the injured fighter was actually one of their own men. The mob wanted blood and it did not matter whose it was.

This is no way to live my life.

Brennus had also had enough. He lowered his longsword and stepped back, ignoring the shouts.

Across the arena, all surviving Dacicus fighters had thrown down their weapons, pleading for mercy. Fewer than fifteen remained living. Twenty-four Magnus gladiators were uninjured; another half-dozen were lying screaming in pain, but would live to fight another day.

Trumpets rang out, silencing the clamour. The portly master of ceremonies stepped forward again.

'Victory goes to the Lu-dus Mag-nus!' he announced.

Brennus, Romulus and the others raised bloody swords in acknowledgement. The responding roars completely drowned out the cries of the wounded and dying. Rome cared not for the victims.

'What a slaughter.' Disgusted, Romulus looked at the open red mouths in the baying crowd. 'Nearly sixty men have died for this?'

Brennus was fully in control of himself now, the battle frenzy replaced by his customary poise. He stared at his right arm, red to the elbow. 'Pompey deserves it more than this poor bastard, I suppose,' he said heavily, nudging the headless Samnite with one foot.

'Yes. He does!' hissed Romulus.

The announcer held up both podgy arms for quiet. 'I give you – the illustrious general Pompey Magnus!'

There was dutiful cheering as Pompey rose to speak again. The middle-aged consul stood in silence for a moment, enjoying the applause. He acknowledged it with regal waves, and the people responded with a more fervent display of gratitude to Pompey. The brutal mass combat had satisfied their bloodlust.

'Knows how to work the crowd as well as Caesar,' said Brennus.

Romulus clenched his fists. 'They are all bastards!' he replied. His exhaustion had been replaced by a desperate desire to show Pompey how it felt to be butchered. But images of the *venator's* death were too vivid. He would end up the same way. A plan was needed.

'People of Rome!' Pompey raised his arms. Enthusiastic screams greeted him. 'What a spectacle we have seen here today! All for you. Citizens of the Republic!' Deafening applause followed.

Pompey smiled, clicking two fingers together. Slaves bearing a bronze tray laden with money bags materialised at his side.

'Let those from the winning side come forward!' The announcer sounded disdainful. 'Only those with no wounds may approach!'

The able-bodied fighters grouped together, heads held high. They walked to stand in front of the box, saluting Pompey with clenched fists. Even Romulus felt a brief surge of pride at having survived the slaughter. It was hard not to.

'You have fought bravely,' Pompey said approvingly. 'Those who show such courage deserve suitable reward.' He picked up a leather bag and tossed it into the air.

Sextus grabbed the first, stepping back with a broad grin. Purses landed until every man had received one. Rapturous cheering continued long after Pompey had finished throwing. People had enjoyed the extravagant contest more than usual. The fighters waved swords, smiled and laughed, unused to such adulation.

It did not last.

With an impatient gesture, the master of ceremonies motioned for them to leave the arena. Their moment of glory was over; the gladiators were mere slaves again.

'It's heavy.' Romulus hefted his prize with both hands. 'How much is in it?'

Brennus shrugged. 'Couple of thousand *sestertii* maybe.'

'A bargain,' Romulus said, full of fury once more. 'We are better than this.' He shook the bag. It made a jingling sound. The price of men's lives.

Brennus shot him a glance. 'Too many ears around still,' he muttered.

Romulus fell silent. There was no point being reckless.

'Enough to buy wine and whores for the next few months!' Sextus was grinning from ear to ear.

'Thanks for getting Romulus out of that tight spot.'

'You saved my hide last year, remember?'

Brennus shrugged. 'Anyone would have done the same.'

'Except they wouldn't,' replied the *scissores* swiftly. 'It's a shame Figulus survived, though. A poisonous snake, that one.'

'Bastard will be stirring up more trouble in no time.'

Brennus watched Figulus with narrowed eyes. 'I know it.'

'Won't be happy until he has killed you,' sighed Sextus. 'And raped Astoria.'

The words were inflammatory.

Brennus raised his sword. 'I'll just go and kill him. Get it over with.'

He was interrupted by Memor, who appeared on the sand alone. 'The fight was over!' he screeched. 'One of the *familia* was pleading for his life. And what did you do?'

The Gaul did not answer.

'You maimed him!'

'He and his sewer rat friends attacked me and Romulus,' replied Brennus. 'They were going to kill us both.'

'It must have been a mistake,' cried Memor, waving his hands. 'They mistook you for Dacicus fighters.' Clearly he had not seen the start of the altercation.

'It was all planned.'

The *lanista* ignored his answer. 'When a man pleads for mercy, *you* do not say what happens.' Memor pointed at the dignitaries' box, shaking with anger. 'Pompey decides!' He waved a fist at the Gaul.

Brennus clenched his jaw.

'All special rights are withdrawn! Astoria can go back to the kitchen where she belongs. I'm taking back your cell too,' Memor sneered. 'Bunk in with some of the others. See how you like it.'

Brennus took a step towards the *lanista*, longsword raised. 'I ought to cut your throat.'

Memor simply lifted a hand.

Archers on top of the hoarding raised drawn bows.

'Do exactly as I say, or get a belly full of arrows.' The *lanista* paused. 'And you might stop that black bitch being sold to the Lupanar tomorrow morning.'

Brennus went rigid.

Memor waited.

Romulus watched the standoff with bated breath. There was no way to stop the *lanista* without also dying.

At last Brennus stepped back.

Memor stared at the big slave for a few moments. Satisfied Brennus wasn't going to take the bait, he stalked from the arena. 'Get back to the cells,' he snarled over his shoulder.

'Son of a whore!' Brennus spat. 'I'll slice him open and make him eat his own guts.'

'It would be good to see that,' Sextus said with a sad smile. 'But you'd be crucified alongside Astoria before the day was over.'

'What can I do?' Brennus' tone was despairing, something Romulus had never heard before. 'I can look after myself, but Astoria needs me.'

'I will care for her.'

'Why?'

'I also hate Memor,' Sextus said calmly. 'Astoria will be safe until you win favour again.'

Hearing this, Romulus nearly said something. They would need allies and it seemed the *scissores* might be of similar mind. But it was a dangerous matter, one to be discussed in private, behind locked doors.

'Take an oath!' Brennus moved closer, eyes fixed on the other's.

'Before all my gods, I swear it.'

The two men clasped forearms, but it was no time for sentimentality.

'Let's get inside before those archers get restless.'

Sextus strode off to gather his men.

Romulus was trying to think of ways to win over enough gladiators to silence Memor for ever. There is no future in this, he thought, gazing at the bloody figures on the sand. Spartacus had the right idea. Seize freedom.

The setting sun had turned the dead a dark shade of crimson. As they watched, the intimidating shape of Charon entered, stopping purposefully by each corpse. Each time the ferryman's hammer came down, Romulus heard the sickening crunch of breaking bone.

He looked away.

'Claiming them for Hades.' Brennus curled his lip. 'Making sure none are playing dead.' He leaned in close. 'Lucky not to be lying there myself. That *retiarius* would have done for me. I'm in your debt, Romulus. Again.'

'It was nothing.' Feeling awkward, he changed the subject. 'Memor really has it in for you, eh?'

'The bastard has been waiting for me to step out of line. This just gave him an excuse to finish it. With Figulus and friends out for blood as well . . .' Brennus wiped his brow. 'Life will be quite interesting from now on.'

'I meant what I said earlier.'

'Freedom?' Brennus' face brightened, then sagged as he thought of Astoria. 'Impossible.'

Romulus sighed. The futility of gladiator life had been brought home as never before by the mass combat. He needed support to have any chance of escape and the Gaul was crucial to this. But Memor's punishment seemed to have knocked the fight out of him. He would have to be patient and work on Brennus gradually. Men would follow more easily if the *ludus'* champion fighter was involved.

Romulus would not rest until he was free.

In the rest days that followed, Memor swaggered round the school, a broad grin on his scarred face. He had received a large sum from Pompey and the victory would have gained the *ludus* considerable respect in the Roman public's eyes.

For three days all the gladiators except Brennus were rewarded with extra rations of food and wine. Prostitutes were allowed to visit their cells. Training sessions for those who had fought were cut to just one hour daily. The baths were open to all, a privilege normally reserved for elite fighters. These gestures were universally acclaimed by the tired men, who had risked their lives yet again for the honour of the *ludus*.

'Out of my sight, you little bastard!' Memor scowled one afternoon as he caught sight of Romulus. The *lanista* suspected he had played a part in the deaths of Gallus and the others but had no proof. 'Plotting to kill more of my best fighters?'

Romulus did not dare answer. He ducked back into the small cell he and Brennus were sharing with two veteran Thracians. The homosexual pair had remained neutral since the fight over Astoria which had started the bloody vendetta. Otho and Antonius were already marginalised by the intolerant *familia* and two more outcasts did not trouble them.

When the quiet offer had come their way, the friends had seized the chance. Thanks to Memor's veiled threats, there had been no other options of accommodation. Life in the *ludus* had suddenly become difficult, and a safe place to sleep made things a little easier. Romulus for one found the Thracians' company quite entertaining. Otho was tall and thin with an ascetic manner. Antonius was plump and effeminate, but deadly with a sword.

'Memor still pissed off?' Brennus had heard the brief altercation. He was lying on a straw mattress, his home for most of the time since the fight. 'Prick.'

Nothing Romulus said seemed to improve his friend's mood. Not even the idea of rebellion, which he could only bring up when they were alone.

'He's never taken Astoria from me before.'

'Sextus is looking after her.'

'Just as well. Old bastard would have tried to screw her otherwise,' said Brennus sourly. 'I don't know what to do. It's bad enough in here!' He rolled his eyes theatrically as Antonius was wont to do when excited.

'They're good men,' Romulus replied, laughing at the caricature. He peered round the door. To his relief, the Thracians were training in the yard. 'Nobody else would take us in. Sextus couldn't.'

'True enough. And the Thracians are risking their necks for us.' None of the other gladiators would have anything to do with them. 'But I'm going crazy being stuck inside.'

'Give it a week or two,' said Romulus bluffly. 'Things will settle down.'

'I don't know. Memor is a vindictive bastard.' The Gaul sighed. 'Wouldn't be surprised if things get worse.'

'We could organise a little something for him.' Romulus mimed a stabbing motion.

'Who would join us?'

'The Spaniard might. Remember what he said after the fight.'

'That makes three,' said Brennus sadly. 'Against all of Rome.'

'The other *scissores* would probably come with him.'

'Take it easy,' frowned the Gaul. 'What you're talking about takes real planning.'

'Let's talk to Sextus then!'

'We'll end up dead if we do this.'

'Sure,' answered Romulus with a shrug. He threw caution to the wind. 'What's new about that? Might as well die free.'

Curious, Brennus looked up.

'If it fails, we can leave Italy. Like Spartacus was going to do. Go a long way away. Somewhere Rome has no influence.'

The Gaul's tanned face brightened, the words resonating within him. 'Now you're talking!' A spark lit in his eyes. 'Six years I have waited for the gods to give me a sign.' He got to his feet, clouting Romulus good-naturedly. 'And they've sent it through you!'

The young man was delighted by his friend's response. 'It's been too long since I smelt the wind, hunted in the forest.' Brennus grew even more animated. 'Let's find the *scissores.*'

'Tomorrow,' cautioned Romulus. 'Memor is going to the slave market for new fighters then.' The school's losses would be easily replaced and the knowledge angered him even more.

'Good.'

Romulus nodded grimly. Perhaps now they could start to recruit men who felt the same way.

'This has given me a real thirst. Why don't we get out of the *ludus* tonight?' Brennus nudged Romulus. 'I'll show you my favourite haunts.'

'We've been confined to quarters. It's not worth the risk.'

'Come on. We deserve it!'

'Why not have some wine here?'

'I'm sick of it.' The Gaul banged on the wall, knocking loose damp plaster.

Romulus could see that Brennus meant it. 'Doesn't Severus owe you a favour?' he asked. The grey-haired guard had been a formidable gladiator in his day, but was now more interested in gambling.

'That old drunk?' Brennus stopped pacing up and down. 'Suppose he does. I've helped him pay off the moneylenders often enough.'

'He's on duty at the gate most nights.'

'Asked me for three thousand *sestertii* yesterday. Took a bashing on chariot racing at the Circus Flaminius.' The Gaul smiled. 'Severus wouldn't dare tell Memor if we went out.'

'What if he checks the cell?' Romulus was still wary.

'No chance of that,' Brennus replied confidently. 'Memor doesn't leave his rooms after sunset.' The Gaul had cheered up immensely at the prospect of going out. 'We'll be back before dawn. Nobody will know a thing.'

'We can't get into any trouble.'

'All right. I won't crack any heads.'

'Promise me.'

'You have my word,' Brennus growled.

Drinks in one of the taverns the Gaul was always talking about appealed to Romulus too. If the serving girls were as his friend described, he could do with a grope of their flesh. Romulus' hormones had been raging for some time. The scantily clad prostitutes visiting the *ludus* recently had driven the teenager wild with lust. The temptation to spend his winnings had been strong, but sheer embarrassment at the lack of privacy had prevented him.

If Romulus was going to lose his virginity, it would be without others watching.

Chapter XVII: The Brawl

Late that night, they left the Thracians snoring in the cell. Creeping into the unlit training yard after Brennus, Romulus closed the door quietly. The *ludus* was silent. Gladiators rose early and went to bed by sunset.

The stars were partially obscured by clouds, affording little light as they padded across to the heavy iron gate that separated the school from the streets of Rome.

'Who's there?' The voice sounded scared. 'It's after hours!'

'Peace, Severus! It's me.'

'Brennus?' An overweight, middle-aged guard emerged from the shadows, hand ready on his sword hilt. 'What do you want at this hour?'

'Me and Romulus thought we'd go for a drink.'

'Now?'

'Never too late for wine, Severus.'

'Memor would cut my throat if he knew I was letting you out.'

'You owe me a few favours.'

The balding gladiator hesitated.

'Come now!' Brennus chuckled knowingly. 'What about the three thousand *sestertii* you asked for?'

Severus' face took on a hunted look. 'How long?'

'A few hours. We'll be back before you know it.'

Severus shuffled his feet.

Brennus went for the kill. 'Those moneylenders are ruthless,' he said. 'You don't want to piss them off.'

The guard quickly took a large bunch of iron keys from his belt and led them to the gate. Picking one, he placed it in the lock, turning with a practised wrist. The door opened without a sound and Romulus knew it must have been oiled.

'You'll have the money by tomorrow morning,' Brennus whispered as they slipped through.

'Just make sure you're back before dawn,' replied Severus. 'Or my life won't be worth living!'

Romulus shivered as the gate clicked shut with an air of finality. Hoping Memor was sound asleep, he warily followed his surefooted friend. Both were armed with swords and wearing dark-coloured *lacernae*.

A crescent moon added only the faintest illumination to the few stars visible. The light was reduced further by the three- and four-storey buildings around them. But in the Stygian gloom, Brennus seemed to have a sixth sense of where they were.

'It's so quiet!'

'Decent folk are all behind locked doors.'

An occasional burst of laughter from behind the blank wall of a house or tavern broke the silence as they trod the dirt of smaller streets. Shop fronts were boarded up, tenement doors barred, temples empty and dark. Mangy dogs lurked here and there, prowling for scraps. A few people scuttled by, eyes averted. Even the *collegia* thugs at each crossroads dared not trouble the Gaul and his companion: two large, obviously armed men.

'If anyone comes close, stare the bastard in the eyes,' said Brennus. 'Nobody out this late is up to any good.'

'Including us?'

The Gaul chuckled. 'Just be ready to fight at a moment's notice.'

Romulus checked his sword was loose in its scabbard. 'Why are there no watchmen?'

'The Senate has been talking about it for years, but they can never come to an agreement.'

A few moments later, Brennus ducked into a narrow alleyway. He turned, beckoning. 'Watch your step.'

Romulus sniffed distastefully. There was an unmistakable odour of human urine and faeces. Gingerly he picked his way after Brennus, trying not to stand in whatever was making the foul smell.

They soon reached a wooden door strengthened with thick iron strips. Music and the sound of men's voices were coming from within.

'Macro! Open up!' Brennus pounded on the timbers with a balled fist. 'Dying of thirst here!'

The din inside died down for a few moments. Brennus lifted his hand, about to demand entrance again when suddenly the door opened. The biggest man Romulus had ever seen stuck a bald head outside.

'How many fucking times have I told you, Brennus? Three quiet knocks.'

'I'm parched, Macro.'

'Don't care if this is the last tavern in Rome.' The doorman beckoned them inside. 'Keep it down the next time.'

'I'll remember.'

Macro sat back on a stool, still grumbling.

'Thank the gods that hulk wasn't sold to a *ludus*,' muttered Brennus. 'Can you imagine fighting him?'

Romulus shook his head. The idea of facing Macro in the arena was terrifying.

He soaked up the atmosphere as they picked their way between small wooden tables. It was the first tavern he had ever visited. Regularly placed rush torches guttered in wall brackets, shedding a dim light. The rough slab floor was covered with broken pottery, half-gnawed bones and spilt wine. A low hum of conversation filled the air.

Groups of off-duty legionaries packed the smoky room, dressed in calf-length brown tunics, belted at the waist. Heavily studded army sandals stuck out everywhere from under tables and benches. Other customers were a mixture of ordinary citizens, traders and lowlife. Some stared curiously at the new arrivals, but most continued drinking and roaring with laughter. A few sang out of tune or played *tesserae*. In one corner was a low stage, where a number of men sat playing musical instruments with varying degrees of skill. Light wrist chains marked them as slaves.

Romulus grinned with excitement. This was far better than being stuck in the *ludus*.

'Let's drink here. Best to be standing if there's trouble.'

Brennus slapped his hand on the wooden counter that ran the length of the back wall. 'Julia! Your finest red wine!'

'I've not seen my favourite gladiator for an age,' said the pretty, dark-haired girl behind the bar. 'Beginning to think you had been injured.'

Brennus laughed. 'The gods are still favouring me.'

She batted her eyelashes. 'Who's this handsome fellow?'

Romulus quickly looked at the floor, aware he had been eyeing Julia's breasts.

'This is Romulus.'

Julia's smile broadened. 'The one you told me about?'

Nodding, Brennus gripped his shoulder. 'Good friend of mine. He'll be a great fighter one day too.' He clouted Romulus on the back, almost flooring him.

'Pleased to meet you. Any friend of Brennus is a friend of mine.'

Romulus blushed bright red, tongue-tied. Apart from Astoria, virtually the only women he had encountered since arriving in the *ludus* were prostitutes.

'Going to keep us standing here?' Brennus had sensed his discomfort. 'Our mouths are bone dry.'

'Of course.' Swiftly Julia placed two wooden beakers in front of them. With a flourish, she produced a small amphora. 'Vintage Falernian! Kept just for you.'

'By Belenus!' Brennus beamed with pleasure. 'You are a marvel, girl.' He slapped down an *aureus*. 'Tell me when that's done. And take at least ten *sestertii* for yourself.'

'Bless you.' The gold coin vanished before Romulus could even blink. 'Call when you need another one.' The barmaid ducked through a low doorway to the cellar and was gone.

'She's beautiful.' Romulus' groin throbbed and he racked his brains for something clever to say the next time Julia appeared.

'Don't even think about it.' Brennus cracked open the wax seal and poured them both a generous measure. 'She belongs to the landlord. Macro gets paid extra to make sure nobody touches her.'

'Who's the owner?'

'Publius, son of Marcus Licinius Crassus. Who happens to be the richest man in Rome. Not someone to piss off.'

Romulus' ears pricked up. 'Crassus?' The sudden memory from his former existence was shocking. Life in the *ludus* left no time for reflection on the past. 'I've been in his house.'

'Really?' Brennus rolled a mouthful of wine round with obvious relish. 'When?'

'Gemellus sent me there once. Not long before I was sold.'

'What did you see?'

'Only the entrance hall. It was pretty amazing – solid marble floor, beautiful statues, you can imagine it. I saw a nobleman too, about your age.'

'Crassus is at least sixty,' mused Brennus. 'So it could have been Publius.'

'The doorman told me he had fought in the slave rebellion.'

'A slave like that under the same roof as the conqueror of Spartacus?' The Gaul lifted thick eyebrows. 'Not very likely.'

'He seemed genuine.'

'The best liars always do.'

'But he knew how it all started,' protested Romulus. 'And he got far too upset to be lying.'

Brennus seemed interested, so Romulus related Pertinax' tale, his own excitement rising in the telling.

'Stirring stuff.' The Gaul raised his cup in a silent toast. 'But look how it ended. Six thousand crucifixes on the Via Appia. That poor bastard stuck in Crassus' service. And us. In the Ludus Magnus.'

'It doesn't have to be like that! Men would follow you and Sextus to fight the Romans,' Romulus urged. 'Spartacus had an army of eighty thousand men at the end, all former slaves. It could work.'

The Gaul's eyes glinted. 'With Memor on the warpath, our life is only going to get harder,' he agreed. 'But this needs plenty of thought. We'll speak to Sextus, see how the land lies. Decide who else to involve.'

'Soon,' warned Romulus.

'I know,' Brennus said heavily, draining his beaker. 'So let's enjoy tonight.'

Pleased, Romulus nodded. He saw there was little point pressing his friend further. Brennus had taken his words on board.

The big gladiator glanced casually around the room.

'Expecting trouble?'

'Call it previous experience.' The Gaul cracked his knuckles. 'Something kicks off in here at least once a night.'

'No fighting, remember?'

'I know. We can just watch.'

Romulus copied Brennus, turning his back on the bar.

It wasn't long before they heard raised voices, as the result of a nearby *petteia* game went against someone's wishes. The carved wooden board flew into the air, scattering black and white stones everywhere. Conversation in the room ceased. Six legionaries, their faces flushed with drink, began pushing and shoving at each other across a table. Insults were traded and a couple of punches thrown before Macro swiftly intervened.

The doorman's approach was simple. He picked up two of the soldiers and cracked their heads together. Dropping the limp bodies like sacks of grain, Macro turned to face the men's companions, who rapidly sat down before suffering the same fate. Disturbance over, any customers watching took an immediate interest in the bottom of their wooden beakers. Macro waved a fist at the group and lumbered back to the door.

Gradually the noise level increased.

Romulus giggled, amused at how the quarrel had been settled and its effect on other drinkers. After three cups, the smooth red Falernian was beginning to taste like nectar. Reaching for the amphora again, he was shocked when Brennus' hand closed over his wrist.

'That's enough.'

'Why?' he asked truculently.

'You're drunk. And we're supposed to be avoiding trouble.'

'I can hold my drink.' Romulus was vaguely aware he was slurring.

'Really?' The Gaul's tone was stern. 'Where did you get the experience?'

There was no reply to the rebuke and Romulus fell into a sulky silence.

Gladiators were only allowed small quantities of wine with their food; served in the Roman tradition, it was heavily watered down. Brennus was used to quaffing the powerful beverage neat, but it was going straight to Romulus' head.

They stood without speaking for some time. Brennus drank more wine, keeping an eye out for trouble. Romulus took surreptitious peeps at Julia. To his embarrassment, the voluptuous slave caught him on several occasions.

Eventually she approached.

Romulus stared at her dumbly, lacking the courage to break the ice.

'What age are you?' Julia's manner was direct.

'Seventeen.' From the corner of his eye he saw Brennus glance over, but thankfully the Gaul did not give away the truth. 'Nearly.'

'So young for a gladiator. Only a year older than me.' Julia sighed. 'How did you end up in the Ludus Magnus?'

'Got sold after my master heard about me training with a sword.' A wave of guilt washed over Romulus, and he clenched his jaw. 'That wasn't so bad. I always wanted to learn how to fight. But the bastard said he would sell Fabiola as well. To a whorehouse.' He spat the last words.

'Fabiola?'

'My twin sister.'

'All that for using a weapon?' Julia clicked her tongue with sympathy. 'Must have been more to it.'

Suddenly Romulus remembered Gemellus' tantrums in the days leading up to his sale, the response when he had read Crassus' reply. Could Julia have a point? Perhaps it wasn't all his fault. The guilt eased slightly and he smiled.

'What about you?'

'Me?' Julia seemed surprised he should ask. 'Born a slave. Sold at twelve for my looks.' She shrugged. 'Should be grateful I wasn't sold to a brothel like your sister.'

'I'm very glad,' Romulus blurted.

'How sweet.' Julia smiled. 'Most men who come in here are only interested in one thing.'

Romulus swallowed hard, trying to stifle the lustful thoughts filling his mind.

'Where is she now?' Julia asked.

'Don't know. Haven't seen her or Mother since.'

'I've heard nothing about my family either.' Julia's face grew sad. 'Perhaps one day Publius will grant me manumission and I can find them.'

'Doesn't sound as if that's likely.'

'No,' she admitted. 'Publius is not a generous man. I need more money than I could ever save. Customers as generous as Brennus are rare.'

'I would buy your freedom,' he said on impulse. 'We get well paid in the *ludus*. Brennus makes a fortune!'

'Why do that?'

Romulus ignored the question. 'You shouldn't be a slave!'

'Neither should the thousands in the houses and workshops of Rome.'

'I like you,' risked Romulus.

'Thank you.' Julia reached out to touch his cheek. 'But save to buy your own freedom.'

Tentatively Romulus raised a hand to hers. It felt warm. To his delight, Julia did not stop him. He guided it down to the bar top and squeezed her palm. They stared at each other, the attraction immediate, strong.

'Don't want to interrupt,' muttered Brennus. 'But Macro has seen what you're up to.'

Romulus released his grip and spun to see the man mountain approaching fast. Julia moved off, responding to the call of a customer. She left a faint whiff of perfume behind.

'No touching the slave girl.' There was no mistaking the threat. The doorman's hand was already on his dagger hilt. 'Do it again and Brennus will be carrying you home in little pieces. Clear?'

Romulus nodded silently, unperturbed. He was too elated at Julia's response.

'She is off limits!' Macro poked a thick forefinger into his chest for emphasis. 'Remember that, *boy*.'

'What are all the soldiers doing here?' With a smoothness Romulus had never seen before, the Gaul intervened. 'Don't normally see them in the city.'

'Crassus' men.'

'Shouldn't they be in camp outside the walls?' To prevent attempts at seizing power, legionaries were still not allowed into the capital in large numbers.

'Senate granted a special dispensation. The general has raised an army. They're on leave till the morning and Publius promised cheap wine in here.' Macro jerked a thumb at the nearest group. 'Tomorrow they march for Brundisium, to take ship for Asia Minor.'

'Why go there?'

'What do you care?' The doorman seemed to have calmed down. He rubbed his shaven head idly, scanning the room for trouble. Finding none, Macro turned back to the Gaul. 'Heard some saying it will begin with an attack on Jerusalem.'

'Jerusalem!' Brennus' eyes lit up. 'Its temples have doors of beaten gold.' There was a Judaean *retiarius* in the *ludus* who told fantastic stories about his homeland.

Romulus wasn't really listening. He glanced towards Julia, who smiled radiantly. His mouth went dry with tension.

'Eh, Romulus?'

'What?' With a guilty start, he gaped at Brennus. 'What did you say?'

'Plundering Jerusalem doesn't sound like a bad idea.' The Gaul elbowed him none too gently.

'Can't hold his wine!' Macro had not noticed what had gone on. 'Keep him in line, Brennus.' With a deep belly laugh, the huge slave stalked back to the door.

'What are you doing?' hissed Brennus as soon as he was out of earshot. 'Staring like that? If that ox sees you again, you *will* regret it.'

'I want to get to know her,' Romulus protested. 'She's lovely.'

'Macro kills men who don't do what he says.'

Romulus was not going to be put off. 'What would you do if Memor took Astoria?'

Brennus was nonplussed. 'Not the same thing.'

'Why?' challenged Romulus. 'What if she had been Memor's bed companion before you saw her?'

'She wasn't. Good point, though.' Brennus grinned. 'Got something in mind?'

'I need to talk to her.' The barmaid had set Romulus' heart racing.

'Forgetting the slight problem of Macro?'

'That's where you come in.'

The Gaul raised an eyebrow.

'Just keep him occupied for a few moments,' pleaded Romulus, forgetting their decision to have a quiet night.

'I'm not fighting that monster,' laughed Brennus. 'I want to keep all my teeth.'

'So pick a fight with someone else.' Romulus indicated the room full of legionaries. 'I don't need long.'

'Your first time, then?'

He poked the Gaul in the ribs. 'Can you do it or not?'

Brennus smiled. 'I never say no to a good brawl. Beats killing men for a change. But make it quick. You saw Macro in action earlier.'

'Thank you.'

Romulus watched with fascination as Brennus decided whom to quarrel with. The big gladiator didn't take long to make up his mind. He winked at Romulus before sauntering over to a group of soldiers arguing loudly about a game of knucklebones.

'Can't agree, boys?' Brennus pointed amiably at the worn pieces of sheep tailbone lying on the tabletop.

'Piss off, barbarian!'

'Who asked you anyway?'

All four legionaries glared at him belligerently.

'Got two fives, a three and a one there.'

'Deaf too, scumbag?'

'Don't be like that,' said Brennus. 'Only being friendly.'

'We don't need any friends.' The biggest soldier, a stocky barrel of a man with a broken nose, pushed back his stool, screeching it off the stone floor. 'Dirty Gaulish bastard.'

'That's not very nice.'

'Oh no?' sneered the legionary.

His friends began to stand up.

'No.' With a heave, Brennus lifted the end of the table, sending everything flying. Bone playing pieces, wooden beakers and an amphora of wine flew up and two soldiers fell cursing to the floor.

Romulus didn't wait to see what happened next. Macro had noticed the brawl and his attention would be taken up until it was settled. He darted to where Julia was standing, lips pursed, her arms folded in clear disapproval.

'Brennus is only doing it to give us a moment.'

'What?' She looked embarrassed. 'Why do that?'

'I like you. Wanted another chance to talk.'

'You don't even know me, Romulus,' she said, flushing. It made her even more attractive. 'I'm not worth anything.'

'Don't say that. You are beautiful.'

'Nobody could want me after what Publius has done.' Julia's chin trembled and she rubbed at a red mark on her neck. It resembled an old burn.

Determination and a surging anger filled Romulus. 'I do,' he said urgently.

'Go, before Brennus gets hurt.'

Romulus risked a glance over his shoulder. The fight was far from over. Two soldiers lay unconscious on the floor, but Brennus was taking plenty of time with the others, keeping them between him and the circling doorman.

'He's fine,' Romulus said cheekily. 'When can I see you?'

At last she smiled, shyly. 'Only time would be when Macro is asleep.'

'When's that?'

'The tavern closes at dawn. Once he has thrown the last customer out and we've cleaned up, Macro goes upstairs for a few hours. I might be able to sneak out then.'

'How about tomorrow morning?' There was one rest day left at the *ludus*. Romulus knew the *lanista* would presume he was still lying low. 'I'll buy you breakfast in the market.'

Romulus had only been to the Forum Olitorium once or twice before, but his memories of cooking meat and exotic fruits there were still vivid. With the winnings from the fight, he could buy Julia anything she wanted. Astoria could give him some good advice before he left. Romulus was desperate to show the barmaid he was not a dull-witted fool like the men who frequented the inn.

Julia seemed scared for a moment. Then her face changed. 'Why not?' she said confidently. 'Sounds lovely!'

'See you in the alley at dawn!' Romulus leaned over the bar and kissed her. Instead of avoiding the contact,

Julia moved closer, lips softly parting before his. They stayed locked together, eyes closed, oblivious.

Then the crash of breaking furniture reached their ears.

Romulus pulled away reluctantly.

'The last soldier is down. Go, or Macro will tear Brennus apart!'

'Till dawn!' Romulus skipped from the bar with exhilaration. The four legionaries lay senseless nearby, surrounded by broken remnants of the stools and table. The Gaul was holding a wooden bench at arm's length, while his huge opponent swung violently at it with a spiked club. A circle of customers had formed around the fight. Men egged the pair on with cheers of encouragement.

'Get him, Macro!'

'Kill the dumb brute!'

'Show the Gaul who's in charge here!'

Romulus tore past. He could tell his friend was starting to enjoy himself.

'Let's go!'

Brennus came to his senses. He flung the long seat at the doorman and bolted for the exit. 'See you another time, Macro!'

Romulus had pushed his way through the jostling onlookers and was already pulling back iron bolts on the door. He took one last glance at Julia, who was watching him anxiously. Then he shot out into the street, the Gaul hot on his heels.

'That got the blood flowing, by Belenus!' Brennus yelled with sheer exuberance. 'How did you get on?'

'We kissed!' Romulus smiled in the darkness, the smell of Julia's perfume strong in his nostrils. 'And I'm meeting her tomorrow.'

'Glad to hear it.' Brennus peered over his shoulder. 'Keep going for a bit. Macro can't run too far.'

'Thank the gods!' said Romulus. 'I trod on some shit in the alleyway.'

'Smells like it!' Chuckling, the Gaul came to a halt. Light flickered from torches on the wall of a building nearby. 'That's about half a mile. Should be enough.'

'You've run from Macro before?' asked Romulus with surprise.

'Many times!'

Shaking his head, Romulus put a hand on Brennus' shoulder. 'So why does he keep letting you in?' he said, inspecting the soles of both sandals.

'I slip him a few *sestertii* now and then. Don't usually start the fights either.' Brennus' voice took on an injured tone. 'I'm a good customer!'

They both laughed, relieved at escaping unscathed. As the adrenalin rush subsided, Romulus took more notice of the nearby arched doorway. Torchlight profiled a giant painted penis jutting either side, clear evidence of what was on offer within. A small hooded and cloaked figure sat in the shadows a short distance from the entrance. Romulus presumed it to be a cripple waiting for alms.

'That a whorehouse?'

'Lupanar, they call it,' said Brennus. 'One of the best in Rome.'

'Tried it?'

'When I was feeling rich.'

A chill ran down Romulus' spine at the thought of Fabiola. 'Ever seen a girl similar to me?'

'Don't think so.' Brennus shrugged. 'But I was very drunk both times. Want to try it?'

'No!' Romulus felt sick. 'My sister could be in there!'

'She's not,' said Brennus reassuringly. 'Would have remembered a young girl with your looks.'

'I've had enough,' muttered Romulus. 'Let's go home.'

'Come on!' Brennus jingled his purse impetuously. 'There's enough here to buy us a good time.'

Romulus paused, remembering the half-naked prostitutes he had seen in the *ludus*.

'We'll just go inside and take a peek.' The Gaul pointed at the entrance. 'The girls are stunning!'

Romulus' groin throbbed. There would be privacy in such an expensive brothel and the chance of Fabiola being inside had to be remote.

Sensing his indecision, Brennus propelled him towards the door. They had almost reached it when a group of nobles clad in richly cut togas emerged, talking loudly. With automatic deference, the gladiators stood to one side, allowing their betters past.

Most did not even notice.

They had almost gone by when a stocky, redheaded man with a hard face stumbled into Romulus.

'Clumsy brute. Watch where you are going!' The middle-aged equestrian swayed gently, giving off a strong smell of wine. 'I used to have men crucified for less on my *latifundium*.'

'Sorry, Master,' said Romulus, cursing instantly at his involuntary admission.

The Gaul tensed, instinctively knowing this man could be more dangerous than many opponents in the arena.

'You are a *slave*?'

Romulus nodded, face completely blank.

'Hurry up, Caelius!' one of the party called out. 'The night is still young!'

'Just a moment.' He adjusted his toga. 'Guard! Get out here!'

'What are you doing, Master?' Romulus said warily.

'He will take you apart, *slave*. Teach you to respect your betters.'

Suddenly Brennus straightened, towering over the other. Cold eyes glinted in dim light, a vein bulged in his neck. 'Don't do that,' he said.

Tension became palpable.

'Another slave?' Caelius looked round for the doorman. 'What will *you* do?'

'I am no slave.'

Romulus was stunned by his friend's words. They meant instant death. His efforts to win the Gaul over had obviously taken seed. But now was not the time. Better to take a beating.

'What did you say?' Caelius spat.

Romulus had opened his mouth to speak when Brennus punched the angry noble in the belly. Caelius went down like a sack of lead, mouth open wide with shock.

Heart racing, Romulus moved closer. 'Let's go!' he hissed.

'What in Jupiter's name is going on?' A slave nearly as big as Macro appeared in the doorway. 'Who called?'

Caelius tried to speak, but a hefty kick from Brennus sent him sprawling deeper into the gutter.

'This fellow just bumped into me. Seems to have had too much wine,' Brennus said, smoothing down his tunic. 'We were coming to visit your beautiful ladies.'

Confused, the doorman gaped at Brennus, then at Caelius. Something did not quite fit.

'Wait a moment,' he growled. At last it sank in. 'You're a gladiator! That famous Gaul!'

'Come on,' urged Romulus. There was still time to flee.

'Caelius! Caelius!' The noble's friends had finally seen what was happening. They came running to his aid.

'Take those rogues into custody!' screeched one.

Brennus' blood was up. 'Know who I am?' he bellowed. 'Don't even think of touching me.'

The guard hesitated, but then the pretence failed. 'Party's over,' he said, reaching for the cudgel on his belt. 'You're a slave like me.'

'Seize him!' yelled an equestrian.

'Ignore those bastards. Let us go,' Romulus urged.

'Huh?' the doorman replied uncertainly. 'But . . .'

'What do you care about bloody patricians?'

'I have to obey.'

'Says who?' Romulus cried. 'Make your own choice!'

'Come on,' said Brennus. 'Join us!'

'Make a run for it!'

'I'd be killed.' Fear filled the slave's eyes and he drew the club. 'Just give in. With luck you'll only get a beating.'

Romulus' heart sank. The equestrians were nearly on

them, all chance of escape gone. Their night out was over.

'No one is laying a hand on me, by Belenus!' Brennus roared, the wine coursing through him. 'I am a free man!'

'What else can we do?' Romulus had meant to flee the scene, not fight. 'They're nobles.'

'Kill a few!'

'No, you idiot!' This was not how he saw things happening. Outside a brothel was no place to start a rebellion.

But it was too late.

Brennus grabbed the doorman by the tunic, delivering an almighty head-butt. With blood pumping from a smashed nose, the hulk reeled away in agony, clutching his face with both hands. The Gaul seized him by the shoulder and leather belt and, with a great heave, threw the man headlong back into the building.

'Turn around, slave!'

Romulus spun quickly.

Covered in mud, Caelius was only five paces away, dagger in hand. He was flanked by his friends, similarly armed.

'Thought patricians didn't carry weapons?' Romulus answered, anger rising. His *gladius* slid from the scabbard.

'They're useful for killing scum,' snarled Caelius, lunging forward.

Romulus dodged the drunken move easily as Brennus swept in from the left and poleaxed the equestrian for the third time.

'You were right,' the Gaul said to Romulus, grinning. 'Try not to kill any, or they'll crucify us for sure!'

Pleased by Brennus' restraint, he barely had time to nod. Caelius' companions attacked in a wave of swinging knives and flapping togas, but Romulus was less intoxicated than the nobles. It was easy to smash the hilt of his sword into the swarm of frenzied faces. He swept the blade's flat edge at any who came too close and they retreated, wary of his blade. Facing down six armed men was an exhilarating feeling.

Romulus felt something pulling on his tunic. It was Caelius. Instinctively he cracked the patrician on the head, seeing him slump unconscious to the dirt from the corner of his eye.

He and Brennus held the group at bay for some time. They batted away drunken thrusts, laughing at how easy it was. Their enemies cursed and spat with rage, but were unable to get within knife range.

The stalemate was not to last. Attracted by the commotion, five slaves came charging out, swords and cudgels in hand. One was a bodyguard, but the rest looked like unfit kitchen workers. It seemed brothels did not need more than two professional doormen.

'Time to leave.' Brennus slammed one of the fatter men against the wall, then landed a punch in his solar plexus. He toppled to the ground with a groan.

'Fighting retreat, eh?' Finally the Gaul drew his longsword.

'About time,' Romulus snapped.

The pair moved closer, edging into the centre of the street, weapons held threateningly in front. 'Stay where you are!' roared Brennus. 'Next man who comes near gets gutted.'

The slaves held back, reluctant to risk injury or death in a fight that wasn't theirs. Three figures were already lying prone in the mud. Sensing the fight was lost, the nobles still standing made obscene gestures at the fighters.

'Run for it!' Brennus sheathed his sword. 'Back to the *ludus* damn quick.'

A cry from the brothel followed into the darkness.

'Murder!' A portly figure stooped over the redheaded man. 'They have killed Caelius!'

'An equestrian has been killed!'

'It was the boy! I saw him,' cried another. 'Send for the *lictor* and his guards!'

'Gods above,' Brennus wheezed. 'What have you done?'

'Me? Nothing,' yelled Romulus. 'You should have just let me take the beating.'

'Couldn't do that. I owe you, remember?'

'Thanks. But save it for when I really need you.'

'It was his arrogance!'

Romulus chuckled knowingly.

'And the wine,' admitted the Gaul. 'But you put the idea in my head.'

'Not the best way to start a rebellion, Brennus.'

His friend's face turned sheepish. 'So what did you kill him for?'

'I didn't!' Romulus took one last despairing look at the chaos behind. 'Belted him across the head, but it wasn't enough to kill.'

'You must have cracked his skull then,' said Brennus. 'It is easily done.'

Inside the brothel, everyone had heard the racket. Fabiola was waiting in the anteroom beside reception when Vettius came flying through the door. He collided with a statue, bringing it to the floor with a crash. Alarmed, she ran out to find the doorman semi-conscious, blood pouring from his nose. Pieces of broken stone were scattered across the mosaic tiles. Clients stood by, looking horrified. The Lupanar was normally an island of calm in the dangerous city. A group of girls they had been eyeing up clung to each other nervously.

'Benignus!' Fabiola screeched. 'Get out here!'

'What's going on?' Jovina emerged from the corridor to the back, lips pursed.

'Don't know, Madam. Someone threw Vettius inside.' Fabiola risked a glance through the doorway. By the light of the torches, she could see two cloaked figures with swords fighting the men who had just left. 'Looks like thieves trying to rob those nobles.'

'Benignus!' Jovina spat a curse. 'Where is that brute?'

The second doorman appeared a few moments later, adjusting his tunic after a visit to relieve himself. 'Madam called?'

Jovina went bright red. 'My customers are being attacked out there. Get Catus and the others!'

Confused, Benignus finally took in Vettius lying prone, Fabiola kneeling close by and the clash of arms outside. He turned and sprinted down the corridor, yelling at the top of his voice.

'And some weapons!' Jovina darted over, bolting the door while they waited. She turned, smiling ingratiatingly at the shocked customers. 'Just a little altercation, gentlemen,' the madam purred. 'Your choice of girl is half-price tonight.'

Scared faces brightened. Soon the men had disappeared, lustful thoughts banishing all else from their minds.

Jovina paced up and down, waiting impatiently for the slaves.

Fabiola rolled a handkerchief, holding it firmly against Vettius' broken nose to stop the bleeding. The Greek surgeon would be able to straighten it later. Eventually his eyes opened, focusing slowly.

'What in Hades is going on?'

'Two slaves tried to come in,' Vettius mumbled. 'Attacked a noble just outside.'

'Slaves?' Fabiola said sharply. That was very unusual. 'Are you sure?'

The doorman nodded. 'Big bastard, one of them. That Gaulish gladiator.'

Benignus came tearing back, the rest on his heels. All were armed with knives, swords or cudgels. The kitchen slaves looked scared. Fighting was not part of their normal duties.

'What are you waiting for?' screamed Jovina. She pulled open the door. 'Get out there!'

The group tumbled outside, more fearful of their owner than of physical danger.

A few moments later, the sounds of clashing weapons ceased. They heard shouts as the robbers ran off, then silence. Abruptly an equestrian began screaming that murder had been done.

Jovina scowled. This night was not going well. Money had already been lost on discounts. Now someone was dead. Bad news like this travelled fast through the city. She peered into the street, checking it was safe, then ventured forth.

Fabiola followed her to the entrance.

Toga-clad figures lay in the dirt, one with a large red stain on his chest. Slaves stood by uncertainly while the surviving nobles roared after their assailants.

The madam took in the scene at a glance. 'Take three of these fools,' she said crisply to Benignus. 'Go to the Forum and bring the *lictor* and his men. Tell him that Rufus Caelius has been murdered.'

The doorman nodded with relief at the command. This situation was beyond his ability to deal with. He reached up and pulled a torch from the wall. Beckoning to the others, Benignus went off at a trot.

Fabiola watched with wide eyes, listening to the irate conversation. Such an attack was unheard of at the brothel and she felt a surge of pleasure at the thought. The equestrians had been arrogant in the extreme, especially the dead red-haired one. He had been very rough with her, almost to the point where she had to call for help. Caelius was no loss as far as Fabiola was concerned.

She sensed movement behind her. Vettius stood in the doorway, weaving slightly.

'You all right?'

He nodded, a strange look in his eyes.

'Vettius?'

332

'Funny thing. The second one was your spitting image.'

Fabiola's stomach turned over. *Romulus!* Joy surged through her at the realisation that her twin was alive. She muttered a swift prayer of thanks to Jupiter. Aware that she must give nothing away, Fabiola instantly spun back to see what the madam was doing. Jovina had an uncanny ability to hear the quietest whisper. Thankfully she was out of earshot, busy trying to placate the nobles.

'Got sold to a gladiator school, didn't he?'

She nodded, emotion welling up at the vivid memory.

'Strong looking type too,' said the doorman, rubbing his nose and wincing. 'Tried to get me to join 'em.'

Pride mixed with grief. Her brother had survived more than a year in the arena. He would be a man by now, with many victories under his belt. People might know who Romulus was at last. She would be able to find out which *ludus* he was in. 'Not a word about this,' she hissed, eyes flashing. 'Or his friend.'

Vettius swallowed. 'Course not,' he said. 'But the others recognised the Gaul too.'

Distraught, Fabiola stared into the darkness. The killing of a noble by a gladiator was an outrage and no effort would be spared to find the man responsible. The *lictores* would soon extract the same information from every witness. Legal evidence from slaves was inadmissible unless obtained by torture and the eunuchs Nepos and Tancinus would bleat like lambs. That meant returning to their school would provide no safety for Romulus and his companion. And even if the pair escaped from the city, they would still be fugitives from justice.

Whatever small chance there had been of finding her brother was completely gone.

Fabiola's spirits fell into the abyss.

They could hear shutters opening above as people woken by the racket looked out.

'What's going on?' a voice called.

Ignoring the shout, they sprinted round a corner, on to a street that Romulus finally recognised.

'Slow down,' the Gaul muttered, breathing heavily. 'Be no pursuit until reinforcements arrive.'

Romulus had been thinking hard. 'Nobody back there knows us,' he said, smiling.

'We are in deep shit.' Brennus seemed not to have heard. 'Nothing for it,' he muttered. 'We must flee. Right now.'

Romulus was confused. 'Leave?'

'Be crucified before sunset if we don't.' Brennus sounded unusually serious.

'Why?'

'The halfwit doorman recognised me! As a gladiator,' replied Brennus. 'How many Gauls my size are there in Rome?'

Romulus felt his life slipping completely out of control. 'I only used the hilt of my sword,' he said faintly. 'I'm sorry.'

'It is done.' There was sadness in Brennus' eyes, but his gaze did not waver. 'By dawn, there will be soldiers searching every school in the city. Find me and they have you. Our time in Rome is over.'

Romulus heard the truth in his friend's words but did

not want to believe it. There would be no slave rebellion. No meeting with Julia.

There was silence before Brennus spoke again.

'Those patrician bastards will kill us both very slowly while listening to our screams of innocence. Seen it too many times before. I'm not waiting for that.' He turned and strode towards the *ludus*.

'Stop!' Romulus hissed. 'What are you going to do?'

'Say goodbye to Astoria and pick up some weapons.' Brennus' teeth flashed white in the semi-darkness. He was exhilarated at the prospect of his journey beginning once again. 'Then I'm heading for Brundisium. Nobody will know me there and I can enlist in Crassus' army. Coming, brother?'

Romulus hesitated, but for the briefest of moments. His one chance of survival was to stick with Brennus. He followed the Gaul through the early morning light to the Ludus Magnus, wondering if he would ever return. If he would ever see Julia again.

Chapter XVIII: Flight

Southern Italy, autumn 55 BC

Abandoning their life in Rome on the spot, the friends crept out of the city's gates at dawn. They first passed south along the Via Appia, between the large tombs where the wealthy were buried. Few of the area's population of cut-price whores and thieves were awake to see them go by. Aware that their appearance would draw attention, they cut into the fields as soon as it was full light. Two heavily armed men who were not legionaries would mean bandits or runaway slaves to most citizens and so the whole journey was made across country, usually in the early mornings or late afternoons. Romulus and Brennus wanted to meet no one and avoided farmhouses and towns at all costs.

A quick raid on the *ludus'* kitchen before leaving provided bread, cheese and vegetables to last several days. Brennus took his bow as well as other weapons, allowing him to hunt for deer and boar as they travelled. Both men carried leather water bags which they filled regularly from streams. The cold weather meant that sleeping rough each night was not easy, but huddling in blankets under rough shelters, the clear sky above them glittering with thousands of stars, was better than crucifixion.

Latifundia, massive estates owned by the rich, dotted Campania and Apulia, the regions south of Rome. Romulus was amazed by the fields and hillsides covered in wheat, vines, olive and fruit trees. At night the groves supplied them with apples, plums and pears, juicy food that the young man had rarely tasted before. In daylight, impotent rage filled Romulus as he spied the countless miserable slaves working the farms, their ankles manacled together. Supervisors stood over each group, their whips ready to use at the slightest opportunity.

Every estate was the same.

Romulus quickly realised that the whole country ran on slave labour. No wonder Rome was so wealthy, when tens of thousands of its subjects had to work for nothing. The two friends had endless debates as they marched, Romulus imagining that they had killed Memor and started a second slave rebellion instead of ruining it all by visiting Publius' tavern. He still had very mixed feelings about that night. Because they had gone out, he had met Julia. Although he knew it was only an infatuation, the thought of her still made his heart flutter. The feeling was mixed with guilt at what might have been. If they had refrained from going out, perhaps they would have been marching past those very *latifundia* by now, freeing the slaves instead of skulking past like animals.

Brennus had not grasped the extent of the Republic's

captive population before either, and was similarly outraged. On their journey he observed workers of every race and creed under the sun. Rome's appetite for slaves was insatiable, fed purely by war, and the annihilation of the Allobroges was obviously far from unique. To end up on Italian *latifundia*, those he saw must have suffered as he had done. It was abhorrent to him, but Brennus felt powerless to change things. He was no Spartacus. A warrior, yes. Not a general. He had been feeling guilty about not escaping the *ludus* sooner, but that was ebbing now. Maybe their rebellion would have succeeded. But more probably it wouldn't have. And how could Ultan's words have made any sense if he was fighting battles up and down the peninsula?

A journey beyond where any Allobroge has gone. The phrase had become Brennus' mantra; everything else paled before it. It was only by seeing the druid's prophecy fulfilled that he could imagine justifying his decision to flee, rather than to defend, his village six years before.

The two friends covered nearly three hundred miles in less than twenty days.

There had been plenty of time to brood.

Seeing the slave population had increased both men's desire to discard all memories of their own captivity. Romulus' and Brennus' brands were permanent evidence of their status and discovery once they were in the army would mean instant crucifixion. After a quick discussion, they agreed that there could only be one solution. Having found a suitable grove in the hills above Brundisium, Brennus had lit a fire and sharpened his dagger until it could shave a man. Encouraging Romulus to bite down on a piece of wood, he had heated the blade over the flames before removing the hated letters 'LM' with a few deft cuts. Blood ran down Romulus' arm in little lines and dripped to the ground. His eyes bulging in pain, he watched as the Gaul closed the wound using a small iron needle and lengths of gut from an unravelled spare bowstring.

Brennus grinned. 'Might not be pretty, but it'll do. Keep it hidden for a while, and if anyone sees, you can say it was from a sword cut.'

The crude sutures would leave a rough scar, nothing like the neat work of the Greek surgeons in Rome who were paid by wealthy ex-slaves to remove their brands. Romulus didn't care. Memor's proof of ownership was gone for ever. But when he pulled out his own knife a moment later and reached for the Gaul's leg, Brennus stopped him.

'We can't both have a freshly stitched wound. Burn mine. Logs fall out of fires all the time.'

Romulus protested weakly, but he knew his friend was right. There was no mercy for escaped slaves. To avoid suspicion, they had to be different. He heated the dagger until the blade was glowing a dull red and then gritting his teeth, applied it to Brennus' calf. An instant smell of burning hair and flesh filled his nostrils.

The huge Gaul grimaced, allowing the searing pain to cleanse away some of the memories of slavery. 'We'll stay here for a while,' he announced with a smile. 'Lick our wounds and get some rest. Then we can go down to the port.'

His smile was infectious and Romulus grinned.

One last ordeal, but now they were truly free.

Brundisium's harbour was humming with activity. A large town, it had been transformed by the arrival of Crassus' army. Thousands of soldiers, tons of equipment and weapons filled the narrow jetties, waiting to embark for Asia Minor. The skyline was a forest of masts. Dozens of triremes rocked gently in the water, tied close together. Sailors swarmed back and forth, cursing the clumsiness of their passengers.

Mules brayed as they were forced down wooden gangways on to ships. Officers barked orders, pushing and shoving men into line. Messengers scurried between units, relaying orders.

Brennus and Romulus worked their way through the throng, searching for somewhere to join up. At length they found a makeshift desk of sacks of flour on the main dock. An old centurion was standing behind the temporary arrangement, bawling orders at new recruits.

He stared calculatingly at the dirty pair as they came to a halt.

'Farmers, eh?'

'That's right, sir.'

Romulus kept silent, taking in the *phalerae* hanging from the moulded leather breastplate and the silver torque round his neck. This was clearly a brave man.

'Well armed, aren't you?' He pointed at the heavy spears, the bow, swords and daggers, the well-made shields.

'We're from Transalpine Gaul, sir,' explained Brennus. 'The bandits are plentiful and we have to know how to fight.'

'Hmmm. Thought you were a Gaul.' The officer eyed Brennus' bulging muscles and the scars on his arms. 'Why come to Brundisium?'

'The great general is leading an army to Jerusalem. I'm told the booty will be good.'

'So all the new recruits say.' The centurion scratched short grey stubble, looking Brennus up and down shrewdly. 'You're not escaped slaves?'

'No, sir.' The Gaul kept a blank face, Romulus copying him. Aping the Roman military cut, both men had cut their hair short that morning.

'Slaves are forbidden to join the military under any circumstances. It is a crime punishable by death. Understand?'

'We are free men, sir.'

The officer grunted, considering the tally on the calf-skin parchment before him. 'And the lad?'

'Fights better than most grown men, sir.'

'Does he, by Jupiter?'

'Taught him myself, sir.'

'A bit young, but I suppose he's as big as most.' The centurion pushed forward a stylus. 'You enlist for three years minimum. Stay with the army for twenty and you'll be granted Roman citizenship. The pay is a hundred *denarii* per year in equal instalments every four months. Depending on the situation.'

'Situation, sir?' Romulus spoke for the first time, affecting Brennus' thick accent as best he could.

'If we're in the middle of a damn war, you don't get paid!'

'A hundred *denarii?*' Romulus turned to his friend

with disbelief. The purse from Pompey alone had contained five times that amount.

Brennus frowned.

The centurion laughed, misinterpreting the remark. 'A lot of money,' he said. 'Crassus' son Publius is a generous man. He wants the finest infantry to fight beside his cavalry.'

Romulus grinned vacuously as if he had only just understood. After all, they weren't joining Crassus' army for the wages.

'You provide your own clothes and weapons. Costs for equipment, food and the burial club get deducted from pay. And when I tell you to do something, do it fast! Otherwise you'll feel this across your backs.' He slapped a vine cane on the sacks of flour. 'I command the cohort, but I'm also your centurion! Clear?'

They nodded.

The officer tapped the parchment with a gnarled forefinger. 'Put your marks here.'

The pair exchanged a long glance. Once they joined, there was no going back. With a shrug, Brennus picked up the stylus in his huge hand and marked the document. Romulus followed suit.

'Good!' The centurion smiled briefly. 'I'm putting you both under my direct command. Names?'

'Brennus, sir. This is Romulus.'

'Romulus?' he said with interest. 'A good Italian name. Who was your father?'

'Roman legionary, sir.' Romulus couldn't think of anything else to say. 'Mother wanted to honour his memory.'

342

'There is a Roman look to you. Should have a warrior's mettle too.' He seemed pleased. 'Call me Senior Centurion Bassius. Wait over there with the rest of the cohort.'

'When do we set sail, Senior Centurion?'

'Tonight. The general's keen to start the campaign immediately.'

Romulus stared at Brundisium, now barely visible through the orange-yellow haze. It was nearly sunset, and the sea had changed from bright blue to a deep navy. A gentle breeze was propelling the Roman fleet away from shore. Other triremes could be made out in the failing light, companions to the one they had embarked on. Dozens of long wooden oars made a smooth sound as they moved in unison to cut the water's surface.

The *Achilles* was a typical low-slung Roman ship with a single cloth sail, three banks of oars and a bronze ram at the prow. The decks were bare except for the captain's cabin at the stern and catapults for attacking enemy ships.

'Good riddance!' Brennus spat over the timbers of the side. 'The bastards won't find us now.'

'When can we return to Italy?'

'A few years. Murder of a noble takes a while to be forgotten.'

Romulus scowled at that prospect. Thoughts of his family, Caelius and Julia had filled his mind on their march south, but he would have to put all such thoughts to one side. It would serve little purpose to spend his time worrying about situations that were now so completely out of his control.

'We should have stayed in the *ludus* that night.'

'Maybe we should.' Brennus looked east, his eyes distant. 'But the gods meant this to happen. I feel it in my bones.'

Romulus followed his gaze. The horizon was formed by the darkening sky's junction with the black sea, making it impossible to see where they met. Beyond lay the unknown, a world Romulus had thought he would never see. But anything seemed possible now.

He came back to the present with a shiver. 'What will happen to Astoria?'

The Gaul's face grew sad. 'Sextus has promised to protect her and if the gods are merciful, we will meet again. But I cannot avoid my destiny. We had no choice but to run and Astoria knows that.' Their farewell had been all too brief and when Brennus had tried to stay longer, the Nubian had kissed him softly and pushed him out the door. Astoria knew how much Ultan's words meant to her lover. *Follow your destiny*, she had whispered.

Brennus sighed heavily.

Romulus knew how he felt.

The consequences of the fight had been devastating for both. Brennus' life as a champion gladiator was over, his woman lost. Romulus was wanted for murder and both were fugitives from justice. Unless Astoria managed to get his message through, Julia would have presumed the worst of him for not showing up. Romulus' plans for a slave rebellion were dust, and although he was free it seemed even more unlikely that he would ever see his family again, let alone rescue them. Instead he was sailing into the east, a soldier in Crassus' army.

That meant Gemellus would go unpunished.

He scowled at the chance train of events that had led them to be sitting on *Achilles'* deck. If only they had not left the *ludus*. If only they had not stopped outside the Lupanar. If only he had not killed a noble.

But he had.

Romulus took a deep breath and let it out slowly. Like Brennus, he would have to place his trust in the gods. In Jupiter, Greatest and Best. He alone could alter the situation now.

'Reef the sail!' The second in command, an experienced *optio*, bellowed at the nearest crew. Roman ships never used sails at night, relying instead on the power of the oars.

The sailors obeyed rapidly, pulling on halyards that gathered the heavy cloth against the crossbar of the mast. When it had been furled to his satisfaction, the *optio* paced *Achilles'* sun-bleached deck, ensuring the catapults had been lashed down and all loose pieces of equipment tidied away.

Low thudding from the drum reached them through the timbers underfoot. Its speed determined how fast the oarsmen had to row. Driven by curiosity, Romulus had already explored the cramped soldiers' quarters on the armoury deck and the tiny, claustrophobic space under that, where two hundred men sat on banks of narrow wooden benches. He shuddered at the thought of permanent confinement in the hot, stale air breathed by so many others. Those on the oars were fed far more than the soldiers would receive daily, but that was little compensation in his opinion. Although the oarsmen were paid well, it was brutal, unremitting work, and if a trireme sank, there was a very real risk of drowning for all below the decks. It was not unheard of for ordinary slaves to be sent to the galleys either.

The freedom Romulus had begun to enjoy suddenly felt quite fragile.

'Nobody will find us, will they?' he whispered to Brennus.

Smiling, the Gaul threw a massive arm round his shoulders. 'We're in the legions now. As long as we can fight, no one gives a damn.'

Romulus glanced across at their new commander who was talking to a fellow centurion and the captain of *Achilles*. He had taken an instant liking to Bassius, whose composed manner was rubbing off on the new recruits. Few seemed to be warriors, but they appeared happy enough sitting on the gently moving deck. It was not surprising that the old officer had picked both him and Brennus for his unit. The two centuries on the trireme, one hundred and sixty men, were mostly Gaulish farmers, dressed in worn tunics and trousers and armed with an assortment of longswords, spears and daggers. The rest of Bassius' cohort he had seen embarking at the port were similar in appearance. The centurion's relaxed attitude to their status was more clear now. Apart from the sailors, the gladiators were almost the only warlike ones on board.

Crassus' need for thousands of mercenary soldiers had meant practically every able-bodied man who presented himself for service had been enlisted. Plenty of landless peasants were in search of employment, victims of Caesar's campaign in Gaul. Whole tribes had been displaced from their lands. News of the campaign must have reached a long way for these farmers to have journeyed to Brundisium.

It was warmer below and many men had chosen to sleep there rather than on the deck where the breeze off the sea blew strong and chill. Romulus and Brennus secured a sheltered spot in the stern and made themselves comfortable. They sat wrapped in woollen blankets, chewing on bread and cheese bought earlier in the bustling market near the harbour.

'Enjoy it.' Brennus shoved a piece into his mouth. 'Could be our last fresh food for a while. It'll be *bucellatum* and *acetum* from now on.'

'What?'

'Hard-tack biscuit – dry, miserable stuff, and sour wine.'

'We should be able to scavenge for supplies in Lydia, don't you think?'

Standing over them was a slightly built man with a thin face and long hair bleached blond by the sun. Gold winked from an earring in his right ear and a small crooked staff hung from one hand.

'Do you mind if I sit?' The stranger carried himself easily.

Brennus sized him up. 'Suit yourself,' he said, shifting over.

Romulus had not noticed the man before, who was of indeterminate age, somewhere between twenty-five and forty. His chest was protected by an unusual hide cuirass covered in linked bronze rings and he wore a short leather-bordered skirt similar to those worn by centurions. A vicious-looking double-headed battleaxe hung from his back by a short strap. Dangling from a narrow belt was a little pouch and on the deck by his feet sat a well used leather pack.

'Have you just joined?'

'What's it to you?' Romulus did not yet feel safe.

The stranger unslung his axe and sat down with a sigh. Reaching into the bag, he pulled out a large piece of dried pork and cut off a few slices with a sharp dagger. 'Care for some?'

The Gaul's eyes lit up. 'Thanks. Don't mind if I do. I'm Brennus and this is Romulus.'

'Tarquinius is my name.'

Romulus proffered a piece of cheese and the newcomer accepted it with a nod.

Brennus pointed at the iron blades of Tarquinius' axe. 'Mean looking weapon.'

'It has its uses,' he replied, rubbing his hand along the wooden shaft with a smile. 'And I'll wager you can handle yourself in a tight spot.'

'I can if I have to!' Brennus slapped the longsword he had taken from the *ludus* and all three laughed.

There was silence as they ate. The sun had set, leaving a thin red line along the horizon to mark its passage. Soon it would be completely dark and overhead the sky was filling with stars.

'There will be terrible storms on the voyage,' said Tarquinius suddenly. 'Twelve ships will be lost, but this one will be safe.'

They both stared at him with shock.

'How can you tell?' asked Romulus nervously.

'It is written in the stars.' His voice was deep and sonorous, almost musical.

He talks like Ultan, thought Brennus.

The breeze strengthened for a moment and Romulus shivered. 'You are a soothsayer?'

'Something like that.' He paused. 'But I can fight too.'

Romulus didn't doubt that. 'Where are you from?'

'Etruria.' There was a faraway look in Tarquinius' eyes. 'North of Rome.'

'A citizen?' Brennus said quickly. 'Why aren't you in a regular legion?'

Tarquinius gazed into his eyes and smiled. 'What are two runaway slaves doing in the army as mercenaries?'

'Keep your voice down!' hissed the big gladiator.

The Etruscan raised an eyebrow.

'We're no slaves,' Brennus muttered.

'Then why has the young man got such a fresh wound on his upper arm?' Tarquinius responded. 'Just where a brand should be.'

Romulus guiltily pulled down his sleeve, but it was too late. Lying down had let the rough fabric of his jerkin ride up his arm, revealing the telltale stitching. 'We got waylaid on our journey,' he muttered. 'The roads are dangerous, especially at night.'

Fortunately no one else seemed to be paying attention. Other soldiers were busy settling down for the night.

Again Tarquinius raised an eyebrow. 'And I thought you were gladiators.'

Their shocked faces told him everything.

'I am . . . was . . . the best fighter in Rome! Bought our freedom with my winnings,' blustered Brennus.

'If you say so.' Tarquinius fingered the gold ring that hung from a chain round his neck. It was decorated with a scarab beetle. 'Nothing to do with the death of a noble, then?' *Olenus has been avenged*, he thought with satisfaction.

They both stiffened.

How can he know about that? thought Romulus with alarm. *He wasn't there.*

There was silence as the Gaul laid a hand on his sword. 'No,' he said stonily.

Tarquinius did not react to the obvious lie. 'I myself have no wish to be known as an Etruscan. I joined the cohort as a Greek.'

'What are you running from?'

'We all have something to hide.' He smiled. 'Let's say that, like you, I had to leave Italy in a hurry.'

They relaxed slightly.

'You speak Greek?' asked Romulus.

'And many other languages.'

'Why are you telling us all this?' Romulus self-consciously rubbed his wound, which would have to remain hidden until it had fully healed.

'Simple. You both look like fighters. More than I can say for those sorry-looking bastards.' Tarquinius jerked his head dismissively behind him. The Gauls were definitely farmers rather than warriors.

Brennus gave them an appraising glance. 'Bassius will knock them into shape. I've seen worse specimens turned into good soldiers.'

'Perhaps. You are the warrior.' Tarquinius reached into the satchel again and produced a small amphora. Pulling the cork with his teeth, he offered it to Brennus.

The Gaul did not accept.

'Don't trust me?' Tarquinius barked with amusement and took a deep swallow before offering it again. 'We have a long journey and many battles lie ahead. Why would I offer you poison?'

'I apologise. I've spent too many years in the *ludus*,' said Brennus, taking the wine. 'You have shared food and drink and I have only been rude in response.' He held out his right hand.

The Etruscan gripped it with a smile and the slight tension that had been present since he introduced himself disappeared.

'And you, Romulus?' The soothsayer's eyes danced. 'Would you be friends also?'

Romulus chose what he said with care. 'I will be your friend if you will be mine.'

'Wise words from one so young!' Tarquinius threw back his head and laughed again, drawing the attention of the nearest Gauls.

They clasped forearms.

For some time, the three sat enjoying Tarquinius' wine, talking about what they might find in Asia Minor. As the air cooled, the other recruits curled up and slept in wool blankets. To Romulus' delight, the Etruscan was full of knowledge about their destination.

'Very hot, I can tell you.'

'Worse than Rome in the summer?'

'Like a baker's oven during Saturnalia. And nothing but sand and rocks as far as you can see.'

'Still better than a crucifix on the Campus Martius,' interjected Brennus.

'True,' replied Tarquinius. 'But Mesopotamia will be like Hades itself.'

'I thought we were going to Jerusalem.'

Tarquinius lowered his voice. 'Not many know it yet, but our general is set on invading the Parthian empire.'

Romulus and Brennus looked at him blankly.

'The Parthians live in the Mesopotamian desert east of Judaea,' explained Tarquinius. 'Beyond the River Euphrates.' Quickly he outlined the geography of the region to them.

Intrigued, Romulus soaked up the information.

'Go on.' Brennus was also interested.

'Rome has been at peace with Parthia for some years, but Crassus intends to change that.'

'How can you know this?' asked the Gaul.

'Before enlisting, I sacrificed a lamb to Tinia. The Romans call him Jupiter,' replied the Etruscan. 'And the liver clearly showed a campaign into Parthia.'

Brennus became less scornful. Ultan had been able to read the future from animals' organs and had accurately predicted many things – including his own tribe's annihilation. He shivered, remembering the druid's last words to him. 'Why, though?' he asked.

'Simple! Seleucia, the Parthian capital, is wealthy beyond compare.'

'But Crassus is already the richest man in Rome,' said Romulus. He had seen the evidence with his own eyes.

'Money is not the only thing driving Crassus. He's tired of Pompey and Caesar's successes. A successful military campaign is the only way to reclaim some glory.' The Etruscan chuckled in the darkness. 'Popularity with the people. Power over the Senate and equestrian class. That is all that matters in Rome.'

Up till then Romulus had been vaguely aware of the politics and intense rivalry between the members of the ruling classes, but as a slave it had affected him little. Life had been a constant battle for survival, affording him no time to ponder deeper meanings and who controlled what. But Tarquinius' words made perfect sense – the nobility were in control of the campaign, just like the gladiator contests they had left behind.

It did not feel right. He had thought they were free.

'So this is just another Roman invasion.' There was palpable anger in Brennus' voice. 'Will they never be satisfied?'

'Only when they have conquered the world,' Tarquinius replied.

The big man stared up at the stars, brooding.

'Nearly four centuries have passed since my people were vanquished. Yet I still grieve,' Tarquinius whispered. 'Just as you must about the passing of your tribe.'

Brennus' face filled with anger.

The Etruscan raised both hands, palms extended. 'I was passing through Transalpine Gaul a while back. Heard about the Allobroges' final battle. They said that thousands of Romans had been killed.'

Pride flared in Brennus' eyes. 'What makes you think I'm an Allobroge?'

Tarquinius smiled. 'Not much. The pigtails you had till very recently. The longsword. The way you talk.'

The Gaul laughed and Romulus relaxed.

The ship's timbers creaked gently as it moved through the water.

Romulus had rarely considered how the Romans were responsible for the suffering of other peoples. Now, seeing the emotion on Brennus' face, the truth hit him hard. The dozen races of fighters in the *ludus* had been there only because of the Republic's belligerent tendencies. Like Tarquinius and Brennus, their tribes had been massacred for their wealth and land. Rome was a state based on war and slavery. Romulus suddenly felt ashamed of his blood.

'Some races are destined to be greater than others and they will stop at nothing to achieve it. Such are the Romans,' said Tarquinius, reading his mind. 'That doesn't make you personally responsible for their actions.'

Romulus sighed, remembering Gemellus' rants about the founding principles of the Republic having long been subverted. All that seemed to matter now was for nobles such as Pompey, Caesar and Crassus to retain power, using the blood of ordinary men and slaves to make them rich. It was a chilling realisation. Romulus swore silently that once the campaign was over, he would never again submit to the Roman system.

'What happens is pre-ordained. When it was time, Etruria fell. Now Rome's influence is growing.'

'Nothing happens by chance?' asked Romulus.

'Nothing,' answered Tarquinius confidently. 'Not even you and your sister being sold. Not this journey. Or your future.'

The hairs on Romulus' neck rose. 'How can you know about Fabiola?'

But the Etruscan was in full flow. 'And all the while, the world keeps turning. We are just swept along with it.'

'Every fool knows that the world is flat!' interjected Brennus.

'No. You know much, but the world is round, not flat. That is how we can travel around it without falling off.'

The Gaul was taken aback. 'Where does this knowledge come from?'

'I spent years of my childhood under a great master, Olenus Aesar.' Tarquinius bowed his head.

Satisfied, Brennus nodded respectfully. The secrets of druidic lore had also been taught to Ultan by his predecessor. Perhaps Tarquinius would be able to shed some light on the old man's prophecy?

'I want to learn things like that,' said Romulus eagerly.

'It will all be revealed.' The Etruscan lay down, stretching out his legs on the deck. 'Can you read and write?'

Romulus hesitated. 'No,' he admitted.

'I will teach you.'

He burned to ask more questions, but Tarquinius had turned away to gaze at the night sky. Romulus lay back on his blanket, enjoying the movement of cool air across his skin. Their new friend's revelations had been incredible. Nobody on *Achilles* had met either of them before today, yet Tarquinius had known about both Fabiola and the Gaul's tribe. And what had happened outside the brothel. Clearly full of mystical ability, the Etruscan could also read and write. These were rare talents.

Being taught to use a stylus would be Romulus' first

step towards real freedom. His doubts about leaving Italy began to dissipate. With two friends like Brennus and Tarquinius, there could be little to worry about.

The Gaul was snoring loudly in the darkness, oblivious. The noise kept Romulus awake for some time.

'Tarquinius?' he whispered, still eager to talk.

'What is it?'

'You know where Brennus and I came from. Our backgrounds.' How I killed Caelius, he thought with a shiver.

'Much of it.'

'So tell me what you are hiding.' Though it was dark Romulus could feel the Etruscan's gaze.

'One day. Not now.'

Curiosity filled him, but there had been an air of finality to Tarquinius' response. Romulus closed his eyes and fell asleep.

Several days into the voyage, the fleet was hit by a powerful storm that sank a dozen triremes and scattered the rest far and wide. Hundreds of legionaries and sailors were drowned, but the *Achilles* did not suffer as much as a scratch to her timbers. Tarquinius said nothing but Brennus began looking at their new friend with awe. Used to tales of rogue soothsayers in the temples, Romulus was less sure. It was autumn, after all.

Whatever the reason for the bad weather, it was an inauspicious start to Crassus' campaign, and rumours of bad luck began to pass between the vessels. Tarquinius did not seem perturbed by these, which seemed to relieve Brennus. But nothing further occurred to worry the superstitious soldiers and Romulus soon forgot about the Etruscan's predictions.

The fleet sailed on, past hundreds of islands forming the coastline of Greece. Seaworthy enough to venture into open water for no more than two or three days, the ships stayed close to shore. The Romans' skill at land warfare did not extend to shipbuilding. Triremes were built to sail along Republican-controlled coasts, keeping the peace – the *pax Romana*.

Every sunset the flotilla dropped anchor, allowing the exhausted oarsmen time to rest. Armed parties were sent ashore to fill water barrels from rivers and streams. The food was just as Brennus predicted – hard tack and sour wine. Few of the new soldiers complained. They were happy just to be fed twice daily.

On a number of occasions, Romulus saw entire beaches covered in the burnt skeletons of ship frames, evidence of the Cilicians crushed by Pompey. The ferocious pirates had preyed on shipping for decades, costing Rome a fortune in lost trade. After a short pursuit around the eastern Mediterranean, Pompey had cornered the renegades ten years previously and crushed them. It had been a hugely popular victory for him.

A few raiders had returned to the area since, but they did not dare attack the vastly superior force. One day Romulus and his companions saw a group of sleek, dangerous looking vessels in the mouth of a small inlet only a few hundred paces away. Dark-skinned men stood watching fearfully from their decks.

But there would be no battle, as Crassus' captains were under strict orders not to delay.

Brennus raised his longsword and beckoned. 'Come and fight!'

'They prey on the weak,' Tarquinius observed. 'Not a fleet with thousands of soldiers.'

'It's been too long since I had a bout!'

The Etruscan turned his gaze back to the pirates.

'There'll be all the fighting you need very soon.' Bassius had heard the outburst and stepped in, thinking he was preventing a quarrel. 'Quieten down.'

'Yes, sir.' The Gaul's face dropped.

'Come on, Brennus.' By now, Romulus knew the tempering effect he had on his friend. 'Show me those moves you were talking about. That all right, Senior Centurion?'

Bassius knew the journey was boring two of his best soldiers. 'I want no injuries,' he said gruffly. 'Cover your weapons.'

The pair hurried to obey. Realising there was going to be some action, the recruits quickly formed a circle on the deck. Brennus and Romulus practised every morning and by now everyone had deduced that they were trained fighters. Both men had already spent time helping Bassius teach the more eager ones some basic techniques.

Brennus crouched down, scowling ferociously. 'Let's take some wind out of your sails.'

Romulus pointed at the Gaul's belly. 'Getting fat with all this lying about!'

Laughing, the big warrior raised his longsword, its lethal edge now covered in leather.

Romulus moved towards him slowly, bare feet sure on the hot deck.

Watching Brennus and his young protégé spar, Tarquinius smiled. It had been many years since he trusted anyone, but the pair of runaways were becoming good friends.

Olenus' words had returned to him many times since their meeting. *A voyage to Lydia by ship. There two gladiators become your friends.* 'You were wrong, Olenus. For once,' the Etruscan whispered wryly. 'I met them on the way. Not when I got there.'

Having sailed hundreds of miles from the heel of Italy to the shores of Asia Minor, Crassus' triremes finally entered a wide, shallow uninhabited bay, filling it from one end to another. A long beach lined the sea's edge. The ground above was a less welcoming burnt ochre. The sun hung in a bright blue windless sky, casting intense heat on sunburnt soldiers and sailors. In the crystal clear water below the *Achilles,* Romulus could see fish swimming round the large stone anchor.

A protective cordon of legionaries was sent ashore to ensure the force landed without danger of attack. Then organised chaos reigned for two days as the army disembarked, carrying tons of equipment and food off by hand. Only the mules, braying and angry as ever, swam to the beach of their own accord.

Bassius' irregulars had to wade in through chest-high water. Unable to swim, Romulus, Brennus and the others pushed uneasily towards the land while Tarquinius swam confidently around them, laughing. Emerging on to the sand, the Etruscan swept back his long hair, drying it with his hands. As he did, Romulus noticed a red triangular mark on the side of his neck.

Quickly Tarquinius let his blond locks fall back into place.

'What's that?'

'Just a birthmark.'

'It's an unusual shape.'

Ignoring him, Tarquinius crouched down, sorting through the items he had placed in a pig's bladder before they jumped off the *Achilles'* deck.

Curiosity filled Romulus, but he got no chance to ask. Bassius was already roaring at them, keen to get his men into marching order.

Crassus supervised the operation from higher ground above the shoreline. An enormous pavilion had been erected, allowing the general every comfort while the soldiers toiled in baking temperatures below. Filled with carpets, tables, beds and partitioned rooms, the leather tent would serve as his command centre for the duration of the campaign. There were even a number of prostitutes, brought by his son Publius to pleasure senior officers.

A red flag – the *vexillum* – hung limply from a pole embedded in the ground. It showed every soldier Crassus' position. Hand-picked legionaries stood guard day and night, while messengers and trumpeters were positioned nearby to relay orders.

Bassius commanded one cohort – six centuries – of irregulars. Ten cohorts had been formed to fight with the regulars and the old centurion's unit had been attached to the Sixth Legion. Once all the men were on dry land, Bassius bellowed and screamed to get them across the sand to their position. The Sixth was already waiting, each well drilled cohort ranked behind the next.

'Move it!' Bassius was unimpressed at the sloppiness of his four hundred and eighty recruits. He and the other centurions had been training them on board, but it was not yet enough. 'By Jupiter, the real soldiers are laughing at us!'

Trumpets sounded once the mercenaries were in place and the front ranks moved forward, following the regulars. Four legions had landed on the same beach weeks before, erecting vast temporary camps some distance inland. The Sixth had not marched for long before reaching them. The playing-card-shaped forts consisted of earthen ramparts the height of a man. Soil used in the construction came from deep trenches that ran round the perimeter. Sentries stood guard in tall wooden watchtowers on the corners. Only one entrance broke the middle of each side. Two straight roads connected the four gates, cutting the camp into equal parts. The legion's headquarters were situated at their intersection and around this every century had an allocated position which never varied.

More commands blared from the *bucinae*. Swiftly half the legion fanned out in a screen around the rest.

'Time for some real work,' Bassius shouted. 'Lay down all equipment except weapons and shovels.'

The senior centurion knew what he was doing. Leading them to a section of what would be the perimeter, he liaised briefly with a regular officer. Soon Bassius' men were sweating and cursing as they dug.

Romulus had seldom seen such industry as he watched

the legionaries nearby digging ditches and ramparts, hundreds of figures working in unison. It seemed soldiers of the Republic were not just fighters, but labourers and engineers as well.

Romulus' pride at being Roman began to return despite the fact that both of his friends' peoples had been crushed by its might. It was hard not to be stirred by the precision and discipline shown by Crassus' army. Every single man seemed to know exactly what to do. Three hours later, line upon line of tents went up in orderly fashion inside the new ramparts' protection. Each century took its place, marked by a unique cloth standard. Bassius positioned the mercenaries beside Publius' cavalry.

On the *Achilles*, they had been issued with a large leather tent used by regular legionaries but it had not been needed until now. Bassius had seemed content that Romulus, Brennus and Tarquinius should serve in the same *contubernium*, a group of eight men who lived and cooked together. The friends had got to know their five comrades on the voyage. Varro, Genucius and Felix were dour peasants from Cisalpine Gaul, driven from their land by the Romans. Joseph and Appius were short, wily men from Egypt, exiled for crimes they would only hint at.

They had not been relaxing round their tents for long when Bassius asked permission of one of the tribunes to start training his cohort. The veteran had had enough of twiddling his thumbs. Flanked by the five other centurions, Bassius stood with hands on hips, glaring at the sweating mercenaries.

'Time to start some proper military training. You've had long enough sitting on your arses.'

Most soldiers looked unhappy but Brennus rubbed his hands with glee.

'Form up! Attention!'

The irregulars quickly shuffled into rank, staring ahead as they had been taught.

'Stand up!' Bassius stalked between the lines, straightening backs, tapping chins with his vine cane. 'Pretend to have spines, even if you haven't!'

At last the old centurion was satisfied and, directing a number of men to carry with them heavy wooden stakes procured from the quartermaster, Bassius led the cohort out of the busy camp, on to the flat ground in front.

Other centurions had similar ideas. The area was full of irregulars running, jumping and sparring with each other. After long weeks at sea, the officers of Crassus' army knew they had to get the men quickly into shape. It would be two months before the whole host was ready to march to the east, a short time to turn farmers into trained soldiers.

'Looks like some time at the *palus* again!'

'Gods above!' laughed Brennus. 'As if we need that. A good run would be more like it.'

Once the stakes had been hammered into the iron-hard ground, Bassius and his comrades began to instruct groups of recruits in basic weapons training. Romulus and his friends only had to cut and thrust at the *palus* once or twice before Bassius judged them hugely experienced. The three stood watching as the bemused Gauls were put through their paces. The veteran had obtained training equipment, wooden swords and wicker shields twice as heavy as the real thing and he worked the sweating men hard. It was the same method taught in gladiator school.

'What do you think you're doing?' Bassius roared at the trio a few moments later. 'No standing around! Four laps of the perimeter. At the trot!'

Romulus stayed beside the grinning Gaul as they ran along the defensive trench around the camp.

Brennus began loosening his shoulders. 'Just what we need,' he said.

Tarquinius remained silent, observing the legions as they moved into position. Romulus could hear him muttering.

'Crassus has too many infantry. Fool!'

'What's wrong?'

'Look.' The Etruscan pointed out the thousands of legionaries training in the hot sun. 'No horsemen.'

Romulus found it hard not to be stirred by the magnificent sight of so many soldiers moving in unison but his eyes narrowed as he saw what Tarquinius meant. The ancient battles mentioned by Cotta had involved large numbers of cavalry. They were a vital part of any army.

'All I have seen are the Gauls beside our tent lines, and a couple of cohorts of Iberians. Barely two thousand.' Tarquinius wiped his brow. 'That's not enough.'

Brennus punched the air with each fist, indicating to Romulus that he copy the action. 'Thirty thousand infantry should crush any enemy,' he panted, still finding it bizarre that he was now serving in the Roman army. An army which had crushed his people.

'Numbers aren't everything. Think about Hannibal,' countered Romulus. 'A lot of his victories against superior forces were thanks to his cavalry.'

Tarquinius was pleased by the insight. 'And the Parthians will have hardly any foot soldiers.'

'So how do they fight?' asked Brennus in surprise.

'Mounted archers. They attack in rapid waves, firing arrows.' Tarquinius plucked an imaginary bowstring. 'Storms of them.'

'Two thousand horse will struggle to contain those,' said Brennus.

'Precisely. And that's before the cataphracts charge.'

The word was unknown to Romulus and Brennus.

'Cataphracts – fully armoured mounts and riders.'

Romulus felt uneasy. 'Surely Crassus knows this too?'

'He is relying on the king of Armenia,' Tarquinius said thoughtfully. 'Artavasdes has up to six thousand cavalry.'

'That's all right then, surely?'

'If Crassus doesn't throw away the opportunity.'

They waited for him to continue. A stiff breeze sprang up and Romulus shivered. The army had seemed invincible.

Seemed.

'What do you mean?' Brennus was also concerned.

'First we have to march across Asia Minor, into Syria and Judaea,' said the Etruscan lightly. 'The stars and sea currents show several possible outcomes.'

Brennus relaxed. During the voyage, he had come to

trust Tarquinius implicitly, his predictions of bad weather and sightings of pirates proving correct virtually every time.

'If Crassus marches us into Armenia with Artavasdes,' Tarquinius continued, 'we could be feasting in Seleucia in eighteen months!'

But Romulus was sceptical of Tarquinius' words, which plainly covered all outcomes. He had yet to be convinced of the soothsayer's power. The young soldier had persuaded himself that Tarquinius must have over-heard him and Brennus talking about the fight outside the brothel. And anticipating the odd storm and the pres-ence of pirates in wild backwaters was hardly proof of mystical ability.

At the mention of Seleucia, Brennus shivered. No Allobroge could ever have travelled that far, he thought. Is that where my journey will end?

They ran on, passing a group of senior officers clus-tered round a stocky man outside one of the camps. None even glanced at the three soldiers passing by. Sunlight reflected brightly off the central figure's gilded breastplate.

Crassus was planning the campaign ahead.

'Our fates are in his hands,' said Romulus.

'It has already been decided,' pronounced Tarquinius. 'Our destinies are not linked for ever. And Crassus' fate is his own.'

Romulus increased his pace. There'd been enough talk of ill omens and bad luck. All he wanted to do was to push himself physically, to forget everything else for a while. His friends would give him guidance when needed. Despite Tarquinius' predictions about the army's shortcomings, it was hard to imagine how such a massive force could possibly fail.

Chapter XIX: Fabiola and Brutus

More than fourteen months pass...
The Lupanar, Rome, spring 53 BC

In the lifetime that had gone by since Gemellus had sold Fabiola, she had grown into an extraordinarily beautiful woman. Sleek black hair fell in a mane to a narrow waist. Piercing blue eyes mesmerised anyone who gazed into them for more than a few heartbeats. A slightly aquiline nose added character to stunning looks. Her full breasts and sinuous figure reminded men of the goddess Venus.

Fabiola had not been in the Lupanar for long before word had spread of her incredible ability to please. After Brutus' first visit, Jovina decided to drop prices for the new girl only a fraction and it was a gamble that paid off richly. Despite her huge expense, she was soon the most popular prostitute.

The old madam began to earn a fortune from Fabiola alone. Within six months, her shrewd purchase from Gemellus had paid for itself many times over. In a rare gesture, Jovina even let Fabiola start keeping a slightly larger percentage than the other women. But her owner was still sharp as a blade. Fabiola was never allowed outside without company, nor was there any mention of manumission.

Her customers ranged from rich merchants to politicians and military officers – every part of the ruling class. Under her spell, many came to see Fabiola at least once a week and she was showered with expensive perfume, dresses and jewellery. Gifts were always welcome, particularly money, which was carefully locked away in an iron trunk. Every month, Benignus or Vettius escorted her to the Forum. There Fabiola deposited the cash with Greek moneylenders, where it earned a small amount of interest. The only way she could see of leaving the Lupanar was to accumulate wealth, and to leave was still her ambition. Fabiola rarely made a withdrawal, unless it was needed to buy information about Romulus.

Since the fateful night when Fabiola had missed seeing her twin outside the brothel, she had left no stone unturned in her search for him. But there seemed to be no sign of Romulus at all. Fabiola's only hope was based on the fact that she was unable to find out much about the inhabitants of the gladiator schools. There were just four in the city and only one of the *lanistae*, the owners of the *ludi*, was a regular visitor to the Lupanar. She was now sure that Romulus was not and had never been in the Ludus Dacicus. Its short, balding *lanista* was so obsessed with Fabiola that he had told her about practically every fighter that had entered the gates of his school. And although she knew it was likely that her brother had long since fled Rome, she longed to discover something – anything – about what had happened to him.

Fabiola learned the art of patience. No matter how long it took, she would wait until the opportunity arrived to discover her brother's fate.

Her climb to such popularity had made her surprisingly few enemies among the prostitutes. From the first day, Fabiola had made a deliberate policy of being friendly to the others – passing on customers, buying gifts, helping the girls who got sick. Some resented the beauty's meteoric rise to success, but they kept quiet. Doormen, cooks – even the madam – approved of Fabiola. She also struck up a quiet friendship with Docilosa, finding her loyal and discreet.

When one woman had several regulars, they were kept carefully apart. Where possible, visiting times were planned, so none even suspected a rival's existence. It was one of Jovina's strictest rules. Jealousy over popular girls had spilled over into bloodshed before and such things were very bad for business.

Sensing its obvious advantage, Fabiola kept rigidly to this arrangement. More than one client had appeared jealous at the mere idea that she saw other men. If they were to be used to the utmost, maximising her position of power, customers needed to relax the instant they walked through the Lupanar's door. Fabiola was not just a prostitute now. Aided by her natural intelligence, she had grown up fast. Sexual pleasure was only part of the experience. She was an expert at massaging tight muscles, washing off daily grime, feeding tasty morsels and making light conversation. While in her company, a customer felt like the most important man in the world. What he didn't realise was just how much information the beautiful young woman was gleaning from every visit.

Fabiola kept aware of current trends. All knowledge was power and a possible escape from the life she secretly detested. Bringing rich and powerful men under her influence could only help this. Learning how senators, members of the magistracy and army bargained and dealt with each other was fascinating. As a slave in Gemellus' house, Fabiola had had no idea of what went on in the world and how Rome was ruled. Now, after countless hours spent in the company of those who controlled the Republic, she understood it intimately.

For more than five years, Pompey, Crassus and Caesar had enjoyed a stranglehold on the reins of power. Each took his turn as consul and the best governorships were carefully shared. Corrupt equestrians took the rest. A small number of politicians, among them the senators Cato and Domitius, remained loyal to the Republic's original ideal – that no one man should have supreme power. But as a tiny minority, they rarely succeeded in slowing the inexorable decline of the Senate's influence.

The triumvirate cleverly kept the ignorant masses happy with frequent *munera* – gladiator games and horse racing. Distributions of grain to those in need were made free. This resulted in massive influxes of the rural poor to Rome, creating an ever greater demand. Imports of wheat from Egypt soared, prices plummeted, Italian farms suffered. More landless peasants arrived in the cities, requiring more food and entertainment.

Desperate for employment, many joined the military, eager to comply with whatever their leaders ordered. Instead of answering to the Senate, legions were now loyal to generals like Caesar and Pompey. Romans were increasingly prepared to fight each other. It was a far cry from the days of farmers who had served the Republic's army each summer. The people's democracy, which had endured for half a millennium, was stealthily being eroded. If Fabiola's clients were right, it was only a matter of time before one of the triumvirate made a bid for absolute control. The balance of power swung this way and that, as deals and alliances between the three rivals were made and broken again.

Nobody knew who would emerge triumphant.

Although she was not lucky enough to have snared one of the triumvirate, there were several potential candidates for Fabiola's ultimate aim: a client to buy her freedom. As the mistress of a rich noble, she would have a real chance to pursue Gemellus and find out who her father was. Fabiola had not yet selected the unknowing customer. It was something that required careful planning. The decision would be life-changing in more ways than one.

One of the most likely was Decimus Brutus. As Julius Caesar's popularity grew with each passing year, so did that of his close allies. Tales of the general's outstanding tactics and victories against overwhelming odds filled Rome's bathhouses, markets and brothels with gossip. There were even stories about Brutus' victories against tribes such as the Veneti.

Fabiola was ecstatic.

Sent home by Caesar to canvass and maintain support

among the equestrians and senators, the taker of Fabiola's virginity had returned permanently from Gaul two years later. Having made regular visits to the Lupanar each time he was in Rome, the staff officer had become totally infatuated with her. Every need and desire of his was slaked and the pillow talk he provided in return was worth more than that of all her other clients put together. It gave Fabiola a window on the thoughts of a military genius, the likes of whom had not been seen in generations.

'What a leader,' Brutus gushed. 'Alexander himself would have been proud to meet Julius Caesar.'

'Such devotion!' Fabiola raked his arm with long fingernails. 'And he deserves it all?'

'Of course.' Brutus' eyes shone with pride. 'You should have seen him last winter in Gaul. One night he slept amongst his men on the frozen ground, wrapped only in his cloak. The next morning, he turned a battle with the Eburones on its head. Sixty thousand tribesmen against seven thousand legionaries! Defeat was imminent until Caesar took a place in the front line. Covered himself in enemy blood. He rallied the men and rolled those savages back.'

Consummate at her job, Fabiola gasped with apparent amazement. She did not care for war and the suffering it caused. Brutus was so excited he did not even notice.

'What does he look like?' she asked idly, wondering if Caesar would ever visit the Lupanar. 'Not fat, like Pompey?'

Brutus laughed. 'Lean as a whippet!' He frowned and stared at her, concentrating. 'You have the same nose.'

'Really?' She batted her eyelashes.

The subject of their father had always been taboo. Just once, not long before Gemellus had sold them, Velvinna had hinted that she'd been raped by a noble. But when the twins had begun asking questions, she had clammed up. 'Not fit for children's ears. I'll tell you in a few years.' There would never be a chance to ask her mother about the rape now. Fabiola knew the merchant had sold Velvinna to the salt mines a few months later. *Curse him.*

'No patrician blood in me,' she sighed, giving nothing away.

Brutus took her hand and kissed it. 'You are the queen of my heart,' he replied. 'That makes you noble.'

This time, the smile was real. Fabiola was genuinely fond of the enthusiastic young staff officer. He *was* the best candidate, she suddenly decided. Her fingers trailed across firm chest muscles, straying towards his groin. 'Thank you, Master,' Fabiola said. Half-closed eyes looked at him seductively for a moment. Then she slid down, tugging off his *licium*.

Brutus moaned in anticipation.

I must see Caesar's face, she thought.

Some months later, Brutus finally persuaded her to attend a gladiator contest sponsored by Pompey. Terrified she would witness Romulus fighting, Fabiola had always refused invitations to the arena. But it seemed a good chance to see one of Rome's destiny-makers in person, so she agreed. Crassus was long gone to the east and

Caesar had not visited Italy for nearly two years, prohibited as a general with a standing army. Pompey was, for the moment, the leading man in the city and he was making the most of it.

On a warm afternoon in early summer, Brutus' largest slaves carried a litter through crowded streets to Pompey's new auditorium on the Campus Martius. Fabiola and the staff officer sat inside, protected from the world by light curtains. A dozen armed guards paced around them, whipping the way clear of eager citizens. Thanks to charges of corruption against the two sitting consuls and the resulting disarray in the Senate, public unrest was on the increase. Brutus left nothing to chance and there was no equality in the manner of their entrance to the stands.

Soon they were sitting in the area reserved for nobles, protected from sunlight by the cloth *velarium*. Fabiola felt quite strange. Life as one of the ruling class was altogether different. Liberating. It strengthened her determination not to remain a slave for much longer.

Fabiola's lover sat on the cushioned wooden seat alongside, a broad grin on his handsome face. They had spent the previous night together. After a long bath, she had given him a lingering massage. Brutus felt like a god.

Other nobles had watched them arrive, nodding at Brutus and eyeing Fabiola curiously. Some had seen her before, but many had not. Excursions tended to be outside the city, to Brutus' villa at Capua. As usual in such situations, men's glances were admiring, women's disapproving. Fabiola ignored both, staring round the arena proudly. One day she would be free. Equal to those who sneered, more than a mere prostitute.

'No sport watching animals being slaughtered,' Brutus said. He had delayed coming until the earlier, boring contests had already finished. Trumpets were now announcing the imminent entrance of gladiators. 'Might as well see some skill.'

Suddenly Fabiola felt worried. What if Romulus appeared in the arena? *Jupiter, Greatest and Best. Keep my brother safe from harm.* The prayer had become a personal mantra over the last three years. She breathed deeply, forcing herself to be calm. If Jupiter was merciful, Romulus would not be one of today's fighters.

The appeal was answered. None of the armoured men who maimed and killed each other in the hour that followed looked remotely like Romulus, but the bloody spectacle was still distressing. Although she fantasised about revenge on Gemellus and the man who had raped her mother, Fabiola did not like violence. The crowd's roars of approval at more brutal moments were sickening. Images of Romulus bleeding on the sand came frequently to mind, images that she had managed to keep from her mind till now. But for all she knew, her twin brother might already be dead. When the display came to an end, Fabiola felt a real sense of relief. There would be a break before two of the most popular gladiators in the city took each other on.

Brutus was chattering on about technique and the skills of various types of fighters.

Fabiola listened vaguely, nodding at regular intervals as if interested. She was having trouble controlling the grief bubbling inside her.

'Course there hasn't been a decent champion since that Gaul disappeared.'

She pricked her ears. 'Who?'

'Brennus, his name was. Size of two men, but skilful with it.' Brutus' face lit up. 'With a legion of soldiers like that Gaul, Caesar could conquer the world.'

'What happened to him?'

'Got ideas above his station. He and another gladiator killed a noble outside the Lupanar about a year ago,' said Brutus.

Fabiola's stomach clenched. *Romulus! He might still be alive.*

'Remember that? Stocky redhead called Caelius, I think.'

'Oh yes,' she said, feigning surprise. 'Broke the doorman's nose too.'

'Complete waste,' sighed Brutus. 'If either shows his face in Rome again, he'll be crucified.'

Fabiola was about to ask more, but a loud fanfare interrupted.

Pompey had arrived.

Chapter XX: Invasion

The Euphrates, Mesopotamia, summer 53 BC

L ike all Roman leaders, Crassus consulted sooth-sayers before momentous occasions and the invasion had begun with sacrifices to the gods. A good omen for crossing the river was crucial.

Just before dawn, an old priest had led a large bull into the open space before Crassus' command tent. Dressed in a plain white robe and surrounded by acolytes, he had watched the unconcerned beast chew some hay. Hundreds of soldiers gradually assembled, picked from every cohort in the army to witness that the campaign had been sanctioned by the gods. Having persuaded Bassius to let them attend, Tarquinius and Romulus stood in their midst.

There was a sigh of expectation when Crassus appeared at the doorway of his tent. The guards snapped to attention, their weapons and armour polished even brighter than usual. The general was a short, grey-haired man in his early sixties with a beaked nose and piercing gaze, clad in a gilded breastplate, red cloak and horsehair-crested helmet. Studded leather straps protected Crassus' groin and upper legs and an ornate sword hung from his belt.

Unlike Pompey and Caesar, his two partners in the triumvirate, Crassus did not have vast military experience. But he was the man who had defeated Spartacus. The unprecedented slave rebellion a generation before had almost brought the Republic to its knees. Only Crassus – and to a lesser extent Pompey – had saved it from ruin.

The general was flanked by Publius and the legates commanding each of the army's seven legions, the officers dressed similarly to their leader.

Remembering Julia's scar, Romulus angrily nudged the Etruscan when he saw Publius.

Concentrating hard, Tarquinius frowned. 'Be quiet and watch.'

The priest looked at Crassus, who nodded once.

Muttering incantations, he approached the bull, which was still chewing contentedly. Two acolytes grabbed the rope around its head, while others pressed in close, preventing escape. Realising far too late that something was wrong, it bellowed angrily. Despite its huge strength, the men extended the bull's head forward, exposing the neck.

From inside his robe, the priest produced a wicked-looking blade. With a quick slash, he cut the throat, releasing a fountain of blood on to the sand. A silver bowl was swiftly placed under the stream, which filled it to the brim. The helpers let go and the bull collapsed, kicking spasmodically. Standing back, the old man peered into the red liquid.

Everyone present held their breath as the contents were studied. Even Crassus remained quiet. The Etruscan stood motionless, his lips moving faintly and Romulus felt a shiver of unease.

The soothsayer stood for a long time, muttering to himself and swirling the blood. Finally he scanned the sky.

'I call on Jupiter, *Optimus Maximus*! I call on Mars *Ultor*, bringer of war!' The priest paused. 'To witness the omens from this sacred beast.' Again he waited, gazing intently.

Crassus anxiously watched his men. It was vital that they thought the campaign would be successful. A slight soldier with blond hair and single gold earring caught his attention. Carrying a large battleaxe, he was dressed like an irregular. The man stared back without fear or deference, apparently ignoring the ceremony.

Crassus felt goose bumps rising on both arms and suddenly remembered the Etruscan bronze liver he had tried to buy many years previously. The soldiers he had sent on that mission had all died shortly afterwards. Terror constricted his throat and he turned away. The mercenary was regarding him as he imagined the ferry-man might.

No one else had noticed.

'The omens are good!'

A great sigh of relief swept through the gathering.

'I see a mighty victory for Rome! Parthia will be crushed!'

Wild cheering broke out.

Crassus turned to his legates with a smile.

'Liar,' hissed Tarquinius. 'The blood showed something else altogether.'

Romulus' face fell.

'I'll tell you later. The ceremony's not over yet.'

They watched as the priest cut open the animal's belly with a sharp knife. More favourable predictions followed as shiny loops of gut came spilling on to the sand, followed by the liver. The climax came once the diaphragm had been cut, allowing access to the chest cavity. Reaching deep into the steaming carcass with his blade, the soothsayer cut and pulled for a few moments. At last he stood and faced the officers, robes saturated with blood, his arms red to the shoulder. In both hands sat the bull's heart, glistening in the rays of the rising sun.

'It beats still! A sign of the power of Crassus' legions!' he yelled.

All the legionaries roared approval.

All except Tarquinius and Romulus.

Arms outstretched, the old man approached Crassus, who waited with an expectant smile. The omens had been good. Soldiers would hear the news from those watching, spreading it through the entire army faster than he ever could.

'Great Crassus, receive the heart. A symbol of your bravery. A sign of victory!' the priest shouted.

Reaching out eagerly, Crassus stepped forwards. This was his moment. But as he took the bloody organ, it slipped from his grasp, landed on the ground and rolled away from him.

There was a sharp intake of breath from Tarquinius. 'Nobody can deny what that means.'

Crassus moaned. The heart was no longer red. Thousands of grains of sand now coated its surface, turning it yellow.

The colour of the desert.

He stared at the priest, whose features were ashen. Everyone watching had gone rigid with shock.

'Say something!'

The old man cleared his throat. 'The omens stand!' he cried. 'In the blood, I saw a mighty victory from the gods!'

The men glanced at each other, many quickly making the sign against evil, others rubbing the lucky amulets that hung from their necks. They had not seen the bowl's contents. What they had seen was Crassus dropping the bull's heart, an ultimate symbol of courage. Hands grew clammy and feet shuffled on the sand. Instead of cheers, an uneasy silence hung in the air.

Looking up, Crassus saw a group of twelve vultures floating on the thermals. He was not the only one to notice. There was no time to lose.

'Soldiers of Rome! Do not be troubled,' he shouted. 'The priest's hands are slippery – just as yours will be with Parthian blood!'

Romulus turned nervously to Tarquinius.

'He is a fraud,' the Etruscan said quietly. 'But do not fear. We may yet survive.'

His comment was hardly reassuring. It seemed impossible that Crassus' army could be defeated, but the sand-covered heart was still lying on the ground before them all.

Gory evidence.

Romulus found himself wanting to believe in Tarquinius. The alternative did not bear thinking about.

Around them, the legionaries were less than convinced. The general tried to rally their spirits, to no avail. With a savage gesture, he dismissed them, retreating into the tent with his officers. Even Crassus had to admit silently that his effort to inspire the troops had been a total failure. And the news would spread fast. It was nothing to worry about, he tried to convince himself.

But the gods were angry.

Romulus looked back at the wide river snaking off into the south. Soon the army's fate would be as clear as the deep waters flowing swiftly past. Having marched into this vast land, Crassus' men were about to enter more unknown, oriental territory.

Fat tendrils of dawn mist hung low over the waterway, concealing clusters of reeds on the banks. It would not be long before the sun burned off the grey veil, revealing the shore. Reaching the river after many days' march had been a huge relief for the thirsty army, but Romulus and thousands of soldiers waiting in silence would not be able to linger or relax. Crassus and his son Publius were leading them southeast.

The Roman host had travelled hundreds of miles from its beachhead on the western corner of Asia Minor. Every major city in its path had paid large sums of money to avoid attack by such a massive force. Jerusalem in particular had yielded a king's ransom, its elders desperate to preserve its ancient wealth. Once winter had passed,

Crassus' legions had crossed Syria to the Euphrates, arriving thirteen months after disembarking from the triremes. By this time, Romulus and Brennus were firm friends with Tarquinius.

The Etruscan had an enormous knowledge of medicine, astrology, history and the mystic arts. Having spent years on campaign with the general Lucullus in Armenia, he was also an experienced fighter. Bassius had quickly noticed his talents and promoted him straight to *optio* so he could help train the recruits. Tarquinius' sharp sense of humour had blended with Brennus' earthy one and his soothsaying ability complemented the Gaul's huge skill with weapons. Under their tuition Romulus had bloomed, improving not just his fitness and swordsmanship, but learning to read and write as well.

The rumours in the ranks were that they were heading for Seleucia on the Tigris. Romulus knew more about the region now from Tarquinius' stories about the Land of the Two Rivers and the kingdoms that had existed there. He had enjoyed many nights of history lessons, hearing about Babylonians, Persians and other exotic races. Romulus' favourite tale was that of Alexander the Great, a man who had marched from Greece to India and back, conquering half the world in the process.

Now the mighty Parthians ruled the deserts. Originally a small but warlike tribe, the fierce warriors had been absorbing defeated kingdoms for generations, growing until Parthia was rivalled in size only by Rome. It was a sparsely populated empire, peopled by nomads. Parthia's wealth came from taxing valuable goods such as silk, jewels and spices carried by traders returning on caravan routes from India and the far east. Aware of Rome's greed, the Parthians guarded this trade jealously.

But it had attracted the attention of Crassus. And, eager for a rapid victory, he was marching into the desert, in a straight line towards Seleucia.

Cursing the strident trumpet calls, the seven legions, five thousand mercenaries and two thousand cavalry had risen well before dawn. Word was still spreading about Crassus' fumble with the heart, so the legionaries had taken down their tents with typical Roman efficiency, packing them swiftly on to pack mules. The regulars were an excellent example of the Republic's ability to organise, but Bassius' men were less used to the job. Cajoled and threatened by turn, eventually the mercenaries were ready to leave.

The tall earthen ramparts thrown up the previous day outside the town of Zeugma were left in place. Dozens of similar camps marked the army's trail way back into Asia Minor, and would prove useful when returning from the conquest of Parthia.

Crassus had seen no reason to depart from custom. The advance had been led by Romulus' cohort and other units, rather than legion regulars. Crossing the river in hundreds of small reed boats built by the engineers had taken time, but it had been achieved with minimal problems. Only two craft had overturned, spilling their passengers into the water. Dragged under by the weight of armour and weapons, the screaming mercenaries had drowned quickly. It was a trifle compared to the massive force now waiting on the eastern bank. As with Alexander's invasion, single men's lives were unimportant.

At the front of every legion stood its standard-bearer, resplendent in his bronze cuirass and wolfskin head-dress. On a wooden pole above each was a silver eagle gripping golden lightning bolts, the legion's awards hanging below. They were potent symbols of power to every soldier and represented the valour and courage of a unit.

The outstretched wings of the eagle nearest Romulus gleamed in the rising sun. Nudging Brennus, he pointed proudly. It seemed a good omen, and judging by the pleased murmurs in the ranks, the men agreed. Something that was badly needed after what had happened earlier. By now, every man in the army knew that Crassus had dropped the bull's heart.

But Rome appeared triumphant again.

'I've seen too many bloody standards like that from the other side of a battlefield,' sniffed the Gaul, hands resting on his longsword.

Tarquinius said nothing, his eyes searching the heavens. He had not spoken since dawn.

Neither of Romulus' friends felt the same way about the eagles. They did not identify with Rome the way he did. Despite what the legions stood for, he found himself instinctively proud of them. Born a slave, now a mercenary, he was still a Roman.

Behind the standard-bearers came the four hundred and eighty legionaries of the first cohort, the most important. They were followed by nine more of equal size, taking the strength of every legion to nearly five thousand men.

Roman soldiers dressed identically. Long brown cloth tunics were covered by chain mail shirts reaching to the thighs; leather *caligae* with nail-studded soles clad their feet. Each carried a heavy, elongated oval *scutum*. Occasionally topped by a simple horsehair crest, bronze helmets with wide hinged cheek flaps and a neck guard protected their heads. Every man was armed with two javelins and his *gladius*. Other equipment and food hung from the yoke, a long forked piece of wood carried over one shoulder.

By contrast, the units of irregulars dressed according to origin. Bassius' men were mostly Gauls, so chain mail, loose tunics and baggy trousers were common. Spears and longswords, elongated rectangular shields and daggers formed their weaponry. Cohorts of Cappadocians in leather armour stood nearby, armed with short swords and round shields. Balearic slingers, African light infantry and Iberian and Gaulish cavalry completed the tally of mercenaries.

Deliberately breaking the treaty forged by Pompey some years before, the army had crossed the Euphrates a number of times the previous autumn, plundering Parthian towns in the vicinity. Crassus was creating a *casus belli*. By its very nature, the campaigning had not progressed more than a few miles inland. Now an altogether different prospect faced the massed lines of legionaries and mercenaries. An unknown world lay before them.

Despite the possibility of alternative routes, they were about to leave the river behind and march into the barren wastes of Mesopotamia. The prospect filled Romulus with unease, but the friends he had grown to love showed no signs of emotion. Brennus leaned forward on his longsword, dwarfing it, while the Etruscan silently contemplated the nearby eagle standard.

Remembering Tarquinius' words, Romulus breathed deeply, looking southeast towards Crassus' first objective – Seleucia, the commercial capital of the Parthian empire. With luck, all would be well.

The *bucinae* sounded at last, signalling forward march. Romulus felt a push in the back. Still thinking, he did not respond immediately and the man in the rank behind shoved again with his shield boss. A Roman army moved like a machine, leaving no time for contemplation.

He noticed Tarquinius looking over his shoulder at the Sixth Legion, the regular unit immediately behind the mercenaries' position. As they watched, the standard-bearer pulled his spiked pole out of the ground, preparing to lead off the first cohort. The man had only taken one step when the wooden staff slipped in his hand, allowing the silver eagle to rotate and face backwards.

Gasps of dismay filled the air and Romulus swallowed hard.

Brennus, who hated all the eagles stood for, squared his jaw.

This was the second bad omen in as many hours.

Tarquinius was smiling faintly. Luckily, most of their comrades had not seen what had happened.

Romulus took a breath of hot desert air. Stay calm, he thought.

The veteran centurion in charge of the Sixth's first cohort instantly seized the initiative. Superstition would not stop him following his orders. 'Forward march!' he bellowed. 'Now!'

Wary of punishment, the legionaries responded

quickly. But muttering continued in their midst as they moved off. There was no time to ask Tarquinius about the importance of what had just happened.

Kicking up a huge cloud of dust, the soldiers picked up speed slowly. Orders rang out as centurions and *optiones* fussed and bothered. Men shuffled, adjusting their loads and preparing to march as each unit got under way. The mules plodded in the rear, carrying food, gold, spare equipment and assault weapons such as catapults. The enormous column stretched for more than ten miles. Any unfortunates who had been selected to guard the baggage train cursed their luck as they swallowed the mouthfuls of choking dust left hanging in the air by the legions that had marched past.

The army advanced without incident all morning. Deep sand muffled the sounds of marching feet, creaking leather and coughing men. Temperatures rose steadily as they passed by the small settlements of the Hellenic population, a people who had been living in the area for hundreds of years.

'Alexander the Great came through here,' said Tarquinius excitedly as a larger village came into view.

Full of interest, Romulus peered at the nearby mud and brick structures. 'How can you tell?'

Tarquinius pointed. 'That temple has Doric columns and statues of Greek gods. And we crossed the river where the Lion of Macedon did. It's marked on my map.'

Romulus grinned, imagining the crack hoplites who had created history. Soldiers who had been to the end of the world and back. It seemed that under Crassus, they were being given a chance to emulate the feat.

'Crassus is no Alexander,' said Tarquinius darkly. 'Far too arrogant. And he lacks real insight.'

'Even the best general can make a mistake,' Romulus argued, recalling one of Cotta's lessons. 'Alexander came to grief against the Indian elephants.'

'But Crassus has made a fatal error before the battle even starts.' The Etruscan smiled. 'It is madness not to follow a river into the desert.'

Romulus' concern about the bad omens returned with a vengeance and he turned again to Tarquinius, who shrugged eloquently.

'The campaign's outcome is still unclear. I need some wind or cloud to know more.'

Romulus looked up at the clear blue sky. The air was completely still.

Tarquinius laughed.

So did Romulus. What else could he do? There was no going back now and despite the uncertainty of their fate, excitement was coursing through his veins.

Brennus remained silent, troubled by guilty memories of his wife and child, of Conall and Brac. If he was to die in this burning hell, it was crucial for him to know that they had not died in vain. That the Allobroges had not been wiped out for nothing. That his whole life had not been wasted.

Terraced fields filled the landscape, irrigated by channels from the Euphrates. Peasants working in the crops stared fearfully at the host. Few dared wave or speak. They held their breath as thirty-five thousand armed men tramped by in an enormous cloud of dust. The noise drowned out every other sound.

An army of that size meant only one thing in any language.

War.

The general rode his favourite black horse in the heavily protected centre of the column. Trumpeters paced behind, ready to relay his orders. Astride a saddle richly adorned with gold filigree, Crassus rode with the easy grace of experience, feet dangling either side, using only the reins for control.

'Good day for an invasion,' said Crassus loudly. 'The gods favour us.'

A chorus of agreement echoed from his senior officers. The veteran legionaries marching either side of them carefully kept their faces blank. Nobody dared mention what had happened earlier.

Crassus glared round at his entourage. None of these lackeys will get in my way, he thought angrily. His time had finally come. After the soldiers had left, that fool of a priest had been crucified beside the dead bull, a clear warning to the remaining augurs not to make mistakes. The image of the sand-covered heart was locked away in the recesses of his mind. It had been nothing more than a slip of the hand; the storms that had sunk so many ships nothing but bad weather. Word about the eagle standard had not yet reached him.

'With Parthia defeated, the Senate will have no option but to grant you a full triumph, sir,' ventured one of his tribunes in an effort to please.

Crassus nodded happily at the glorious prospect of riding in a chariot through the streets of Rome, a laurel wreath on his head. He would finally be equal to his partners in the triumvirate. It was mere circumstance that had brought the rivals together, not friendship, and it had seemed a good idea at first. Sharing power for more than five years had not stopped them from continually vying for dominance. None had succeeded thus far, but Crassus had suffered more setbacks than the other two.

Thanks to Pompey's propaganda, his lead role in crushing the slave rebellion had been obscured, his rightful triumph downgraded to a parade on foot. Crassus had lived for years in the shadow of the other's military success. It galled him immensely. Whilst Pompey's career had been illustrious, he also had an uncanny ability to claim victories that were not his. It was really Lucullus who had defeated Mithridates and Tigranes in Asia Minor, Crassus thought bitterly. Not that fat fool Pompey. *The same will not happen here in Parthia. The glory will be mine. All of it.*

He began reflecting on Julius Caesar, who had also started well by subjugating Gaul and Belgica, making himself incredibly wealthy at the same time. Now it seemed Caesar's ambition knew no bounds. Crassus cursed. It had been a mistake to help the young noble with those huge loans. The usual tactic of keeping men in his power by refusing to accept repayment of owed money had backfired when Caesar had paid off his debt in typically confident style, sending a train of mules to Crassus' house not long before he had left for Asia Minor. Hundreds of leather bags carried by the pack animals had contained the entire outstanding amount, down to the last *sestertius*. There had been little Crassus could do other than accept. He scowled at the manner in which he had been outmanoeuvred by Caesar, a man nearly half his age. Never again.

No one will be able to deny my brilliance when Seleucia falls, Crassus thought. I will seize power in Rome. Alone.

Cassius Longinus, the boldest of his legates, kicked his heels into his horse's ribs and came alongside. The soldier's scarred face was concerned.

'Permission to speak, sir?'

'What is it?' Crassus forced himself to be polite. Most of the senior officers did not have nearly as much experience as this man. Longinus was a veteran of many wars, from Gaul to North Africa.

'About Armenia, sir.'

'We have spoken about this already, Legate.'

'I know, sir, but . . .'

'Following Artavasdes' suggestion of marching north to the Armenian mountains and then south again would take three months.' Crassus gripped his reins. 'This way to Seleucia takes only four weeks.'

Longinus paused, considering his words. 'Odd that he refused to accompany us, don't you think? The king of Armenia is a proven loyal subject.'

An awkward silence hung in the air, broken by the distant braying of the mule train. Every officer knew Crassus was not fond of advice.

'He withdrew the instant we mentioned our intended route,' added Longinus.

'These are not Romans we are dealing with!'

Displeased, Crassus spat on the sand, the moisture disappearing before it coloured the yellow grains. 'You can't trust them.'

'Precisely, sir,' whispered Longinus. He glared at Ariamnes, the richly dressed Nabataean riding on the edge of the group.

The warrior rode his white mount with arrogant ease, its saddle even more ornate than the general's, the reins braided with gold thread. Above the horse's head a plume of peacock feathers waved gently in the breeze. Bareheaded, Ariamnes wore a leather coat over his chain mail and his long black hair framed gold earrings dangling from both ears. Richly decorated quivers were strapped to both sides of the saddle and a wickedly curved bow hung over his right shoulder.

'Why believe that perfumed snake? Artavasdes is more worthy than a Nabataean *chieftain*,' muttered Longinus.

Crassus smiled. 'Ariamnes might have poor taste in scent, but the man has over six thousand cavalry. And he offered to guide us directly to Seleucia. That is the way I want to go.' He waved in the warrior's direction. 'Forget Artavasdes!'

'And water for the men, sir?'

The legates looked up. It had been an unspoken worry among all of them.

Longinus sensed their unease. 'The Tigris flows south out of the Armenian hills, sir. All the way to Seleucia.'

'Enough!' bellowed Crassus. 'The march will not be long. Ariamnes says the Parthians are already running scared. Isn't that right?' he called out.

The Nabataean turned and rode back, his horse prancing across the sand. Nearer the pair, he bowed from the waist. Fixing the general with dark, kohl-rimmed eyes, Ariamnes brought his left hand up to his heart.

'The enemy faded away the instant your legions crossed the river, Excellency.'

'See?' Crassus beamed. 'Nothing can withstand my army!'

Longinus scowled at the brown-skinned warrior. With his oiled ringlets of hair, perfume and curved bow, the man reeked of treachery. And Crassus could not – or would not – see it. Gritting his teeth, the legate trotted off to remonstrate with Publius, who was riding with his Gaulish cavalry on the right flank.

But Caesar's former lieutenant in Gaul was having none of it. He wanted his own part of the victory. 'My father is a hero, Legate,' the stocky noble said jovially. 'He delivered Rome from Spartacus. Saved the Republic.'

And the fool hasn't led an army into battle since, thought Longinus.

'Trust his judgement. He has a nose for gold like I have for a virgin!'

'We do not have enough cavalry to fight the Parthian archers and cataphracts,' insisted Longinus.

'Two thousand Gauls and Iberians and Ariamnes' six thousand horsemen should be more than sufficient.'

'You trust these Nabataeans to fight for us like the Armenians have?'

'What kind of son does not trust his own father?'

His pleas were falling on deaf ears. Wishing the battle-hardened Julius Caesar was in charge instead, Longinus galloped off to the front.

Chapter XXI: Parthia

S ince leaving the coast of Asia Minor many months previously, the army's journey had gradually taken it further inland, away from cooling sea breezes. Daytime temperatures climbed steadily, reaching new heights in Syria and Mesopotamia. Initially Crassus had used common sense by following the course of rivers and streams, and the legions had covered most of the march without too much discomfort. But not any more.

Now the brief cool of dawn had faded away, leaving soldiers at the sun's mercy. The yellow orb quickly climbed to fill the entire sky, blasting the ground below. Irrigated fields with their sheltering palm trees grew sparser, then died away completely. Five miles from the Euphrates, all signs of habitation had disappeared. Soon afterwards, the narrow road the legions were following led off between lines of undulating dunes and came to an abrupt end.

The view that awaited them was shocking.

As far as the eye could see, a vast emptiness stretched. It was a burning wasteland and a great sigh of anticipation escaped men's throats. Spirits fell and the cohort's momentum was suddenly stalled by deep sand which was far harder to march in.

'Crassus has lost his mind!' said Brennus furiously. 'Nobody can survive out there.'

'Quite similar to Hades,' commented Tarquinius. 'But if the Greeks did it, we can.'

'Not a living thing. Just sand.' At the limits of Romulus' vision danced a shimmering haze. It was like nothing he had ever seen before.

'What are you waiting for? Sluggards!' screamed Bassius, the *phalerae* on his chest clinking. 'Forward march! Now!'

The Roman army's formidable discipline prevailed. With a deep intake of breath, the mercenaries entered the desert's oven-like heat. It was not long before the soldiers' feet were burning through the soles of their *caligae*. Chain mail shirts grew uncomfortably hot to touch. Exposed skin began to burn. Despite strict orders to conserve water, men began taking surreptitious gulps from their gourds.

Romulus was about to do the same when Tarquinius stopped him.

'Save it. The next waterhole is more than a day's march.'

'I'm parched,' he protested.

'The man's right,' added Brennus. 'Stay thirsty.'

Without breaking step, Tarquinius stooped to the ground and picked up three smooth pebbles, passing one to each of them before popping the last in his own mouth. 'Put it under your tongue.'

Brennus raised his eyebrows. 'Have you gone mad?'

'Do as I say,' Tarquinius said with an enigmatic smile.

Both men obeyed and were amazed when moisture instantly developed in their mouths.

'See?' Tarquinius chuckled. 'Stick with me and you'll go far!'

Silently Brennus clapped the Etruscan on the shoulder. He was glad that the soothsayer was full of surprises.

Reassured by his friends' guidance, Romulus strode ahead, full of youthful enthusiasm. The young soldier felt even surer that with Brennus and Tarquinius nearby, little could go wrong. Seleucia would fall in a matter of days, making them rich. Then all he needed was proof of his innocence so he could return to Rome. Quite how that would be achieved was unclear, but he had unfinished business there. Rescuing his mother and Fabiola. Finding Julia. Killing Gemellus.

Starting a slave rebellion.

They had been marching for much of the afternoon when they were alerted by a cry from the front.

'Enemy ahead!'

All eyes turned to the southeast.

Romulus peered at the confusion of sand and rocks but could see nothing.

Brennus squinted into the blinding light. 'There!' he pointed. 'To the right of the lead cavalrymen. Must be a mile away.'

Beyond the Gaul's outstretched hand, Romulus could just make out a faint puff of smoke curling up into the haze.

Slowly the dust cloud grew larger until it was visible

to all. The thunder of horses' hooves carried through the hot, still air. As soon as the senior officers had been notified, the halt was sounded. With sighs of relief, men grounded javelins and shields, waiting for orders.

'Stay put. Drink some water, but not too much!' Bassius paced up and down the cohort, encouraging his soldiers. 'The cavalry will check it out before we have to worry.'

'Nowhere to go anyway, sir. Unless it's the next sand dune?'

The anonymous comment raised a laugh from those who could hear.

'Silence in the ranks!' roared Bassius.

Responding to further trumpet calls, the cavalry nearest the enemy took off. Their fair skin, flowing hair and moustaches clearly marked them as Gauls. Some wore chain mail but many had no armour, relying instead on their speed and agility. They were not gone for long, most returning to their position while a decurion rode back to the centre of the column to report.

'What did you see?' bellowed Brennus as the officer cantered by.

Bassius glared at the indiscipline but remained silent, keen as anyone else to know what was happening.

'A few hundred Parthians,' replied the decurion dismissively.

Murmurs of excitement rippled through the cohort.

The news did not seem to alarm Crassus. Moments later, the advance sounded once more. Romulus found himself picking up pace as the marching speed perceptibly increased. Sight of the enemy had reduced the daunting prospect of desert wastes.

The group of horsemen soon came into sight, riding to within a quarter of a mile of the Roman vanguard. The Parthians pulled across their path, sitting astride short, agile ponies. Each man wore a light jerkin, decorated trousers covered by chaps and a conical leather hat. Large case-like quivers hung from the left sides of their belts. All were carrying deeply curved composite bows, similar to those of the Nabataeans.

'They're not even wearing armour,' said Brennus contemptuously.

It was hard to feel scared. If these horse archers were all the Parthians had to offer, then the huge Roman army had little to fear.

'They're just skirmishers,' observed Tarquinius. 'Here to soften us up for the cataphracts.'

It sounded ominous.

'Those bows are made with layers of wood, horn and sinew. Gives them twice the power of any other.'

Brennus' eyes narrowed. If he could send an arrow from a Gaulish bow through chain mail, what would the Parthian weapons be able to do? A shiver ran down his spine at the thought.

Tarquinius was about to continue, but Bassius came striding past, vine cane at the ready.

The Parthians sat motionless until Publius responded to the challenge. He ordered the charge. But his men had only ridden a hundred paces before the enemy turned tail and galloped away, leaving the heavier horses floundering behind. When the Gauls reined in to

conserve their mounts' energy, the archers began taunt-
ing them.

Watching carefully, Publius held his men in check.

Suddenly a wave of arrows snaked into the air. Falling
in a deadly shower, it knocked many Gaulish riders to
the sand. Enraged, three troops immediately broke off
and charged straight at the Parthians.

'Where's their discipline? The fools think they can ride
them down,' said Tarquinius. 'The Parthians are not
infantry!'

Fascinated, Romulus watched as the irregular cavalry
thundered towards the archers, trailing clouds of dust.
Used to smashing aside opposition with ease, the Gauls
roared and whooped. He could imagine how terrifying
such an attack would be for foot soldiers. Lacking
mounted units of its own, the Republic relied on
conquered tribes like Gauls and Iberians to provide its
horsemen. Carrying lances or javelins and long slashing
swords, the cavalry served as a battering ram to break up
enemy formations.

The ill-disciplined charge was precisely what the
Parthians desired. As the Gauls closed in, they trotted
off, turning gracefully in the saddle to fire at their
pursuers. Swarms of arrows filled the air and Romulus
gaped in amazement at their accuracy. Within moments,
only thirty Gauls of the ninety who had charged were
left alive. Corpses littered the ground, staining it red with
blood. Dozens of riderless horses galloped about
aimlessly, many bucking and kicking in pain from their
wounds. The survivors reined in and fled, losing more
men as they did. Sounding the recall, Publius retreated

to the main column, leaving the Parthians victorious.

Not a single warrior had been killed.

'The bastards didn't even look where they were riding.' There was respect in Brennus' voice.

'I told you they weren't infantry.'

'Have you seen them before?' asked Romulus.

'Heard rumours in Armenia. They're famous for turning in the saddle and loosing. It's called the "Parthian shot".'

'Those Gauls didn't stand a chance.'

'Attacks by the archers weaken an enemy. And when they are in disarray the heavy cavalry get sent in.' Tarquinius grimaced. 'Then they repeat it.'

'Discipline!' cried Brennus. 'The Roman shield wall can take anything if the soldiers stand fast.' He thumped his shield robustly and immediately began to doubt his own words.

Tarquinius said nothing. It was unsettling.

Romulus found it nearly impossible to ignore the dead Gauls, men whose lack of restraint had got them killed. Their bodies were a grim reminder of what happened to those who disobeyed orders. Romulus hoped it would teach Crassus to conserve his cavalry. The Etruscan's veiled comments about the lack of Roman horsemen were starting to make sense and Romulus' unease grew.

High above in the azure sky, the vultures were circling.

Tarquinius studied them for a long time.

Puzzled, Romulus stared up at the broad wingtips silhouetted against the sun. Twelve vultures. No more than he might see on any other day. But when the

Etruscan lowered his gaze at last, both he and Brennus noticed that he seemed very troubled.

'Were you ever wrong, Olenus?' Tarquinius said to himself. 'Twelve.'

'What did you see?' asked Romulus.

'I'm not sure,' answered Tarquinius vaguely.

It was obvious he was holding something back.

Romulus began to speak again and Brennus lifted a finger to his lips, trying to forget Ultan's prophecy. 'The man will tell us when he's ready,' he said. 'Not before.' Now that he was more than a thousand miles from Transalpine Gaul, the big man found he did not want to know if his death was imminent.

Romulus shrugged fatalistically. No point pressing the matter. The Etruscan's predictions had got them this far.

Romulus wiped the sweat off his face. 'How much longer before they stand and face us?' he said angrily. 'Why won't the bastards fight?'

Far in the distance, a line of riders danced along the horizon.

The enemy horsemen had pulled away after the abortive Gaulish attack, giving Crassus time to think. But the general would only advance and the hot mercenaries were still trudging through deep sand.

'They've gone for more arrows,' replied the Etruscan.

Brennus smiled thinly. 'Be back soon then.'

Romulus shook a fist at the Parthians. 'Come back and fight!' he roared.

'It's a simple plan, really.' Tarquinius indicated the men around them. 'They're just tiring us out.'

One day in the furnace-like heat had taken a huge toll on Crassus' army. Instead of marching in regulation close order, most cohorts had now sagged apart. The sun beat down, sapping strength from the men. Their water bags long since empty, the weaker men were beginning to sway as they walked, while others leaned on their comrades' shoulders. Figures fell out of rank to collapse on the sand. Kicked and beaten by their officers, most struggled to their feet, while some lay unnoticed and were left to die. Such poor discipline would not normally have been tolerated, but the exhausted centurions had given up shouting. It was enough that the legions were still moving forward, although under the weight of his chain mail, shield, javelins and equipment, every soldier was struggling. Except Brennus.

Publius' Gauls rode beside the slowly moving column, their large horses also beginning to look tired. In stark comparison, the Nabataeans' mounts pranced along, riders chattering busily to each other.

Brennus pointed. 'Easy for them, eh?'

'You'll be glad of the Nabataeans when we're facing the main Parthian army,' said Romulus.

'I suppose. But I don't trust them,' the Gaul growled. 'Forever sniggering and laughing. Look!'

Romulus didn't like the sly glances being cast in their direction either.

'A couple of thousand Gaulish cavalry would be more use.'

'Not if they perform like those fools back there,' said Tarquinius dryly.

In an attempt to find relief from one of many blisters,

Romulus hefted his yoke from one shoulder to another and narrowly missed the head of the man immediately behind.

'Watch what you're doing,' the soldier swore. 'Or you'll feel the tip of my *gladius*.'

Romulus ignored him. 'Why didn't we travel through Armenia?' he asked again. 'Crassus must have known that would be easier.' Tarquinius had not been slow to share his discontent when it became evident the army was not taking the longer, safer route.

'Impatience. This way to Seleucia takes only four weeks.'

'A month in this hell?' Brennus rolled his eyes. 'What about water?'

'Resen, one of my people's ancestral cities, lies the other way,' added the Etruscan regretfully. He lowered his voice. 'And fewer men would have died in the mountains.'

Romulus noticed him glance up at the vultures and his suspicions grew further.

Tarquinius gestured at the Parthians in the distance. 'We should have been facing that lot on our terms, not theirs.'

'True,' replied the Gaul. 'Broken terrain would suit us far better.'

'Precisely.'

'It's what we did to the Romans in the first year,' mused Brennus. 'Attacked them on our own ground.'

'And now the Parthians are doing it to us,' Romulus chipped in. 'Crassus needs to start using the Nabataeans as protection.'

Brennus nodded approvingly at the observation while a dark shadow passed unseen over Tarquinius' face. His wish to travel east was being fulfilled, but it would be at far greater cost than the haruspex had first thought.

True to form, Tarquinius' words were prophetic. In the hours that followed, groups of Parthian archers rode in close, attempting to goad the Gauls into pursuit. If Publius' cavalry responded, more arrow storms rained down. If they did not, the enemy horsemen used them as target practice. Without bows, there was little the Gauls could do to retaliate and after a number of assaults, they had lost scores of men.

The Nabataeans seemed immune to temptation. Volleys of shafts were released if the Parthians came near, a tactic that worked well. Crassus finally realised this and Ariamnes was ordered to split his cavalry, placing half on each side of the army as a protective screen. The mercenaries were heartened by their allies' presence.

Slowly the army ground forward into the sandy waste-land.

But the Parthians immediately adapted the method of harassment. Groups of riders began picking areas the Nabataeans were not protecting at that exact time and their sudden charges from behind large dunes were harder to predict. Men on the outside of each rank became experts at spotting dust clouds driven up by the enemy's horses, early warning that an attack was imminent.

'Halt! Shields up!' echoed along the line throughout the afternoon. 'Form testudo!'

Despite their exhaustion, the soldiers had learned to

respond fast. Each side of the Roman column would become a wall of shields, the men inside lifting theirs to form a roof, creating cover for all.

But no matter how fast they responded, fresh screams always rang out as the showers of Parthian arrows came scything down, the shafts finding gaps in the testudo and the men who'd obeyed orders too late. The enemy quickly realised that aiming both above and below the shields was even more effective. Soldiers dropped to the ground clutching throats, arms and legs. The hiss of arrows competed with shrieks of agony in a terrible crescendo.

Romulus was glad Brennus had insisted that they buy heavy legionary *scuta*. The Gaulish tribesmen of his cohort carried traditional elongated rectangular shields far thinner than standard army issue and it soon became evident that they were more susceptible to the enemy bows. If the Parthians came within less than fifty paces their arrows penetrated either type with ease. Further away, only the Gauls' shields were vulnerable. It was small consolation. All day the Parthians remained tantalisingly out of range of Roman *pila,* which were ineffective beyond thirty paces. Fortunately their assaults did not last long, as the enemy were driven off by Nabataean charges or pulled back when they had used all their shafts.

By mid-afternoon more than forty mercenaries had been killed and injured. The dead sprawled in the sand, fresh meat for the vultures above. As the army marched past, the wounded were left with a few guards. When the baggage train arrived, they were loaded into the wagons, their screams and cries adding to the general sense of fear and unease.

And the sun beat down mercilessly, an oven from which there was no escape. Crassus' army was being drained of its ability to fight.

Romulus' first taste of battlefield combat was not what he'd expected. Cotta's lessons about armies meeting on a flat plain and lines of men clashing in shield walls were far from this. He ground his teeth as comrades continued falling to Parthian arrows. Even fights in the arena seemed easy now. There they were one on one, man to man. The tactic of wearing down an opponent was new to him. It was torture enduring attacks without being able to fight back.

Matters came to a head for Romulus when a lone Parthian archer returned after his comrades had just been driven off. Riding parallel, he began firing shafts at the irregulars from just outside javelin range. Half a dozen arrows later, five men lay dead and another had been maimed. The marching soldiers cringed behind their shields, each hoping he would not be next.

'Son of a whore!' Romulus yelled. He prepared himself to break rank, but Brennus quickly pulled him back.

'Wait!'

'I can kill him,' Romulus said, taking a deep breath. It was time to take a stand: too many of their comrades had been slain.

'He'll loose three arrows before you go ten steps!'

Romulus shook off the Gaul's hand proudly. 'I'm a man, not a boy, Brennus. I make my own decisions.'

The comment sank home more than he could know and Brennus released his grip. *The lad's just like Brac,* he thought.

Tarquinius did not look surprised.

Hefting the *pila* he had been training with for months, Romulus stepped out of formation.

'Get back into line, soldier!' yelled Bassius.

Ignoring the order, Romulus stabbed his second *pilum* into the sand and locked eyes with the Parthian. The archer's confidence was now so great that his horse had slowed to a walk and he smiled as Romulus drew back to throw.

Brennus held his breath but the arrogant rider did not even raise his bow in response.

'Waste of time,' said a soldier two ranks behind. 'He's too far away.'

The centurion was about to bellow again, but paused.

With a grunt of effort, Romulus hurled the javelin. It curved upwards in a huge arc before coming down to skewer the Parthian through the chest. There was a roar of approval as the archer toppled slowly off his horse. It was an incredible throw and the mercenaries' spirits visibly lifted.

Romulus resumed his position and Brennus clapped him on the shoulder. 'Fine shot.'

He flushed with pleasure.

By late afternoon, the dreadful heat began to abate and the Parthians finally pulled away. Only fifteen miles had been covered instead of the regulation twenty, but Crassus called a halt before even more men collapsed. Despite their total exhaustion, every other soldier had to help build a marching camp.

'Thank the gods we dug yesterday,' remarked Tarquinius when the order came.

Brennus allowed himself a gulp from his water container. 'It'll be us again tomorrow.'

Grateful not to dig the hot sand, the mercenary cohort fanned out in a curved screen with half the Sixth Legion. Their job was to protect the remainder as the camp was built. The unlucky legionaries shed heavy yokes, cursing loudly as they got to work with shovels.

Across the desert plain other legions were doing the same. By sunset, the earth ramparts and defensive trenches had been finished. Even after extreme ordeals, the strenuous training and harsh discipline meant the army could still function. Rome could install civilisation anywhere.

As evening passed, the sun changed in colour. It went from yellow to orange, finally turning to blood red. Sitting by his tent, Romulus stared at the horizon, an uneasy feeling in his belly. The day had seen no real combat. Apart from his amazing javelin throw, all the skirmishing had gone the Parthians' way. Despite Tarquinius' warnings, it had been a revelation. With rare exceptions, the stories of warfare he had been weaned on consisted of crushing defeats for anyone foolish enough to resist the Republic. It didn't matter who it was – the rebel king Jugurtha in Africa, Hannibal of Carthage – all came to grief at the hands of Rome.

But the sunburnt, exhausted men he could see looked incapable of a major battle. Slack faces stared into space, tired jaws chewed dry food, sunburnt bodies lay everywhere, weapons dropped alongside. Crassus' soldiers did not seem to care what happened to them.

A shiver of fear ran down Romulus' spine. How could an army composed almost entirely of infantry beat one of only cavalry? 'How can Crassus win?' he said out loud.

The Etruscan stopped chewing. 'Simple. By drawing the Parthians into a fixed battle, facing a deep line of soldiers. And when that happens, our horsemen need to be on the wings.'

'Stops the army being flanked,' added Brennus.

'What would the infantry do?'

'Weather the storm,' replied Tarquinius. 'Shelter behind their shields with the front ranks on their knees.'

Romulus winced. 'To protect their lower legs from arrows?'

'Correct.'

'If they stand fast, it would allow the cavalry to peel round to the enemy's rear in a pincer movement.' Brennus thumped one fist into the other. 'Then we'll crush them with a charge on the centre.'

'And the cataphracts?'

Tarquinius grimaced. 'If they are sent in before the Parthians get flanked, things will be very difficult.' He sighed. 'It should all be down to our cavalry.'

Brennus frowned. 'If the mangy bastards don't disappear beforehand!'

'Indeed.'

Romulus looked sharply at the Etruscan. 'What is it?'

'Brennus is right not to trust the Nabataeans. I have been watching our new allies and studying the sky above.' Tarquinius sighed. 'They will probably leave tomorrow.'

'Treacherous savages,' muttered the Gaul.

'How can you be so sure?' asked Romulus.

'Nothing is absolutely certain,' the Etruscan replied. 'But the Nabataeans are no friends of Rome.'

'So what will happen?'

'We must wait. Time will tell,' replied Tarquinius calmly.

'And if there are twelve vultures above us tomorrow?' blurted Romulus.

The Etruscan glanced at him shrewdly. 'Twelve is the Etruscans' sacred number. Often it appears with other signs, which can be good. Or bad.'

Romulus shivered.

Unrolling his blanket, Brennus smiled reassuringly. He had come to the conclusion that Ultan's prophecy had to mean something positive. Since escaping his life as a gladiator and travelling to the east, he had survived storms, battles and fiery deserts. Seen incredible cities like Jerusalem and Damascus. Made friends with a powerful soothsayer. He was learning new things every day. It had to be better than killing men in the arena on a daily basis. 'Don't worry,' he said to Romulus. 'The gods will protect us.' He lay down and was asleep within moments.

Romulus breathed in cool desert air. He had grown quite used to his friend's tendency to only partially answer questions. Although Tarquinius' reticence was frustrating, most of his predictions had been correct so far, forcing the young man to start believing what he said. If the Nabataeans left, the army's only defence against the Parthians would be the irregular cavalry and each soldier's *scutum*, and both had already been shown to be ineffective. It was a sobering thought.

He watched Tarquinius gaze silently at the stars, sure that the soothsayer knew what was going to happen.

Increasingly Romulus thought he did as well.

Chapter XXII: Politics

Campus Martius, Rome, summer 53 BC

While the nobles smiled and nodded, the crowd yelled with anticipation. Brutus' face stayed neutral. The wooden steps creaked as hobnailed *caligae* clattered up. Burly legionaries in full armour appeared, gazing round suspiciously. Satisfied there was no threat, one beckoned to the men at the foot of the stairs. Several senior military officers, resplendent in gilt breastplates and red cloaks, preceded Pompey. It was all designed to impress. Shouts of approval filled the arena as the tribunes acknowledged the people.

'Pompey is on a mission,' whispered Brutus. 'To remain more popular than Caesar and Crassus. With all the unrest in the city, he's plotting to become sole consul.'

'Can he do that?'

It was one of Rome's most sacred laws that power should always be shared between two men. And although the consulships had been monopolised by the

413

triumvirate and their allies for years, no one had dared to promote any other change.

Smiling at those around them, Brutus pressed his lips against her ear. 'Of course,' he said quietly. 'He's deliberately letting the violence from the street gangs spiral out of control. Soon the Senate will have no option but to offer him power. With Crassus in the east, no one else has the soldiers.'

Fabiola made a face. In her lover's eyes there was only one man to lead the Republic.

Caesar. Who was stuck in Gaul, mopping up pockets of tribal resistance.

There was a last clamour from the trumpets. Everyone waited in silence for the master of ceremonies to stand forth.

'Citizens of Rome!'

Loud cheers split the air.

'I give you – the *editor* of these games! Pom-pey Magnus!'

As the praise for Pompey went on and on, Brutus rolled his eyes.

Yet the crude tactic worked. The audience went wild.

A stocky man of medium height with a thick fringe of white hair emerged into the box. His round face was dominated by prominent eyes and a squashed, bulbous nose. Unlike his officers, Pompey wore a white purple-edged toga, mark of the equestrian class. It did not yet pay for leaders to appear in military dress in Rome.

'But Pompey *is* a canny soldier,' added Brutus. 'It'll be a close match when he comes up against Caesar.'

Fabiola turned to him. 'Civil war?' There had been rumours for months.

'Be quiet!' hissed Brutus. 'Do not say those words in public.'

Pompey moved to stand where all could see and raised his right arm, waving slowly to the citizens. When the rapturous applause died down, he took his seat on a purple cushion in the front row.

Moments later, the final pair of gladiators walked on to the sand below. It was a long, skilful contest to the death between a *secutor* and a *retiarius*. Even Fabiola had to admire the lethal display of martial skill. While watching, she prayed silently that the big Gaul was still with her brother, would protect him from danger. Where they were, the gods only knew.

Brutus explained their moves as the two well-matched men lunged and slashed at each other. To compensate for his lack of armour, the fisherman was more experienced than the *secutor*, who could defend himself against trident thrusts with his shield. The *retiarius* had only speed and agility to avoid his opponent's razor-sharp blade.

Time passed and finally the fisherman drew first blood, a wily throw half covering the *secutor* with his weighted net. Instantly the trident swept forward, plunging deep into the other's right thigh.

Thinking the end was near, the crowd roared.

Desperately the hunter threw himself forward as the barbed prongs ripped clear of his flesh. Groaning in pain, he reached up with his sword and slashed the *retiarius* across the belly as he fell.

His opponent also slumped to his knees.

Blood dripped on to the sand from both men.

There was a pause while the two wounded fighters dragged air into their chests, struggling for the energy to continue. People in the audience screamed encouragement, throwing pieces of bread and fruit at them. The *secutor* was first to stand, throwing off the net and raising his weapon. With a struggle, the *retiarius* also got up, holding his stomach with one hand, gory trident with the other.

'It will be over soon,' said Brutus, pointing. Both were clearly badly hurt.

Fabiola closed her eyes, imagining Romulus.

The staff officer leaned forward and tapped the shoulder of the portly man in front. 'Ten thousand *sestertii* on the *retiarius*, Fabius,' he said, his eyes glinting.

Fabius half turned, an amazed look on his red face. 'His guts are about to fall out, Brutus!'

'Scared to lose?'

'You're on,' laughed Fabius and the pair gripped forearms.

Fabiola pouted and caressed Brutus' neck. 'You're wasting money,' she whispered in his ear.

He winked. 'Never underestimate a fisherman – especially a wounded one.'

Although the *secutor* could not move fast, he was still armed with sword and shield. Shuffling after the *retiarius,* he cut and slashed rapidly, parrying occasional trident thrusts with little difficulty. The fisherman made sporadic attempts to retrieve his net but was blocked every time. He seemed quite weak, barely fending off the hunter's aggressive efforts.

Different sections of the crowd shouted their support for each man. Typically, most were backing the fighter who seemed more likely to win.

The *secutor*.

Watching intently, Brutus stayed quiet amidst the clamour. Fabiola held on to his arm, wishing she could stop the barbaric display and save a man's life.

Weakened by his injury, the *retiarius* slowed even further and the hunter redoubled his efforts, trying to get in a mortal blow. Tiring himself out, he paused for a moment, confident the other would not attack. The fisherman groaned and blood oozed from between his fingers.

Silence fell on the arena.

The audience held its breath as the *secutor* prepared to end the fight.

Suddenly the *retiarius* gasped and looked over his enemy's shoulder. Confused, the hunter's gaze turned away for a single heartbeat.

It was enough.

The armoured fighter spun back, eyes widening in horror as the trident drove deep into his throat. Hanging off the sharp tines, he made a loud choking noise and dropped both sword and shield. The fisherman quickly released his weapon and let the dead man fall to the sand. Swaying gently, he received the crowd's approval with glazed eyes before collapsing on top of his opponent.

Brutus was delighted. 'The oldest trick in the book,' he crowed, poking Fabius in the back.

The fat noble grimaced at the unexpected turn of

events. 'A slave will bring you the money in the morning,' he muttered with poor grace before turning back to his companions.

Fabiola's eyes were drawn to the *retiarius*, who was still lying across the dead *secutor*. No one else even gave him a glance. He was a slave. 'Will he live?' she asked anxiously.

'Of course,' replied Brutus, patting her arm. 'Only army surgeons are better than those in the gladiator schools. He'll need dozens of stitches in the muscle and skin, but within two months that fisherman will be back in the arena, good as new.'

Fabiola smiled, but inside she was boiling with rage. One brave man had just died and another had been badly wounded. For what? The mob's amusement, nothing more. And when he recovered, the survivor would have to endure it all over again. As Romulus must have until he fled after the fight outside the brothel.

Never let the savages catch you alive, brother, she prayed. There is no mercy in Rome.

Afterwards, Brutus took her to the house of a political ally on the Palatine hill. Gracchus Maximus, a senator with close links to Caesar, had invited him to a feast.

On the journey from the Campus Martius, Fabiola brought up the subject of the triumvirate again. Away from other nobles, Brutus seemed more at ease.

'Since the death of Julia, Pompey's wife, relations have become very strained.' He frowned. 'It was a tragedy.'

The death of a woman during childbirth was all too common and that of Caesar's only daughter had weakened the strong bond between him and Pompey.

'The loss of a child is hard to bear,' said Fabiola, thinking of her mother.

'Because he is not in the city, Caesar needs Pompey to fight his corner here. Fortunately the general still respects their agreement enough to do that. But it won't be for ever.'

'Surely the revolt in Gaul will keep Caesar completely tied up?' News had reached Rome that the previously localised unrest was spreading. A young chieftain named Vercingetorix was rallying the tribes under one banner.

'Not for long,' replied Brutus briskly. 'And it keeps his legions battle-ready while most of Pompey's do nothing but play dice in Greece and Hispania.'

Fabiola concealed her surprise. She had not known it had come to this already. Men were preparing for civil war.

The litter came to a halt, ending the conversation.

Apart from Brutus' villa and Gemellus' *domus*, Fabiola had not been in any large houses. As befitted an extremely wealthy man, Gracchus Maximus' residence was enormous. A high, plain wall guarded its exterior, the only entrance a pair of wooden doors strengthened with iron studs. One of Brutus' guards rapped on the portal with his sword hilt. The demand was answered immediately and they alighted, leaving their slaves outside. Entering a grand *atrium*, Brutus and Fabiola were welcomed by the shaven-headed major-domo, who bowed and guided them into the house proper.

Each room that followed was more magnificent than the last. Gold candelabras held hosts of burning candles, illuminating graceful statues in alcoves along the painted walls. Beautiful mosaics were laid out everywhere, even in the hallways. Fountains in the garden murmured gently through open doors.

Reaching the palatial banqueting hall, Fabiola's eyes momentarily widened. Its floor consisted of one huge image, decorated in a circular fashion with scenes from Greek mythology. Hundreds of thousands of tiny clay pieces had been laid in intricate patterns to form a richly coloured picture. Surrounded by lesser gods, Zeus occupied the centre of the design. It was a more stunning piece of art than anything Fabiola had ever seen. Perhaps the villa she dreamt of could look like this.

The room was crowded with nobles mingling, and slaves serving food and drink. Loud conversation filled the air. If the chance presented itself, this would be a good situation to meet potential clients. Great care would have to be taken to avoid Brutus noticing. As the majordomo led them towards Maximus, Fabiola's eye was caught by a large statue on a plinth occupying a prominent position near the entrance.

Brutus followed her gaze. 'Julius Caesar – my general,' he stated proudly.

Carved from white marble, the painted figure was taller than a man. Caesar was regally depicted in a toga, a thick sweep of cloth covering the right arm. The hair was cut short in military style, the jaw shaven. The face blankly watching the guests was long and thin, the nose aquiline.

'I've never seen a better likeness,' said Brutus with pleasure. 'He could be here in the room.'

Fabiola was lost for words. Before them was an older version of Romulus, in stone. Since Brutus' casual comment months before, she had spent hours gazing into the mirror, wondering about her half-theory.

Could Caesar be their father?

'What is it?'

'Nothing at all,' laughed Fabiola brightly. 'Please introduce me to Maximus. I want to meet everyone who knows the great man.'

He took her arm and they threaded their way through the crowd. Fabiola's beauty turned heads every step of the way. Brutus nodded and smiled, exchanging handshakes and cordial words with the nobles and senators they passed. It was at such times that much of Rome's political business was conducted. She could see that Brutus was an adept at it.

Fabiola's mind was in complete turmoil. Could one of the triumvirate have raped her mother seventeen years before?

Maximus beckoned when he saw Brutus, who proudly introduced her as his lover. There was no mention of the Lupanar. Although their distinguished-looking host probably knew her background, he inclined his head graciously at Fabiola. She rewarded him with a radiant smile, aware that he had been more respectful to a prostitute than most would be. It was a sign of Brutus' stature.

Fabiola breathed deeply, returning the bows from passing guests. It was taking considerable self-control to remain calm and she was glad when Brutus began muttering in Maximus' ear. No doubt this was the main reason for the day's outing. Like Pompey, Caesar's men were busy plotting the future of Rome.

She let the room's noise wash over her.

Somehow I will find out if Caesar is the one, Fabiola thought. And the gods help him if he is.

A week later . . .

Memor moaned.

Pompeia had been good at her job, but this new girl was incredible. He had been getting bored with the redhead. When Fabiola had joined them unasked in the baths a few weeks previously, the *lanista* had been pleased. Presumably it was a gift from Jovina. Occasionally the shrewd madam gave regular customers a treat. It was good business.

The theory was completely wrong.

Mad with lust, he shoved upwards, trying to get the teasing mouth to take his jutting penis inside.

Fabiola looked up carefully. Memor's eyes were closed, his wiry body relaxed. She licked the tip of his shaft and a groan emanated from the top of the bed.

'Don't stop!'

Obediently she bobbed her head up and down, prolonging the pleasure.

Memor writhed on the sweat-stained covers, gasping with ecstasy.

It had taken months of persuasion for Pompeia to give up the best customer she had gained in years. Despite having been in the brothel longer, the redhead had far fewer regulars than Fabiola. Although Pompeia tried hard, it was difficult not to be jealous. Fully aware of this, Fabiola took care of her as if she were family. The borrowed perfume had been replaced a dozen times; jewellery and little gifts of money regularly appeared in her room. Troublesome customers vanished, helped discreetly by the doormen.

Pompeia agreed to Fabiola's initial requests, asking Memor about young boys sold into the *ludus*. Frustratingly, the answers were never more than vague. It seemed the *lanista* did not talk business with prostitutes. But Fabiola became fixated with the idea that he knew something. Leads from other clients since her arrival had all proved fruitless. It seemed Romulus had vanished without trace after the brawl outside the brothel.

Memor was her only chance. After all, he ran the largest gladiator school in Rome.

Knowing Pompeia would not have the same personal reasons to obtain information, Fabiola finally asked if she could take on the *lanista* as a customer. The redhead refused. Friendship in the Lupanar only went so far.

'He gives good tips.' Pompeia's tone was whingeing. 'What do you need more clients for anyway?'

'You know why. This means a lot to me.'

Pompeia pouted, but did not answer.

She had tried almost everything. 'Will money help?' Fabiola asked desperately.

There was instant interest. 'How much?'

She threw caution to the wind. 'Twenty-five thousand *sestertii.*'

Pompeia's eyes widened. It was far more than she had imagined, half a lifetime's tips. Fabiola must be even better than she'd thought. 'Memor might know nothing,' she said with a twinge of guilt.

Fabiola closed her eyes. Jupiter guide me, she thought. It only took a moment. 'He does. I know it.'

Pompeia flushed. 'If you're sure . . .'

Fabiola smiled at the price, which was less than half of her savings. She did not care if finding Romulus used up every last coin she had.

But the *lanista* had proved a hard nut to crack. All the usual wiles to make a customer talk had failed miserably. Pompeia had not been exaggerating. Memor was easily irritated and Fabiola quickly learned not to ask too many questions. Coupling with the scarred old man was most unpleasant; something about his casual brutality left her cold. But the new client took to Fabiola with gusto. A month went by with a virtually wordless visit every single week. She began to think that her carefully saved money had been wasted. When Memor had not appeared for a while it had been a relief.

Then he had returned. Intense preparation for a big fight had left no time for relaxation. As soon as it was over, Memor had returned to his favourite girl.

It was now or never. She had made his pleasure last longer than ever before. Every time he thrust into her mouth, desperate to come, Fabiola had slowed down the rhythm, teasing him with tongue and fingers. She knew the *lanista* could not take much more.

'Master?'

Memor's eyes opened with a start. 'What's wrong?'

'Nothing, Master.' She held his penis tightly with one

hand, prolonging the moment. 'Ever had a fighter called Romulus in your school?' She took him into her mouth again.

He gasped. 'Who?'

'Romulus. My cousin, Master.'

'Troublesome son of a whore!' Memor pushed her head down.

Hope flared inside. A short time later, Fabiola paused again.

'Is he still in the *ludus*?'

'Little bastard's long gone,' said Memor, momentarily distracted. 'He helped my best gladiator kill an important noble about two years back.'

Fabiola's pulse quickened.

'That Gaul was worth a fortune,' muttered Memor.

At the time, the comment passed her by.

She began stroking him up and down gently and the *lanista* moaned. 'What happened to them, Master?'

'Rumour was they joined Crassus' army.' He jerked upright and gripped Fabiola's hair. The look on his scarred face was terrifying. 'Unless you know something?'

Fabiola opened her eyes wide. 'I never liked him, Master. He was a bully.' She bent her head to finish the job and Memor fell back, sighing with satisfaction.

Hope. There was still hope in Fabiola's heart.

Chapter XXIII: Ariamnes

Parthia, summer 53 BC

Next day came far too soon for the soldiers of Crassus' army. The dawn sky rapidly changed to a clear blue, and the temperature began to soar. It would be another scorching march. Crassus had risen before sunrise, woken by a troubling nightmare about the unhappy episode with the bull's heart. He knew that the story had spread like wildfire through the legions and a distinct feeling of unease had been palpable since among the men. This had been increased by equally fast moving reports that the eagle of the Sixth had reversed as it had left the Euphrates. Even senior officers now seemed to be affected. Only Publius and the Nabataean continued to show confidence in him.

But driven by his burning urge to become the leading force in Rome and to crush Pompey and Caesar, Crassus remained convinced he would be victorious. The previous day's losses had been minor and a few hundred horse archers were certainly nothing to worry about. After all, had he not conquered Spartacus and his army? The slaves had numbered more than eighty thousand. Today, all his veteran legions had to face was a fraction of that number. And they were savages. Crassus laughed out loud. In a few short weeks Seleucia would fall, proving his vision. His leadership.

Desiring more details of Parthia's wealth – soon to be *his* wealth – Crassus had summoned Ariamnes to his side. The chieftain found him eating dates on a couch under gently moving palm leaves fanned by slaves.

The Nabataean bowed deeply. 'Your Excellency wished to see me?'

'Repeat what you said about Seleucia's riches.' Crassus was never bored by the story.

Again Ariamnes bowed low. 'Most is found in the palaces of King Orodes, the wealthiest man in Parthia. Many chambers have walls covered with beaten silver or huge silk banners. The fountains are filled with precious stones and there are countless gold statues with opals and rubies for eyes.' He paused for effect. 'The treasure store alone is said to fill a dozen rooms.'

Crassus smiled. 'Rome will never forget the triumphal parade from this campaign!'

Ariamnes was about to reply when the pair saw Longinus approaching. The legate was followed closely by a swarthy figure in leather armour. A curved sword hung from the man's belt and a small round shield from one arm. The fine layer of dust covering him from head to toe could not conceal the grey sheen of exhaustion on his skin.

Obviously agitated, Longinus came to a halt and saluted.

Crassus curled his lip with distaste, Ariamnes swiftly copying the gesture.

'One of our patrols has just brought him in, sir. A messenger from Artavasdes,' said Longinus, looking daggers at the Nabataean. 'He's ridden day and night to reach us.'

Crassus frowned. 'Not an impostor then?'

'He carries a document stamped with the royal seal.'

'What does the Armenian want now?' snapped Crassus.

'The king has been attacked by a large Parthian force north of here. Even if Artavasdes wished to join us now, he could not.'

Ariamnes' eyes darted to Crassus.

'Continue.' The general's voice was ice cold.

'Artavasdes calls on us for aid.' Wary of continuing, Longinus paused.

'There is more?'

'He still wants us to march on Parthia through Armenia, sir.'

'That dog wants *me* to retreat? And help him?' roared Crassus. 'When Seleucia's riches lie at my feet?'

'It's a safer route, sir,' tried the legate, but it was obvious his commander had no intention of helping the client king.

Crassus' face darkened.

'May I offer my humble opinion?' interjected Ariamnes smoothly.

Bodies stiff with tension, both men turned to him.

'Excellency, Orodes must have assumed that you would march through the mountains. He has sent his army north, but they have encountered Artavasdes instead.'

'That would explain the small numbers of Parthians yesterday,' beamed Crassus.

'A delaying tactic and nothing more,' Ariamnes continued. 'And all that stands between us and the capital.'

Longinus was unconvinced. 'What proof have you?'

'Patience, Legate,' Crassus said calmly. 'Let him speak.'

The Nabataean threw a sidelong glance at Longinus. 'Yesterday my scouts outflanked the horse archers and reconnoitred for miles to the southeast. There was no evidence of more Parthian forces. Orodes *must* have taken his men north.'

'Why did you not tell us before?' said Longinus acidly. 'This smells of treachery.'

Ariamnes looked hurt. 'But I am myself offering to lead another search.'

Crassus nodded approvingly.

The Nabataean noticed Longinus' fingers tighten around the hilt of his sword.

'We will return at the slightest sign of enemy activity. But I suspect the route to Seleucia is already clear.' Ariamnes pointedly ignored the legate. 'Would that please Your Excellency?'

A huge smile spread across Crassus' face. 'And the scouts found no signs of the Parthians?'

'None at all, Excellency.'

Longinus was unable to contain himself. 'Do not trust this snake, sir! I know it's a trap. Why not return to the Euphrates and join Artavasdes? With over ten thousand cavalry, we would smash any opposition.'

'Silence!' screamed Crassus. 'Are you in league with that damned Armenian?'

'Of course not,' muttered Longinus, stunned by Crassus' monumental arrogance.

'Then shut your mouth. Unless you want to end your career in the ranks.'

Longinus struggled to contain his rage. With a crisp salute, he turned to leave but suddenly bent towards Ariamnes. 'Prove treacherous and I will crucify you myself,' he whispered before marching away.

'So. Today we shall sweep aside these gnats who have been annoying my men,' declared Crassus.

The Nabataean smiled.

Shortly afterwards, Romulus and Tarquinius watched as the long column of Nabataean cavalry rode eastwards.

'He's just letting them all go?'

'We will not see them again,' said the Etruscan, peering at the fine layer of cloud positioned in the sky high above the departing horsemen.

Romulus shook his head in disbelief.

'I predicted that one.' Brennus was sharpening the longsword again. 'The general is a fool.'

'Ariamnes is very persuasive and simply told Crassus what he wanted to hear,' observed the Etruscan.

'We have only two thousand cavalry left now,' said Romulus. 'How many Parthian horsemen will there be?'

'Up to five times that number.'

Romulus frowned, trying to calculate the number of arrows that many archers could loose.

Tarquinius checked there was nobody else within

earshot. 'Thousands will lose their lives in the coming battle.'

The Gaul's face darkened. 'What about us?'

'So many spirits were leaving this existence . . .' The Etruscan seemed unusually troubled. 'It is difficult to be precise,' he admitted. 'But I feel sure that two of us will survive, because I have seen our friendship endure past the bloodshed and killing.'

Brennus prepared himself for the worst. Let me die bravely, he thought. With honour, protecting Romulus and Tarquinius. So I can meet Brac and my uncle in paradise with no shame. Tell Liath that this time I did not run when my loved ones needed me. A lump formed in his throat and he swallowed hard, struggling to quell the guilt that still ruled him.

Romulus scowled. How could any man see the spirits of the dead? Obviously plenty of men would die fighting the Parthians, but to know exactly which ones? It was not possible. He looked up to find Tarquinius' eyes on him, his gaze piercing. Unnerved, Romulus found himself unable to meet it. Perhaps it was his turn to die. His stomach lurched and he quickly threw up a prayer to Jupiter to protect them all.

'And the rest of the cohort?' asked the big warrior.

Tarquinius was reluctant to answer but Brennus persisted.

Silence.

The Gaul blanched. 'Every single one?'

'Virtually all.'

'Sometimes you see too much,' Brennus said, shivering. He stared at the unsuspecting mercenaries preparing for another day in this furnace. It was chilling to imagine them all being killed, and it reminded him strongly of the last time he had seen his fellow Allobroge warriors readying themselves for battle.

As always after the Etruscan's predictions, images of Fabiola and his mother filled Romulus' mind. He longed to ask about them, but dared not. If Tarquinius revealed something dark or evil, the young man was not sure he could refuse to believe it as well. Their fragile memories were sacred, even intrinsic to his survival. They helped him to continue marching into this wilderness.

The sun climbed fast from the horizon, bringing its heat to bear with renewed vengeance. The Nabataean cavalry had not been gone for long before trumpets sounded to break camp. Discipline was still strong and the army was soon ready to move. At the front stood the irregular cohorts, followed by five legions and the baggage train. Two legions now protected the rear, leaving the Gaulish and Iberian cavalry on the flanks. It was a thin protective screen for the number of infantry.

Bassius listened carefully to the last series of commands. 'Time to go. I want twenty miles from you today.'

Following the Nabataeans' hoof prints, two troops of Gauls galloped off in front.

The soldiers marched after them into the empty desert. The horizon remained clear of enemy horsemen and their spirits rose. But as the hours passed without a single cloud to provide respite from the burning sun, the enemy was forgotten as the extreme heat again took its terrible toll on the footsore Romans. Many had drunk all their water the day before and, contrary to Crassus' opinion, the mules had been carrying enough for only some of the soldiers. As thirst levels increased, the rest had no option but to keep walking. The three friends sucked grimly on pebbles, hoarding the remaining liquid in their leather bags as if it was gold.

And then it seemed as if the gods had remembered Crassus' army. Half a dozen Gauls came riding back with news that there was a river ahead. The legions' speed almost doubled, and quickly they made out the typical desert haze that formed over water in the distance.

Patches of reeds on the banks were trampled flat as thirsty mercenaries tramped into the shallow rivulet. Men flopped down headlong in an effort to get cool. But Romulus and his comrades were not allowed long to fill their containers.

'Did I say stop? Or fall out? No!' Bassius roared. 'Keep marching! Bastards!'

Relishing the feeling on his weary muscles, Romulus splashed through the calf-high water. 'A rest would be good,' he muttered, careful not to let the centurion hear.

'Some chance!' Brennus drained his bag, stooping to fill it immediately. 'Drink as much as you can.'

'There'll be no rest for a while.' Tarquinius pointed ahead.

Romulus and the Gaul tore their attention from the refreshing liquid.

All the scouts were riding back at the gallop.

Romulus saw Brennus' hand reaching for his sword. Automatically he did the same, sweat forming on his brow.

The Gauls rushed past the mercenaries, heading directly to Crassus' position. Moments later the *bucinae* blared with a stridency the men had not heard before.

'Hear that? Enemy in sight! Double time!'

The cohort responded with as much urgency as they could muster, pounding up the river bank, each man hoping the Gauls were wrong.

For the rest of his days, Romulus would remember the sight that greeted him.

On a flat plain in the middle distance sat the Parthian army, a formation nearly a mile across. Their appearance distorted by the haze, thousands of men on horseback waited patiently for the Romans. Huge, brightly coloured banners swirled in the hot air, making them appear even more alien. The noise of pounding drums and clanging bells reached the legions as signallers relayed messages to and fro.

It was an immensely intimidating sight for the exhausted Roman soldiers. Sunburnt faces went pale and oaths were spat. More than one mercenary looked west to the Euphrates and safety.

'Jupiter's balls!' swore Brennus. 'No infantry at all?'

'I told you there would be none,' replied Tarquinius.

There was a short silence. The Gaul visibly braced himself. 'We'll cope,' he said simply. 'We'll have to.'

The Etruscan's dark eyes were calm. 'It will all be clear by nightfall.'

They nodded grimly. With a battle to fight, there was little point entertaining fearful thoughts. It was courage and Roman *gladii* that they needed now.

'What are those?' Romulus pointed at tall humped

creatures with long necks and legs, standing behind the enemy lines.

'Camels. The Parthians use them as mules,' explained Tarquinius. 'And they'll be carrying spare arrows, so those bastard archers don't run out. With that many of them, each man will have hundreds of shafts. Real trouble.'

'Because our damn shields are practically useless,' said Brennus, thumping his *scutum.*

The Etruscan nodded. 'The warriors train with those composite bows every day, my friend. Remember what they did yesterday.'

'But we are free men now.' Brennus clapped Romulus on the shoulder. 'If the gods will it, we shall die together – with our swords in our hands and the sun on our faces. Better than in the arena for that bastard Memor.'

'True.' Romulus met the Gaul's gaze squarely. Mention of the *lanista* made him remember Cotta's lessons. 'Spartacus wouldn't have worried about facing the Parthians,' he said. 'He always had plenty of horsemen.'

'That Thracian had far more ability than Crassus,' agreed Tarquinius. 'He only got beaten because Crixus, his second-in-command, wouldn't leave Italy. Spartacus would never have led his men into a mess like this.'

Romulus sank into a reverie, imagining himself in charge of the army, Tarquinius and Brennus by his side. Keeping the cavalry on the wings would be the most urgent task, to prevent the legions being outflanked while they formed up. Then the centre could make a tactical withdrawal as the Parthians attacked, allowing the cavalry to enfold the enemy. It was how Hannibal had won so many of his battles against Rome.

Tarquinius regarded him keenly. 'Crassus will not think of trying Carthaginian tactics. The fool thinks all we have to do is advance and the Parthians will flee.'

Romulus was stunned. 'Men like you two should be in charge,' he blurted.

Tarquinius inclined his head. 'And you, Romulus.'

He flushed with delight.

'We'd do a better job than Crassus,' chuckled Brennus.

'That would not be difficult.' Tarquinius squinted at the Parthians, counting under his breath.

Bassius ordered his men to take up a defensive position on the ridge. One cohort could do little but wait for the rest of the army to catch up. Not a man moved from the Parthian force. Their trap sprung, the enemy was content to let the Romans take up battle formation.

'Shows how confident their leader is. They could be riding in and showering us with arrows.'

'Maybe he wants to fight Crassus in single combat!' joked the Gaul. 'We could put our feet up and watch.'

'It'll be common soldiers bleeding today,' said Tarquinius. 'Not leaders.'

Reconciling himself to his fate, Brennus shrugged his massive shoulders. '*Lanistae*. Generals. Whoever. They give the orders. Men like us die.'

Keeping the Etruscan's reassuring words uppermost in his mind, Romulus prayed to Jupiter, his guide since childhood.

You did not need to be a soothsayer to know that thousands would die in the forthcoming battle.

And possibly one of them.

'Where is Ariamnes?' Crassus sat bolt upright in the saddle, his face pinched with anger.

Nobody answered.

There had been no sign of the Nabataeans since dawn. With the full Parthian army in sight, it was obvious that the Romans' erstwhile ally would not be returning.

Ariamnes was a traitor.

'Son of a whore! I will have him disembowelled. Then crucified.'

Longinus tactfully cleared his throat. 'What are your orders, sir?'

Crassus glared at him, but, unwilling to acknowledge any mistakes, his eyes dropped away. 'Cavalry on the wings. Cohorts in one square formation,' the general blustered, picking the boldest tactic he could think of. 'That rabble will take one look at us and flee.'

The grizzled legate gasped. 'And leave gaps between the units?'

'Those are my orders. Is that clear?' said Crassus, bunching his jaw. Although he could immediately see what Longinus meant, his monumental pride was still smarting at the exposure of Ariamnes' treachery. 'This way their greater numbers of horse cannot flank us.'

'Yes, but it also allows those bastards to ride between us,' replied Longinus, expecting his fellow officers to voice their support. None was forthcoming. The legate glared at them, then continued undeterred. 'Sir, solid lines would be better. Then only a small number of men could be attacked at one time.'

Crassus' eyes bulged. 'Are you questioning my orders again?'

'Merely offering advice.'

'Insubordination!' Crassus cried. The black cloak he had donned that morning clung to his back, soaked in sweat. The legionaries on guard nearby eyed it uneasily. Black was the colour of death. 'Get into position, Legate, before I have you whipped.'

Longinus' jaw clenched. Few people would dare speak to a senior officer in such a manner. 'You are making a big mistake, *sir*,' he said insolently. The general needed him too much to follow through on the threat. 'Solid lines would be best.'

Crassus glanced at the others. 'Anyone care to agree?'

There was silence. His subordinates had been well picked.

'Consider your career finished,' said Crassus. 'If you survive the battle!'

'See what the Senate says about this back in Rome. They still have some power.' Longinus snorted with contempt and rode away, swallowing his anger. Crassus' arrogance would not stop them smashing the Parthians. He would sort out his problems with the general later. Longinus tried to put the bull's heart, the reversed eagle standard and the black cloak out of his mind.

'What are you all waiting for?' Spittle flew from Crassus' lips. 'Get out of my sight!'

The legates hastened to obey.

There was a battle to win.

Chapter XXIV: Publius and Surena

It took nearly half the afternoon for every legion to reach the plain. The desert horsemen sat in the shimmering haze, waiting patiently. Drums and bells kept up a relentless din. The outlandish sound was mindful of wild animals' roars intermingled with the sound of thunder.

It was terrifying.

Having waited the longest, the mercenaries were worst affected by the melting temperatures. Few had any water left and again men began to collapse from dehydration and heat exhaustion. The stronger soldiers did what they could for their comrades before battle commenced. Bassius stalked up and down, cajoling and threatening by turn. His sheer drive helped rally spirits that had fallen to a new low.

With Crassus' army finally in place, a staccato series of notes sounded from the *bucinae*. The waiting was over.

'You heard!' screamed the centurions. 'Get into position!'

Following routines that had been practised many

439

times, the legions fanned out across the plain in a massive four-sided formation. Simultaneously each cohort formed into another hollow square, three men deep, forty in length and breadth. A hundred paces separated each from its neighbours in front and behind. Crassus, his officers and two veteran cohorts took their position in the empty middle along with the baggage train while the Gaulish and Iberian cavalry moved to sit on the wings. It was a most unusual formation for the start of a battle.

'What is he doing?' Romulus frowned. It was clear what would happen as soon as the attack began.

'Crassus thinks we might be completely outflanked,' said Brennus. 'This prevents it.'

'But not much else,' added Romulus, imagining how the Parthians would respond.

'He is a fool!' Tarquinius peered round angrily. 'Those archers will simply ride between the cohorts and pick us off with ease.'

It was unsettling that they could all see what would happen but Crassus could not. Any respect for authority Romulus had left was disappearing fast.

The Parthian leader was still in no hurry to attack. He waited until the Roman army had stopped manoeuvring.

At an unseen signal, the drums began pounding a heavy, rhythmic beat, different from before. The bells also changed tempo, their volume making even speech impossible. The noise went on and on, intimidating with its sheer energy. Exhausted by sunstroke and the incredible temperature, the dazed soldiers could only stare at the enemy, unsure what to do.

Suddenly, the clamour stopped.

A large group of horsemen in the Parthian centre separated from the rest. Slowly they moved forward to within a few hundred paces of the Roman front ranks, halting in unison.

Romulus peered into the haze. 'Who are they?'

'The cataphracts.' There was respect in Tarquinius' voice. 'Their elite heavy cavalry.'

'Long spears like Greek hoplites carry would soon sort them out,' said Romulus fiercely. 'If we had any.'

'Or a defensive ditch,' added the Gaul.

Tarquinius nodded approvingly.

The weary Romans stared miserably at the enemy, unable to do more than bake in the intense heat. It was almost a relief when the instruments started up again. With a flourish, the Parthian riders whipped off their cloaks, revealing chain mail from neck to mid-thigh. In each soldier's right hand was a heavy lance. The horses were also covered in armour, creating an immense wall of metal. Sunlight bounced off thousands of iron rings, reflecting towards the Romans in waves of blinding light.

Crassus' soldiers found it impossible to look directly at the cataphracts and the dazzling light wasn't the only reason. Fear was creeping into men's hearts.

'Amazing.' Tarquinius pointed excitedly. 'The *andabatae* in the arena were a mockery of the real thing.'

Romulus had only heard of the mounted gladiators who wore helmets with no eyeholes.

'Roman savages,' said the Gaul. 'Sending blind men into the arena to fight.'

'These riders are a different proposition,' pronounced the Etruscan.

Romulus was amazed by the mail rippling down the horses' flanks. He had never seen anything like it.

The cataphracts waited, maximising their terrifying effect. The drums kept up their dreadful din, deepening the sense of impending doom. Mercenaries and legionaries shifted uneasily from foot to foot. The unease in Crassus' army was becoming palpable, spreading to every man. Normally it was the Romans who scared their enemies by standing in silence before battle.

'Might have a decent fight today.' Brennus hefted his spear impatiently, eager to end their wait. 'Those bastards actually look dangerous.'

Tarquinius smiled humourlessly.

Wishing the battle would just start, Romulus checked his sword was loose in its scabbard, his *pilum* head securely attached to the shaft. Stay calm, he thought.

For what seemed an eternity, the two armies faced each other, soaking up the intense heat. The tension was unbearable.

And then the noise stopped. Immediately the horse archers moved forward while the heavy cavalry remained where they were.

'Prepare for an enemy charge,' ordered Bassius. 'Close order!'

The mercenaries had been well trained. Quickly the men readied their *pila* and spears and moved closer, standing shoulder to shoulder. Like tiny cogs in a big machine, thousands of soldiers across the battlefield did the same. Their shields overlapping, the formations presented the Parthians with dozens of armoured squares.

The enemy urged their mounts to a trot, followed by a gallop. The earth shook with the thunder of hooves and Romulus felt his stomach clench. The previous day's attacks would be as nothing compared to this.

Just as Tarquinius had predicted, the horsemen split smoothly into columns, aiming at gaps between the cohorts. Fear grew palpable in the ranks, men sweated heavily and hands grew clammy on javelin shafts. Behind him, Romulus heard a man vomiting. He ignored the sound, lifting his *scutum* higher, squinting at the approaching riders.

Battle was about to commence.

The Parthians rode closer and closer. Soon they could see horses' nostrils flaring, the archers' faces tense as they drew back bowstrings.

Romulus' remaining *pilum* felt burning hot.

'Ready javelins!' There was no trace of fear in Bassius' voice. 'Wait till my command!'

Every man's right arm went back, ready for the order to release.

Before it could come, the Parthians fired a volley. It was from much closer range than the day before. Until that moment, the mercenaries had no idea just how powerful the enemy's composite bows were. Waves of arrows swept through the air, punching through Roman *scuta* like they were made of parchment. The front rank dissolved, cut down to a man.

Miraculously, Bassius alone remained standing, shield peppered with arrows. 'Aim short! Loose!' he screamed.

With a heave, Romulus and the men of the second two ranks swung forward, launching their *pila* in low curving arcs. They fell in a flurry of wood and metal, finding targets at last. From such a short distance, Roman javelins were also lethal. Horses fell screaming to the sand, throwing their riders. Dozens of warriors were hit, but the force of the charge was such that they were carried past to safety.

Another brutal volley scythed into the side of the cohort before Bassius had time to respond. And then the Parthians were gone, galloping off to attack another square. The noise of hooves died away, to be replaced by screams.

At least eighty men lay strewn across the hot sand.

Romulus gaped at the sight. Scores of soldiers had been killed outright by arrows which had passed through shield and chain mail, ripping into soft flesh beneath. *Scuta* lay pinned to prone bodies all around and a dense network of wooden shafts peppered the ground. So many had been injured that Romulus looked himself over in disbelief. He had not suffered so much as a scratch. Neither had his friends.

'They can do that all day,' Tarquinius said calmly.

His face grim, Brennus muttered and cursed.

Through clouds of dust, other cohorts were now being subjected to the same attacks as the archers swept around the Roman formations. For the moment, Bassius' depleted unit was an island of calm in the midst of chaos.

'Romulus! Get over here.'

Bassius was waving to him, his face knotted in pain. An arrow-riddled *scutum* hung from his left arm.

'What can I do, sir?'

'Cut out this damn thing!' The senior centurion swung

out his wounded arm. A barbed head was protruding just below the elbow.

Romulus winced.

'Came clean through the shield.' Bassius shook his head. 'Thirty years of war, and I have never seen a bow as powerful.'

Romulus took the arrow in both hands and snapped it in two near the point. Bassius grunted in pain as the young soldier pulled the shaft backwards. The *scutum* fell from his grip and a fresh run of blood came from the two small wounds. Using a piece of cloth ripped from his tunic, Romulus bound the area tightly.

'Good lad,' said Bassius, picking up the shield again.

'You can't fight like that, sir.'

The centurion ignored him, moving back into position. 'Form square! There'll be another attack very soon.'

Romulus rejoined the ranks, wishing Bassius was in charge of more than a cohort. Officers like him were worth far more than Crassus.

A momentary calm fell on the battlefield as the Parthian archers withdrew, leaving mayhem behind.

'They've only gone to replenish their arrows.' Tarquinius watched the flocks of vultures gathering above. 'Crassus must seize this chance. The whole army should be in a continuous line, eight or ten ranks deep.' He indicated the battered units. 'Not like this. It's a massacre, not a battle.'

'How many casualties?' Crassus punched a fist into his palm. Unsettled, his horse skittered sideways, ears flattening.

'Still being counted, sir.' The junior tribune spoke with trepidation. 'But at least a tenth of every cohort.'

'A tenth of my army dead or wounded?'

'Yes, sir.'

'How many Parthians have been killed?'

'Not sure, sir.' The young officer was pale with fear. 'A few hundred, perhaps.'

'Get out of my sight,' Crassus spluttered. 'Before I have you executed!'

'It's hardly his fault, sir,' said Longinus, who had disobeyed orders yet again to come and remonstrate.

Hands twitching on his reins, Crassus glared at the legate. Nothing was being said about their argument before the battle started. Even he had realised what was more important now.

'What are your orders? The Parthians will attack again soon.'

'Send word to Publius,' cried Crassus abruptly, a wild look in his eyes. 'He must advance on the Parthian right with his cavalry and four cohorts of mercenaries. Create a diversion.'

Longinus paused. It was not what he would do.

'Is that clear?' The general's voice was suddenly calm. Too calm. Crassus glanced at the officer in charge of his guards.

The centurion laid a hand on his *gladius*.

Longinus saw the gesture and knew instantly what it meant. Any man who questioned Crassus' orders would now be killed. The legate saluted stiffly and paced over to the nearby scouts.

'When Publius has driven them back, we will charge the enemy's centre,' yelled Crassus after him.

Longinus did not reply. He was wondering what difference the ridiculous tactic would make. How could an army of infantry led by an arrogant madman beat a mobile enemy with no interest in fixed battle?

Romulus' cohort heard Crassus' orders when the messenger arrived moments later. *Bucinae* repeated the commands, common practice in battle to ensure they were passed on accurately. At once the Gaulish cavalry fanned out in front of Bassius' mercenaries, while the nearest cohort of Cappadocians moved to stand on their right. Two more came in to the rear, forming an arrow head of cavalry, reinforced by a large square of foot soldiers behind.

Bassius grinned at his men. 'All right! This is a chance to show the whole army what we are capable of. Leave the yokes!'

'Take only water flasks,' said Tarquinius, stuffing something inside his tunic. 'We will not return to this position.'

His two friends quickly discarded all their equipment.

They did not have long to wait. Even Crassus knew that the time before another devastating Parthian attack was diminishing. The exhausted men could not withstand many like it.

Cavalry trumpets blared a staccato series of notes.

Publius assumed his position at the front of his cavalry. The noble's short figure and brown hair were unremarkable, but his determined face and strong jaw drew attention. 'Advance!' he cried, pointing straight at the Parthians. 'For Rome and for Gaul!'

Urging their mounts forward, the tribesmen cheered loudly, kicking up sand and stones. Bassius and other centurions shouted at the mercenaries to follow.

'Let's show those bastards the sharp edge of our swords!'

There was a muted roar as tired bodies pushed into a trot behind the tough old officer. Despite his wound, Bassius seemed indestructible and his appetite for battle inspired everyone to follow.

'Ready *pila*!'

They ran with their arms cocked, heads bowed to avoid the clouds of dust from the horses' hooves. Romulus glanced at his friends from time to time. Having used both javelins in the first attack, Tarquinius slung his shield on his back, holding the double-headed axe firmly in both hands. Incredibly, he was smiling. Brennus' face was calm, his gaze focused.

Romulus' spirits rose and he laughed with the madness of it. The arena had been replaced by something even deadlier, but it no longer mattered. By his side were the two mentors who had become his family. Men he would die for and who would die for him. It was a good feeling. Romulus readied the *pilum* he had picked off the ground, ready to accept the gods' will.

With enormous effort, the cohort managed to keep up with the trotting horses. Marching on burning sand had been hard enough without having to run. Hot air scorched the soldiers' throats with every breath.

'Not much further,' panted Romulus when they had gone about five hundred paces.

The enemy's right flank was coming within the range of the Gauls' spears.

Tarquinius slowed down, his eyes narrowing.

Suddenly Publius ordered a full charge, and the infantry found themselves being left behind.

'Double time!' Bassius threw his arm forward. 'Let's take these fuckers!'

The men responded with superhuman effort to keep up. But instead of standing to meet the cavalry, the Parthians turned and fled.

Publius was taken in. 'Charge! Charge!' he screamed in exultation and his men pushed their mounts harder.

Three of the mercenary cohorts fell even further behind, but Bassius' did not. His soldiers kept pace with the old centurion, now running as if Cerberus himself was after him.

In apparent disarray, the entire Parthian right flank fell back, drawing on the Roman attack. Convinced he had scared them into retreating, Publius heedlessly led the Gauls onward.

He did not see the Parthian commander's gesture.

Almost as one, hundreds of archers turned, drawing their lethal bows to full stretch. With a guttural cry, the officer swept down his arm. Arrows shot forward in a dark swarm, hissing through the air to land with soft thumping sounds. Dozens of Gauls were knocked to the ground. Without pausing for breath, the Parthians loosed for a second time. Feathering man and mount without distinction, the torrent of missiles brought the charge to a juddering halt.

Bassius' men reached the mounds of bodies within

moments. It was a horrific sight: the sand covered with dead and injured riders, horses rearing in agony with wooden shafts protruding from chests, rumps, eyes. Many stampeded into the distance, trampling everything underfoot. The deadly rain was still falling, slaughtering the Gauls. Survivors milled about, horseless and bewildered.

Desperately trying to rally his cavalry, Publius was wheeling in circles at the front. Quite abruptly he released the reins and toppled slowly from the saddle, clutching his throat. An arrow had taken him through the neck.

A huge cry of dismay went up from the remaining Gauls.

The situation was hopeless. Brennus realised it at once and looked to the rear, seeking a way out. But it was too late. Hundreds of Parthians were already sweeping round to envelop Bassius' mercenaries and the remnants of Publius' horsemen.

The old centurion had also seen their escape route disappear. 'Form testudo!' he cried.

Discipline still holding, the mercenaries clumped together. Shields clattered off each other, the metal bosses glinting as an armoured square took shape. Men along the sides formed a wall of *scuta* while those in the middle crouched low, covering their heads completely. The testudo was not an attacking formation, but an extremely effective defensive one – against everything except Parthian arrows.

They watched from behind their shields while the Gauls were cut to pieces. Unable to retreat and unwilling to advance, Publius' cavalry was annihilated before their eyes.

As the last tribesmen fell, warriors began to close in on the testudo. Romulus saw a Parthian jump down beside the body of Crassus' son, knife in hand. There was a huge cheer a few moments later as he stood, Publius' bloody head dangling from his fist. A second warrior rode over and fixed the gory trophy to the tip of his spear.

Fear mushroomed, infecting all. Gazing fixedly at Publius' head, a handful of soldiers broke away from the testudo's protection. They were instantly cut down, striking terror into the rest.

The square wobbled and began to fall apart.

'Close up!' screamed Bassius, but his orders were to no avail. More mercenaries broke free, dropping their heavy shields.

'Publius is dead!' they shouted.

The cohorts behind were still advancing, had not even reached the Parthians. Suddenly the air was filled with cries of panic. Dozens of soldiers appeared through the dust, fleeing in blind panic towards them.

The Cappadocians did what most would do. They turned and ran.

The advance became a retreat as four cohorts bolted heedlessly towards the Roman lines. Straight into another screen of waiting Parthians.

All had fled save the twenty men around Bassius.

'Form testudo!' There was a note of pride in the senior centurion's voice.

Romulus, Brennus, Tarquinius and the remaining mercenaries moved closer to make a small square.

'Roman soldiers do not run!' Bassius yelled. 'Especially when the whole army is watching!' He pointed at the enemy. 'We will stand and fight!'

Through clouds of sand and grit, Romulus saw Parthians riding rings round the fleeing mercenaries. Arrows scythed through the air, cutting them down. Curved swords flashed in the sunlight, opening gaping wounds in men's backs. Hooves trampled the fallen into the sand, face down. Few of the terrified soldiers even lifted their weapons to retaliate.

The group watched helplessly as what had been a rout now became a slaughter. It was over very quickly. Except for those huddled with Bassius, Publius' cavalry and the four cohorts had been completely destroyed in a stunning example of battle tactics.

The sun beat down, unrelenting. Not a cloud was visible. The air was windless. Oppressive. Dead.

Under the raised *scuta*, the temperature was climbing fast. It would soon be unbearable. But Parthian arrows awaited any who stood up.

'Anyone got water?' asked Felix hopefully. The little Gaul who shared the friends' tent was one of the few to stand fast.

Romulus handed over his water bag, still a quarter full.

Felix took a mouthful and passed it back. 'That won't last much longer.'

'Doesn't need to,' muttered one of the others. 'Elysium is waiting for us.'

'We'll take plenty of them too,' said Felix grimly.

'That's the spirit,' bellowed Bassius.

Hearing this, the mercenaries roared at the tops of their voices. They would die bravely. Like warriors. Like Romans.

Horrifying screams echoed all around them as wounded men thrashed about. Blood saturated the yellow sand, turning it a deep red. Innumerable corpses lay scattered like broken dolls.

Crouching behind shields they now knew to be useless, the survivors waited for the inevitable attack. As the dust began to settle, hundreds of Parthians rode in from all sides. They were boxed in completely.

But no arrows were launched as a lone rider in fine robes rode towards the testudo, his horse picking its way delicately between the bodies. The Parthian officer reined in at a safe distance and watched them, his eyes inscrutable.

'Bastards!' cried Bassius. 'Come and get us!'

As Romulus and his comrades screamed their rage and defiance, he and Brennus exchanged a meaningful look. When the Parthian gave the order, death would take all of them. It would be no glorious end – just a volley from the lethal composite bows. There would still be no surrender.

Farewell, Mother. The gods be with you, Fabiola.

A journey beyond where any Allobroge has gone. And here at least I can die without having to run from my loved ones.

The dark-skinned man stared long and hard. Outnumbered and surrounded by mounds of their own dead, his enemies still had not laid down their weapons. Speaking in an unfamiliar tongue, he pointed back towards Crassus' army.

'What is he saying?'

'Probably telling us to run. Son of a whore,' said Felix, curling his lip. 'So they can kill us too.'

The Parthian gestured again at the Roman lines.

Tarquinius turned to Bassius. 'We can go, sir.'

The senior centurion regarded him blankly while the others gaped.

'You understand him?' hissed Romulus.

'Parthian is very similar to ancient Etruscan,' he muttered.

'The bastards could have killed us five times over,' admitted Bassius.

Tarquinius called out in the same language and the officer listened carefully before replying.

With raised eyebrows, Bassius waited until the brief conversation had finished. 'What was that about, *Optio*?'

'I asked him who he was, sir.'

'And?'

'He is Surena, the leader of the Parthian army.'

There was a collective sharp intake of breath.

Tarquinius raised his voice. 'Surena said we are all brave men, who do not deserve to die today. He is giving us safe passage.'

Heads lifted at the prospect of survival and Brennus let out a great sigh. His journey was not over.

'Can we trust him?' asked Felix.

'We haven't a chance in Hades waiting here,' said Bassius grimly. 'Break testudo! Form up in two files!'

The soldiers lowered their shields with trepidation, fully expecting a volley of arrows to be loosed.

Nothing happened.

Impassive bearded faces surrounded the twenty survivors of three thousand. Silently the riders nearest the Roman legions pulled apart, opening an avenue wide enough for men to pass through two abreast.

It seemed too good to be true.

'Follow me, boys! Nice and slowly,' announced the centurion calmly. 'We can't let the bastards think we're scared.' Bassius moved off between the ranks of archers, his head held high. Despite his wound and the crushing defeat, the veteran's spirit burned undimmed, and his men followed gladly. Romulus could have sworn some of the warriors inclined their heads with respect as the ragged mercenaries passed, their *scuta* and javelins held in the marching position.

They had to tramp over the fallen to get by and every soldier following Bassius knew what their fate would be. But with Parthian horsemen watching from a few paces away, there was nothing they could do.

When the injured realised that some of their comrades were escaping, desperate calls for help rang out. 'Help me up,' cried one, his left leg pinned to the ground by an arrow. 'I can make it back.'

Romulus' heart filled with pity. It was one of the men from their century. Before he could move out of rank, Brennus' huge fist grabbed him.

'He's one of ours!'

'Don't even think about it!' the Gaul hissed. 'They'll gut you like a fish.'

'We are the only ones who stood our ground,' agreed Tarquinius.

Romulus watched the nearest warriors. One gave him a wolfish grin as he slid easily from the saddle, a long curved dagger in his hand.

Staring helplessly at the approaching Parthian, the mercenary panicked. 'Don't leave me here!'

'You don't even know his name,' said Tarquinius. 'Will you try and save the rest of them too?'

'He ran, leaving us to die,' growled Brennus. 'Coward.'

Romulus hardened his heart with difficulty. 'May the gods give you swift passage.'

'No!' screamed the injured soldier. 'Don't ki . . .' There was an abrupt silence, replaced by a soft spraying noise.

Romulus turned back.

The man's throat had been cut. His expression was most startled as both his carotid arteries showered the sand in a crimson fountain. Toppling slowly to one side, the mercenary's body twitched a few times and lay still.

Cries of fear rang out as the remainder realised what was about to happen. Yet it was only what they would have done to enemy survivors in the same circumstances.

'Eyes to the front!' roared Bassius. 'They are all dead men.'

Romulus did his best to ignore what they were leaving behind. The Parthians moved amongst the fallen like wraiths, killing without mercy, silencing the screams. Only Bassius and his twenty men were being allowed to go free.

'We have survived one great danger,' said Tarquinius reassuringly.

Romulus shook his head, forcing himself to believe. What else was there to hold on to?

The walk back to the Roman lines seemed to take forever. But not a single arrow followed the tiny remnant of the mercenary cohort. Surena had been true to his word. Unlike Crassus, who had flouted a peace treaty in his quest for fame and riches.

As they drew nearer, it was obvious that the army had finally been marshalled into one continuous front.

Romulus nudged Tarquinius. 'The general has read your mind.'

'Too late,' replied the Etruscan. 'The cataphracts will charge soon. One thousand of them.'

Romulus shuddered. Could anything be more terrible than what he had just witnessed? Brennus saw the young man faltering. 'The gods must be protecting us,' he said bluffly. 'We're still here!' The Gaul's mind was still spinning at being alive. But only through divine intervention could they have survived the lunacy of that charge.

Just twenty to thirty paces had been left between cohorts now, allowing each to manoeuvre without leaving space for the Parthians to utilise the gaps. Crassus had placed a huge number of centurions in the front ranks. He knew it was imperative that the legions withstand the next attack and was relying on the seasoned officers' ability to hold the soldiers steady and raise their morale. It was a tactic resorted to only when stakes were high.

When the group were within javelin range, a great cry went up from the legionaries. Tarquinius pointed; they peered to see what the noise was about.

Surena had been generous in letting the mercenaries go, but he was now about to use his greatest weapon against Crassus. A troop of cataphracts had ridden into the centre of the ground between the armies. Their chain mail glinted and flashed in the sunlight: a magnificent sight. But this time they had a different purpose. In the lead, a rider brandished Publius' head on a spear, brutal evidence of what the Romans could expect.

The enemy horsemen rode close enough to let every soldier see exactly whose head had been taken. Another roar of despair rent the air. The Romans had lost not just half their cavalry and two thousand infantry.

Crassus' son had been slain.

Behind the Roman centre, Crassus heard the outcry, but failed to respond. Having watched Publius' cavalry charge being cut to pieces, the general's spirits had plummeted. His son's fate was unknown and there was little chance of any help in deciding the legions' next move. Other than that troublesome Longinus, none of his senior officers seemed to have any idea what to do. Their intimidation had been too thorough. But Crassus was damned if he would listen to a mere legate.

Unsure what to do next, he pushed his horse up to the back ranks, to find out what was going on. Waves of fear rippled through the men at the sight of his black cloak. It was a bad omen to wear this colour at any time, let alone when leading an army into battle.

Ignoring the frightened soldiers, Crassus focused with difficulty on the cataphracts riding past. Publius' blood-soaked features bobbed up and down on the spear.

Crassus froze in shock. Then, overcome by grief, the arrogant general disappeared; a shrunken man sagged over his pommel. Great sobs racked the would-be Alexander.

Making the most of their trophy, the Parthians moved on.

Remembering all the bad omens, legionaries nearby glanced at Crassus nervously. The repeated signs from above had affected even those who weren't superstitious. The storms at sea. The bull's heart. An eagle standard turning to face the rear. Vultures following the column for days. The Nabataeans' treachery. And now Publius was dead.

It was obvious. The gods had damned Crassus' campaign.

The huge army stood motionless, the trumpets silent as Publius' head continued its ghastly journey along the front lines. Then men began to waver and break rank, looking for ways of escape. Positioned to their rear, junior officers armed with long staffs beat them back into position, but could not stem the rising fear. Cold fingers of terror were stealing into exhausted hearts and it was contagious. The soldiers needed immediate leadership, but none was forthcoming.

The murmurs began, spread, rose to panic-stricken shouts.

'The general has lost his mind with grief!'

'Crassus has gone mad!'

'Fall back!'

'Shut your damn mouths!' screamed the centurion near Romulus, wielding his cane viciously. 'The next man to mention retreat will end with my *gladius* in his belly! Stand fast.'

Cowed by their officers, most of the legionaries fell silent. Discipline was still holding – just.

The troop of cataphracts returned to the Parthian lines. Their quivers refilled, thousands of horse archers immediately began moving towards the Romans. After his master stroke of displaying Publius' head, Surena was now going for the jugular.

At last Crassus came to his senses and took in the approaching enemy. 'Close order!' he croaked. 'Launch javelins at twenty paces. No more!'

The messenger by his side scuttled over to the trumpeters. If the orders weren't relayed fast, the Parthians would be on them.

'What then, general?' One tribune had plucked up enough courage to speak.

Surprised rather than angry, Crassus waved his hands vaguely in the air. 'Weather this attack. Shower the Parthians with *pila*. That'll drive them off.'

The tribune looked confused. 'But their arrows have a greater range than javelins.'

'Do as I say,' said Crassus dully. 'Nothing can withstand Rome's legions.'

The officer withdrew, eyes bulging with alarm.

Crassus had lost his mind.

Unsure exactly where to go, Bassius led his men to the position held by the Sixth Legion, right of the Roman centre.

'You've no time to reach the other mercenaries,' shouted a centurion as they came closer. 'Against regulations, but bring your boys in alongside mine.'

'Very good, comrade. You heard the officer!' Bassius ordered. 'Six men wide, three deep. Move!'

The group quickly formed up beside the regulars. The barrel-chested centurion who had spoken leaned over to grip Bassius' forearm.

'Gaius Peregrinus Sido. First Centurion, First Cohort.'

'Marcus Aemilius Bassius. Senior Centurion, Fourth Cohort of Gaulish mercenaries. And veteran of the Fifth.'

'That was a massacre out there,' said Sido. 'You did well to survive.'

'The bastards led us into a trap, pure and simple. Their right flank fled, then they swept round and enveloped us. Publius never saw it coming.'

Sido whistled with respect. 'Why are you not dead?'

'We didn't run like the rest,' shrugged Bassius. 'And the Parthian leader let us go.'

'Mars above! That should get you a few drinks back home.'

'I hope so,' laughed Bassius grimly, eyeing the Parthian archers. It would only be moments before they reached the Roman lines.

'Our *pila* don't have the range of their bows,' said Sido heavily. 'What can we do?'

'We'll need to hold the bastards off till sunset,' replied Bassius. 'Then fall back to Carrhae under cover of darkness and head for the mountains tomorrow.'

'Retreat?' Sido sighed. 'We can't fight those sons of whores in the open, that's for sure.'

'Crassus had better see it that way damn quick, or it will mean death for all of us.'

Since the cataphracts had ridden past, there had been no commands from the centre. Finally the *bucinae* blared a series of short notes.

'Close ranks! Prepare for attack!'

The men at the front needed no prompting. Shields slammed together while the soldiers behind held theirs angled overhead. There was nothing else to do. Legionary *scuta* could resist normal missiles, but as every man knew only too well, the Parthian bows were different.

Clouds of dust rose from the horses, filling the atmosphere with a fine choking powder. With the Romans in a continuous line, the archers were unable to ride around each cohort as before. Now they would have to ride along the enemy's front and far fewer could attack at any one time.

This provided Crassus' legions with only a shade more respite. A wave of riders swept in, releasing hundreds of shafts from fifty paces. The Roman officers did not order volleys of javelins. There was no point. As the Parthian assault withdrew, it was immediately replaced by another. Storms of arrows rained upon the beleaguered army, piercing wood, metal and flesh without distinction.

Screams of pain rose up as the barbed tips penetrated *scuta*, taking out eyes and pinning feet to the sand. And every soldier that fell created a hole in the shield wall. Into these gaps came scores more missiles, the Parthians using every opportunity to decimate their foes. The Romans cowered under their shields with gritted teeth, praying.

Several of Bassius' mercenaries fell wounded in the prolonged onslaught. Following the centurion's lead, the others snapped the shafts off and pulled them out when they could. Men roared in agony as blood poured from their wounds. The air was filled with the moans, galloping hooves and the hiss of feathered shafts: a terrifying cacophony.

Romulus had grown used to the shrieking, but the number of combatants was far greater than he could have ever imagined. This was death on a grand scale, the sheer magnitude of slaughter impossible to comprehend. Cannae must have been something like this, he thought. A battle that the Republic had lost.

The attacks lasted as long as the enemy had arrows. Whenever the Parthians had exhausted their supply, they simply rode back to the camel train for more. There were enough archers to ensure that any breaks were few and far between. At various stages, the frustrated centurions ordered javelins be thrown, but the horsemen were rarely close enough. Hundreds of *pila* flew through the air to land on the sand, wasted and useless.

After hours of this endless cycle, Roman morale was falling fast. In the ranks of the Sixth alone, nearly a thousand men had been killed. Hundreds more lay injured on the baking hot sand. The air was now thick with dread and the officers were finding it increasingly difficult to keep their units in position.

On the left wing, the Iberian cavalry had fled, unwilling to suffer the same fate as the Gauls. With no sign of Ariamnes and his Nabataeans, the Romans retained no horsemen at all. The rest of Crassus' army had been battered to a pulp, left unable to respond in any way.

Cohort after cohort stood reeling under the onslaught. Parched. Exhausted. Wavering. And about to run.

But instead of another attack, the drums and bells began to sound. While the noise rose in an unearthly crescendo, the horse archers pulled back. Unsure what was happening, the uninjured Roman soldiers waited, their nerves wire-taut. Thanks to the dust cloud that had taken up a permanent place between the two forces, the Parthian army was invisible to them.

For what seemed an eternity, nothing happened.

Then the instruments fell abruptly silent. Surena was a shrewd judge of men and it was time for the hammer blow.

Beneath Romulus' feet the sand began to tremble. Still nothing could be discerned before them.

Then he knew.

'Cataphracts!'

The senior centurion stared at Romulus blankly.

'A charge by heavy cavalry, sir!'

Bassius turned to Sido and swore. 'They will smash us apart! Everyone still with *pila* to the front.'

The other centurion nodded jerkily. He had seen the cataphracts and could well imagine their capability.

'All men with javelins move forward! Hurry!'

Brennus pushed his way through, keen to get to grips with the enemy. He was sure now that his journey was being watched over by the gods themselves. Therefore there was a purpose to it – to all he had sacrificed. Now it was time to fight.

Having thrown their *pila* already, Romulus and Tarquinius stayed put.

'Other ranks, close up,' ordered Bassius. 'Use your spears to stab the horses' bellies. Gut them! Take their fucking eyes out! Rip the riders off!'

'Stand fast!' Sido raised a bloody *gladius* in the air. 'For Rome!'

The soldiers managed a ragged cheer and hurriedly formed up. Romulus and Tarquinius found themselves in the second rank, a few paces behind Brennus. The Gaul had elbowed his way to stand near the two centurions.

The ground shook from the drumming of hooves and a low thunder filled the air. Bassius had just enough time to shout, 'Shields up! *Pila* ready!' before the Parthians emerged from the concealing gloom. Riding in a wedge formation, the desert horsemen were already at full gallop. In response to a shouted order, their heavy lances lowered as one. The centurions had no chance to order a volley of javelins. With devastating force, a thousand heavy cavalry punched into the Roman lines. Sido and those at the front were smashed aside or trampled underfoot while the men behind received a lance in the chest.

Romulus watched in horror as the unstoppable tide poured through the cohort's centre, driving all before it. He struggled to reach the fighting, but the press was so great there was little to do but watch. Here and there a soldier stabbed a horse in the eye with a *pilum*. The mounts reared up in pain, their hooves dashing out the brains of those nearby. Cataphracts clutched frantically at the reins as vengeful legionaries pulled them from the saddle. There was no mercy. Swords ripped into Parthian throats; blood gushed on the sand.

He glimpsed Brennus pulling a mailed warrior down with brute force and stabbing him in the face. Bassius and a few others managed to hamstring half a dozen horses, dispatching the riders with ease. And somehow Tarquinius had wormed his way through the tightly packed ranks to the fighting. Romulus had seen his friend use the battleaxe on several occasions, but never tired of watching the Etruscan's skill and grace. The sinewy figure spun and chopped, wielding the massive weapon with ease. Its curved iron heads flashed to and fro and Parthians screamed as hands and arms were severed. Horses went down thrashing, their back legs slashed to pieces.

Tarquinius was not merely a soothsayer.

But for the most part the Parthian attack had been successful. As the cataphracts smashed through the rear ranks, a great hole was left gaping in the Sixth Legion. Hundreds of casualties sprawled on the bloody sand, howling in agony. Lances and bent *pila* jutted from the dead of both sides. In the section where Romulus and his friends were positioned, all the regular centurions had been killed, leaving the soldiers leaderless and confused.

The sheer power of the charge had destroyed more than the Roman line. It was the final straw for legionaries whose confidence had been steadily eroded all day. Many were veterans who had fought against every enemy the Republic could find and tasted victory in many countries. But Crassus had presented them with a foe they could not fight on equal terms: horse archers who killed from a distance; heavy cavalry which trampled with impunity.

The cataphracts turned on the open ground behind the army. Cries of terror greeted them as they pounded the sand back towards the Romans. Driving through another part of the Sixth, the mailed riders hacked scores more infantry to pieces with their long swords, then disappeared into the clouds of dust.

Everyone knew they would be back.

Another assault by the archers followed. Shortly after that, the cataphracts hit the Tenth Legion alongside the Sixth. The charge had the same devastating effect. When it was over, the survivors stood reeling with shock, their heads turning involuntarily, hopefully, hopelessly to the rear.

It was only a matter of time before Crassus' army broke and ran.

Chapter XXV: Treachery

The Lupanar, Rome, summer 53 BC

Fabiola tapped a finger against her teeth, half wishing that she had not asked Docilosa to search another girl's room. It had felt wrong: yet another violation. Other than the tiny chambers granted them by Jovina, the prostitutes had little to call their own. She pushed away the troubling thought. Too many snide comments had been thrown in her direction recently. And the recent gossip in the bathing area was much more troubling than usual. Instead of the normal chatter about clients' requests, the tips that had been left or not left and whose prayers had been answered, the women were whispering in little groups, unsettled by the bad feeling in the brothel.

By now, Fabiola was used to the jealousy that occurred when a new, rich client asked for her by name, declining even a look at Jovina's selection of prostitutes. To minimise bad feeling over these fairly frequent occasions, Fabiola always made sure to pass on some of her larger tips in the direction of other women. She had long since discovered that nothing sweetened opinion like a bag of *sestertii*. But when Fabiola had actually overheard a muttered conversation through a half-open door two days before, it had been time to enlist Docilosa's help. There had been real vitriol in what had been said. Fear began to creep into Fabiola's heart for the first time since she had been dragged away from Gemellus' house. She had only just discovered that Romulus might still be alive, and life had suddenly become very precious.

So the older woman had gone in the previous night, when all the prostitutes were busy. No one would have passed much comment if they saw her entering a bedroom anyway. Docilosa cleaned and tidied for everyone in the Lupanar.

And Fabiola's decision to ask her had proved astute.

'You're sure?' she asked.

Docilosa scowled. 'What else would it be? A single tiny bottle, hidden under a loose tile in the floor,' she replied. 'But I couldn't risk taking it to show you.'

'Perhaps it was perfume?' Fabiola did not want to admit what was plain to both.

There was a derisive snort. 'I took out a drop of the liquid using a fine twig,' the older woman went on. 'Then dripped it on a piece of bread that was lying on the table.'

Fabiola's respect for Docilosa shot up.

'I left the crust by that little crack in the bottom of the garden wall. You know the one?'

'Where the mice come out,' she said dully, knowing now what Docilosa would say. Fabiola had often watched, quietly amused at the tiny creatures scurrying in and out through the hole, busily searching for food. The brothel's resident cats could only kill so many of the ubiquitous rodents, something that endlessly irritated Jovina.

There was a pause.

'I stepped back and waited. It wasn't long before one appeared. Ate the bread in a flash.' Docilosa stared at Fabiola grimly. 'The mouse took no more than two steps before it fell down dead.'

The black-haired girl's stomach constricted and she stepped to the door, opening it to check that there was nobody eavesdropping in the corridor. Relieved to see no one, she closed it quietly and turned to Docilosa. 'Poison.'

The word hung in the air like a black cloud.

'She's not to be trusted,' spat Docilosa. 'I've said it from the beginning.'

It was impossible to argue. The proof was lying outside in the garden.

Fabiola sighed. Relations with Pompeia had been strained for some time, but she had not thought it would come to this. Despite her best efforts, the redhead had become a dangerous enemy. Jealousy had turned the woman who had made Fabiola most welcome on her first day in the Lupanar into someone who wanted her dead.

It had started off so well. Aware that she would need allies to survive her new life, Fabiola had been quick to replace Pompeia's lent perfume, and the two had become good friends. Claudia, the blonde Goth, had also proved to be essentially decent. Forming a little group, they soon spent all their free time together, Pompeia and Claudia freely dispensing advice that the young newcomer soaked up. Desperate to become the best, to win clients and influence over them so she could rescue Romulus and her mother, Fabiola was soon driving customers wild. As her popularity began to increase, Claudia had shrugged fatalistically. The blonde had a few devoted clients, nobles who liked being tied up and dominated. In a strange way, this seemed to satisfy Claudia.

But the highly-strung Pompeia had been less philosophical. She had been in the brothel for nearly five years, yet Fabiola had gained more regulars than Pompeia inside twelve months. One of her best tippers had even gone to Fabiola in preference to her. That was too much to bear. Their friendship began to sour, and soon it had reached the point where each barely acknowledged the other's presence. Trying to remain on good terms with both, Claudia did her best not to get involved. Of course Jovina had been quick to notice the bad feeling, and had taken Fabiola and Pompeia aside separately. The Lupanar was her domain and she guarded it jealously. 'I want no trouble,' the old crone had threatened. 'Men always notice when girls are bitchy with each other. They don't like it, and that's bad for business. It must end now.'

Fabiola had been happy to let matters lie.

Pompeia obviously had not.

Denarii chinked off each other as Fabiola handed over a small purse.

Docilosa judged its weight instantly. 'That's far too much,' she protested.

Fabiola laughed. 'For saving my life? I can never thank

you enough.' She leaned forward and kissed Docilosa's cheek.

This produced a rare smile.

'I'll just have to spend more time in the kitchen,' said Fabiola brightly. 'Watch all my meals being prepared.' She didn't think it likely that Catus or the other slaves would be prepared to poison her. Pompeia would need to come into the cooking area on some pretext. Do the dirty work herself. Jovina allowed the prostitutes to order food whenever they were not working and so the kitchen was always a hive of activity. It would not be that difficult to come down the corridor and lace a plate waiting on the work surface by the door. Another girl looking for a morsel to eat would attract little attention.

Fabiola suddenly felt very uneasy. It was horrible knowing that Pompeia wanted her dead. While she did not like all of the other women, Fabiola did not actually want to harm any of them. Neither could she understand the degree of jealousy that would drive someone to kill another over such a trivial matter. Despite the shocking revelation, Fabiola had no wish to murder Pompeia in return. It was not that she was scared of doing so. After all, she desperately wanted a man to die.

Gemellus.

The fat merchant had done unspeakable things to her mother for years. He deserved a slow, painful death. And her own father also deserved a trip to Hades: a noble who had raped a slave just because he could. In comparison to the subjects of Fabiola's deep-rooted hate, Pompeia seemed pathetic. Laughable. She poked herself. There was real danger here. If the redhead was determined enough to make threats and buy poison, Fabiola had to assume that she was prepared to use the deadly liquid too.

Life in the brothel had become perilous and the task of monitoring her food being cooked would not pass unnoticed. Poisoning was a common method of killing an enemy in Rome and the cooks would understand why Fabiola was watching them work. Rumours would start and then Pompeia would find out she knew. She could not refuse to eat food from the kitchen either. Jovina would hear about that instantly. A frisson of fear snaked up Fabiola's spine.

Something had to be done. Soon.

Fabiola bit her lip, momentarily unsure how to respond. She would have to think about this. Offer extra prayers to Jupiter and hope for inspiration. For some reason, she felt sure that the most powerful Roman god would provide her with a sign.

Docilosa grinned infectiously. It was a rare sight. Fabiola looked enquiringly at the older woman, wondering what had pleased her so much.

'I poured every last drop down the sewer,' announced Docilosa triumphantly. 'Washed the bottle out thoroughly and filled it with fresh water from the well.'

Fabiola's heart soared at the unexpected revelation. 'The gods must have sent you to me!'

'The bitch will think that she was ripped off by whatever lowlife sold her the poison.'

'Or that I'm immortal.'

They both giggled.

Docilosa's face gradually turned serious again. 'What

are you going to do, Fabiola? Pompeia's a vindictive one. She won't stop at this, you know.'

Fabiola nodded. Docilosa's shrewd action would have bought her a reprieve, nothing more. 'Leave it with me,' she said, affecting a confidence that was not wholly there. 'I'll come up with something.'

But things were to get worse.

Two days later, Fabiola entered her room at dawn, tired from a busy night's work. There had been more customers than she usually had to entertain, but it had been worth the effort. She had three gold *aurei* to add to her savings and the last client had turned out to be a newly elected quaestor. Someone who might prove to be useful in the future. Ambitious politicians were always a good catch and Fabiola had driven the man completely crazy before allowing him to climax.

He would be back. Soon.

She smiled. Most men were so easy to manipulate.

After a good wash, Fabiola normally just stripped naked and fell on to her bed to catch a few hours of well-deserved sleep. For reasons that she could never explain afterwards, something made the black-haired girl study the plain woollen bedspread as she prepared to throw it back.

It looked strange. Lumpy.

Fabiola's pulse quickened and she froze on the spot, her eyes taking in the thick, coiled shape under the covers. Then it moved slightly and she had to stifle a scream.

Pompeia was not to be put off.

Tiptoeing into the corridor, Fabiola shut the door

quietly and went in search of the doormen. They would know what to do.

When the pair heard, their reaction was so violent that Fabiola had to tell one of them to stay by the front door. It was just before dawn and, with all the customers gone, everyone had finally gone to bed. Both men pounding through the house would have drawn too much attention. Ordering Vettius to follow her quietly, Fabiola walked back to her room. She took deep breaths, releasing the terror that had filled her at the first sight of the shape on her cot. All would be well.

Outside the door, the shaven-headed hulk gently pushed her aside. 'Leave this to me,' he said, gripping his metal-studded club. 'There were plenty of snakes where I grew up.'

Fabiola did not argue. She watched as Vettius peered inside, checking first that there was nothing on the floor.

'It hasn't moved,' he said without turning his head. 'Stay here until I tell you it's safe.'

Fabiola squeezed his huge hand, suddenly worried that she was endangering a man she regarded as a real friend. 'Be careful.'

He looked back and winked at her. 'Jupiter will protect me.'

There was silence as Vettius entered the small chamber, his weapon poised in his right hand. Creeping to the bed, he quickly lifted the edge of the straw mattress nearest the wall and tipped the whole thing on to the stone floor. Vettius smashed down on the pile of sheets and blankets with repeated blows of his club, keeping his feet well clear in case the snake escaped. Fabiola was relieved that the noise he made was muffled somewhat by her bedding. It was important to minimise the number of people who knew what was going on.

After a few moments, he grunted with satisfaction, nudging at a red stain that was appearing through the wool of Fabiola's blanket.

'Come in.'

Glancing to left and right, Fabiola shot in and closed the door. 'Is it dead?' she asked nervously.

Vettius flipped over the bedspread, revealing a thick brown shape as long as a man's arm. Twitches still spasmed through the snake, but its head was a bloody mess.

Fabiola shuddered at what would have happened if she had climbed into bed as usual. Jupiter be thanked, she thought to herself.

The doorman studied the chequered pattern on the serpent's back for a moment. 'Never seen this type before,' he pronounced.

'So it's not native to Italy.'

Vettius shook his head.

'It must be poisonous,' mused Fabiola. 'Why else would it be in my bed?'

Vettius took her words in gradually. 'Who would do this?' he hissed, his face darkening. 'Everyone here loves you.'

'Keep your voice down,' Fabiola answered sharply, already concerned that his blows might have been heard outside the room.

Embarrassed, Vettius bobbed his head.

'Some women are jealous of me.'

'But to do this?' Vettius pointed angrily at the mashed snake on the floor.

Fabiola considered briefly whether she should tell the doorman about Docilosa's discovery. Then she imagined the sensation of being bitten as she clambered under the covers. Of dying before she found out what had happened to Romulus.

'It was Pompeia.'

He gasped disbelievingly. 'You're friends with her!'

'Not for some time.' Fabiola was not surprised at his ignorance. Vettius and Benignus did not usually notice the intricacies of the interactions between the women. Quickly she told him about the tiny bottle that Docilosa had found under the tiles of Pompeia's floor.

'Just say the word,' Vettius muttered, clenching his fists. 'We'll sort the bitch out. Take her for a little stroll by the Tiber one night.'

'No,' Fabiola replied firmly. 'That would be too easy. And too obvious. Jovina must not suspect anything or we'll both end up on a cross.'

'But that's the second time,' Vettius snarled, stamping on the snake's head to emphasise his point. 'Lupanar girls are supposed to look after each other.'

Fabiola did not say, but the snake made it three. There had been another occasion, months before, when a trio of thugs had surprised her and Benignus as they walked to the Forum to deposit her savings. She had been suspicious even then at the manner of the attack, which had obviously been planned. Generally robberies in daylight were opportunistic affairs, but the men that day had foolishly followed the pair the instant they had left the brothel. Someone had given them information. And there had been no attempt to steal her money, a significant detail that had passed the huge doorman by. Instead the thieves had immediately borne down on Fabiola with drawn daggers. Quickly pushing her behind him, Benignus had left no chance of interrogating the lowlifes for information. He had been enraged at the threat to his Fabiola. Leaving one with a broken neck and the other spilling the contents of his belly into the gutter, Benignus had pursued the last into the crowd, returning a few moments later with a satisfied smile. And a bloody knife.

Now there could be no doubt. A daylight assassination attempt. Poison stored secretly. The rumours that were running through the brothel. A venomous snake in her bed. Coincidence could have nothing to do with it.

Fabiola had racked her brains to work out who might be responsible. There were few possible candidates. To her knowledge, not one client that had visited her had ever left unsatisfied. It was not Jovina either. Money meant everything to the old madam and Fabiola was her best earner. The doormen adored her. Catus and the kitchen slaves simply had no reason to want her dead. That only left the other women and Fabiola could read virtually all of them like a book. Cowed by their enforced prostitution, most were happy enough to live in Fabiola's shadow.

Pompeia. It could only be Pompeia.

Jealousy had overwhelmed the redhead completely. And when attacks outside the Lupanar walls had failed, she had resorted to more stealthy ways of trying to kill her enemy.

'You two are supposed to protect us, not make us disappear,' Fabiola said, patting Vettius' heavily muscled arm. Befriending the two doormen had been one of the best moves she had ever made. She knew both would die rather than let her come to harm.

Vettius grinned in response, but he was still plainly worried. 'I've been with Pompeia when she goes out,' he replied. 'Didn't think much of it before, but the slut's been talking to members of the *collegia*. And Milo's gangs. She's even been to the temple of Orcus recently.' The doorman made the sign against evil. 'Only one reason to go in there.'

Vettius' words were worrying. People went to worship the god of death if they had malicious feelings towards someone. Swarms of vendors outside sold small squares of lead sheet to visitors, and nearby scribes would write whatever damning words their customers required. Fabiola had heard that the large pool inside the shrine's walls was full of the tiny folded curses. She shivered at the thought and muttered a quick prayer to Jupiter for his continued protection.

'Let me kill her.'

At last she felt rage building inside her. This had gone far enough. 'I'll do it,' Fabiola said, meeting Vettius' gaze squarely.

He had opened his mouth to reply when Fabiola pointed at the now motionless snake.

'Cut the head off that thing for me.'

Pulling a vicious-looking dagger from his belt, Vettius hurried to obey. When he was done, he looked up.

'Leave me the knife too.'

Vettius smiled and handed it over.

Fabiola gripped the bone hilt tightly, steeling her resolve, imagining Romulus killing to stay alive, first as a gladiator and then as a soldier. The chilling thought helped to give her strength. It seemed that things were not much different here in the Lupanar. Despite Pompeia's treachery, Fabiola remained focused on her one driving purpose in life: to save her brother. In her profession, there was only one way to achieve that: by gaining influence over the rich and powerful.

And no one would get in her way.

Chapter XXVI: Retreat

Parthia, summer 53 BC

Late in the afternoon, Crassus called together his seven legates. For reasons best known to Surena, the Parthians had not attacked for a while. Perhaps he was allowing his men a well-earned rest. The Roman general still possessed enough reason to utilise the breathing space this granted. Crassus' lack of cavalry was rendering the invincible legions helpless. Something had to be done. Fast.

Desperate for ideas, Crassus' bloodshot eyes moved around searchingly. Six of the red-cloaked officers avoided his gaze, staring down at the hot sand. Only Longinus had the courage to return it.

'What shall we do?' Crassus' voice cracked with emotion. 'If we stay, they will butcher us.'

'Another charge and the men will crack, sir,' said Longinus immediately. 'Only one thing to do. Retreat.'

There were reluctant nods all round. The situation was dire. Roman armies rarely fled the field, but in this

481

burning desert hell, the rulebook had been rewritten.

'With the baggage train gone, there is no more water. We *must* fall back to Carrhae.' Longinus spoke with utter conviction.

The others muttered in agreement. Carrhae had deep wells and thick earth walls. It would provide some respite from the lethal Parthian arrows.

'And after that?'

It seemed the death of Publius had rendered the general unable to make any decisions.

'Head north. The broken ground in the mountains will help us. With luck, we may find Artavasdes.'

Crassus' eyes closed. His campaign was in ruins, the plans of equalling Caesar and Pompey dust. 'Sound the retreat,' he whispered.

'The wounded, sir?'

'Leave them.'

'Are you sure, sir?' asked Comitianus, commander of the Sixth. 'I have over five hundred casualties.'

'Do what I say!' screamed Crassus.

'He's right. For once. They would slow us down too much,' said Longinus harshly. 'We have no choice.'

They did not argue further and the grizzled legate barked an order at the nearest soldiers.

Moments later, trumpets sounded the ominous notes that no legionary ever liked to hear. The injured stirred frantically, knowing what was about to happen. Five of Bassius' mercenaries could no longer walk and had been placed at the rear. As the retreat died away, the senior centurion moved to stand by the wounded.

'You have fought bravely today, boys.' Bassius flashed

a rare smile. 'Not many options left, though. We have to leave right now and none of you can march. So you can take your chances here,' he paused, 'or choose a swift death.'

The words hung in the hot air.

Unwilling to meet their comrades' eyes, the rest of the men looked at the ground. It was a brutal decision, but the Parthians would be less merciful.

'I'm not ready for Hades yet, sir,' said one, a dark-skinned Egyptian. A bloody bandage was wrapped roughly around his left thigh. 'I'll take a few with me.'

A second soldier also chose to stay, but the remaining three were very badly hurt. Too weak to retreat or fight, they had no choice but the last. Muttering briefly with each other, they pulled themselves upright.

'Make it quick, sir,' one said.

Bassius nodded without replying.

A lump formed in Romulus' throat. He had dispatched opponents in the arena but they had rarely been people he'd known, trained or fought with. This trio of men had been with them since boarding the *Achilles,* a lifetime ago. After nearly two years of campaigning, Romulus knew the wounded well enough to really grieve their passing.

The centurion firmly gripped each man's hand once. As he moved to stand behind, all three bowed their heads, exposing their necks. They were receiving a soldier's death, an honourable way to die.

Bassius' *gladius* hissed from the scabbard. He raised it high, holding the hilt in both hands, the razor-sharp tip pointing towards the ground. With a swift motion the centurion stabbed down and cut the spinal cord. Death was instant: the first body crumpled without a murmur. Silently Bassius moved on to the second and third. The mercy killings did not take long; clearly the veteran had performed this grisly task before.

All over the Roman lines, the same act was being repeated by any officers of conscience. But the Parthians had no intention of letting their enemies retreat in good order and another attack began before everyone could be dealt with.

Quickly Bassius organised his new command of exhausted men into a square. With Sido and five other centurions killed, the veteran had assumed control of the regular cohort as well. None of the dazed junior officers questioned the unusual move. Bassius nodded farewell to the Egyptian and his companion. The pair were sitting back to back, swords at the ready.

Eyes full of tears, Romulus could not look back.

'They are brave men.' There was real respect in Tarquinius' face. 'And this is how they have decided to die.'

'Doesn't make it any easier to leave them,' he retorted.

'Stay if you wish,' said the Etruscan. 'That is your choice. Perhaps this is why I could not be sure about all three of us surviving?' His dark eyes were unreadable.

'Now is not the time for you to die,' added Brennus confidently. 'What purpose would it serve?'

Romulus briefly considered the idea. It did seem pointless. The wounded had freely chosen how they would end their lives and dying with them would prove nothing. There were still many things he wanted to achieve. With a heavy heart, he marched away.

Bassius' incredible willpower held his mixed group together as they left the battlefield behind. To the soldiers' relief, Parthian horsemen did not pursue them for long. Romulus eventually glanced round to see groups of warriors riding in circles, whooping with glee. One waved a familiar shape in the air. It was the ultimate disgrace – a legion's silver eagle, fallen into enemy hands. At the sight, his spirits fell even further.

Beneath the horses' hooves, the huge plain was covered with dead and injured as far as one could see. It was a charnel house. Flies swarmed on to dry staring eyes, gaping mouths, bleeding sword cuts. Nearly fifteen thousand Roman soldiers would never return to Italy. Above them, clouds of vultures now hung on the thermals. The air was filled with the smell of manure, blood and sweat. It had been a bad day for the Republic.

'Lots of men are still alive.'

'We can't help them now,' said Brennus sadly.

'Olenus saw this seventeen years ago,' uttered Tarquinius with some satisfaction. 'He would have liked to see the Romans come to this.'

Romulus was shocked. 'Those are our comrades!'

'What do I care?' the Etruscan replied. 'Rome butchered my people and devastated our cities.'

'But not those men! They did not!'

To his surprise, Tarquinius was nonplussed. 'Wise words,' he admitted. 'May their suffering be short.'

Placated by the compromise from someone who hated all that the Republic stood for, Romulus could still not block out the screams. And there was only one person responsible for it all, he thought angrily.

Crassus.

'Your teacher predicted this battle?' Brennus was amazed.

'And he saw us on a long march to the east,' revealed the Etruscan. 'I had begun to doubt his prediction, but now . . .'

Their eyes widened.

'The gods work in strange ways,' Brennus muttered.

Romulus sighed. There would be no easy return to Rome.

'It is not completely certain.' A faraway look appeared in Tarquinius' eyes, one that Romulus and the Gaul had come to know well. 'The army may yet return to the Euphrates. Much still depends on Crassus.'

'Gods above! Why go that way?' Romulus gestured truculently into the desert. 'Safety. Italy. Everything lies to our west.'

'We would see temples built by Alexander.' For a moment, Tarquinius seemed unaware of their presence. 'And the great city of Barbaricum on the Indian Ocean.'

'Beyond where any Allobroge has ever gone,' whispered Brennus. 'Or will ever go.'

'No one can avoid destiny, Brennus,' said Tarquinius suddenly.

The Gaul went pale beneath his tan.

'Brennus?' Romulus had never seen his friend like this.

'The druid told me that the day I left the village,' he whispered.

'Druids. Haruspices,' announced Tarquinius, clapping

the Gaul on the back. 'We are one and the same thing.'

Brennus nodded, full of awe.

He missed the sadness that flitted across Tarquinius' face.

He knows what will happen, thought Romulus. But this was not the time for long conversations. It was time to retreat, or die.

The sun was low in the sky, but hours remained before darkness would offer the exhausted Romans any protection. Slowly the legions limped away from the devastation, harassed by occasional arrows from zealous Parthians. Most warriors remained behind, however, killing the Roman wounded and looting the dead.

It was a bitter irony. Untold numbers were still dying on the battlefield, giving their comrades the opportunity to escape.

The defeated army straggled north to the walls of Carrhae; at every step, injured soldiers fell by the wayside. Few had any strength left to help those who collapsed. Anyone not strong enough to march simply perished. Holding his cohort together with roars and screams, Bassius even used the flat of his sword to keep the exhausted men moving. Romulus' respect for him grew even further.

Carrhae was a desert town that existed purely because of its deep subterranean wells. Knowing the settlement would prove useful when the invasion began, Crassus had sent in an occupying force the year before. Its small encampment outside the thick earthen walls was ignored as the thousands of defeated Roman troops reached Carrhae. Men poured through the gates in a great tide, seizing houses and food from the unfortunate residents. The brutal thrusts of *gladii* instantly ended any resistance.

The majority had to camp outside. A few centurions tried to insist that the temporary ditches and ramparts that traditionally followed a day's march were built. They failed. The soldiers had been through too much to spend three hours digging hot sand. It was all the officers could do to get sentries positioned a few hundred paces into the desert.

The sun had set and with it temperatures dropped sharply, a stiff breeze adding to the chill. Outside the town, those not fortunate enough to have found cover spent the night huddled together in the open. All the tents had been lost with the baggage train. Now the injured began to die of cold, dehydration and fatigue. There was nothing anyone could do.

Romulus and his friends commandeered a miserable mud-walled hut, turning the residents on to the street rather than killing them. Soon they lay sleeping like dead men. Not even the danger of a Parthian attack was enough to keep them awake.

Elsewhere in the town, the largest building had belonged to the local chieftain before Roman occupation and was now the quarters for the garrison commander. Crassus gathered the legates there for a council of war.

The bare walls, dirt floor and rough wooden furniture revealed that Carrhae was far from wealthy. Rush torches guttered from brackets, casting flickering shadows on the weary figures. The six bloodstained officers sat with blank faces, some with head in hands, beakers of water and loaves of hard bread untouched before them. It was a far cry from Crassus' luxurious command tent, long since disappeared with the mules.

Nobody knew what to say or do. The legates were stunned. Defeat was not something that Roman soldiers were used to. Instead of achieving a crushing victory and the sacking of Seleucia, they had succumbed to Parthian wrath. They were stranded deep in enemy territory, their army in tatters.

Crassus sat quietly on a low stool, taking no part in what little conversation was going on. Simply calling the officers together seemed to have taken up the last of his energy. Beside him sat the garrison commander, overawed by the presence of so many senior figures. Prefect Gaius Quintus Coponius had not seen the extent of the slaughter, but the fleeing Iberian cavalry had brought him the shocking news on their way back to the Euphrates. Later he had witnessed the beaten legionaries staggering into the town. It was not a sight he would forget.

Longinus strode into the room, energy radiating from him.

Few looked up.

The tough soldier came to a halt in front of Crassus and saluted crisply. 'I have done the rounds. The Eighth has lost about a third of its number. Now that they've had water and some rest, my men are in reasonable shape.'

Crassus sat quite still, his eyes closed.

'Sir?'

Still silence.

'What have you decided?' demanded Longinus.

Comitianus cleared his throat. 'We have not come to an agreement yet.' He would not meet the other's eyes. 'What do you say?'

'There is only one real option.' Longinus let the words sink in. 'Retreat to the river immediately. We can reach it before dawn.'

'My soldiers cannot march tonight,' replied one legate.

There were murmurs of agreement.

Unsurprised, Longinus glanced at Comitianus.

'What about Armenia?' the commander of the Sixth ventured.

'The legate is right, sir.' Coponius' tone wavered. 'Retreating to the mountains makes a lot of sense. There are plenty of streams and the broken ground would make it awkward for the Parthians' horses.'

'The mountains?' Crassus gazed round the room longingly. 'Where is Publius?'

There was no answer.

'Gone, sir,' said Longinus at last. 'To Elysium.'

'*Dead*?'

Longinus nodded.

A sob escaped Crassus' lips and he bent his neck, ignoring those around him.

The spirited officer had seen enough. 'With your permission, sir,' he said, 'I would like to lead the army to safety. Tonight.'

Crassus rocked on his stool and stared at the floor.

Longinus raised his voice. 'We should retreat under the cover of darkness.'

There was no response. Crassus, the liberator of Rome, was nothing but a shell.

Longinus turned to face the others. 'Stay with him,' he said dismissively, 'or follow me. The Eighth is marching to the Euphrates in an hour.'

Nervous muttering filled the room. He waited, fingers impatiently tapping his sword hilt.

'There is a local who has aided us on many occasions, sir,' began the prefect, eager to please.

Longinus raised an eyebrow.

'Andromachus has proved reliable since we first took Carrhae. Many Parthian attacks have been foiled because of his information.'

'Let me guess.' Longinus' voice dripped with sarcasm. 'This *Andromachus* can guide us to safety.'

'So he says, sir.'

'Where have I heard that before?'

Coponius was not to be deterred. 'Apparently the mountains are only five to six hours' march, sir.'

'Are they, by Jupiter?' said Longinus acidly.

But the legates began whispering with excitement.

Even Crassus lifted his head.

'I know the way to the river!' Longinus bunched a fist. 'These savages are all treacherous sons of whores. We can trust none of them. Remember Ariamnes?'

There was an ominous silence.

'Publius,' Crassus broke in. 'Where is Publius?'

The officers were paralysed with indecision.

At length Comitianus plucked up the courage to speak. 'Armenia seems a better option,' he said uncertainly. 'That road to the river is totally flat.'

'It's at least a day's march to the mountains by my reckoning. We can make the Euphrates overnight,' urged Longinus. 'Who is with me?'

Nobody met his eye.

The veteran was no longer prepared to tolerate their spineless attitude. 'Fools! You will be massacred.' He stalked out, red cloak flowing in the faint breeze.

There was a brief, uneasy pause before the group began asking Coponius eagerly about possible salvation. The brave legate was forgotten. It was the only way the rest could reconcile themselves to staying with Crassus.

The commander of the Eighth was as good as his word. Within the hour, Longinus' legion had gone, marching into the desert in virtual silence. Only the occasional clash of spear against shield betrayed its departure. Few of the exhausted survivors bothered to watch.

Romulus heard the tramp of feet, jingling mail and muted coughs and got up straight away. Brennus was snoring peacefully, but the Etruscan's eyes were open. Together they walked to the main gate.

'The Eighth is leaving,' said Romulus. 'Should we go too?'

The Etruscan's face was enigmatic in the moonlight. 'The penalty for deserting is crucifixion. We should stay.'

Romulus frowned. It wasn't likely the tired sentries would even notice if three more men fled the town. Discipline was at an all-time low.

'What about the stars?'

'They're not telling me much.'

Romulus shrugged, content to trust his friend. Brennus seemed set on following Tarquinius to the ends of the world if necessary. The big man was like a father to him and that was enough reason to stay.

The pair returned to the hut, where they found Brennus awake.

'What's happening?'

'The Eighth is heading for Zeugma.'

'Be easy to slip over the wall. No one would see.'

'No,' said Tarquinius firmly. 'It is less than a day's march to the mountains and safety. The men can manage that after a good rest.'

'It seems cowardly fleeing at night.' Brennus lay back on the dirt floor, closing his eyes. 'I need a good sleep anyway.'

Romulus pictured the lines of legionaries marching into the darkness. The Eighth had still looked proud, disciplined. Not like the rabble in and around Carrhae. His stomach turned over. Surely it was wiser to retreat when the Parthians could not use their deadly bows? What advantage was there in waiting until the morning? It didn't seem to make sense, but the Etruscan knew best. Wearier than he could ever remember, Romulus closed his eyes and fell asleep instantly.

The haruspex did not speak again before dawn. He sat by the open door, brooding and studying the night sky. Tarquinius did not like misleading his friends, but there was no other way. Olenus had been right all those years before.

By mid-morning, everyone knew that they should have followed Longinus to the Euphrates. Instead of marching west, the legates had elected to follow Coponius'

493

guide north towards Armenia. Crassus had not given a single command since the previous night and rode his horse in a silent daze. After four hours in the cauldron of fire, the men had reached the limits of endurance. There had been no sign of the Parthians, nor of the promised mountains. Worst of all, no rivers or oases. Most soldiers had emptied their water containers within a few miles and once again, thirst had become the enemy.

Sensing the soldiers' need for a rest, the legates finally ordered a halt. Men collapsed on to the ground, not caring that it was hot enough to burn. Fearing mutiny, the centurions did not attempt to move them for some time.

Eventually Bassius and the officers began to pace up and down, vine canes in hand. Armenia would get no nearer like this.

'Get up! Lazy bastards!' The words were the same, but since the superhuman effort of bringing the Second Cohort to safety, Bassius had lost his vigour. It seemed his last reserves had been spent, leaving only willpower to keep him going.

The legionaries moaned but did as he said. Bassius had earned their respect during the retreat and they were still willing to follow. Other centurions had more difficulty, but at last the battered army managed to get moving.

Its speed was now painfully slow and as the column ground on, ever more soldiers began to fall out of rank from sheer exhaustion. Some managed to struggle up, but the weaker ones remained sprawled on the baking sand. Cries for help filled the air, but few men had the strength to carry another. It was easier to look away. Tears again formed in Romulus' eyes when he recognised legionaries he had fought with during the campaign. Only Brennus' iron grip on his shoulder prevented him from trying to help many.

And so it went on. Half-dead figures littered the army's trail, left to cook in the sun. Clouds of vultures swiftly descended when it had passed. Loud, eager cries rose from the ugly birds as fights took place over the best pickings. Whether they waited until their prey was dead no one could tell.

At length the legions neared the base of an enormous dune that ran across their path, its sheer bulk halting their progress. Nearly a quarter of a mile of sand rose steeply into the air. The soldiers groaned aloud. It would be a long, hard slog.

'Climb!' The centurions roared, pointing upwards. 'Move!'

The front ranks shifted their yokes and began ascending. For the moment all they could do was obey. Maybe the promised mountains would be visible from the top.

Within fifty paces, Romulus saw a telltale cloud rising from behind the slope.

'Trouble.' Stomach churning, he nudged Brennus.

Suddenly everyone saw the dust. The army came to an abrupt standstill. Officers screamed in vain as the legionaries stared up with fascinated horror.

When Parthian archers emerged on top of the dune, a wordless moan escaped men's throats. They would be going no further. As the tired soldiers waited, awestruck, the entire ridge filled with the enemy.

'We're finished,' swore Romulus. 'Can't fight them, can we? Might as well lie down and die now.'

A little shocked, Brennus regained his composure quickly. 'Can't be as bad as it looks,' he said.

Romulus spun to face Tarquinius, who regarded him steadily. The young soldier was furious. 'Did you know this would happen?' he snapped.

'No.' It was impossible to tell if the Etruscan was lying or not.

'Really? There are thousands of the bastards up there,' yelled Romulus. 'How could you miss seeing them?'

'The art of haruspicy is an uncertain one,' replied Tarquinius with a shrug. 'I've told you that before.'

Romulus' spirits plummeted. How could they live through another battle like the day before?

Then the Etruscan pointed.

A party of horsemen was making its way down the slope, hands held aloft to show they carried no weapons.

Romulus peered at the riders suspiciously. 'Are they offering parley?'

'Looks like it,' answered Brennus calmly.

'The breeze is more favourable now,' added Tarquinius. 'Although thousands more men will die today.'

'It's time to talk,' Romulus grumbled. 'We don't stand a chance otherwise.'

The friends held their breath as the Parthians came closer, the horses picking their way through the thick sand.

Crassus' position was obvious from the number of

standards and red-cloaked officers, and the riders halted a hundred paces from it. They waited expectantly.

To Romulus' surprise, there was no response.

Men began to grow angry. The endless marching in blistering heat, exhaustion and the lack of water had been followed by the death of thousands at the hands of an unreachable enemy. Now, even when they were about to be slaughtered, it seemed that their leader would not talk to the Parthians. His arrogance had not completely evaporated.

With no cavalry remaining, Crassus had to rely on his bodyguards to carry orders. At last a pair of this elite came trotting along the column, sweating heavily in their gilded breastplates and leather skirts.

'Prepare for battle!' one wheezed every few steps. 'Back to the flat ground. Form a continuous line.'

'Piss off, son of a whore!'

'Who said that?' Both men skidded to a halt, hands on their swords.

'Go and fight those bastard Parthians yourself!'

There was an angry roar and more insults were thrown. So far, these hand-picked soldiers had seen no combat at all, which generated huge resentment among the rank and file.

'Where's the ranking centurion?' The more senior bodyguard, an *optio*, tried to regain control.

Silently Bassius came forward, his *phalerae* prominent.

'Nobody disobeys a direct order from Marcus Licinius Crassus. Arrest those men!'

'You can call me *sir*. I didn't spend sixteen damn years in the legions for nothing!'

'Sir.'

'Go and do it yourself,' declared Bassius. 'You piece of shit.'

Huge cheers erupted from his men.

'Refusing to obey orders, Centurion?'

Bassius ignored him. 'Why has Crassus not sent a party to negotiate?'

More delighted shouts rose from the surrounding legionaries.

The two guards were blind to diplomacy.

'Crassus does not parley with desert savages.'

Bassius whipped out his *gladius*, placing its razor sharp tip under the *optio*'s chin.

'Tell the general to go and talk with the Parthians. Himself.' He half turned. 'That right, boys?'

A swelling roar of approval moved down the line, the soldiers drumming their swords off *scuta* to show support. Those further away guessed what was going on and joined in. Romulus and Brennus did likewise. What was the point of dying in the Mesopotamian desert? They might as well retreat to Syria and survive.

A faint breeze had sprung up and Tarquinius saw that a number of small clouds had appeared in the sky. Engrossed with the standoff, no one else saw him frown. There were twelve.

The *optio* was a brave man. 'Crassus ignores demands from scum.'

'I've fought in more than ten wars, you miserable dog,' said Bassius, pressing harder with his *gladius* and breaking the skin. A drop of blood rolled down the iron.

He winced but did not back away.

'Crassus had best do what we say.' Bassius paused. 'Or he might end up like Publius.'

The *optio* glanced at his comrade.

Dozens of legionaries tensed and the second soldier carefully let go of his sword hilt. The men around them pounded harder on their shields. Crassus had promised them everything but delivered only hardship and death. Thousands of Parthians now waited to complete their annihilation. If the general would not parley, they would take matters into their own hands.

'You heard them.' The old centurion gestured at the column's centre. 'Now go and tell Crassus.'

Slowly the two guards moved away from the raised weapon and stalked back to Crassus' position. Bassius watched for a few moments before stepping into line.

'Jupiter!' Romulus let out a breath. 'Ever seen anything like that?'

Brennus shook his head. 'Shows just how bad it is, for a man like Bassius to mutiny.'

'Crassus decimated a unit that ran from Spartacus,' said Tarquinius. 'Interesting to see what he does about this.'

'He'll talk. If the fool doesn't,' replied Brennus calmly, 'the entire army will rise up.'

The Gaul was right. Crassus finally realised that his soldiers had suffered enough. The racket alone would have conveyed their depth of anger and it was not long before a party detached itself from the centre. Led by the swarthy Andromachus, Crassus and his legates rode across the sand towards the waiting Parthians, their heads bowed. Even the horsehair plumes on the officers' helmets were sagging. Not a sound broke the silence as the sun beat down on the dramatic scene. Motionless, the archers sat high above. Watching. Waiting. Ready to attack.

For some time the two groups talked, their words inaudible because of the distance. With Andromachus acting as interpreter, Crassus and his officers listened to Surena's terms.

Romulus clenched his jaw. 'Let's hope that the fool gets us a safe pass, or we will all be food for vultures.'

'They will be wanting guarantees that he won't invade again,' said Tarquinius.

'What kind?' asked Romulus.

Brennus spat on the hot sand. 'Prisoners.'

The young man's stomach lurched. Was this what Tarquinius had meant? Romulus had no time to dwell on the disconcerting thought.

Above them, a vicious mêlée suddenly broke out. Andromachus and the Parthians had produced concealed weapons and killed three legates. While the soldiers watched helplessly, Crassus was knocked from his horse with a blow to the head. Instantly two warriors jumped down and threw his senseless body on to a horse. Leaving their companions to finish off the remaining Romans, they galloped away up the dune.

The stunned legionaries watched as their sole chance of salvation disappeared. One senior officer had managed to pull his horse around and ride back, but the others lay lifeless on the sand.

The army had been left with only one legate.

'We are done for,' groaned a voice nearby.

Brennus drew his longsword, his face calm.

'Treacherous bastards,' said Romulus bitterly.

'They must have been planning it all along,' remarked Tarquinius. 'That I did not see.'

The horsemen above had already split into two files, each aiming at one side of the Roman column. Surena had prepared the final blow.

Romulus pulled his *gladius* free, regretting that he would never get revenge on Gemellus. They would be lucky to survive the next hour.

Then Tarquinius glanced at the sky and to his relief, spoke with absolute certainty. 'We three will not die today.' He lowered his voice. 'Many will. But not us.'

A great gust of relief escaped Romulus' lips.

Brennus grinned from ear to ear, his faith stronger than ever.

There was a collective moan when the soldiers realised that the previous day's slaughter was about to be repeated. What seemed like hope had only been deceit.

Centurions and junior officers seized the initiative, ordering retreat down the slope. With Crassus gone, there would be no clear orders from the trumpeters. Men shuffled desperately to the flat ground, peering over their shoulders. A ragged line, three ranks deep, assembled in close formation at the bottom of the dune. Shields were raised against the storm of deadly missiles that would soon be hissing down.

Crassus' once proud army huddled together, preparing to die under the burning Mesopotamian sun. Few legionaries had any will to fight remaining.

The one-sided battle did not last long. Countless

Parthian arrows filled the air, punching through *scuta*, decimating those beneath. With no means of retaliation, all the soldiers could do was to be killed where they stood. Any who broke and ran were butchered within a few steps. Soon Roman casualties sprawled on the hot sand in their hundreds.

By the time cataphracts were sent in for the first time, the end was nigh. The heavy cavalry pounded down the slope, ploughing into the Roman centre. Lances ripped into men's chests, horses trampled bodies into the ground, swords hacked deep into flesh. A massive gap remained where their unstoppable momentum had carried the Parthians through.

The legionaries could not take much more before they were utterly routed.

The one surviving legate ordered his legion's eagle dipped to show the desire to surrender. Romulus would never forget the symbol of Roman military might being lowered to the sand. Since he had first seen them in Brundisium, proudly borne aloft by the standard-bearers, the silver birds had stirred Romulus' blood. As a slave and then a gladiator, he had never encountered anything to really inspire him. His worship of Jupiter was like that of everyone else – hope and belief in the intangible. But the eagles were solid metal, and hard evidence of the Republic's military might: something for him to have faith in. After all, he was a Roman. His mother was Italian and so was the bastard who had raped her. Why should he not follow the eagle into battle as the regular legionaries did?

He saw many break down in tears at the shame of the

defeat. Some officers attacked the Parthians blindly, preferring to die fighting than live with the ignominy, but most soldiers surrendered with relief. The desert warriors surrounded the beaten Romans, their sweating horses pressing in close. The survivors were herded together like sheep while dark brown eyes stared from behind fully drawn bows. None dared resist any longer. These were arrows that had defeated an army of thirty-five thousand men.

All unit standards, potent symbols of power, were seized and the Parthians forced everyone to throw down their swords. Those not swift enough to obey were killed on the spot. Brennus dropped his longsword with reluctance, but the Etruscan seemed less concerned about his battleaxe and Romulus soon knew why. Groups of archers dismounted and began to pick up the weapons, tying them together in bundles. Camels were being loaded with the *gladii* and remaining *pila*. The weapons were going with the captives, evidence that their fate had already been decided. Tarquinius expected to retrieve his axe later. It gave Romulus hope.

But nearly half the force involved in the final battle had been killed. The remainder – approximately ten thousand legionaries and mercenaries – were now prisoners. Defeated and dejected, the soldiers were left with nothing but their clothes and armour. Once disarmed, it was simple for the Parthians to tie ropes round each man's neck.

In long lines of human misery, they were marched south towards Seleucia. As he trudged away, Romulus did not look back at the carnage.

Behind him, hundreds of vultures were starting to land.

Chapter XXVII: Crassus

Seleucia, capital of the Parthian Empire, summer 53 BC

Life in the circular stockade where Romulus and hundreds of soldiers were incarcerated had become almost routine. Positioned near a great brick archway leading into the city, the prison of thick logs was twice Brennus' height. The men sat miserably on hard dirt inside, packed so tightly they were barely able to stretch out their legs. Rumour had it that the other captives were being held in many similar locations around Seleucia. Even unarmed, the Parthians did not trust the Romans in very large groups.

Replaced by new suffering, Carrhae and the terrible march south had already become a distant memory. Freezing nights followed the searing hot days, increasing the hardship for wounded and whole alike. There was no shelter in the compound. The Roman soldiers shivered together in the dark and burned in the sun. All known officers had been taken elsewhere, leaving only a few low-rankers to rally spirits.

Tarquinius seemed content to wait, making few comments about wind or weather. No one else knew what their fate would be. They had been spared so far, but it still seemed likely the Parthians would execute them all. Thousands of comrades had been left to rot in the desert, a shame each man felt keenly. It was Roman custom to inter the dead with pomp and ceremony. Normally only criminals were left in the open and Romulus could vividly recall the putrid smell from corpses littering the pits on the eastern slopes of the Esquiline. Only the gods knew what Carrhae would have been like.

The prisoners were fed barely enough to survive. Chaos descended each time the guards shoved inside to leave provisions on the ground. Men were reduced to beasts, fighting over stale crusts and brackish water. It was thanks to Tarquinius' increasing stature that the friends ate and drank at all. Helped by Romulus, the Etruscan moved tirelessly among the sick every day, cleaning wounds and administering herbs from a small leather pouch that he had miraculously saved from their captors. As soldiers became aware of his mystical ability, respect for the Etruscan soared even higher and food was kept back for him. It was through someone like the haruspex that a way might be found out of the hell they were in.

Many of the injured succumbed to dehydration and the bloated corpses were only hauled away by the Parthians if the prisoners carried them to the gate. To prevent disease spreading to the nearby city, the guards had constructed a huge pyre, constantly ablaze to cope with the number of dead. At night its ghostly light revealed thin, hungry faces. The smell of burning flesh was all-pervading, its acrid odour adding to the men's distress.

'Bastards should have executed us,' raged Romulus at dawn on the twelfth day. 'A few weeks and we'll all end up like them.'

More than twenty legionaries lay dead nearby.

'Patience,' counselled Tarquinius. 'The air is moving. Soon we will know more.'

Romulus nodded reluctantly but Felix was enraged at the sight of his comrades' corpses. 'What I'd give for a weapon,' he said, thumping the timbers with frustration.

The little Gaul's action caught the eye of a guard, who waved his spear in a clear gesture to stand back.

'Quiet!' hissed Brennus. He would wait as long as Tarquinius was happy to. 'You don't want to die like that legionary.'

The decomposing figure hanging from the T-shaped wooden structure outside was a brutal example of Parthian discipline. Two days before, a burly veteran of the Sixth had spat at the feet of a guard. He had been dragged outside immediately and fastened to a cross.

With thick iron nails driven through his feet, the soldier had been unable to stand for long. Nor could he hang from his transfixed hands. Shifting from one agonising position to another, the victim was soon screaming. The cruel spectacle had carried on for half the morning. Satisfied that the prisoners had seen enough, the guard had abruptly ended the man's suffering with a spear thrust and had left his body in place to serve as a reminder.

Felix sat down.

The Parthian resumed his patrol around the perimeter.

'We are still alive. That means they have something planned,' said the Etruscan.

'Public execution,' growled Felix. 'That's what the Gauls would do.'

'Not for us ordinary soldiers.'

Romulus remained unconvinced. 'In Rome we'd end up in the arena. Are these savages any different?'

'They have no gladiators, no beast hunts. This is not Italy.' Tarquinius was emphatic. 'Listen!'

The Parthian bells and drums had not stopped since dawn. Since their arrival in Seleucia there had been triumphant noises most days, but this was different. Growing ever louder, the clamour had an ominous feel to it. The temperature had been climbing steadily as the sun rose into the clear blue sky and the sweating soldiers were beginning to feel uneasy.

Brennus got to his feet, looking towards the maze of streets that led into the city. 'It's getting nearer.'

Silence hung over the stockade as the din approached. Dirty, bandaged and sunburnt, the survivors of the Sixth got to their feet one by one as the guards chattered excitedly outside.

'What is it, Tarquinius?' Like many, Felix had realised the Etruscan had knowledge of the Parthians.

Eager for any information, a cluster of men formed around him.

Tarquinius rubbed his chin thoughtfully. 'There has been no formal celebration yet.'

'What about Crassus?' asked Romulus. Since the

battle, there had been no sign of their general. No doubt he would play an important part.

The Etruscan was about to answer when a group of fifty unusually tall warriors emerged from the brick archway into the open area before the compound. Clad in chain mail and wearing polished spiked helmets, each bore a heavy spear and round shield. They were followed closely by dozens of Parthians in robes, playing instruments. The procession came to an orderly halt, but the harsh music carried on relentlessly.

More than one man made the sign against evil.

'Elite bodyguards,' muttered Tarquinius. 'King Orodes has decided our fate.'

'You know.' Romulus glanced at the Etruscan, who smiled enigmatically.

He ground his teeth.

'Have you seen something else?' said Brennus.

'I told you before. We are going on a long march to the east.'

Alarmed by the revelation, the soldiers stared fearfully at the haruspex.

'Where Alexander led the greatest army ever seen.' By now, Tarquinius had told many stories of the Greek's legendary march into the unknown, three centuries before.

Most faces dropped even further but Romulus had found the tales fascinating. Anticipation coursed through his veins.

'We may be glad that they passed east.' Tarquinius patted the tiny leather pouch hidden in his waistband which contained the herbs and the ancient map they had seen only once before. Along with his scarab ring and the *lituus*, it was the only personal possession he had managed to retain after capture. 'One of Alexander's soldiers made this. And it passed into my hands for a reason,' he whispered.

They were interrupted as the newcomers' leader began loudly addressing the guards. Heavy ropes were immediately picked up, the same ones that had been used on the prisoners after the battle. Fear, ever present among them, rose. When one of the gates was half opened, the legionaries' frightened muttering grew even louder. There had been some security in the confined space. What now?

Flanked by several burly warriors with lowered spears, the captain in charge entered the compound and directed those nearest to walk outside. With great reluctance the soldiers obeyed. As they emerged, ropes were tied around their necks. Soon a long file had formed. Counting carefully, the Parthians inside the stockade gestured at more captives to follow.

One man had endured enough. Clad in the distinctive breastplate of an *optio*, he had been missed when the officers were removed. As the guard pointed with his spear, the *optio* deliberately shoved him in the chest.

'What's the fool doing?' hissed Romulus. 'He must know what they'll do.'

Tarquinius regarded him steadily. 'Choosing his own fate. It is something we can all do.'

Romulus remembered Bassius' mercy killings and the two mercenaries who had stayed behind at Carrhae. Self-determination was a powerful concept and he struggled to comprehend it.

A swift order rang out and the sentry drove his spear point deep into the man's belly. He doubled over with a scream, hands clutching the shaft. They watched as the guard knelt and drew a thin-bladed dagger. Two others held the *optio*'s arms. As shrieks of agony rent the air, the Parthian captain glared at the remaining soldiers.

The sentry stood up and swung his arm, throwing something through the air. Two glistening eyeballs, their nerves still dangling, landed nearby and Romulus recoiled in disgust, still astonished that anyone could choose such suffering.

Nobody resisted when the officer motioned again for them to walk outside. Romulus shuffled silently past the *optio*. Inevitably he found his gaze drawn to the mutilated writhing creature, hands clutching its bloody sockets. The low moans filled him with pity, and he clenched his fists.

'No man should have to endure a fate such as that,' he whispered.

'Do not presume to judge another,' replied Tarquinius. 'That *optio* could have walked outside with us. He chose not to.'

'No one can decide another's path,' agreed the Gaul, his tone sombre. Bright in his mind was the image of his uncle, choosing to die to save another. Brennus.

Romulus looked at his friends in turn. Their words resounded inside him.

When fifty soldiers had been assembled, the Parthian commander signalled his guards to stop. As with the sacrifice of the bull, only a few were required as witnesses. Word would spread fast to the remainder.

Led by the cataphracts and musicians, the column got under way. The legionaries shuffled miserably together, urged on by kicks and spear butts.

They passed under the immense archway, which was as big as any Romulus had seen in Italy. But it was the exception rather than the rule. Lined by single-storey mud huts, Seleucia's streets were narrow. Constructed of sun-hardened bricks, the tiny dwellings made up the majority of structures. Just an occasional, plain temple was taller. As in Rome, everything was built very close together, the alleyways between filled with rubbish and human waste. Romulus saw no signs of aqueducts or public toilets. It was a simply built city; the Parthians were clearly not a nation of engineers. They were nomadic desert warriors.

Only the arch and the structure of what must have been King Orodes' residence were impressive enough to exist in Rome. Bare ground extended for some distance around the high, fortified walls of the palace. Towers sat on each corner, with archers patrolling the battlements between. A troop of cataphracts sat on horses beside ornate metal gates, staring impassively as the legionaries filed by. Few could look at the mailed warriors without a shudder of fear.

As he passed, Tarquinius peered through gaps in the metalwork.

'Don't draw their attention!' hissed Brennus.

'They don't care,' replied the Etruscan casually, craning his neck. 'I want a glimpse of the gold Crassus was after. The place is supposed to be dripping with it.'

But one cataphract had seen enough: dropping his lance tip towards Tarquinius, he then forcefully jerked it away.

To Romulus' relief, the haruspex ducked his head and shuffled on.

There was little space for the captives to pass through the waiting crowds. Everyone in Seleucia wanted to revel in the Romans' humiliation. Jeers and shrieks of scorn rang in their ears as they stumbled along. Romulus kept his gaze firmly on the rutted mud beneath his feet. One glance at the brown hate-filled faces had been sufficient. What was to come would be bad enough without drawing more attention to himself.

Sharp-edged stones and pebbles flew in low arcs, cutting and bruising their bodies. Rotten vegetables – even the contents of chamber pots – rained down. Snot-nosed children in dirty rags darted in and out of the press to kick at the men. One soldier had his cheek raked open by the nails of a thin woman who stepped into his path. When he tried to stop her, a guard clubbed him unconscious. The crone crowed in triumph, spitting on the limp figure. Legionaries in front and behind were forced to carry their comrade.

The filth-covered prisoners were driven through the streets for what seemed an eternity, allowing the stunning victory over Crassus' huge army to be savoured by all. At last they reached a large open area, similar in size to Rome's Campus Martius. The temperature soared as the small amount of shade was left behind. Few dared look up as they were forced towards the centre, away from the jeers and missiles. Guards led the way, viciously beating back those foolish enough to block their path.

Beside a great fire, dozens of Parthians were toiling busily, feeding the hungry flames with logs. An empty stage sat close by. Blows and kicks urged the confused soldiers to stand before it. They formed in weary, beaten lines, wondering, dreading, what was to come. As time passed, more groups arrived, brought from other compounds around the city. Soon there were hundreds of Romans watching – the representatives of ten thousand.

Romulus had decided no one would see him look beaten. If he was about to be executed, it would be a proud end. Brennus seemed content that Tarquinius was not alarmed. Thus he and his mentors were relatively at ease with their fate, in contrast to the half-starved, sunburnt legionaries waiting for death beside them. The awful defeat at Carrhae had shattered their confidence. Heads hung low; quiet sobs racked the weakest. There was even a faint smell of urine as the tension of the situation grew too great for some.

Gradually the mob's abuse died away. Even the drums and bells fell silent. A new sound filled the air, one that instinctively drew attention. Moans of agony were coming from beyond the surrounding crowd.

Dozens of wooden crosses were being erected around the area. From the vertical section of each hung a Roman officer, suspended by ropes holding his forearms to the horizontal crossbar. Periodically the victims pushed up on nailed feet to relieve the pressure on their upper bodies. Then the pain grew too great and they slumped down again, groaning. It was a vicious cycle that would end in total dehydration or suffocation. Death could take days, especially if the victim was physically strong.

The crowd shouted and laughed, their focus drawn away from the other prisoners. Stones flew at the crucified men. Fresh screams rang out when they found targets. Guards prodded the helpless officers with spears, laughing when blood was drawn. Cries of glee filled the air. The brutal spectacle continued in this fashion for some time. The ordinary soldiers watched appalled, each imagining his own fate.

Felix pointed. 'There's Bassius. Poor bastard.'

Romulus and Brennus stared at the veteran who was hanging nearby, his eyes closed. Despite the agonising ordeal, not a sound was passing the centurion's lips. Never had Bassius' courage been more evident.

Brennus tugged at the cord around his neck. 'I'm going to put him out of his misery.'

'And end up on a cross yourself?' responded Tarquinius.

Romulus swore. The same idea had been in his mind but they could never reach Bassius without being killed first.

'He won't last long,' interjected Felix. 'Crucifixion saps a wounded man's strength very quickly.'

'The Romans taught them how to crucify,' said the Etruscan.

Romulus had no answer. He felt shame and disgust that his own people could have passed on such a barbaric torture. But while slaves and criminals were routinely killed this way in Italy, he had never seen it in such numbers. Then he remembered how Crassus had killed the survivors of Spartacus' army. Rome was as cruel as Parthia.

Brennus spat angrily, preparing to snap his bindings. Images of Conall dying beneath a dozen *gladii* filled his mind again. Now another valiant man needed to be saved. He had journeyed far enough.

'Your choice, Brennus.' Tarquinius' voice cut in. 'We still have a long road before us.'

The big warrior turned, real anguish in his eyes. 'Bassius is a brave soldier. He saved our lives! And he doesn't deserve to die like an animal.'

'Help him then.'

There was a pause before Brennus sighed heavily. 'Ultan foretold a very long journey. So have you.'

'Bassius will die anyway,' said Tarquinius gently. 'Conall and Brac would have too. There is nothing you could have done to change any of it.'

Brennus' eyes widened. 'You know about my family?'

The Etruscan nodded.

'I have not spoken their names for eight years.'

'Brac was a brave warrior, just like his father. But their time had come.'

The hairs on Romulus' neck rose. He had only ever gleaned hints of the Gaul's past before.

Brennus looked distraught.

'There will be a day when your friends need you.' The Etruscan's voice was deep. 'A time for Brennus to stand and fight. Against terrible odds.'

There was a long silence.

'No one could win such a battle. Except Brennus.'

'It will happen far from here?' His tone was urgent, almost frantic.

'At the very edge of the world.'

Brennus smiled slowly and released the rope. 'Ultan was a mighty druid. As are you, Tarquinius. The gods will take our centurion straight to Elysium.'

'Be sure of it.'

Romulus could still remember the glance Tarquinius had given the Gaul as they retreated towards Carrhae. Concern for Brennus filled the young soldier's heart as he pieced the comments together, but then he saw Tarquinius eyeing the fire.

'What is it for?'

The Etruscan nodded at a squat iron cauldron perched in the middle of the blaze. Sweating men in leather aprons were labouring to keep the flames burning hotly beneath it. Every so often one would lean over and stir the contents with a long-handled ladle.

'A while ago they dropped in a gold ingot.'

Romulus felt a shiver run down his spine.

The drums began again, but this time the din did not last for long. A flat-bed wagon arrived, pulled by mules and surrounded by heavy cavalry, magnificent in their chain mail. On either side strode a number of guards masquerading as *lictores*. Each held a *fasces*, the Roman symbol of justice. But unlike those used in Italy, the bundles of rods they carried were decorated with money bags and their axes with officers' heads.

'This has all been planned,' he muttered.

'It's a parody of a military triumph,' explained the Etruscan. 'And it mocks Crassus' greed for riches.'

There was a collective gasp when the soldiers saw Crassus standing in the cart, tied to a wooden frame by the neck and arms. On his head rested a laurel wreath while his lips and cheeks had been painted with ochre and white lead. A brightly coloured woman's robe completed the indignity, its fabric soaked with human waste and rotten vegetables. The general's eyes were closed, his face resigned. It had been a long journey.

The prostitutes who had accompanied the senior officers were also present. Stripped naked, cut and bruised, they wailed and clung to each other. During the campaign, Romulus had seen many rapes. And every time he had, awful images of Gemellus grunting on top of his mother had flooded back. It was part of war, but Romulus shuddered at what the women must have endured since Carrhae.

When the mules came to a halt, screams of fear rang out.

Parthian warriors swarmed on to the cart and the prostitutes were dragged by the hair on to the stage and shoved down on their knees. Whimpers were met with blows and kicks. Soon only the occasional sob escaped them.

A tall bearded man in a black robe climbed into view and gestured for silence. The crowd obeyed and the priest began speaking in a low, deep voice. Palpable anger could be heard in every word. His speech drove the watching Parthians into a frenzy and they swarmed forward at the prisoners. Guards had to use real force to drive them back, wounding many with their spears.

'Rabble-rousing,' said Brennus. 'So the real entertainment can begin.'

'He is talking about what happens to any who threaten Parthia.' The Etruscan translated quickly. 'Crassus was the aggressor. But their mighty gods helped them defeat the Roman invaders. Now they require a reward.'

Romulus looked at the stage and shivered. The campaign had been damned from the start and only a fool would have disregarded the plethora of bad omens. But Crassus had ignored every last one, his monumental arrogance leading thousands of men to their deaths. He was still revolted by what was about to happen to their general. But there was nothing he could do. The young soldier breathed deeply to calm himself.

At last the bearded priest finished, content the audience understood the impending ritual. Only moans from the crucified officers and prostitutes now broke the eerie silence.

Every legionary's gaze was fixed on Crassus and the unfortunate women. A faint smile played across the priest's lips as he drew a long dagger from his belt. Moving to stand behind the first whore, he spoke a few more words.

Loud cheers rose up.

She twisted round to see, crying in anticipation and terror. Brutally her head was wrenched back to face the mob. With a smooth movement, he slashed the woman's throat.

Abruptly, the screams stopped.

Arms and legs jerked spasmodically as a fountain of blood sprayed from the gaping neck wound, covering guards and prisoners alike. The Parthian released his grip and a warrior propelled the corpse off the stage with a huge kick. Roman soldiers scattered to avoid the mutilated body landing on them.

One by one, the prostitutes suffered the same fate. Soon only Crassus remained alive. The platform ran with blood, bodies lay heaped in front, but still the crowd bayed for more.

Parthia wanted its revenge.

'Savages,' growled Brennus.

Romulus was thinking of Fabiola. For all he knew, she might have been one of the women killed. His hard-won calm was gone: he was seething. Suddenly all he wanted was to be free. To call no man master. Not Gemellus. Not Memor, Crassus or any Parthian. He glanced at the nearest guards, wondering how fast they would react if attacked. He could choose his own fate.

'You will return to Rome,' hissed Tarquinius. 'I have seen your destiny. It does not end here.'

They locked eyes as a deafening roll of drums announced the end of the ritual.

Stay strong. Like Fabiola. I will survive.

'Look.' The Gaul gestured at the stage.

The guards did not bother to untie the last prisoner. Instead they picked up the frame and placed it on the platform. A deep, almost primeval roar greeted the action.

It was time for Crassus to pay.

Sensing the end, he screamed and kicked his legs futilely. The ropes binding him were thick and strong and soon Crassus sagged against the rough timbers, his face grey with exhaustion and fear. During the struggle, his wreath had tipped sideways over one eye and the warriors pointed, smirking.

Again the priest began to speak, a tirade of fury against the man who had invaded Parthia. As spittle flew from his lips, the spectators howled with anger and surged against the guards' crossed spears once more. Tarquinius considered translating the words, but the soldiers around him needed little explanation of what was going on. And only a handful looked sorry for Crassus.

When the Parthian had finished his oration, he waited for silence to fall. Finally the mob fell back.

The general looked up and focused on the mass of ragged prisoners. By their uniforms, he knew they could only be Roman soldiers.

Yet all that greeted him were insults.

Crassus' head slumped as the certainty of his fate began to sink in. Even his own men would not save him.

Anger still burned within Romulus. He could have happily killed Crassus in combat, but a public display like this went totally against his nature. It was as brutal as the worst depravities of the arena. He glanced at Brennus and could tell the Gaul felt the same way.

As always, Tarquinius seemed completely calm.

A smith leaned over the fire and dipped a ladle into the cauldron. Fat white globules of molten gold spilled from the lip as it emerged, narrowly missing his feet. With arms outstretched, he walked slowly towards the stage.

The crowd shrieked with anticipation and Romulus looked away.

Two guards bent Crassus' head backwards, forcing his

chin up on to an angled wooden crossbar. Using loops of rope, it was bound to face the sky. The priest moved alongside and inserted a small metal vice between the prisoner's jaws. He cranked it open, baring teeth and tongue.

Crassus screamed as he realised what was about to happen. He continued wailing as the smith ascended the steps, his burning load held at arm's length.

The priest gestured impatiently.

'Gold cools fast,' said Tarquinius.

Crassus' eyes flicked from side to side as the heat approached and the frame jerked as he tried frantically to get away.

The ladle rose high above his head and paused.

To shouts of approval, the bearded Parthian chanted a deep, resonant series of words.

'He is calling on the gods to receive the offering,' muttered Tarquinius. 'It symbolises victory over the Republic. Shows Parthia is not to be trifled with.'

The smith's hand began to tremble from holding the heavy weight. Suddenly a fat bead of gold tipped out, falling into one of Crassus' eyes. The globe ruptured, and a bellow of pain like Romulus had never heard split the air. A mixture of clear fluid and blood spurted on to the general's cheek.

Crassus' other eye held a look of utter terror. Urine formed in a puddle between his feet.

The priest intoned a last prayer and made an abrupt motion with his right hand.

An inarticulate moan escaped Crassus' lips as the gold poured down in a stream of molten fire. With a sizzling noise audible to all, the boiling liquid emptied into his gaping mouth, silencing the general for ever. His body shuddered and spasmed with the unbelievable agony of the ordeal. Steam rose in little spirals as flesh reached cooking point. Only the tightness of the bonds prevented Crassus from breaking free. At last the precious metal reached heart and lungs, burning the vital organs into stasis.

He slumped and hung limply from the frame.

Crassus was dead.

The watching Parthians went into a frenzy. Nothing could be heard except the clamouring shouts, clanging bells and thudding drumbeats.

Many soldiers vomited at the sight. Others had closed their eyes rather than witness the savage execution. A few shed tears. Romulus swore silently that whatever the cost, he would escape.

When the crowd had quietened, the priest stabbed a finger at Crassus' body, yelling at the prisoners. At his words, there was again silence.

The spectacle was not over.

Tarquinius leaned forward. 'He is offering us a choice.'

The soldiers nearby pricked their ears.

'What kind of choice?' growled Brennus.

'A cross each.' The Etruscan indicated the officers. 'Or the fire, if we prefer.'

'Is that it?' spat Felix. 'I'd sooner die fighting.' He tugged at his neck rope.

Angry shouts of agreement rang out.

'There is another option.'

Seeing Tarquinius translating his words, the priest smiled and pointed eastwards with his dagger.

Everyone turned to the Etruscan.

'We can join the Parthian army and fight their enemies.'

'Wage war for them?' Felix was incredulous.

'Same job. Different masters,' said Brennus. After the horror of the executions, he had recovered his poise. 'Where?'

'The far borders of their empire.'

'To the east,' the big Gaul added calmly.

Tarquinius nodded.

Romulus was also unperturbed but the legionaries were terrified.

'Can we trust them?' Felix scowled as guards prodded Crassus' limp body with spears.

'Make your own choice,' said Tarquinius. 'They have left us alive this long and shown us Crassus' death as an example.' He turned to face the men behind and shouted out their choices.

When Tarquinius had finished, the bearded priest called to him again.

'We must choose now!' cried the Etruscan. 'If you want crucifixion, raise your right hand!'

Not one hand went up.

'Do you want to die like Crassus?'

No reaction.

Tarquinius paused. Sweat was rolling down his face, but he was utterly controlled as he delivered the ultimatum.

Romulus frowned. The Etruscan was almost too calm.

'Join the Parthian army?'

Silence filled the air. Even the crucified officers' groans

were inaudible. The crowd watched with bated breath.

Romulus raised his eyebrows at Brennus.

The Gaul raised his right hand. 'It is the only sensible choice,' he said. 'This way we stay alive.' *And I will meet my destiny.*

He lifted an arm in the air and Tarquinius did the same.

Around them a sea of hands rose as the other prisoners slowly accepted their fate. It was unlikely that their comrades in the stockades would argue with their decision.

The priest nodded with satisfaction.

Ten thousand legionaries would march east.

Chapter XXVIII: Manumission

Rome, autumn 53 BC

It had taken a while for Fabiola to decide on the best method of dealing with Pompeia. There had been time to think while she washed her bloody bedding and Vettius disposed of the snake's body down the sewer. After that, acting normally and secure in the knowledge that Vettius was staying within earshot, Fabiola had calmly joined the group of women in the baths.

Pompeia's face had first turned grey with shock; then it had flushed with anger. But with so many others present, she could do nothing. There had been an uneasy silence as the other prostitutes watched the two enemies. Feigning complete ignorance, Fabiola filled the air with bright conversation about the forthcoming public holiday, which often saw even more business than usual. Gradually the atmosphere relaxed.

As Fabiola suspected, Pompeia was not to be put off. This was exactly what she wanted. The redhead soon made her excuses, climbed out of the warm water and went to the madam. With Benignus eavesdropping, Fabiola quickly knew that Pompeia had managed to wheedle permission from Jovina to leave the brothel later. Apparently she wanted to consult a soothsayer about her best client. Of course she really wanted to know whether it was still possible to kill Fabiola, even perhaps to buy more poison. The black-haired girl smiled grimly at that thought. It seemed that after three failed attempts at murder, the gods were indeed watching over her. She could only pray that they were doing the same for Romulus.

When the solution finally came to her, Fabiola creased her face in apparent pain. Complaining of a violent stomach ache, she left the bathing area and retired to her room. Several noisy visits to the toilet later, everyone within earshot knew that Fabiola was suffering from a bout of food poisoning. Shortly after that, her face touched with a dusting of white lead, Fabiola had begged one of the other women to inform Jovina that she might not be able to work that night.

The hours before sunset were generally quiet ones. Fabiola knelt alone before her altar to Jupiter, praying for it to remain so. She needed an opportunity to get out of the brothel without being seen. This was the most risky part of her endeavour. Her alibi would rest on the fact that everyone thought she was in her room, as sick as a dog.

The gods were smiling on Fabiola still.

Peace fell on the Lupanar as the prostitutes rested and slept in their cells. Not a single customer appeared that afternoon either and Jovina retired to her room for a rare nap. None of the bored women in the anteroom beside reception was paying attention as Pompeia left, accompanied by Vettius. A few moments later, Fabiola stole past, wearing a long cloak with the hood raised. Benignus remained by the entrance, nervously turning his club in his hands. Both doormen wanted to be part of Fabiola's plan, but one had to stay behind and Vettius had refused to do so. The proof of the redhead's treachery had enraged him so much that he insisted on being her chaperon when she left.

It was a simple matter for Fabiola to follow the pair from a distance.

Once the divination was over, Vettius knew where she would be waiting.

Still musing over the favourable prediction given her by the soothsayer, Pompeia barely had time to protest before she found herself in an alleyway, ten steps off the narrow street that led back towards the brothel. Twice her size, Vettius was well used to manhandling rich clients out of the brothel without hurting them.

Immediately the noise of oxen pulling carts and traders touting for business seemed further away. The poor amount of light that had been on offer fell to a dim twilight that made it hard to see. Broken pottery and rotten vegetables covered the rough ground, mixed with human waste, dirty straw and spent charcoal from the braziers that kept the miserable *insulae* warm. A mangy dog that was nosing about for food barked once and ran off, startled by the intrusion.

Thinking Vettius wanted his way with her, Pompeia

turned coy. 'Never knew you were interested, big man.' She flashed a practised smile. 'Here's not the place, though. Come to my room tomorrow morning after I've finished work. You'll not regret it.'

The doorman did not reply. With a blank face, he pushed the redhead deeper into the alley. Always useful in street fights, a sheathed *gladius* hung from a strap over his right shoulder.

'Can't wait? Typical man.' Without protesting further, Pompeia came to a halt and began to shrug off her robe. 'Come on, then. It's cleaner here.'

Something flew through the air to land at her feet.

Even in the poor light, it was recognisable as a snake's head. Pompeia screamed and jumped back, her mouth open wide with shock.

The look on her former friend's face told Fabiola all she needed to know. She stepped out of the shadows, raising Vettius' dagger threateningly.

Pompeia's features turned ashen. This was no easy coupling to keep the doorman sweet. She backed away, her feet unsteady on rubbish and shards of terracotta. 'Please,' she begged. 'Don't hurt me.'

'Why not?' Fabiola barked. 'You've tried to do the same to me. Three times. And I've done nothing to you.'

Fat tears of self-pity formed in the corners of Pompeia's eyes. 'You take all the best customers,' she whimpered.

'There are plenty to go around,' Fabiola hissed. 'And I'm only doing it for my brother.'

'He's long dead,' replied Pompeia viciously. 'The augur swore it.' Despite the magnitude of the situation, vitriol still filled her.

Knowing the remark could well be true, rage over-whelmed Fabiola. Without even thinking, her dagger whipped up and pricked the redhead's throat. It was very gratifying to see terror in Pompeia's eyes. Yet Fabiola was still loath to kill her. She breathed deeply, calming herself. There had to be another way.

Pompeia sensed a chance. 'Kill me and you'll be executed,' she spat. 'You know what Jovina's like.'

She did not realise it, but the comment was her death sentence.

The account of a prostitute who had tried to murder the old madam years before was well known. First she had been tortured with hot irons, and then blinded. Finally, the unfortunate woman had been crucified on the Campus Martius while everyone in the Lupanar had been forced to watch. The story kept all the slaves in line. Almost all.

Fabiola knew now that there was no other way. Pompeia was so twisted with malice that she could never be trusted. The whole plan would have to be followed. Looking down at the mangled snake's head, she hardened her heart. There would have been no mercy for her.

'Fool,' Fabiola announced quietly. 'Jovina thinks I am in bed with an upset stomach.'

Pompeia's mouth opened and closed.

'And Vettius did his best to fight off the *collegia* thugs, but there's only so much one man can do against eight others.'

Panic-stricken, the redhead's eyes turned to the door-man.

Drawing the *gladius*, Vettius shrugged eloquently,

drawing its edge along his left forearm. Blood welled from the long cut and he smiled at the pain. 'The madam will need evidence that I was attacked,' he said mildly. 'I'll walk into a couple of pillars on the way back just to make sure.'

Realising that her fate was sealed, Pompeia screamed. It was a futile gesture. There was no chance that anyone would come to her aid. Few citizens were brave enough to intervene in street disputes, let alone venture into tiny alleys. She moved uncertainly a few steps forward, and then back.

There was no escape.

Vettius was blocking one end of the alleyway; Fabiola stood at the other. Both had set, determined stares.

The redhead opened her mouth to cry out again. It was the last thing she did.

Darting in, Fabiola slashed Pompeia's throat wide open with her dagger. She stepped back quickly as blood poured from the gaping wound. With a startled expression distorting her pale features, Pompeia slumped silently to the dirt and rolled to lie face down between Fabiola and the huge doorman. Red liquid pooled around her.

'My brother is alive.' Clinging to that hope, Fabiola spat on the corpse. This is how Romulus must have felt in the arena, she thought. *Kill or be killed.* It was as simple as that.

Vettius was filled with awe. He had always known that Fabiola was clever and beautiful, but here was graphic evidence of her ruthlessness. She was not just a helpless woman who needed his protection. Here was someone to follow: someone to lead him. He was brought back to reality by Fabiola's voice.

'Let me bind that before you lose too much blood.' Producing a piece of cloth, Fabiola wound it tightly around Vettius' arm.

He smiled his thanks as she leaned in and kissed him on the cheek. There was an unspoken bond between them now.

'Wait here for a while. I need time to get back without being noticed.'

Vettius nodded.

'Make plenty of noise when you get inside,' ordered Fabiola. 'I'll be able to get up from my sickbed, hear you tell Jovina what happened to poor Pompeia.'

'Yes, Mistress.'

It was only later that Fabiola remembered how the doorman had addressed her.

He was her follower now, rather than Jovina's.

There had been little that Jovina could say when Vettius staggered into the brothel, covered in blood. His story had been most compelling and, wary of more trouble, the madam immediately banned all the prostitutes from leaving until further notice.

Fabiola's satisfaction at ridding herself of Pompeia and her threats did not last for long. The redhead's barbed comment about Romulus being dead had sunk deeper than she had realised and worry began to consume Fabiola day and night. Her prayers to Jupiter grew even more fervent. Thus far, the news from the east had been quite encouraging: the city was full of tales about minor skirmishes and the riches extorted from cities that Crassus' army had passed. Fabiola tried to use this to calm her fears for Romulus. With no large battles taking place, the risk of many men being killed was surely low. But everyone in Rome knew that Crassus would not rest with mere intimidation. He was bent on one thing: military success.

And it was common knowledge that his target was Parthia.

Fabiola felt sick when she thought about it.

Things got even worse when word reached Rome of the crushing defeat at Carrhae. Longinus had led the Eighth across the Euphrates to safety, his rank senior enough to mean that his account could be relied upon. Publius and twenty thousand soldiers had been slain, ten thousand taken prisoner and seven eagles lost. Adding insult to injury, Crassus was now a helpless captive in Seleucia. The triumvirate had been reduced to two.

While the news would have pleased Pompey and Caesar, it was devastating for Fabiola. Romulus was surely among the dead. Even if he wasn't, she would never see him again, lost to the savage east. Since entering the Lupanar, she had hidden all emotion from everyone, but the awful certainty of her brother's fate broke something inside Fabiola.

For weeks she managed to conceal the sadness from everyone, even Brutus. She laughed and smiled, entertaining clients with her customary panache while the grief inside her knew no bounds. Rather than diminishing as time passed, it grew: a deep, inconsolable gloom. Their mother was long dead, a nameless victim of the salt mines, and now Romulus had joined her. It became harder and harder for Fabiola to remain composed. The clever young woman was losing the will to carry on.

What point is there in living? I am nothing. No one. A prostitute, she thought bitterly. A slave with no living family, apart from the bastard who fathered us. And while the prospect of revenge on the noble who had raped her mother still appealed, she knew it was a hopeless quest. All Fabiola had to go on was a statue of Caesar that she had seen once in Maximus' house. Using the embers of her desire for revenge, she continued working numbly, haunted constantly by thoughts of Romulus. Of how Gemellus had dragged him away to the *ludus*. How close they had come to meeting the night of the brawl outside the Lupanar. How she might have found him more quickly if she had taken on Memor as a client sooner. Guilt ravaged Fabiola from dawn till dusk.

When a new girl from Judaea arrived in the brothel, it had seemed a good opportunity to find out about where Romulus had died. A way to start letting the sadness go. But the tales of the eastern deserts were terrifying: the boiling heat, the lack of water, the natives with lethal bows. Fabiola's imagination was flooded with vivid images, each more gruesome than the last. She began to sleep badly and suffer from nightmares. Soon she was taking mandrake just to get some rest at night.

Late one morning Fabiola was still lying in bed, avoiding the world. Two miserable months had passed in this fashion. Despite being offered a better one by Jovina, she had retained the original tiny room given her on the very first day in the brothel. It was comforting to her. Fabiola's favourite clothes hung from iron hooks on the walls; bottles of makeup and perfume sat on a low table alongside. A shrine now took up one corner; on it sat a statue of Jupiter, surrounded by dozens of votive candles. Over the years, Fabiola had spent countless hours on her knees before it, praying for her family. She had also been generous with her donations at the huge temple on the Capitoline Hill.

All her efforts had been in vain.

Romulus and her mother were gone.

As far as Fabiola was aware, there were no regular clients coming to see her until that evening. It was a small consolation as she had slept little, thanks to a graphic nightmare about Romulus being disembowelled by a slashing Parthian sword. She still couldn't banish the image from her mind.

'Romulus.' Her head slumped and Fabiola let a tear form in her eye. Another followed, and another. Then the dam burst. Grief overcame her and she began to sob, deep surges of anguish erupting from the depths of her soul. She hadn't cried since her first day in the brothel. Now she couldn't stop.

She cried for her mother. For Romulus. For her own lost innocence. Even for Juba, who had always been friendly to her.

The gentle knock startled her.

'Fabiola?' The voice was Docilosa's.

She gulped, wiping her eyes with the edge of the blanket. 'What is it?'

'Brutus is here. He wants to see you.'

Her lover wasn't due to visit for two days. How could she bear to appear happy? 'Now?'

Docilosa opened the door and peered in. She took one look and entered, closing it quietly behind her.

Over the previous four years, the older woman had proved herself reliable on many occasions, running errands, buying items outside the *ludus* and feeding Fabiola snippets about Jovina. Fabiola had come to trust Docilosa more than any of the prostitutes. Caught up in the race for popularity, none could be completely relied upon. Not after Pompeia.

'What's wrong?' Docilosa sat down on the bed, taking Fabiola's hand in hers.

She sobbed even harder.

'Tell me.' Docilosa's voice was kind but firm.

It all poured out. Every last detail, from Velvinna's rape to Gemellus' nightly visits. Romulus training with Juba and his sale to the *ludus*. Her own arrival in the Lupanar.

Docilosa listened without saying a word. When Fabiola had finished, she leaned forward and softly kissed her on the forehead. The gesture meant more to the young woman than anything had in her entire life.

'My poor child. You have been through so much.' Docilosa sighed, her eyes dark with sorrow. 'Life can be very hard. But it goes on.'

'What's the point?' asked Fabiola dully.

Docilosa took her by the arm. 'That handsome noble out there is the point! Brutus would do anything for you.' She smoothed Fabiola's lustrous hair. 'He would, you know.'

Fabiola knew Docilosa's words were true. Brutus was indeed a kind, decent man and she was genuinely fond of him. To jeopardise in any way her best chance of a life outside the Lupanar would be very foolish.

'Dry those eyes and get dressed,' said Docilosa. 'You mustn't keep him waiting.'

Feeling more composed, Fabiola nodded and did as she was told. Being able to open her heart to a sympathetic ear had lifted some of the weight from her shoulders. Docilosa helped her choose a low-cut silk robe and apply some ochre and perfume. Thanks to her good complexion, Fabiola had not yet resorted to using lead.

'Thank you,' she said warmly.

Docilosa nodded. 'You remind me of what my own daughter might have been like.'

Fabiola felt a pang of guilt. She had never asked. 'What happened to her?'

'Sabina was taken from me when she was six,' replied Docilosa in a flat tone. 'Sold to one of the temples as an acolyte.'

'Have you seen her since?'

Docilosa shook her head. Tears formed in her eyes.

Fabiola reached out and hugged her. 'Bless you,' she whispered.

With a little smile, Docilosa regained control of herself. 'Go on,' she said brightly. 'He's in the usual place.'

Fabiola disappeared up the corridor.

Her lover was waiting in the bedroom where they had first slept together. It was the only one that Brutus would use and Jovina was happy to allow this privilege.

Customers as rich or as frequent as the staff officer were uncommon.

'What a surprise!' Fabiola swept in, making sure her cleavage was on full view.

A powerful smell of incense filled the air and only two oil lamps had been lit. Rose petals covered the bedspread. Docilosa had done well to prepare the chamber at such short notice.

Brutus stood up, surprising her. Normally they tumbled straight on to the bed. He seemed unusually serious.

'Is everything all right?' she asked, slightly worried. 'Shouldn't have taken me so long to get ready, but I wasn't expecting you today.'

He smiled as she kissed him. 'It's not that.'

'What then?' Fabiola said, sweeping her lashes down, hoping he would not notice her reddened eyes.

'I've been talking to Jovina.'

He had her attention now. Generally Brutus' conversations with the old crone tended to last no longer than it took him to pay her. He did not like the madam either.

'About what?'

He could contain himself no longer. Brutus took his right hand from behind his back.

Fabiola stared at the rolled parchment he was holding for a moment. Then the blood drained from her cheeks. 'Is that . . .?'

He nodded. 'Your *manumissio*.'

Fabiola's heart pounded as she took it. Of all the things she had expected today, the document naming her as a free woman was not one of them. Her spirits rose from the dark pit at the thought of leaving behind the Lupanar for ever. With all its tawdry luxury and grandeur, it was still just a brothel full of expensive whores. Perhaps Docilosa had known something, she thought. Life does carry on.

Taking a deep breath, Fabiola looked up. 'Why now?'

Brutus was embarrassed. 'It should have been long ago,' he muttered. 'But I've been so busy. You know how it is: the situation between Caesar and Pompey changes every damn day.'

Laying a hand on his arm, Fabiola smiled radiantly. It was a smile she knew he loved. 'What changed, my love?'

'Things are deteriorating in the city faster than ever.' He frowned. 'Clodius slipped Caesar's leash long ago and Milo has never really called anyone master. Their gangs control the city almost completely now. Elections are being postponed because officials who preside over them are at risk of their lives. Rome is becoming too dangerous.'

Fabiola nodded. Since the news of Crassus' defeat and capture, public violence had escalated sharply. Murder on the streets was even more commonplace now; rioting and the burning of public buildings were a daily occurrence. As rough and tumble politicians like Clodius Pulcher and Titus Milo entered the race for power, Rome's future seemed increasingly dark. With Caesar bogged down in Gaul, Pompey was staying neutral, waiting for the Senate to beg for his help.

'I want you somewhere safe,' said Brutus. 'Out of the city until things calm down. It seemed like a good time to buy your freedom.'

Fabiola's heart soared at the thought. 'May the gods bless you for ever,' she said and kissed him again.

Delighted by her response, Brutus immediately began talking about his new villa in Pompeii and the improvements that could be made to it. As she listened, Fabiola's guilt returned with a vengeance. Freed for just a few heartbeats, she was already forgetting about Romulus. Tears filled her eyes and she turned away.

Brutus stopped mid-sentence. 'Fabiola?'

'It's nothing. I . . .' she managed, her chin wobbling.

He stroked her face. 'You must tell me what's wrong. I can help.'

As always, Fabiola was touched by his concern. 'It's my twin brother,' she said sadly.

'You have a brother? A slave?' Brutus laughed. 'I'll set him free too!'

'You can't.'

The noble smiled gently. 'He couldn't cost more than you did.'

She began to ask and he put a finger to her lips.

'Jovina drives a hard bargain,' was all he would say. 'Tell me about your brother.'

'Romulus was a soldier in Crassus' army.'

Brutus looked confused.

Without revealing her sources, Fabiola explained what she had learned from Memor and Vettius about Romulus' escape from the *ludus* and his likely part in the invasion of Parthia.

Brutus had seen plenty of combat in Gaul and had intimate experience of the common soldier's terrible lot. Having heard the account of Carrhae, he knew it was highly unlikely that Romulus was alive. Racking his brains for what to say, Brutus patted her arm awkwardly.

Neither spoke for a moment.

Suddenly Brutus' face brightened. 'He could be one of the captives,' he said bluffly. 'Let things settle down for a few months and we'll see about sending an envoy to the east. Might be able to buy him back.'

While obviously bravado, it was deeply tempting to believe his reassuring words. Desperate for something to hold on to apart from revenge, Fabiola let herself do that. She thought of the ten thousand prisoners taken by the Parthians. No one knew what their fate would be. Except the gods. She closed her eyes, praying as she had never done before.

Jupiter, keep my brother safe from harm.

Once the initial euphoria at receiving her manumission had cleared, Fabiola had asked Brutus for another favour. He had been delighted to oblige, the price for a mere kitchen slave scarcely ruffling the surface of his coffers. Thanks to his campaigns in Gaul with Caesar, Brutus was richer than ever. Freeing Docilosa meant that Fabiola had an ally to take with her to her lover's villa. She would not be alone when Brutus had business in Rome. Fabiola had also asked Brutus to buy the two doormen, but Jovina had refused point blank. They were worth too much to her.

Fabiola's departure from the Lupanar was a memory she would cherish for the rest of her life. Jovina had fawned and sighed, sorry to see her best earner leave; the other women had laughed and cried by turn; surprisingly, Claudia had sulked, finally jealous of her friend's good fortune. Touching Fabiola's heart, it had been Benignus and Vettius who had been the most upset. 'Don't forget us,' Vettius had muttered, looking at the floor. She would not. Men as reliable as the two huge slaves were hard to find.

The day after her manumission, the lovers travelled to Ostia, Rome's port. Tied up by one of the jetties was the *Ajax*, Brutus' low-slung liburnian. Smaller than a trireme, with two banks of oars, the fast boat was his pride and joy. Keeping its jutting prow driving straight into the waves, *Ajax'* captain stayed close to shore to avoid being swept out to sea by the stormy weather. Encouraged by the constant pounding of the drum, the hundred slaves on the oars worked hard to carry Brutus and Fabiola down the coast. Their destination was Pompeii, in the popular bay of Neapolis. It was about six days' journey to the south.

Fabiola did not like travelling by ship. Protected from the rain and wind by a thick fabric canopy, sitting in luxury by a glowing brazier, she was uncomfortably reminded of life's fragility by the water pounding off the hull. But Brutus was in his element and spent the voyage recounting his campaigns in Gaul.

Fabiola was intrigued by the full details of Caesar's battles. If only half of what Brutus told her was true, his general really was an amazing leader and tactician. Pompey would have his work cut out winning the race for power. By the sixth day, Brutus had still not spoken of the Venetians' rebellion three years previously, an uprising that had been put down thanks to his expertise and ability. When she gently reminded him of it, Brutus had the grace to blush. His modest, unassuming manner was one of the things Fabiola liked most.

'The Veneti had surrendered to us twelve months before,' he began. 'But during the long winter, the tribe's druids persuaded their chieftains to seize a group of our officers who were out requisitioning supplies. The dogs thought they could get a huge ransom for them and retreated to their strongholds, which were built on islands in tidal estuaries. We couldn't approach them by land, except at low tide.'

Fabiola had never heard all the story before. She nodded encouragingly.

Once started, it did not take much to keep Brutus talking. 'When spring came, we built a fleet of triremes on the River Liger and sailed up the coast. Really caught the bastards by surprise!'

Fabiola braced herself for a moment as the *Ajax* hung on the crest of a wave before sweeping down into the trough. 'Is it much further?' she asked.

Brutus immediately called out to the captain, a gnarly old Greek in bare feet, who was alternating his time at the rudder with spells on the deck bellowing at the slaves. He listened carefully to the reply. 'Not long now, my love. We passed Misenum and the mouth of the bay a while ago.'

Fabiola smiled. 'Didn't the Venetians have proper seagoing vessels?'

'They did! Big, deep-bottomed craft with huge sails that were far superior to ours,' said Brutus, grinning triumphantly. 'But Mars blessed us with flat calm weather and we rowed in one afternoon, hemming them against the jetties and cliffs below the villages. Just to make sure, I had ordered dozens of scythes tied on long poles and the sailors were able to cut their rigging to pieces.'

His lover gasped admiringly.

'Our boarding parties swarmed over and we took the settlements in double-quick time. Freed the officers too.' Brutus sighed. 'Caesar wanted an example made of the Veneti, though. We executed all their leaders and sold the whole tribe into slavery.'

Fabiola adjusted the pearl-encrusted gold brooch which held up her hair and tried not to imagine the scene: the cries from injured and dying warriors on the ships; the sea red with blood and full of bobbing corpses. Thatched roofs on fire, women and children screaming as they were beaten and tied with ropes, new slaves to make Rome even richer. It was hard to justify anything that Caesar did in its name. There should be more to life than warfare and slavery.

Sensing her unease, Brutus took Fabiola's hand. 'War is brutal, my darling. But once Caesar is in power alone, he will have no need to conquer anywhere else. The Republic will be at peace once more.'

Your general has butchered and pillaged an entire nation to pay his debts to Crassus and make himself rich, Fabiola thought bitterly. That certainly makes him cold-blooded enough to have raped a lone slave eighteen years ago.

I need to meet him. Find out if he really is the one.

'When will I be introduced to Caesar at last?' She batted her eyelashes. 'I want to see the reason for all this adulation.'

As was his recent custom, Caesar was overwintering at Ravenna, two hundred miles north of Rome. Once Fabiola was settled in the villa, the staff officer would be taking the liburnian up the coast to consult with his master.

'He has spoken of his desire to meet you also,' said Brutus, looking pleased. His expression changed abruptly. 'But it won't be any time soon. Those damned Optimates in the Senate are putting a lot of pressure on Pompey to break faith and recall him to the city. They want Caesar to stand trial for exceeding his jurisdiction as proconsul in Gaul.'

'Cato and his henchmen?'

Brutus scowled in response.

Fabiola knew a lot about the young senator who had made it his life's mission to defend the Republic from what he saw as rapacious opportunists. He and other politicians who felt the same way called themselves the Optimates, the best men. Caesar was their number one enemy. A former quaestor, Cato was an excellent public speaker and lived as austerely as his main foe, often wearing black because aspiring politicians wore purple. He had even visited the Lupanar with friends once. Unusually for a noble customer, he had refused all Jovina's offers of women and boys, relaxing in the baths instead. It was a restrained decision that had gained Fabiola's admiration as she had listened to his stimulating conversation from her hiding place.

'And his crony, Domitius.' He grimaced. 'Caesar is slowly being pushed into a corner.'

'But he won't give up control of his legions.'

'Why should he?' Brutus cried. 'After all he's done for Rome?'

Fabiola nodded, remembering the recent gossip. Caesar would be treated worse than a dog if he came back to the city as a civilian. 'What if Pompey disbands his?'

'The crafty sons of whores won't ask him to do that.' Brutus thumped a fist into his palm. 'Double standards.'

She sighed. Two powerful nobles wrestling for control, both with massive armies at their disposal and a weakened Senate caught in the middle. It did seem as if the Republic was heading inexorably towards civil war.

It was not long before the liburnian reached Pompeii, bumping against the timbers of the dock and allowing the exhausted slaves to slump over their shipped oars, work done. As a few sailors used boathooks to hold the *Ajax* in place, others clambered on to the jetty with ropes, tying them securely to large stone bollards. Brutus muttered a few words to the captain, making sure that his ship would be ready to leave at a moment's notice. Carefully holding her dress with one hand, Fabiola let the staff officer help her up off the ship. Docilosa followed close behind.

Positioned a short distance south of the city, Pompeii's harbour was much smaller than that of Ostia. Fishing vessels rocked in the water alongside the larger shapes of naval triremes. Heavily laden barges filled the opening of the River Sarnus around which the curtain walls had been built. Pompeii was a busy trading port. A ferry packed with passengers furled its sails as it followed them in, pausing on the journey from Misenum to Surrentum at the other end of the bay.

Dominating the city and harbour, almost overhanging them, was Vesuvius. Fabiola stared up at the huge mountain, taking in the grey clouds covering its peak, the forests greening its upper slopes, the farms and empty fields below. It was an imposing sight.

'They say Vulcan himself lives up there,' said Brutus. 'Not so sure myself.' He laughed. 'The crater at the top is a miserable damn place. Boiling hot in summer, covered in snow at this time of year. No sign of a god anywhere. But it doesn't stop the locals trying to appease him at Vulcanalia. More fish are thrown into the bonfires that week than get eaten here in a year. Superstitious peasants!'

The noble cared little for any deities except Mars, the god of war.

Fabiola shivered, pulling closer her woollen cloak. There was a strong smell of rotting fish and human waste in the cold air. She looked down into the dark water and made a face.

'Sewage from the town,' declared Brutus. 'Don't worry. There's none of that at the villa. It has proper drains that lead half a mile away.'

Eight slaves had been waiting miserably on the exposed dock for their arrival. A large litter stood beside them. Leaving the newly freed Docilosa to supervise the offloading of their luggage, Fabiola and Brutus climbed in and set off for the villa.

Pompeii's streets were almost deserted. Those who were out hurried by on their way to the baths or the market, their necks hunched against the biting wind. An old augur tottered along, holding his blunt-peaked hat tightly to prevent it blowing away. Ragged children ran past, screaming with glee at the bread that they had stolen. Angry shouts followed them.

The forum was a decent size for a rural town, although it was a work in progress. An unfinished temple to Jupiter occupied the position of prominence in the square, flanked by the usual theatre, public library and other shrines. Statues of the gods were dotted in front of many buildings. A covered market filled most of the open space, the stallholders' cries muted by the bad weather.

The litter bumped and swayed its way north out of the city for some time. Seemingly unaware that Fabiola was tired from the voyage, Brutus chattered about the villa that they were approaching.

'It was originally built by a noble family. But a rich pleb bought the place when they fell on hard times nearly thirty years ago,' Brutus said. He winked. 'They got on the wrong side of Sulla.'

She laughed dutifully at his macabre joke. Thousands of people had died under the dictator's rule.

'The augurs say that bad luck follows bad men. Or maybe it's because the merchant lived on the Aventine.' Brutus shrugged. 'He had to put the villa on the market two winters ago when there weren't many buyers about.' He smiled. 'I got it for a song.'

'A merchant?' said Fabiola, leaning forward with sudden interest. 'From the Aventine?'

He looked surprised. 'Yes. Old, smelly and fat. Why?'

'What was his name?'

Brutus ran a hand through his short brown hair, thinking.

Her heart raced as she waited.

'Gemellus?' He paused. 'Yes, it was Gemellus.'

Fabiola's composure slipped and she gasped with delight. The idea that she was the new mistress of her former owner's villa was a dream come true.

'You know him?' asked Brutus curiously.

She took his hand and squeezed it. 'He sold me to the Lupanar.'

'The bastard!' Sudden rage from Brutus was rare and shocking.

'I would never have met you otherwise,' she said coyly.

'True.' Calming down, he peered out of the litter. 'If it's any consolation, I've heard that his business has gone down the sewer completely now. He lost an absolute fortune when shiploads of beasts that he had bought for the circus sank on the way over from Egypt.'

A pang of sadness hit Fabiola. She could remember fantasising with Romulus about trapping wild animals with the *bestiarius*. It seemed a lifetime ago.

'The moneylenders were hounding him from dawn till dusk by the end,' Brutus added. 'Even had to sell his house on the Aventine.'

Relief began to replace the pain. And as the high wall surrounding her new home finally came into sight, Fabiola knew that Jupiter, in the inexplicable way of the gods, was taking care of her in some way.

Revenge had been granted: Gemellus had become one of the homeless who clogged Rome's streets, begging for alms from the rich. As someone who valued money above all else, the merchant's life had been ruined more completely than by a swift knife between the ribs down an alleyway. It was a suitable punishment, she thought, although it would have been even sweeter to have knocked on Gemellus' door and informed him that she, Fabiola, was to have his beloved villa. Her only regret was that Romulus and her mother were not present to share her joy. But they would be watching her from the other side.

Now, as the lover of a powerful noble, Fabiola could concentrate fully on discovering the identity of her father. Brutus, whether he knew it or not, was the key. He would happily facilitate her entry into Roman society at the highest level, an equal to those who had once sneered. The clues would be there somewhere. They could even be close to home.

It would take time, but Fabiola would not rest until her mother had been avenged.

Chapter XXIX: The March

East of Seleucia, autumn 53 BC

The desolate landscape stretched into infinity.

Behind the soldiers, an immense range of mountains ran from north to south, the snow-capped tops a stark contrast to the sandy plain far below. It had taken weeks to negotiate countless narrow passes, icy streams and winding paths along cliff edges. Hundreds of legionaries had perished in landslides or died of exposure. The bare slopes had provided little in the way of fuel and the occasional goat brought down by an arrow could not feed everyone. Dried meat, unleavened bread and sheer determination had carried the remaining prisoners over the jagged peaks.

That and the instant execution awaiting any man refusing to march. Parthian discipline was even harsher than Roman.

The column of over nine thousand soldiers had excitedly made its way down a winding track that morning. Just reaching flat ground had felt like success. Low dunes rose smoothly on either side as another desert prepared to welcome them. The sky was clear of clouds, its only inhabitants the ubiquitous vultures.

But the wilderness was not as intimidating as before Carrhae. These men had been through unbelievable suffering, seen unimaginable things. This was just another trial to be endured. Survived.

Romulus adjusted the cloth covering his head and wiped away sweat. Like that of everyone else, the young soldier's helmet dangled from the yoke over one shoulder. There was little need to wear it, with no enemies for hundreds of miles.

Brennus and Tarquinius marched confidently beside him. During the passage of the mountains, their survival skills had helped keep the remaining men of the Sixth alive. The pelts of the wolves Tarquinius had trapped served as blankets and Brennus had regularly brought down goats or antelope with a bow he had procured from a guard.

With all senior officers dead, a power vacuum had been left in the ranks. Soldiers needed someone in charge and with so many men from different legions, it had been difficult to organise the Roman prisoners. Sensibly the Parthian officers who had been placed in command banded together the men who had served in the same unit, but there had been an inevitable reluctance to obey more than basic orders since leaving the capital two months earlier.

Many legionaries now looked to Tarquinius as an unofficial leader. He had been treating the wounded for months, and his ability to predict the future was also well known throughout the column. The Etruscan's understanding of the Parthian language had naturally attracted their captors' attention. The mystical skills he showed also earned respect. In recognition, Tarquinius had been made the equivalent of a centurion, answering to the officer commanding one of the reformed cohorts. Although the haruspex was not a regular, taking orders from one of their own was easier to stomach.

So far, the Etruscan's cohort was the only one to have been re-armed, a source of real pride for Romulus and Brennus. But only Tarquinius knew why. The rest were relieved not to have to carry any more for a time. A train of mules behind carried the remaining weapons, food and water.

'When will we reach Margiana?' asked Romulus.

'Five to six weeks,' replied the Etruscan.

He groaned. Located on the northeast border of the Parthian empire, their destination never seemed to get any nearer.

'At least those bastards have to walk too.' Brennus indicated the warriors to either side of the column.

The prisoners might outnumber the Parthians twenty to one, but it meant little. They were now more than a thousand miles northeast of Seleucia and there was nowhere to go, no point in resisting. Only the dark-skinned natives knew the exact locations of the life-saving waterholes in the vast emptiness of sand and the Romans had no choice but to follow. Without water no one could survive.

'Why didn't they send cataphracts to guard us?' asked Romulus.

'Rome doesn't accept defeat easily,' said Brennus. 'Orodes is probably saving them in case of another attack.'

Tarquinius chuckled. 'The king might not know it, but nobody wants revenge. Caesar won't be too happy having lost his sponsor, but he's far too busy with other matters. And Pompey will be delighted that Crassus is out of the equation. This will let him concentrate on Caesar.'

Romulus sighed. Italian politics meant little here. 'If Rome doesn't retaliate, how can there be any chance of returning home?' he muttered. 'We are in the middle of nowhere, heading for the ends of the earth.'

'We will make our own way back,' whispered Tarquinius.

The Gaul did not hear the comment. 'We are the Forgotten Legion!' he cried cynically, pointing forward.

All eyes followed his outstretched arm.

Pacorus, the Parthian officer in charge, had shrewdly obtained one silver eagle from the booty after Carrhae. While the others decorated Orodes' palace, his was constantly positioned at the head of the column.

Brennus stabbed a finger at the metal bird again, recognising its significance. The standard was vital to the Parthian's new command and had become the soldiers' most important possession. A growl of pride left men's throats. There had been little to cheer about since Carrhae – till now.

The guards listened curiously, but did not respond straight away. Discipline was less strict now than when they had left the city. Enough men had been executed to keep the rest in line. But until an enemy was in sight, their new-found trust only went so far.

Tarquinius smiled. 'A good name.'

'It has a certain ring to it,' Romulus admitted.

'Good!' Brennus paused, turning to face the ranks following. 'The Forgotten Legion!'

Quickly the Gaul's cry was taken up and the sound rose into hot, windless air.

As roars surged down the column, many Parthians became alarmed and began to reach for their weapons. This had never happened before.

Pacorus was riding nearby and he leaned over in the saddle to speak to Tarquinius. When the answer came, the commander smiled and barked a response. The warriors relaxed at his words. Spurring his horse to the front, Pacorus went to check for signs of other travellers. He was not one to lead from behind.

'What did he want?' asked Romulus.

'To know why we shouted. I told him we were the Forgotten Legion and he replied that much was expected of us.'

Brennus grinned, pleased at the response to his cry.

'He also said that our gods have forsaken us.'

'They turned their backs when we crossed the river,' said Felix. The resourceful little Gaul had attached himself to the trio after leaving Seleucia.

'Maybe on some,' replied Brennus seriously. 'But not on the Forgotten Legion.'

'Perhaps you're right.' Felix made the sign against evil. 'We're still alive!'

Romulus agreed and silently thanked Jupiter for his

protection. Something made him glance at the Etruscan, who had a faint smile playing on his lips. Nothing about the trek eastwards ever upset him, which he found strange. Although Brennus now seemed content with his lot, every other man worried about marching further from the known world. But Tarquinius positively relished it. Every few days he would write notes on the ancient map, describing what he had seen and explaining them to Romulus if he asked. Thanks to these lessons, the young soldier had also come to enjoy the journey and to respect the burning deserts and mighty peaks they had crossed. The image of Alexander in his mind had grown to near mythical status. The Lion of Macedon must have been an extraordinary leader, he thought. Perhaps Tarquinius is retracing his steps.

'Alexander was one of the most charismatic leaders ever seen,' said the Etruscan.

Romulus jumped. 'Crassus didn't try to inspire us at all, did he?'

'The fool did not,' he replied. 'So the bad omens affected the men badly. If they had loved their leader as Alexander's did, they might have overcome their fear.'

The words came to Romulus out of nowhere. 'Lead by example. As you do, treating the sick and injured.'

Tarquinius' lips twitched and he squinted into the clear blue sky. 'And the omens for the rest of the journey are good. All the way to Margiana and Scythia.'

Despite the intense heat, Brennus did not dare to ask if those places were where he would save his friends. He did not want to know exactly when the slate had to be wiped clean. Brennus shoved away the thought and kept marching.

Romulus watched from the corner of his eye. It was obvious that Brennus never talked about their destination and he was convinced Tarquinius knew something about the Gaul's fate that he was keeping quiet. But living in such close proximity with hundreds of men rarely afforded an occasion to speak in private. Even when one did arise, Romulus was not sure he wanted to ask either friend. It felt sufficiently strange that the Etruscan knew so much. Romulus had known Tarquinius for two years, but was only now getting used to his extraordinary abilities. He was forever using sky, birds and wind as ways to accurately reveal past and future events. Every so often Tarquinius would explain what he was doing and Romulus could now predict simple things such as the next rain shower. It was fascinating knowledge and he concentrated hard every time the haruspex revealed anything new. But Tarquinius kept many things to himself still. 'Much of what I know is sacred,' he would say regretfully. 'And should only be revealed to a trained soothsayer.'

Romulus was mostly content with this. Life was simpler not knowing everything that would happen. It was enough to be told that he would survive the Parthian army. This left room in his heart for the dream of returning to Rome.

Finding his family.

During the long march, Romulus had gone through periods of blaming his mother for her awful predicament. She could have killed Gemellus any time he was in her bed. But she had not. Why? Anger filled him when he thought of how easily the fat merchant could have been silenced for ever. But eventually her reasoning became clear. She was not a trained fighter like him. Velvinna had been a mother with two young children; she had done everything in her power to protect them. She had let Gemellus rape her over and over again for the sake of the twins' safety. This bitter realisation had filled Romulus with shame and self-disgust. How could he not have appreciated his mother's sacrifice before? It made him even more determined to kill Gemellus. But it was hard not to lose hope. Unlike Brennus, he still struggled to believe some of Tarquinius' more incredible predictions. From all practical points of view, going home now seemed impossible.

'Margiana?' said Felix. 'Never heard of it.'

'Trust me,' Tarquinius replied archly. 'It exists.'

'What is it like?'

'Green landscape. Wide rivers and fertile land.'

Felix gestured at the desert. 'Anything'd be better than this hell.'

Romulus laughed. As well as being one of the few survivors of Bassius' cohort, Felix was good company.

'So who lives there?' said Brennus.

'Descendants of the Greeks, meaning they are civilised people. And nomads. Men with yellow skin, black hair and slanted eyes.'

'Sound like demons,' muttered Felix.

'They bleed like anyone else.'

'How do they fight?' Brennus was ever the pragmatist. He would always be a warrior.

'With bows. From horseback.'

There was a collective groan.

'And not friendly with Parthia either?'

Tarquinius shook his head.

'Marched to the far side of the world to be massacred,' said Felix sarcastically. 'Again.'

'Not if I have anything to do with it,' Tarquinius replied. 'We need to cover each shield with silk.'

'What? The material the Parthians make their banners from?' asked the Gaul. The huge, brightly coloured flags had helped to terrify Crassus' soldiers before Carrhae.

'The same. It will stop those.' The Etruscan pointed at the shafts in Brennus' quiver.

The spirits of those within earshot lifted at the prospect of surviving the arrow storms that had slaughtered their comrades at Carrhae.

Romulus had occasionally seen noble ladies at the arena dressed in softly shining robes. 'Costs a fortune, doesn't it?' he said.

'Not if we liberate a caravan load of the stuff.'

Brennus and Romulus were now openly curious.

'In twelve days we will cross paths with Judaean traders returning from India,' remarked Tarquinius.

Parthia was virtually empty, populated only by small nomadic tribes, and since leaving Seleucia there had been few others crossing the wilderness. But by now no one reacted to the Etruscan's second sight. If Tarquinius said something was going to happen, it would.

'That is a long journey,' said Romulus with surprise. He knew from the ancient map that India was even further than Margiana. To discover that men would make the trip by choice was a surprise. 'It must be worth while.'

Tarquinius smiled enigmatically.

Brennus began to grow impatient and the Etruscan relented.

'They will be carrying spices mostly. And a lot of silk.'

'For us to cover our *scuta*,' said Brennus thoughtfully. 'Pacorus might need some convincing. And Orodes won't be too pleased if his captains start stealing from traders.'

Tarquinius looked shocked. 'Who said we would rob anyone?'

Brennus snorted. 'How else can you part Judaeans from their goods?'

'I will buy the fabric.'

'Need more than the gold head on that,' replied the Gaul, nodding at the *lituus* dangling from Tarquinius' belt.

Since Pacorus had realised the Etruscan's worth, Tarquinius had stopped hiding his symbol of power. Remembering stories of haruspices from childhood, other soldiers regarded the staff with awe and it gave their cohort a special place in the Forgotten Legion.

Even Romulus felt dubious. Silk was the most precious of commodities. Only small amounts reached the markets in Rome, transported distances that few could even imagine. The amount required to cover over nine thousand shields would cost a King's ransom.

'So how will you buy it?' the Gaul asked.

Tarquinius would not answer. 'I need to talk to Pacorus,' he announced.

Brennus rolled his eyes.

'He won't tell us,' said Romulus. 'You should know that by now.'

The Gaul laughed.

Well used to Tarquinius' secretive nature, Romulus did not ask either. They had survived Carrhae, marched east for over a thousand miles with few mishaps. Despite an apparent lack of funds, he felt reassured by the prediction. The wise haruspex would win over Pacorus and get them the silk to give them a way of fighting new enemies. Getting back to Rome might seem impossible, but this did not. He strode forward confidently, the hot sand crunching beneath the soles of his sandals.

Tarquinius was as good as his word. That night, he left the others huddled by a tiny fire, eating bread and dried goat meat. Once the legionaries had sworn allegiance to Parthia, their captors had begun to treat them better and they were now fed a reasonable amount every day. There was no point starving men who would be expected to fight for the empire.

Making his way quietly through the darkness, the Etruscan observed the resting soldiers. Although they were captives, there was still good discipline, a sense of order. The cloth tents had been placed in neat lines, century by century. Even temporary ramparts had been thrown up, with pairs of sentries marching vigilantly round the perimeter. It looked like a typical army camp, except that this was further from Rome than any legionary had ever ventured.

Since the prisoners had realised they were not to be killed out of hand, their spirits had been rising. They would fight well, especially when Tarquinius revealed a new protection against the tribes' lethal arrows.

'Halt!' Burly warriors levelled spears at the Etruscan. Pacorus kept Parthians stationed around his tent at night. 'Who goes there?'

'The haruspex.'

Fear filled their eyes. 'What do you want?' one asked.

'A word with Pacorus.'

They conferred with each other for a moment.

'Wait here,' the first guard said curtly. Leaving his companions to watch Tarquinius, he entered the large tent a few steps away. He was not gone long. Lifting the cloth flap, he jerked his head.

Tarquinius approached, ducking a little to enter. The warrior lingered at the opening, clutching his weapon nervously.

In stark contrast to the Romans' accommodation, the interior of Pacorus' tent was richly decorated. Thick wool carpets covered the floor and a brazier smoked in one corner, providing warmth against the night air. Oil-soaked torches burned in deep plates, casting long shadows. Reclining cushions lay scattered about, but weapons stacked on a wooden stand were a reminder of the journey's real purpose. Slaves were cooking on a fire, and standing by with platters of food and drink. The tempting smell of roasting meat filled the tent.

The Etruscan's mouth watered. It had been a long time since he had tasted fresh lamb. Memories of Olenus at the cave flooded back and Tarquinius offered up a prayer of thanks for the wisdom the old man had imparted. Because of his abilities, the haruspex knew what was about to happen.

Pacorus was seated cross-legged by the brazier. Waving

a half-gnawed bone, he gestured at Tarquinius to sit. The Parthian did not seem at all surprised to see him. 'Share my food,' he said, nodding brusquely at the nearest servant.

Beard greasy with fat, Pacorus' eyes danced with interest. He had shed his normal loose jerkin for an expensive robe and baggy white cotton trousers. Soft leather slippers with pointed toes poked from under his muscled legs. The gold belt circling his waist was delicate, yet a pair of curved daggers hung from it. First and foremost, Pacorus was a warrior.

Tarquinius sat down, taking the offered meat and a wooden beaker which contained some good wine. There was silence as he ate and drank. When the Etruscan looked up, Pacorus was eyeing him closely.

'How are my new troops?' said the Parthian. 'Ready to obey their master?'

'They have little choice.'

Pacorus leaned forward. 'Tell me. Will the legionaries fight for me? Or will they run, as at Carrhae?'

'I can only answer for my cohort.' Tarquinius spoke confidently. After Pacorus had granted his request to re-arm the legionaries of his unit, their spirits had risen immeasurably. All it had taken to convince the Parthian was an accurate prediction of which mountain passes were blocked with snow. This valuable information had probably saved lives and certainly shaved several days off their journey. 'They will fight to the last man rather than suffer defeat again.'

Pacorus sat back, looking satisfied. In the manner of enemies who are being polite, the pair spent a short time discussing the journey and border areas. Tarquinius quickly learned that the entire eastern region was full of unrest and that the Forgotten Legion would have its work cut out restoring peace.

'Why have you come?' Pacorus finally asked.

The Etruscan did not prevaricate. 'I have a proposition for you.'

Pacorus lifted a hand and a bowl of warm water carried by a slave instantly appeared. Cleaning his fingers and face, he smiled. 'The prisoner has a proposition for the captor.'

Tarquinius inclined his head.

Annoyed at the lack of deference, the Parthian's manner became less friendly. 'So?'

'Soon a caravan of Judaeans will cross our path.'

'They will be returning from India.' Pacorus picked an orange from a silver tray and began peeling it. 'What has this to do with us?'

'A large part of their cargo will be silk.'

'It usually is.'

Tarquinius changed tack. 'What is the Forgotten Legion's main duty?'

He smiled at the name. 'To defend the empire from hostile tribes. Bactrians, Sogdians and Scythians.'

'Whose warriors use composite bows like the Parthians.'

Pacorus was becoming visibly irritated with Tarquinius' vague manner.

'Your arrows butchered our men at Carrhae. And so will those of the nomads if we do not have a plan,' Tarquinius said.

'Go on,' said the commander icily.

'Orodes will not be pleased if his new border garrison is wiped out shortly after its arrival. That would allow fresh raids into Parthia.'

Pacorus ate a segment of orange, chewing thoughtfully. 'What do you propose?'

'Silk is very strong.'

The Parthian was confused.

'Wrap layers of it over the men's shields,' continued Tarquinius smoothly, 'and no shaft will penetrate.'

'How can you be sure?' Pacorus asked.

'I know many things.'

Pacorus could see where this was going. 'Merchants are taxed as they enter both Antiochia and Seleucia,' he said. 'And the king does not tolerate the robbing of honest travellers.' Most of Parthia's wealth was derived from the tolls imposed on those returning from the east.

'We will not steal from anyone,' replied Tarquinius.

'How will we pay for it then?' snapped the Parthian.

Tarquinius reached into his tunic and produced the leather pouch. Undoing the drawstring, he dropped an enormous ruby into one palm. It had been worn next to his heart ever since he had removed it from the hilt of Tarquin's sword. After seventeen years, the time had finally come to use Olenus' priceless gift. 'This will buy all the silk we need.'

Pacorus pursed his lips. 'I see the *lituus* is not all you managed to retain.'

Tarquinius said nothing.

The Parthian eyed the gemstone greedily and his right

hand moved towards one of his daggers. 'I can take that very easily.'

'But you won't.'

'You are alone and unarmed.' He glanced at his guard. 'There are ten more of my men outside.'

'I would curse you for ever.' Tarquinius' dark eyes glinted in the torchlight as he tucked away the little bag. 'And my cohort might not be too happy either.'

Pacorus swallowed. The blond-haired soldier had helped the column pass safely through the mountains. He could predict landslides days in advance and storms before they appeared in the sky. It was rumoured that he'd even predicted his own side's defeat at Carrhae.

Smiling, the Etruscan walked over to one of the silk partitions that separated the tent into sections. 'May I demonstrate?'

Pacorus nodded.

Tarquinius took down the piece of coloured fabric and wrapped it several times around a square cushion. He paced fifty steps to the end of the long tent, the killing distance that had cut the legions to pieces. Placing it on the floor, he walked back, picking up a deeply curved horn bow and quiver from the wooden stand.

The warrior by the entrance instantly lunged forward, spear at the ready.

Pacorus barked an order and he moved back.

Reaching his host, the haruspex studied the weapon carefully. 'This is very well made,' he commented, testing its draw. 'Powerful too.'

'A good bow takes weeks to build,' said Pacorus. 'The

horn and sinew must be just the right thickness and the wood well seasoned.'

Turning towards the target, Tarquinius pulled out an arrow and fitted it to the string. Raising his arms, he paused, half turning.

The Parthian sucked in a breath.

Tarquinius swung away, content the point had been made. He drew back to full stretch, closing one eye and aiming carefully in the dim light. With a grunt, he released. The shaft hissed through the air, landing with a thump.

'Bring it here!' Pacorus shouted.

The guard picked up the cushion, an amazed look on his face. He walked to the commander, bowed and handed it to him.

Pacorus stared, fascinated. The arrow had only penetrated two fingers' depth into the filling. With a gentle tug, he pulled it free. The barbed head was completely covered in fabric.

Silk that was hardly torn or damaged.

The Parthian goggled.

'Wrap half a dozen layers of that over a *scutum*,' Tarquinius pronounced, 'and you have an army that can withstand any arrow.'

New respect for the haruspex filled Pacorus' eyes.

'You saw Roman discipline at Carrhae before the cataphracts charged. Legionaries are the finest infantry in the world,' said Tarquinius. 'With silk on our shields, the Forgotten Legion will be unbeatable.'

'Those tribes outnumber us.'

'They do not stand a chance,' repeated Tarquinius.

'Why tell me this?'

'My friends and I have no wish to die. We were lucky to survive the last battle.' Tarquinius raised his eyebrows expressively. 'Facing those bows a second time . . .'

Pacorus was intrigued. Unknown to the Etruscan, his new command from Orodes was a double-edged sword. Historically the horse archers and cataphracts had been able to keep the steppe nomads at bay. But the war with Rome had depleted Parthia's border forces to dangerously low levels and there had been news recently of incursions deep into the empire. Facing marauding tribes with few bowmen of his own had been worrying Pacorus since leaving Seleucia.

The Parthian poured more wine.

'There's your caravan,' said Brennus, shielding his eyes from the sun.

Romulus grinned. Both of them had been impatiently scanning the horizon since Tarquinius' night visit to Pacorus.

Exactly twelve days had passed.

Dust billowed into hot air in the middle distance. It was never difficult to spot movement on the flat plain that had replaced the sand dunes. A long line of camels could just be made out, stretching back into the haze.

Pacorus spotted the animals too and bellowed for the column to halt. The drums beat further commands. Most soldiers had learned basic Parthian orders by now and obeyed promptly. Recognising that new troops would fight best the way they had been trained, the shrewd officer had already learned many Roman manoeuvres from

Tarquinius. A day earlier, he had taken the step of arming all the prisoners again. Again, no one but the Etruscan knew why. Despite their initial enjoyment at marching unburdened, the legionaries were proud to carry javelins, swords and shields once more.

Responding to the calls, the cohorts fanned out in a defensive line, six across, three deep, with two protecting the baggage train at the rear. Everyone grounded weapons and *scuta*, taking sips of water as they waited. Lean and fit, the Roman soldiers had become used to marching in the heat, and exhaustion was no longer an issue. Deep in Parthian territory, few worried at what was approaching.

Some time passed. Gradually the train grew near enough to make out more details. There were about thirty single-humped animals, walking with a distinctive rolling motion. Heavy cloth panniers hung from the sides of each.

'Extraordinary beasts. They can go for days without water,' commented Tarquinius.

Romulus studied them closely as they drew nearer. At Carrhae, the camels had been too far away to see properly.

A party of fifty men accompanied the beasts of burden. Most looked like bodyguards, hired to protect the merchants and their goods. All wore long robes and head-dresses to protect against the sun and most carried a spear and bow. A few wore swords. They showed little signs of discipline. Several scouts rode nervously alongside, their job of reporting the Romans' presence done.

Tarquinius gave them a quick glance. 'Mixture of

Indians, Greeks and Parthians. Enough protection against most bandits.'

'Half a century would take them out,' said Romulus.

'There'll be no need,' smiled Brennus. 'Look at them.'

The caravan came to a halt a short distance away and the dust began to settle. Camels roared loudly, glad of a rest.

It was obvious that the newcomers were nervous. Hands gripped weapons tightly, feet stamped on hot sand. Dark eyes shifted uneasily in sweaty faces. There was nothing the traders could do when faced with such overwhelming force. The plain was flat for miles on end.

'I suppose we're not a common sight,' observed Romulus wryly.

Everyone laughed. Ten thousand legionaries in the middle of Parthia would seem bizarre to other travellers.

Eventually a short man in a grimy white robe began to approach them, his hands held high in a gesture of peace. Three guards followed with dragging feet. Halfway over to the legions, the figure stopped, waiting for a response.

Pacorus glanced at Tarquinius. 'Squad of ten men!' he barked. 'Form up and follow me!'

The Etruscan saluted crisply and led Brennus, Romulus, Felix and seven others to stand in line behind the Parthian. With the legionaries marching to his rear, Pacorus walked his horse slowly across the sand and halted twenty paces from the other party. Tarquinius shouted an order and the files re-formed, facing forwards, *scuta* at the ready.

The old man in the dirty robe leaned on a well-worn

staff, surveying the approaching soldiers. Straggling white hair framed a shrewd face with a large hooked nose. His skin was a deep nut brown, the result of years in the sun. He seemed visibly relieved to find a Parthian in charge.

'Who are you?' demanded Pacorus. 'And where are you bound?'

'My name is Isaac,' replied the stranger swiftly. 'I am a merchant travelling to Syria via Seleucia.' He paused for a moment before daring to ask. 'Who might you be, Excellency?'

Pacorus chuckled. 'An officer of King Orodes' army.' He turned in the saddle, gesturing at the massed cohorts. 'And here are his latest recruits.'

Isaac's mouth opened and closed. 'They look like legionaries.'

'Old eyes do not deceive,' said Pacorus. 'Some months ago, we crushed a huge Roman army west of the capital. These are the survivors. The Forgotten Legion.'

The trader concealed his shock at the news of such an invasion. 'Good news indeed,' he smoothly replied. 'So it is safe to continue our journey?'

'Of course.' Pacorus bowed his head. 'After you have shared my hospitality. The king would wish it, I am sure.'

Isaac smiled, revealing decaying teeth. Not all Parthians could be trusted, but the offer had left no room for refusal.

'A day of rest would be welcome,' the Judaean said, turning and crying out in a high-pitched voice at the men by the camels.

Despite the fact that it was only midday, Pacorus called for camp to be built. Most soldiers complained bitterly about having to dig much earlier than normal. It was extremely hard labour to construct a rampart and ditch under the sun's full heat, but those in Romulus' cohort said little. They could tell the haruspex was plotting something.

A few hundred paces away, the camels had been tethered to pegs in the ground. Angry brays filled the air as they demanded food. Unfamiliar with the bizarre-looking creatures, the Romans stared with fascination. The camels' protuberant eyes, long lashes and wide lips gave an impression of real intelligence, but the humped animals also had vicious tempers, kicking and spitting at anyone who came too close.

Guards and traders had worked together to set up large roomy tents. Stacks of goods were carried inside the biggest. Making the most of the situation, Isaac was setting up full camp as well.

Romulus could hardly contain his excitement. Since Seleucia there had been little of interest apart from weapons training and Tarquinius' continuous lessons and the inquisitive young soldier was frequently bored. The long days of marching were tedious. The desert had been replaced by mountains, and yet more sandy wasteland had soon followed. There was almost no daily variation. The possibility of hearing stories from further east and seeing exotic goods was intoxicating.

Hours passed and the temporary earthworks went up as they had so many times before. Tents were pitched and the tired soldiers threw themselves inside, desperate for shade. A few drops of water washed dust from dry throats. It had been a hard lesson, but everyone knew how to conserve liquid as if it was gold. Every man in the Forgotten Legion now knew Tarquinius' trick of sucking on pebbles.

Pacorus waited until early evening before inviting the Judaean to his spacious pavilion. The baking heat had begun to subside as the sun fell in the sky and a faint breeze sprang up. The commander supplemented his Parthian guards with the ten legionaries, while a further century waited nearby, a show of force designed to intimidate.

The two groups of sentries stared at each other with thinly veiled suspicion. Until they had fought against a common enemy, little would change. Too much blood had been shed on both sides.

Soon afterwards Tarquinius was ordered inside while Brennus and Romulus stood close to the tent wall, trying to hear what might be said. To his frustration, Pacorus and the haruspex talked in muted voices.

'How is he going to do it?' muttered Felix.

Romulus had also been racking his brains to work it out.

'Trust him.' Since Seleucia, nothing could shake Brennus' convictions.

The short Gaul grumbled and fell silent while Romulus craned his head, still trying to hear snippets of the conversation.

They waited for some time, swatting at flies and glaring at the nearby Parthians.

'Here he is!'

The merchant was approaching, followed by three companions, while a solitary guard took up the rear. Reaching the entrance, Isaac spoke briefly with the Parthian sentries before entering with his party.

Pacorus bowed graciously as the Judaean came inside. 'Parthia welcomes honest traders.'

'My thanks, Excellency.' Isaac responded more slowly. He was here under duress, but had to keep up the pretence.

Servants moved forward, offering wine, fruits and meat. The old man drained two cups without pause, then polished off a small plate of food. Chewing on a piece of lamb, he peered at Tarquinius curiously.

The Etruscan pointedly ignored him.

'How long has your journey taken?' Pacorus asked when it seemed his guest had eaten plenty.

'In total?' The Judaean cackled. 'Two years so far, Excellency. India. Scythia. Margiana.'

'Your camels are heavily laden.'

'It has been a good trip,' admitted Isaac grudgingly. 'And it might make a small profit. If I return safe to Damascus.'

'What are you carrying?' Tarquinius spoke for the first time.

The merchant frowned at the question. Unsure of the blond soldier's status, Isaac raised an eyebrow at Pacorus, who nodded.

'Myrrh, *olibanum* and silk. Some ivory and indigo.' These goods commanded huge prices in Rome, but Isaac made them sound utterly worthless.

'Anything else?'

Isaac's face took on a hunted look.

'Well?' Pacorus' voice was less friendly now. 'All goods must be declared to royal officials.'

'Some gemstones, Excellency,' he said reluctantly. 'Lapis, agate. A few diamonds.'

'Do you know much about jewels?' shot Tarquinius.

The Judaean's eyes flickered. 'I have some knowledge.'

'How much indigo?'

'Three *modii*.' Isaac's lips pursed at the interrogation and he turned to Pacorus for support. 'All taxes due were paid in full, Excellency. At Antiochia.'

The Parthian smiled.

'One *modius* would be enough purple dye for a thousand togas!' Tarquinius blew out his cheeks. 'Make you a wealthy man.'

'First the dyers in Tyre must be paid,' protested Isaac. 'They will rob me blind!'

'That will still leave a tidy amount, old man,' said Pacorus dryly.

'I risk my life crossing half the world, Excellency,' Isaac muttered. 'Can I not make a little money?'

'Of course,' Tarquinius laughed, raising both hands placatingly. 'What quantity of silk have you got?'

Sensing interest, there was an instant change in the merchant's demeanour. 'Over a hundred bales of the very best fabric,' he said slyly. 'Want to see?'

The Etruscan glanced at Pacorus, to indicate that the officer was in apparent command.

'Show us.'

Isaac spoke eagerly to his compatriots. Hurrying from

the tent, the men quickly returned with two large cloth-wrapped bundles. Walking towards them, the Judaeans expertly unrolled the bales. Clouds of dust rose as the heavy covering came away, but the cream silk within was still clean. Even the tent's dim light could not dampen the glistening sheen from the fabric.

'Worth its weight in gold,' whispered Tarquinius, moving closer. He felt the sheet with a finger and thumb. 'Is it all the same thickness?'

Isaac began to extol the qualities of his merchandise.

Tarquinius dropped the pretence. 'We want the lot.'

The Judaean was shocked. 'All of it?'

He nodded.

'That silk is worth a fortune,' Isaac protested before bowing towards Pacorus. 'And I doubt very much if it is in your . . . price range.'

Tarquinius reached into his tunic. 'Look at this,' he said, opening the leather pouch.

Warily Isaac extended a grimy hand.

The ruby dropped into his outstretched palm.

'That should pay for everything,' said the Etruscan.

For a moment the Judaean was speechless. It was larger than a hen's egg.

Tarquinius chuckled knowingly.

'I'm not sure this is top quality,' Isaac raised the gem to the light, one eye closed. 'I can see some imperfections.'

'It is worth more than your whole caravan,' snapped Tarquinius. 'And you know it.'

'Take the ruby,' Pacorus' voice was cold. 'The silk is ours.'

'And the myrrh,' added Tarquinius.

Isaac knew when to take a bargain. 'Of course, Excellency,' he fawned. The stone had already disappeared into his robe. 'They are yours. The goods only need to be carried here from my camp.'

He turned to go.

'Stay,' said Tarquinius. There was no mistaking his tone. 'Until we have seen all the silk.'

The old trader stopped dead. 'Indeed, indeed.' He spat an order at his men, who scurried from the tent.

Tarquinius turned to Pacorus. 'It is strong and thick. And these bales should cover five thousand shields.'

'That's only half of them.'

'It will be more than enough.' The Etruscan stared at the commander, dark eyes piercing. 'I have already seen a mighty victory over the Sogdians.'

'They say you predicted the Roman defeat before Carrhae.'

'Weeks before.'

Pacorus smiled.

Chapter XXX: Margiana

Margiana, autumn 53 BC

Spanning fifteen hundred miles, the journey from Seleucia had taken in all terrains and weather types. It had been an extraordinary experience for the legionaries, Crassus' campaign having provided little skill at survival in such environments. Encouraged by Tarquinius, surviving *optiones* and harsh Parthian discipline, the prisoners had toughened up beyond measure. Three months later, fitter than ever before, muscled, tanned dark brown, the men were recognisable only by their tattered uniforms. New cloth standards had been fashioned for each century and five thousand *scuta* covered with silk. Tarquinius had been busy each night, supervising the soldiers as they stitched multiple layers in place. Helmets and spear tips flashed in the sunlight; neat ranks marched in step for twenty miles every day. The trumpeters were still being used, but Pacorus had also trained the men to recognise new commands from the drums.

The Forgotten Legion was now an intimidating sight, but there had been no action on the long march. As the soldiers had soon discovered, few people lived in the vast emptiness of central Parthia. No one had complained. The memory of Carrhae was still raw.

Some weeks after the encounter with Isaac, the flat, arid terrain had been replaced by a range of hills covered in scrubby bushes and trees. Marching through them, the legionaries entered the green plains of Margiana. To their delight, there were frequent watercourses, fed from the mountains visible on all sides. This was inhabitable land, the polar opposite of the wastes left behind. It reminded Romulus of the countryside he had seen while journeying from Rome to Brundisium.

Water bottles were now full every day, the game plentiful and temperatures acceptable. Each night the men's bellies were stuffed with meat. The Parthian guards relaxed. Life had become more enjoyable. Even the cloud of vultures that had followed them all the way from Seleucia thinned out and disappeared.

The attention of the gods had been drawn away from the Forgotten Legion.

'You were right!' Felix stared at the verdant scenery with delight. 'Rivers. Fertile soil. There are farms here.'

'Told you,' answered Brennus with a smile. 'Trust Tarquinius.'

Felix shook his head in amazement.

Cultivated areas and clusters of low mud huts were common. Several villages had been spotted, but Pacorus did not enter them. He was deliberately keeping a low profile. There had been only one stop, lasting several days, near a small Hellenic-looking town surrounded by a protective wall.

Tarquinius and the Parthian had gone in alone, and had placed an order with every blacksmith to be found. Margianian iron was renowned in Parthia for its quality and was used to forge the cataphracts' armour. On the third afternoon they had returned, their mules laden with thousands of long spears. The weapons had immediately been issued to half the men and training had begun the next morning. New manoeuvres were taught, soldiers grumbling as they were organised into strange formations.

Nobody was told why. But Brennus and Romulus suspected. As usual, the Etruscan would not say.

Wishing to reach the border quickly, Pacorus led the Forgotten Legion in a northeasterly direction across Margiana until they had reached rolling grassland. Filled with abundant wildlife, the virgin green landscape stretched as far as the eye could see. Antelope were sighted daily, allowing hunting parties to provide the army with even more fresh meat. To vary their diet, Romulus and Brennus caught fish from streams.

Occasionally they saw encampments of large, round tents with pointed roofs. Herds of horses, sheep and goats spread out around the settlements, grazing the lush pasture. Men and boys on horseback kept watch over the animals. Just as Tarquinius had described, the tribesmen were squat people with yellow skin, black hair and slanted eyes.

'Outlandish-looking folk,' commented Brennus as they passed a sizeable group of tents. 'But they seem peaceful enough.'

The riders nearby reined in and watched impassively as the column marched past. Their rough cloth jerkins and trousers were covered in autumn mud and they carried only the ubiquitous bows and hunting knives. Few legionaries bothered to look. The locals were of no consequence.

Tarquinius nodded. 'They are practically settled. But the nomadic Sogdians who raid this area look very similar.'

Brennus stared curiously at the riders' flat noses and high cheekbones. 'I'll wager they've not set eyes on too many of us.'

'Or seen a man your size!' said Romulus.

They both laughed.

'Their ancestors would have.' Tarquinius always had more information. 'Alexander founded the city of Antiochia not far from here and it is still the capital of Margiana. Most of the trade from the east passes through its gates.'

'Local legends tell of mighty soldiers with pale skin and blond hair who crushed all before them.' Pacorus had overheard the comment as he rode by.

Those who could understand some Parthian looked round with interest.

'Greeks!' said Romulus, imagining the army that had marched so far from home, nearly three centuries before. As ever, the thought fired his imagination.

It was old news to Tarquinius.

'This area has only been under our control for a generation,' the Parthian officer continued. 'The inhabitants don't like us and rebellions are common. And tribes from the north think the grasslands are theirs to graze, the towns free to plunder. The Forgotten Legion's job is to teach them different.'

'Plenty of fighting then, sir?' There was a glint in Brennus' eye.

'Quite likely,' revealed Pacorus. 'And very soon.'

Romulus felt a surge of pride to hear the name being used and from their reactions, other men felt the same way too. They were still Roman soldiers. The eagle still led from the front. Holding on to their identity had been a crucial part of survival. Without it they were nothing. Prisoners with no future, banished to the ends of the earth.

'We are needed at the border,' Tarquinius said unexpectedly.

Pacorus' mouth opened. 'Messengers brought word this morning,' he admitted gloomily. 'Been a raid by Sogdian tribesmen. Thousands of the bastards. They've hit several towns north of the capital. Burned them to the ground.'

'The men are ready, sir.' The Etruscan indicated the silk on every shield, the long spears. 'If I could have a word . . .'

'Why?' asked the Parthian suspiciously.

'Got a surprise for the enemy.'

Pacorus beckoned.

Everyone watched with bated breath as the Etruscan broke ranks to confer with their commanding officer. Tarquinius spoke urgently, gesturing with his hands while the other listened. The conversation did not last long.

Pacorus barked an order at the trumpeters, who immediately signalled the men with silk-covered shields to halt.

'This plan had better work, soothsayer.'

'It will,' said Tarquinius calmly.

Moments later, the Parthian second-in-command led away the other half of the legion to the west, towards Antiochia. When the men with Tarquinius realised their comrades were not also heading for battle, insults filled the air. Soldiers marching away responded with laughs and jeers.

'Where are they going?' asked Felix.

'To defend the capital.' The Etruscan smiled. 'And set up camp. There'll be no ditches to dig when we return.'

'From where?' said Felix dubiously.

'The river forming the border.'

Questions flew thick and fast as men clamoured to know more.

But Tarquinius would not answer and stepped back into line, fixing his eyes on the horizon.

Trumpets blared stridently and drums pounded. Officers listened, then roared the commands. The soldiers moved off, thousands of iron-shod sandals grinding the grass flat.

'Sons of whores have probably escaped.' Pacorus stared into the haze. 'We got here too late.'

Long grass extended south to the horizon. In the distance, a range of low hills ran from left to right. Clumps of trees provided the only variation in the panorama. Birds sang overhead, competing with the hum of countless insects. The air was still, carrying every

582

sound. Some distance away, a herd of antelope nervously watched the soldiers. It did not take long for them to move away, grazing as they went. Bright sunshine lit up the fertile land, but there was no sign of human inhabitants. This was too near Sogdia.

It was fierce tribesmen from the bare steppes that the Forgotten Legion was waiting for.

'There's been no sign of their passage,' Tarquinius reassured him.

Behind the legion's massed ranks stood the Parthian guards, the trumpeters and drummers. At their backs ran a broad, swiftly moving river. Muddy tracks near their position led down the bank into the water, good sign of a crossing point. The hoof prints mostly led out, into Margiana. It was clear that few horses had passed north in recent days.

The Parthian glanced at the ford yet again.

'You said yourself it would take them three days to get here.'

Pacorus grunted irritably.

'Only been a couple.' Despite the nature of the relationship, Tarquinius was careful to address the Parthian respectfully.

Pacorus changed the subject. 'The men did well.' Marching over fifty miles in two days had been an ordeal. 'Are they still ready to fight?'

'Of course, sir.' Again Tarquinius indicated the long spears carried by the legionaries. Fitted with barbed iron heads, the thick shafts were twice the length of normal *pila*.

The swarthy warrior nodded with approval.

'Is this definitely the only safe ford?' asked the Etruscan, checking.

'For thirty miles in either direction.' Pacorus scowled. 'They must cross here!'

Tarquinius fell silent. He did not move for so long that the Parthian began shifting nervously in his saddle. At length the haruspex smiled.

'They will be here by early afternoon.' It was unspoken, but there was no doubt now who was more powerful. 'No later.'

'You are sure?'

'Yes.'

Pacorus eyed the nearest grove of trees. 'And the hidden men?'

'They will not move until the trumpets sound, sir.'

Silence fell. There was nothing more to do but wait.

As usual, Tarquinius was correct. The sun had just passed its zenith when the few scouts returned at a gallop. Shortly after that, a large dust cloud appeared in the distance. Laden with spoils, the Sogdians were returning to their homeland. They would be careless, arrogant with success. From conversation with Pacorus, the Etruscan knew it was unlikely there had been any opposition to the raid. Parthia's armed forces in Margiana were at dangerously low levels and towns to the south would have paid dearly for their lack of defences. The tribesmen would hardly be expecting to meet thousands of legionaries blocking the route north.

Nine of the cohorts were arranged in battle formation, a good distance from the river. Five were in the centre, a pair on each wing. Soldiers in each ranked sixty across, eight deep. Men in the front four rows held long spears, those behind carried *pila* and every *scutum* was covered in silk. Small gaps between the units left room to manoeuvre once fighting started. Acting as reserves, the Parthian warriors were situated to the rear while the tenth cohort was hidden in trees five hundred paces in front, slightly off to one side.

Bucinae sounded as the Forgotten Legion moved into final position. Cohorts on the flanks moved forward a short distance, creating a curve in the defensive line.

They were ready.

'They're coming!' Romulus peered anxiously through thick summer leaves. 'I can't see anything, though.'

'Patience.' Brennus sharpened his longsword with a whetstone. The Etruscan had managed to obtain the items from Pacorus, the blade a souvenir from Carrhae. The Gaul now wore it in a scabbard across his broad back while a *gladius* hung from his belt, vital for close combat. 'Plenty of time yet. Won't be our turn till the end.'

Romulus sighed, never having watched a battle from the sidelines before. The grove faced south, wide enough to conceal five hundred men from view. They could remain hidden until the Sogdians had engaged with the other cohorts.

The soldiers behind them were ready to fight, their faces set. It had been months since they had seen any action and most were eager to change that. The men had fought together under Crassus because it was their duty, but Carrhae and a fifteen-hundred-mile march had forged strong bonds between all of the prisoners. Now they would gladly fight and die for each other – because there was no one else.

Their stout commander Darius was one of the more likeable Parthians. He too had heard the trumpets. Riding over, he dismounted, tying his horse's reins to a low branch. 'We will teach these dogs a lesson,' he said in poor Latin. 'For invading Parthian territory.'

Romulus grinned. Few of the new officers had bothered to learn their soldiers' language but Darius was an exception.

Brennus swung the longsword back and forth. 'Just let us at the bastards!' he replied, wondering if they had reached the end of the world. *No one could win such a battle. Except Brennus.* Tarquinius' words resonated through him. If the time was now, Brennus was ready.

Darius stood back a little, clearly awed by the Gaul's huge muscles and strange weapon. 'You are a Roman?'

'No!' Brennus swept back his pigtails angrily. 'I am an Allobroge, sir.'

The Parthian looked at him blankly.

'A Gaul. Different tribe, sir.'

'Why fight for Rome? Money?'

'That's a long story. We were slaves.' Brennus laughed, winking at Romulus. 'Gladiators.'

Darius rolled his tongue round the unfamiliar word. 'Gladi . . . ators?'

'We were paid to fight others while people watched. It is a sport in Rome.'

'Professional fighters! And now you are Parthian soldiers.'

Brennus and Romulus exchanged a glance.

The Sogdians arrived some time after the scouts. From their hidden position, Romulus and the others had a grandstand view of what transpired.

As predicted, there were several thousand tribesmen in the large war band. The column was fifteen or twenty men wide and extended back for some distance. Following in the rear came shepherds driving flocks of stolen sheep and goats, food for the coming winter. Yellow-skinned, black-haired and squat, the warriors halted their small, agile ponies not far from the grove. Most wore fur hats, leather jerkins and trousers and carried composite bows, round shields and swords. Every mount was heavily laden with bags of booty.

Consternation reigned when the raiders drew near enough to take in the Forgotten Legion. Yanking their reins back violently, the Sogdians pulled up, conferring in loud voices. The racket was audible even to the hidden cohort. Arms waved angrily, threats were made, weapons drawn. The warriors were not happy. It was not until a group of riders from the back galloped up that things calmed down.

One of the newcomers, a swarthy thickset figure with a beard, seemed to be in charge. Quarrelling men fell back in obvious deference when he spoke. The leader sat calmly contemplating the nine cohorts and conferring with his officers.

'He wouldn't have been expecting resistance this close to the border,' chuckled Darius. 'Been no troops here since the moment Orodes heard Crassus was thinking of invasion.'

The Sogdian leader was no coward. There was only a brief pause before he made a chopping gesture straight at the river. A group of two hundred warriors clad in metal helmets and chain mail waited with their chief while the remainder immediately rode forward in a sweeping curve that would carry them across the Roman front.

A flock of birds scattered into the air, startled by the noise of drumming hooves. Bows already half drawn, the bunched tribesmen charged at the Forgotten Legion.

An order rang out. Men in the front rank dropped to their knees, protecting the lower legs. Thousands of *scuta* clattered together as each cohort formed a testudo. It did not appear remotely threatening.

The riders smiled with contempt. Bowstrings were drawn taut as they came within killing range and grunts of effort accompanied the release. Hissing sounds reached Romulus as swarms of arrows flew towards the silk-covered shields. It was an awful noise, vividly evoking the carnage of Carrhae. But Tarquinius had trained the men well. Not a chink showed in the wall of fabric facing the archers.

The shafts landed in one great shower.

Romulus closed his eyes, unable to watch.

Brennus laughed, alarming him. 'By Belenus, look!' he whispered. 'It worked.'

Muted cheering was heard from the Roman lines. Sogdian arrows jutted from every *scutum*, but not one had gone right through.

Romulus was delighted. The Etruscan had related the tale of Isaac's silk and the ruby to them afterwards. Obviously the purchase had been well worth it.

Excited whispers broke out as the legionaries took in the impossible.

'Silence!' glared Darius. 'It's not over yet.'

Reluctantly the men obeyed.

The enemy leader was most displeased. Roaring with anger, he sent in another attack straight after the first. It made no difference. His riders withdrew without inflicting a single casualty, most of their shafts now wasted. As they fell back, the Romans began beating sword hilts off their *scuta*, mocking the enemy.

Access to the ford was still denied and there was no camel train for the Sogdians to replenish their arrows.

It was time for the heavy cavalry. The Sogdian shouted commands at the mailed warriors round him, then at the bowmen. Visors clanged down, curved swords were drawn, shields lifted high.

Darius looked worried. This was what had broken Crassus' soldiers once before. But there was no doubt in Romulus' and Brennus' eyes. The relentless training of the men by the Etruscan was about to pay off.

Intent on smashing straight through to the river, the armoured horsemen formed a great wedge and charged forward, followed by the entire contingent.

Tarquinius and Pacorus were ready.

As Romulus watched, each testudo broke up smoothly and both flanks moved forward, forming an even greater curve in the line. Four ranks of long spears emerged from every cohort, poking out in a bristling hedge of sharp metal. Men behind readied their *pila* in welcome for the raiders. It was a totally different approach to normal Roman tactics.

The Sogdians had never fought defenders in such close, disciplined formation. Any enemies who did not flee after one or two volleys always broke before a charge. Ignoring the Roman response, they thundered down on the armoured squares with whoops and yells. Dust rose in thick clouds, mounts' nostrils flared with effort, the ground shook.

'Horses will never ride on to that,' said Brennus, pointing at the dense network of metal and wood. 'They are too intelligent.'

'That haruspex is a genius,' exclaimed Darius as he saw what was about to happen. 'Carrhae would have ended differently if your general had listened to him.'

'He never got the chance, sir,' replied Romulus regretfully. 'Tarquinius was just a simple soldier then.'

'And now he fights for us. The gods must be thanked!'

A tremendous noise went up as hundreds of horses reached the Roman positions. Desperate to avoid the deadly iron points, they skidded to a stop, rearing up and unseating many riders. Those in the vanguard were driven on to the spears by the crush from behind. The air filled with Sogdian screams as men were impaled on the impenetrable wall of metal. Their steeds fared no better. In some areas legionaries were driven back, the lines buckling with pressure. But the sheer number of long shafts projecting forward was enough to withstand the combined weight of men and animals. The charge came to an abrupt halt. Dozens of warriors had been killed or wounded while the remainder milled about aimlessly, unable to reach the enemy.

'Time for a volley,' hissed Brennus. 'Only the ones at the front have chain mail.'

The words had barely left his lips when the soldiers with *pila* drew back and released. A dark cloud of javelins flew in a low arc overhead to rain down on the densely packed Sogdians.

At such close range and against men with no armour, the Roman *pilum* was deadly. Scores of Sogdians fell from the saddle to be trampled underfoot. Horses which had been hit spun in circles, kicking madly. Desperate to escape, others turned and bolted. Used to easy victories over poorly armed townspeople, it was too much for the tribesmen. The survivors turned and fled to safety.

There was little mercy for the fallen. As soon as the Sogdians were some distance away, legionaries darted forward into the piles of bodies, killing the wounded. The gruesome task completed, the ranks swiftly re-formed, once more presenting an unforgiving wall of shields.

Romulus could barely contain himself. The new tactics adopted by Tarquinius were revolutionary. A buzz of excitement shot through his cohort as word spread to the back.

'The fool is going to try again,' announced Brennus.

The Sogdian chief was rallying his war band, preparing for another charge.

'The nearest ford is a day's journey away,' explained Darius. 'More, on tired mounts. They'll try again before doing that. Just what we want.' He turned to the nearby officers. 'Prepare to advance!'

Pacorus' trumpets sounded when the enemy riders had

covered exactly half the distance to the legionaries. It was the signal they had been waiting for.

'Forward!' shouted the stout Parthian, urging his horse forward. 'Double time!' He trotted through the covering trees, out into the open.

Romulus, Brennus and five hundred eager men followed.

Totally absorbed in their attack, the Sogdians were not looking to the rear. Every rider pressed forward, those at the front attempting to cut a way past the long spears. As the tenth cohort pelted after Darius, the Roman flanks moved in closer, boxing in the tribesmen on three sides. Soon the entire force was involved in the fighting. There was no possible escape for the enemy.

Except to the south.

Swords rang on *scuta*, urging them on. The sound was coupled with shouts and cries, trumpet blasts, the scream of orders. As in the first attack, most horses had stalled, balking at the prospect of impalement. But the sheer momentum of the charge had carried a few warriors through the defensive shield wall, face to face with the Romans. Their mounts were quickly hamstrung, the riders hauled down and dispatched. Sogdian heads began to turn to the rear, seeking an escape from the lethal spears. Fear filled their eyes as some men saw what was about to happen.

Darius roared encouragement over his shoulder. 'Quickly! We must close the gap!'

Faces purple from running in full armour and carrying heavy *scuta,* the soldiers redoubled their efforts. Already they had covered more than half the ground.

'Spread out! Hundred men across. Five deep!'

Flowing smoothly, the cohort changed shape. Some of the running figures slowed while others increased their speed. It was one of many routines that had been practised countless times a lifetime before, when the legionaries fought for Rome.

Moments later, the first ranks reached the edge of the right flank. Locked in desperate combat, most Sogdians had still not seen the danger. Their chief was at the front of the mêlée, trying to batter a route through to the river.

Then the trap closed.

Darius' men were completely blocking the way out of the 'bull's horns'. Romulus grinned, remembering Cotta's lessons. Tarquinius was using the tactic employed by Hannibal at Cannae, when more than fifty thousand Romans had lost their lives.

Chests heaving, he and Brennus waved at the nearest soldiers.

Grinning broadly, they raised weapons in salute.

The Sogdians were dead men. In close combat, nobody on earth was as dangerous as the legionary. Every Roman knew it.

After the humiliation of Carrhae, it was exhilarating.

'Close order!' Junior officers pushed the men nearer to each other. 'Forward! At the double!'

Shields were raised, narrowing the gaps between till only the sharp blades of *gladii* protruded. The long spears had been too unwieldy to run with. Protected by crested bronze helmets, lines of hard faces were visible over the *scuta*. Romulus and his comrades advanced quickly, on to an enemy who was beginning to realise that there was no way out.

Screams of terror greeted the Forgotten Legion.

In the Roman centre, Tarquinius' eyes glinted.

Some of the Sogdians wheeled their mounts and charged at Darius' soldiers. Launched at the run, a swift volley of *pila* broke up the attempt to escape and soon there was no space for the horses to do more than turn on the spot. The cohort pressed closer, swords searching for homes in Sogdian flesh.

It was bloody and exhausting work. When the men in Darius' front ranks grew tired, they simply closed the shield wall completely. Held at bay by the press of bodies and the spears of the other three sides, the enemy could do nothing. But the Sogdians did not give in easily. Eager to fight still, many dismounted, shoving their way forwards on foot to hack at the legionaries.

Romulus fought with Brennus on one side of him and Felix on the other, each protected by the man on his left. The young soldier's sword felt like a living thing in his hand as warrior after warrior fell beneath it. Their lines moved forward relentlessly, compressing the Sogdians ever more tightly. *Gladii* stabbed back and forth, cutting deep with every stroke and covering their arms with blood. It was impossible to miss. Shrieks filled the air, rendering the officers' orders and the trumpets almost inaudible. It did not matter. The repetitive motion was hypnotic, its result absolutely lethal.

But the Sogdians were not completely beaten. Their leader finally managed to rally fifty of his mailed warriors together, using the space left by his own dead. Turning their horses' heads to the south, they drove forward at

Darius' men. Attacking the legionaries without the long spears was their only chance of escape.

Romulus' eyes widened as the frantic mounts pounded straight towards them. The impact would be massive.

'Close order!' roared Darius. 'Rear ranks, move in tight!'

Scuta slammed off each other and the men braced themselves. But nobody backed away. This would be a minor setback only; the battle's outcome was already certain.

And then the enemy was upon them. Horses crashed into the Roman shield wall, smashing it asunder. Romulus was thrown to one side, knocking his head as he went down. Half stunned, he fell on top of Felix. For a few moments he lay, unaware of his surroundings. Then he realised that the little Gaul was shaking his shoulder and shouting at him.

'Brennus!' Felix' eyes were wild. 'It's Brennus!'

Romulus' stomach lurched and he clambered to his feet, trying to make sense of the maelstrom of flashing swords, fighting men and sweating mounts all around him. Gradually he saw that somehow the rear ranks had not given way before the Sogdian charge. This amazing effort had confined the group of enemy warriors within the ranks of the cohort, creating a confusing mass of animals and humans. There were no longer discernible lines among the legionaries, no lines of battle. It was simply a matter of hacking at the nearest enemy.

'There!' cried Felix, pointing frantically.

Romulus took it in instantly. Brennus had also been bowled over by a horse and in the time it had taken him to get up, he had been surrounded by the Sogdians who were still trying to break out to freedom. At least ten riders ringed the Gaul, slashing downwards at him with long cavalry blades. He could see that Brennus was fighting more slowly than usual.

'Come on!' Romulus yelled, noting the deep wound on his friend's right arm. His sword arm. 'We haven't got long.'

Felix nodded grimly and together they launched themselves at the warriors, immediately hauling two from the saddle. The men were dispatched with swift *gladius* thrusts. Their horses turned and bolted, opening up the way through the mêlée. Romulus snatched a Sogdian lance from its dead owner and shoved it deep into the side of the rider nearest him. Keeping a firm grip on the shaft, he pulled it free as the screaming man fell away out of view. The young soldier used it to kill another warrior before a large Sogdian engaged him. Between sword thrusts, Romulus cast desperate glances at Brennus. The Gaul was holding his own. Only just. There were several new flesh wounds on his arms and face, but strangely Brennus did not seem scared.

Quickly, Romulus hamstrung his opponent's horse, hacking off the man's left arm as his mount went down kicking. Was this what Tarquinius had been sad about during the retreat from Carrhae: Brennus dying alone, surrounded by his own comrades? Fear constricted his throat. This could not be the time. Not Brennus. Not now.

By now, Felix had maimed another Sogdian and three of the others had been killed by legionaries on either side of them. Only the chief and one bodyguard remained.

Seeing Romulus and Felix bearing down, the leader barked an order at his warrior, jerking his head in their direction. It seemed he wanted to kill Brennus.

As the Sogdian's trained horse reared up and struck out with its forefeet, the big Gaul smiled, confident he was out of range. But he was close enough for one hoof to catch the front of his helmet. Brennus instantly dropped to his knees, his eyes glazed. With a cruel smile, the chief drew back his lance. In slow motion, Romulus saw what was about to happen. But the bodyguard was between them. Without thinking, he threw himself forward, rolling between the Sogdian's mount's legs. He hoped Felix would see what he was doing and keep the warrior occupied. Romulus came up fast, drawing his dagger.

Incredibly, Brennus had managed to ward off one spear thrust but his reactions were painfully sluggish. The next blow would be the last. Romulus did not pause. He drew back his right arm and heaved forwards, throwing his knife at the small area of exposed flesh above the Sogdian leader's chain mail and below his helmet. It was an impossible shot, aimed at a man on a moving horse, in the midst of a pitched battle.

But the blade flew with all Romulus' force and skill. It flew with his love for Brennus. And drove deep into the chief's neck. Killed instantly, the bearded warrior toppled from the saddle.

Romulus let out a huge breath. His heart was pounding wildly, but Brennus was still alive.

'Romulus?' Brennus mumbled. He smiled broadly and toppled over, unconscious before he hit the ground.

The young soldier darted to stand over his friend, ready to defend him against all comers. Fortunately the fighting had moved on as the remaining raiders were cut down one by one. He was quickly joined by Felix, who had left the bodyguard in a bleeding heap nearby.

'A fine shot,' said the little Gaul, respect in his eyes. 'Saved his life, I reckon.'

Romulus swallowed, imagining how he would have felt if the dagger had missed. But it had not. He laughed with relief. Today was a good day after all.

By the time the sun had begun to drop in the sky, it was all over. A small number of warriors had managed to break out, forcing through to the river. But the vast majority would never trouble Margiana again. Sogdian corpses were piled in heaps between dead horses. Spear shafts and bent *pila* jutted from bloody flesh, animal and human. Countless mouths hung slackly, dry eyes stared, loops of intestine spilled carelessly from open bellies. Clouds of flies covered the bodies and the ground was churned to mud, turned red in many places. Overhead, vultures and eagles were gathering.

As his battle frenzy faded away, Romulus found himself deeply troubled by the number of men who had been killed. After all, he had no quarrel with Sogdian tribesmen. But there was little he could do about it. Until he and his friends were completely free, they were soldiers in the Parthian army, and had to fight her enemies. It all came back to Brennus' advice from years before. *Kill or be killed.*

He kept silent as the legionaries reassembled by the river bank. Brennus and the other injured men were having their wounds attended to while others went downstream to wash off the blood and slake their terrible thirst. Close combat was exhausting work.

Pacorus was delighted. While his guards collected the booty from the dead, he sat on his stallion, gazing happily at the carnage. 'Many casualties?'

'Thirty or forty killed,' replied Tarquinius. 'Few dozen injured, but most will survive.'

'An outstanding victory!' declared the Parthian, his arrogance returning. 'Orodes will be pleased with my tactics.'

The Etruscan chuckled to himself.

'Other tribes will hear of this.' Pacorus waved his hands excitedly. 'Make them think again before threatening Parthia.'

There was a pause before Tarquinius spoke. 'The king of Scythia is a determined man. News of our success will not halt his plans to invade next year.'

Pacorus' smile disappeared. 'You have seen this?'

'And an attack by the Indians will follow soon afterwards.'

'With elephants?'

'Yes.'

The commander blanched. 'Normally we drive off those monsters with volleys of arrows.' His voice tailed off. Only a few dozen of the Parthian guards were archers.

Tarquinius stared east, waiting.

'Have you a plan, soothsayer?' The tone was pleading.

'Of course.' Tarquinius' dark eyes bored into him. 'But there will be a price to pay.'

There was silence as Pacorus stared at the piles of Sogdian bodies again. Without the haruspex, he would have no chance against new waves of invaders.

'Tell me,' he said heavily.

Late that evening, hundreds of celebrating legionaries packed the parade ground just inside the camp's north gate. As soon as the ramparts and defensive ditches had been built, Pacorus had rewarded his men with an issue of local spirits. The alcohol was disappearing fast as the victorious soldiers let the tensions of battle slip away. To fill their empty bellies, whole sheep were being cooked on spits over great fires at one end of the open area. The bemused guards stood watching, content now that the prisoners had fought bravely for Parthia.

Roars of laughter, loud conversation and singing competed to drown each other out. Drunken figures fell unnoticed to the ground while their companions wrestled each other or played dice. It was the first time in many months that the Romans had had a real reason to rejoice, and they were going to make the most of it.

The men of the Forgotten Legion had no idea what the future might hold. It was probably death, but tonight they did not care.

The surgeon had stitched Brennus' wound and now a heavy bandage covered his upper right arm. It would be weeks before he could fight again but it did not mean he could not enjoy the night with a few cups of spirit. Beside him, Romulus swigged his allotted measure happily, remembering the night in Publius' tavern. And Julia. Neither man had drunk much when Tarquinius appeared at the edge of the raucous gathering. Beckoning to them, the Etruscan led the way to the eastern gate. They followed curiously. Sentries saluted and waved them through the portal with broad smiles. Nobody would question the haruspex after the stunning victory that day. Everyone knew it was thanks to Tarquinius.

The three friends walked in silence along the river bank until they were a good distance from the marching camp and the sounds of revelry. A gentle breeze cooled the sweat on their faces and ruffled the water flowing past. It was a beautiful night with a clear, glittering sky. Far to the east lay a range of snow-covered peaks, visible now the heat haze had gone.

'The Qilian mountains,' said Tarquinius, halting by a grassy knoll. He flopped down, patting the ground beside him. Comfortable in each other's company, the soothsayer, warrior and young soldier sat back, watching shooting stars pass across the heavens. Spending time with his mentors at this time of day was a routine that Romulus had grown to love.

'Remember when I told you it took years to become a great fighter?' said Brennus suddenly.

Romulus nodded, recalling his burning desire to be the best in the *ludus*. So that he could kill Gemellus. An age ago, in Rome.

The Gaul threw a massive arm round his shoulders. 'I was watching you fight today,' he said with a smile. 'You're nearly there. A year or two and you'll be better than me.'

Romulus was astonished. 'I could never be as strong as you.'

'Not as strong, maybe. But more skilful.' There was real respect in Brennus' eyes.

Romulus met the look squarely. 'Much of it is thanks to you.'

Brennus tightened his grip. 'You're like a son to me,' he growled.

Emotion welled up inside Romulus and he hugged the Gaul fiercely.

In the darkness they could not see Tarquinius' face. But Romulus did not care. He felt huge relief that Brennus was still alive. Still with him.

For some time no one spoke, and they listened happily to the bats that were swooping and diving over the river. The land was at peace, delivered from the Sogdians by the Forgotten Legion's courage.

Having witnessed Brennus survive against all the odds, Romulus imagined returning to Rome one day and finding his family. It seemed possible now.

Brennus felt contentment at the thought of how similar Ultan's and Tarquinius' predictions had been. His guilt and pain were greatly eased, for it was proof to him that the gods would deliver his redemption one day. Not here. At the edge of the world.

With memories of Olenus uppermost, Tarquinius asked that his urge to discover more about the Etruscans' origins be fulfilled. Strangely, his once constant thirst for knowledge had been diminishing for some time and the haruspex knew it was due to the growing emotions he felt for his companions. Since Olenus he had loved no one. But without Tarquinius becoming aware of it, the brave, generous Gaul and the eager young man had become very dear to him. Romulus felt like . . . what? A son to him. He laughed. How very human; how very . . . ordinary; but how good that felt.

The others looked at Tarquinius questioningly but he was deep in thought.

How could he have forgotten Olenus' words? *You will pass on much information.* Romulus had been right there under his nose all along. Someone he could begin to instruct in the ancient art. A tiny sigh of satisfaction escaped his lips and he began to speak at last.

'Our journey will continue for years.' His eyes turned to the horizon, and their gaze followed his.

East.

'There will be more battles. And mortal danger.'

The hairs on their necks prickled, but neither Romulus nor Brennus asked more.

They were alive. For the moment, that was enough.

Author's Note

Interested readers may read that the more exotic classes of gladiators mentioned (*dimachaerii*, *laquearii* and *scissores*) were introduced in Imperial times rather than during the Republic. My use of them in this novel was merely to make the scenes in the arena more colourful. Although it is commonly thought that every gladiator fight was to the death, this is now thought not to be the case. In many cases, the fighters were simply too valuable to be wasted in such a way. It was more common for mortal combat to be reserved for special occasions or for the last bout of the day.

The Etruscans were a mysterious people who ruled large parts of central Italy from about 700 BC until they were overthrown by the Romans in the mid 450s BC. Although they owed much to Greek influence, many of their customs did not originate from there. They had a more eastern flavour. Many theories are still extant about the Etruscans' exact origins: the area of Lydia in western Asia Minor; Egypt; and even further afield in Mesopotamia. Fond of music, dance and feasting, the self-styled Rasenna also practised divination from the livers of sacrificed animals. Games such as horse-racing, wrestling and gladiator fights were very popular. Despite their subjugation, they were not to be forgotten. Many Etruscan customs were swiftly subsumed into Roman civilisation.

It is a matter of historical fact that Crassus led an enormous host all the way from Italy to Parthia, only for it to be annihilated. Rome rarely suffered such a comprehensive defeat, and the lesson was not lost on its leaders. Cavalry soon became a feature of every Roman army. The term 'parting shot' derives from the 'Parthian shot' that devastated Crassus' soldiers at Carrhae.

Many reports maintain that the arrogant general was killed during the supposed parley with the Parthians, but I have taken the liberty of having him taken prisoner. The manner of Crassus' execution matches his greed and is similar to that of an unpopular Roman governor in Asia Minor some years previously.

We also know from contemporary text that ten thousand legionaries were marched to Margiana to serve as border guards. One can only imagine what it must have been like to be so far from home, in a time when such distance was utterly final. Little information has passed down about the fate of the Roman prisoners, although some assert that they went on to serve as mercenaries for the Huns.

Glossary

acetum – sour wine, the most common beverage served to Roman soldiers.

aedile (pl. aediles) – an officer responsible for maintaining the streets of Rome; overseeing religious affairs; seeing to the upkeep of public order; looking after the corn supply and the provision of public games and entertainments.

Aesculapius – son of Apollo, the god of health and the protector of doctors.

amphora (pl. amphorae) – a large, two-handled clay vessel with a narrow neck used to store wine, olive oil and other produce. It was also a unit of measurement, equivalent to eighty pounds of wine.

andabatae – heavily armoured fighters on horseback who wore visored helmets without eyeholes. This class of gladiator would have been heavily handicapped and was possibly used more for comedic value than anything else.

as (pl. asses) – a small copper coin, originally worth one-fifth of a sestertius.

atrium – the large chamber immediately after the entrance hall in a Roman house or domus. Frequently built on a grand scale, this was the social and religious centre of the house. It had an opening in the roof and a pool, the impluvium, to catch the subsequent rain-water that entered.

auletos – a popular instrument among the Etruscans, the double flute is often depicted in images on the walls of tombs.

aureus (pl. aurei) – a small gold coin worth twenty-five denarii. Until the time of the early empire, it was minted infrequently.

ballista (pl. ballistae) – a two-armed Roman catapult which looked like a crossbow on a stand. It operated via a different principle however, utilising the force from the tightly coiled sinew rope holding the arms rather than the tension in them. Ballistae varied in size, from man portable versions to enormous engines that required wagons and mules to move them around. They fired either bolts or stones with great force and precision. Favourite types had nicknames like 'onager', the wild ass, named for its kick, and 'scorpion', called such its sting.

basilicae – huge covered markets in the Roman Forum; also where judicial, commercial and governmental activities took place. Public trials were conducted here, while lawyers, scribes and moneylenders worked side by side from little stalls. Many official announcements were made in the basilicae.

Belenus – the Gaulish god of light. He was also the god of cattle and sheep.

bestiarius (pl. bestiarii) – men who hunted and captured animals for the arena in Rome. A highly dangerous occupation, it was also very lucrative. The more exotic the animals – for example elephants, hippopotami, giraffes and rhinoceroses – the higher the premium commanded. The mind boggles at the labour required, and hazards involved, to bring such animals from their natural habitat to Rome. In later times the term bestiarii was also used to mean venatores.

bucellatum – hard-tack biscuit, a common Roman army ration when on campaign. Made of flour, salt, olive oil and as little water as possible, bucellatum was baked in an oven to form very hard, dry 'cakes'.

bucina (pl. bucinae) – a military trumpet. The Romans used a number of types of instruments, among them the tuba, the cornu and the bucina. These were used for many purposes, from waking the troops each morning, to sounding the charge, the halt or the retreat. We are uncertain how the different instruments were used –

whether in unison or one after another, for example. To simplify matters, I have used just one of them – the bucina.

bulla (pl. bullae) – a pendant, consisting of a rounded box containing an amulet. Supposed to protect the new-born child against evil spirits, they were given as gifts and worn by boys until manhood, and by girls until marriage. Poorer citizens would use ones made of leather or cloth, while wealthier parents gifted bullae of gold.

caldarium (pl. caldaria) – an intensely hot room in Roman bath complexes. Used like a modern day sauna, most also had a hot plunge pool. The caldarium was heated by hot air which flowed through hollow bricks in the walls and under the raised floor. The source of the piped heat was the hypocaustum, a furnace constantly kept hot by slaves.

caligae – heavy leather sandals worn by the Roman soldier. Sturdily constructed in three layers – a sole, insole and upper, caligae resembled an open-toed boot. The straps could be tightened to make the fit more close. Dozens of metal studs on the sole gave the sandals good grip; these could also be replaced when necessary. In colder climes, such as Britain, socks were often worn as well.

casus belli – the justification for acts of war.

cella (pl. cellae) – the windowless, rectangular central room in a temple dedicated to a god. It usually had a statue of the relevant deity, and often had an altar for offerings as well.

Cerberus – the monstrous three-headed hound which guarded the entrance to Hades. He allowed the spirits of the dead to enter, but none to leave.

collegia – former trade groups which had historically existed at every crossroads in Rome. They were surprisingly egalitarian, open to citizens, freedmen and slaves alike. Thanks to their supposed links to organised crime, the collegia were abolished in 64 BC. But in 58 BC, they were cleverly resurrected by Clodius Pulcher, the people's tribune, and reorganised along military lines. As their patron, Clodius gained huge control over Rome's streets.

congiaria – free distributions of grain and money to the poor.

consul – one of two annually elected chief magistrates, appointed by the people and ratified by the Senate. Effective rulers of Rome for twelve months, they were in charge of civil and military matters and led the Republic's armies into war. Each could negate the other and both were supposed to heed the wishes of the Senate. No man was supposed to serve as consul more than once. But by the end of the second century BC, powerful nobles such as Marius, Cinna and Sulla were holding on to the position for years on end. This dangerously weakened Rome's democracy.

contubernium – a group of eight legionaries who shared a tent and ate together.

cursus honorum – the nobles' career path. In theory, the sequence of offices could not be skipped. A Roman male of the upper classes often started his career with a spell in the army as a staff officer. By the time of Sulla, the age limits had been raised to slow down the number of ambitious young men moving into the cursus after military service. Now, the rank of quaestor could be attained no earlier than the age of thirty. One could be made praetor by thirty-nine and then, for the lucky few, the post of consul was possible three years later. While useful on a curriculum vitae, the positions of aedile and tribune were not mandatory to move upwards on the cursus.

decurion – cavalry officer in charge of ten men. In later times, the decurion commanded a turma, a unit of about 30 men.

denarius (pl. denarii) – the staple coin of the Roman Republic. Made from silver, it was worth four sestertii, or ten asses (later sixteen). The less common gold aureus was worth twenty-five denarii.

dimachaerus (pl. dimachaerii) – a gladiator of the later Empire, who fought without a shield, using two swords or knives instead. Little more is known about this class of fighter.

Disciplina Etrusca – the ancient Etruscan volumes containing the lore of haruspicy. There were three sets of volumes: the Libri Haruspicini – regarding divination from animals' organs; the Libri Fulgurates – allowing interpretation of thunder and lightning; the Libri Rituales – concerned Etruscan rituals and consecrations for temples, cities and armies. The Romans stole editions of these books from the Etruscan cities that they conquered, and revered them highly, keeping them under lock and key in the temple of Jupiter in Rome. They were consulted only in times of great need. Anyone who was caught trying to read or use them without permission was sewn in a sack and dropped into the River Tiber.

domus – a wealthy Roman's home. Typically it faced inwards, presenting a blank wall to the outside world. Built in a long, rectangular shape, the domus consisted of two inner-light sources: the atrium at the front and the colonnaded garden to the rear. These were separated by the large reception area of the tablinum. Around the atrium were bedrooms, offices, store-rooms and shrines to a family's ancestors, while the chambers around the garden were often banqueting halls and further reception areas.

editor (pl. editores) – the sponsor of a munus, a gladiatorial contest. Once part of the obligatory rituals to honour the dead, such munera had by the late Republic become a way of winning favour with the Roman people. The lavishness of the spectacle reflected the depth of the editor's desire to please.

equites – the 'knights' or equestrian class were originally the citizens who could afford to equip themselves as cavalrymen in the early Roman army. By late Republican times the title was defunct, but it had been adopted by those who occupied the class just below that of the senators. Some senatorial families also continued to use the term.

familia – by taking the gladiator's oath, a fighter became part of the familia gladiatoria, the tight-knit group that would be his only family, often until death.

fasces – a bundle of rods bound together around an axe. The symbol of justice, it was carried by a lictor, a group of whom walked in front of all senior magistrates. Quite probably Etruscan in origin, the fasces symbolised the right of the authorities to punish and execute lawbreakers.

Fortuna – the goddess of luck and good fortune. Like all deities, she was notoriously fickle.

frigidarium (pl. frigidaria) – a room in Roman baths containing a cold plunge pool. It was often the last chamber in a bathing complex.

gladius (pl. gladii) – little information remains about the 'Spanish' sword of the Republican army, the gladius hispaniensis, with its waisted blade. I have therefore used the 'Pompeii' variation of the gladius as it is the shape most people are familiar with. This was a short 420–500 mm (16.5–20 in) straight-edged sword with a 'V' shaped point. About 42–55 mm (1.6–2.2 in) wide, it was an extremely well balanced weapon for both cutting and thrusting. The shaped hilt was made of bone and protected by a pommel and guard of wood. The gladius was worn on the right, except by centurions and other senior officers, who wore it on the left. It was actually quite easy to draw with the right hand, and was probably positioned like this to avoid entanglement with the scutum while being unsheathed.

haruspex (pl. haruspices) – a soothsayer. A man trained to divine in many ways, from the inspection of animal entrails to the shapes of clouds and the way birds fly. As the perceived source of blood, and therefore life itself, the liver was particularly valued for its divinatory possibilities. In addition, many natural phenomena – thunder, lightning, wind – could be used to interpret the present, past and future. The bronze liver mentioned in the book really exists – it was found in a field at Piacenza, Italy in 1877.

hora quarta – the fourth hour; hora undecima – the eleventh hour. Roman time was divided into two periods of twelve hours, those of daylight and of night time. The first of the day, hora prima, started at sunrise. Great inaccuracies were present in the Romans' methods used to measure time. The main instrument used was a sundial, which meant that the latitude of the location defined day length. Thus the time in Rome was quite different to Sicily, far to the south. In addition, varying day length throughout the year meant that daylight hours in the winter were shorter than in the summer.

We must therefore assume that time was more elastic in ancient times. The Romans also devised the clepsydra, or water clock. By using a transparent water vessel with a regular intake, it was possible to mark the level of water for each daylight hour, and then to use it at night or during fog.

hypocaustum – the heating system which was powered by a furnace from outside. Underfloor concrete channels, or brick columns supporting a raised floor, allowed hot air from the furnace to heat rooms. Hollow box-tiles could be placed in the walls to channel even more heat vertically.

insulae (sing. insula) – high-rise (three-, four- or even five-storey) blocks of flats in which most Roman citizens lived. As early as 218 BC, Livy recorded the tale of an ox which escaped from the market and scaled the stairs of an insula before hurling itself to its death from the third floor. The ground level of each insula often comprised a taberna, or shop, which opened right onto the street via a large arched doorway. The shopkeeper and his family lived and slept in the room above. Built on top of this was floor after floor of cenaculae, the plebeians' flats. Cramped, poorly lit, heated only by braziers, and often dangerously constructed, the cenaculae had no running water or sanitation. Access to the flats was made via staircases built on the outside of the building.

Jupiter – often referred to as 'Optimus Maximus' – 'Greatest and Best'. Most powerful of the Roman gods, he was responsible for weather, especially storms. Jupiter was the brother as well as the husband of Juno.

Juno – sister and wife of Jupiter, she was the goddess of marriage and women.

lacerna (pl. lacernae) – originally a military cloak, it was usually a dark colour. Made of dyed wool, it was light-weight, open-sided and had a hood.

lanista (pl. lanistae) – a gladiator trainer, often the owner of a ludus, a gladiator school.

laquearius (pl. laquearii) – a little-known sub-class of the retiarius. Dressed in the same manner as a retiarius, the laquearius probably fought with a trident but used a lasso instead of a net.

latifundium (pl. latifundia) – a large estate, usually owned by Roman nobility, and which utilised large numbers of slaves as labour. The origin of the latifundium was during the second century BC, when vast areas of land were confiscated from Italian peoples defeated by Rome, such as the Samnites.

liburnian – a faster and smaller ship than the trireme, the liburnian was adapted by the Romans from its origins with the Liburnian people of Illyricum (modern-day Croatia). With two banks of oars, it was a bireme rather than a trireme. It could travel under sail, by the power of its oars or using both.

licium – linen loincloth worn by nobles. It is likely that all classes wore a variant of this: unlike the Greeks, the Romans did not believe in unnecessary public nudity.

lictor (pl. lictores) – a magistrates' enforcer. Only strongly built citizens could apply for this job, essentially the bodyguards for the consuls, praetors and other senior Roman magistrates. Such officials were accompanied at all times in public by set numbers of lictores (the number depended on their rank). Each lictor carried a fasces – the symbol of justice – a bundle of rods enclosing an axe. Other duties included the arresting and punishment of wrongdoers.

lituus – a small, crooked staff carried by haruspices. It was a symbol of their office and used in various rituals.

ludus (pl. ludi) – a gladiator school.

manica (pl. manicae) – an arm guard used by gladiators. It was usually made of layered materials such as durable linen and leather, or metal.

manumissio – during the Republic, the act of freeing a slave was actually quite complex. It was usually done in one of three ways: by claim to the praetor, during the sacrifices of the five-yearly lustrum, or by a testamentary clause in a will. A slave could not be freed until at least the age of thirty and continued to have formal duties to their former master after manumission. During the empire, the process was made much more simple. It became possible to verbally grant manumission at a feast, using the guests as witnesses. By allowing Brutus to grant Fabiola's freedom in private, I have therefore taken a small liberty.

Mare Nostrum – literally 'our sea'. The Roman colloquial term for the Mediterranean Sea.

Mars – the god of war. All spoils of war were consecrated to him, and no Roman commander would go on campaign without having visited the temple of Mars to ask for the god's protection and blessing.

Minerva – the goddess of war and also of wisdom.

modius (pl. modii) – an official Roman dry measure of approximately 8.6 litres (just over 15 pints). To prevent malpractice, all weights and measures (wet and dry) in Rome were standardised.

modus operandi – manner of working or operating.

munus (pl. munera) – a gladiatorial combat, staged originally during celebrations honouring the death of someone. Their popularity meant that by the late Roman Republic, the munera were being staged regularly by rival politicians, to win the public's favour and to upstage each other.

murmillo (pl. murmillones) – one of the most familiar types of gladiator. The bronze, crested helmet was very distinctive, with a broad brim, a bulging face-plate and grillwork eyeholes. The crest was often fitted with feathered crests, and may also have been fashioned in a fish shape. The murmillo wore a manica on the right arm, and a greave on the left leg; like the legionary, he carried a heavy rectangular shield and was armed with a gladius. His only garments were the subligaria, an intricately folded linen undercloth, and the balteus, a wide, protective belt. In Republican times, the most common opponent for the murmillo was the secutor, although this later became the retiarius.

olibanum – frankincense, an aromatic resin used in incense as well as perfume. Highly valued in ancient times, the best olibanum was reportedly grown in modern-day Oman, Yemen and Somalia. For obvious reasons, I have not used today's name as it refers to the Franks who reintroduced it to Europe in the Middle Ages.

optio (pl. optiones) – the officer who ranked immediately below a centurion; the second-in-command of a century.

palus – a 1.82 m (6 ft) wooden post buried in the ground. Trainee gladiators and legionaries were taught swordsmanship by aiming blows at it.

Periplus (of the Erythraean Sea) – a priceless historical document from approximately the first century AD. Clearly written by someone familiar with the area, the

Periplus describes the navigation and trading opportunities along the entire coast of the Red Sea to eastern Africa and as far east as India. It mentions safe harbours, dangerous areas, and the best places to buy valuable goods such as tortoise shell, ivory and spices. I have changed its origins and contents slightly to fit in with the story.

petteia – meaning among other things, 'pebbles'. This ancient Greek board game was played on differing sized boards, using black and white pieces that started the game on opposite sides. A contest of great skill, the objective was to capture or immobilise an opponent's pieces by sandwiching them between two others.

phalera (pl. phalerae) – a sculpted disc-like decoration for bravery which was worn on a chest harness, over a Roman soldier's armour. Phalerae were commonly made of bronze, but could be made of more precious metals as well.

pilum (pl. pila) – the Roman javelin. It consisted of a wooden shaft approximately 4 ft (1.2 m) long, joined to a thin iron shank approximately 2 ft (0.6 m) long, and was topped by a small pyramidal point. The javelin was heavy and when launched, all of its weight was concentrated behind the head, giving it tremendous penetrative force. It could strike through a shield to injure the man carrying it, or lodge in the shield, making it impossible to use. The range of the pilum was about 100 ft (30 m), although the effective range was probably about half this distance.

praetor – senior magistrates who administered justice in Rome and in its overseas possessions such as Sardinia, Sicily and Spain. They could also hold military commands and initiate legislation. The main understudy to the consuls, the praetor convened the Senate in their absence.

Priapus – the god of gardens and fields, a symbol of fertility. Often pictured with a huge erect penis.

quaestor – administrators and assistants to the senior magistrates. Elected by the Senate, their main roles were in the finances of the state. One of the positions used to climb the cursus honorum, and from which a noble could become a senator.

retiarius (pl. retiarii) – the fisherman, or net and trident fighter, named after the rete, or net. Also an easily recognisable class of gladiator, the retiarius wore only a subligaria. His sole protection consisted of the galerus, a metal shoulder-guard, which was attached to the top edge of a manica on his left arm. His weapons were the weighted net, a trident and a dagger. With less equipment to weigh him down, the retiarius was far more mobile than many other gladiators, and without a helmet, was also instantly recognisable. This may have accounted for the low status of this class of fighter.

rudis – the wooden gladius which symbolised the freedom that could be granted to a gladiator who pleased an editor sufficiently, or who had earned enough victories in the arena to qualify for it. Not all gladiators were condemned to die in combat: prisoners of war and criminals usually were, but slaves who had committed a crime were granted the rudis if they survived for three years as a gladiator. After a further two years, they could be set free.

Samnite – a class of fighter based on the Samnite people who occupied the central Apennines, but were finally defeated by Rome in the third century BC. Some accounts describe them with triple-disc metal breastplates, but other depictions have the Samnites barechested. Plumed helmets and greaves were common, as was the typical wide gladiatorial belt. Carrying round or rectangular shields, they usually fought with spears.

scissores – a mysterious type of gladiator from the Eastern empire, probably a variant of the murmillo. There seems to be dissent about the weapons carried by the scissores, so to avoid controversy, I have taken the liberty of giving Sextus and his comrades axes.

scutum (pl. scuta) – an elongated oval Roman army shield, about 1.2 m (4 ft) tall and 0.75 m (2 ft 6in) wide. It was made from two layers of wood, the pieces laid at right angles to each other; it was then covered with linen or canvas, and leather. The scutum was heavy, weighing between 6 to 10 kgs (12–22 lbs). A large metal boss decorated its centre, with the horizontal grip placed behind this. Decorative designs were often painted on the front, and a leather cover was used to protect the shield when not in use, e.g. while marching.

secutor (pl. secutores) – the pursuer, or hunter class of gladiator. Also called the contraretiarius, the secutor fought the fisherman, the retiarius. Virtually the only difference between the secutor and the murmillo was the smooth-surfaced helmet, which was without a brim and had a small, plain crest, probably to make it more difficult for the retiarius' net to catch a hold. Unlike other types of gladiator, the secutor's helmet had small eyeholes, making it very difficult to see. This was possibly to reduce the chances of the heavily-armoured fighter quickly overcoming the retiarius.

sestertius (pl. sestertii) – a brass coin, it was worth four asses; or a quarter of a denarius; or one hundredth of an aureus. Its name 'two units and a half third one' comes from its original value, two and a half asses. By the time of the late Roman Republic, its use was becoming more common.

stola – a long, loose tunic, with or without sleeves, worn by women.

strigil – a small, curved iron tool used to clean the skin after bathing. First perfumed oil would be rubbed in, and then the strigil was used to scrape off the combination of sweat, dirt and oil.

tablinum – the office or reception area beyond the atrium. The tablinum usually opened onto an enclosed colonnaded garden.

tepidarium – the largest area in a Roman baths and often where bathers met and talked. Containing a large, warm pool, it was a place to linger.

tesserae – the game of dice. It was very popular among all classes of the population in Rome.

tesserarius – one of the junior officers in a century, whose duties included commanding the guard. The name originates from the tessera tablet on which was written the password for the day.

testudo – the famous Roman square formation, formed by legionaries in the middle raising their scuta over their heads while those at the sides formed a shield wall. The testudo, or tortoise, was used to resist missile attack or to protect soldiers while they undermined the walls of towns under siege. The formation's strength was reputedly tested during military training by driving a cart pulled by mules over the top of it.

Thracian – like most gladiators, this class had its origins with one of Rome's enemies – Thrace (modern-day Bulgaria). Armed with a small square shield with a convex surface, this fighter wore greaves on both legs and occasionally, fasciae – protectors on the thighs. The right arm was covered by a manica. A Hellenistic type helmet was worn, with a broad curving brim and cheek guards.

tribune – senior staff officer within a legion; also one of ten political positions in Rome, where they served as 'tribunes of the people', defending the rights of the plebeians. The tribunes could also veto measures taken by the Senate or consuls, except in times of war. To assault a tribune was a crime of the highest order.

trireme – the classic Roman warship, which was powered by a single sail and three banks of oars. Each oar was rowed by one man, who was free born, not a slave. Exceptionally manoeuvrable, and capable of up to eight knots under sail or for short bursts when rowed, the trireme also had a bronze ram at the prow. This was used to damage or even sink enemy ships. Small catapults were also mounted on the deck. Each trireme was crewed by up to 30 men and had up to 200 rowers; it also carried up to 60 marines (in a reduced century), giving it a very large crew in proportion to its size. This limited its range, and made their main uses those of troop transports and protectors of coastlines.

unctor – a masseur, often a slave.

velarium – cloth awning positioned over the seats of the rich at the arena. It protected them from the worst of the sun's heat and allowed Roman women to remain fair-skinned, a most important quality.

venator (pl. venatores) – a trained beast-fighter. They hunted animals like antelope, wild goats and giraffe and more dangerous ones such as lions, tigers, bears and elephants. Typically the lowest class of gladiator, the venatores provided the warm-up acts in the morning, before the main attraction of man to man combats later in the day.

vexillum (pl. vexilla) – a distinctive, usually red, flag which was used to denote the commander's position in camp or in battle. Vexilla were also used by detachments serving away from their units.

vilicus – slave foreman or farm manager. Commonly a slave, the vilicus was sometimes a paid worker, whose job it was to make sure that the returns on a farm were as large as possible. This was most often done by treating the slaves brutally.

Now read a chapter from
the next novel in
The Forgotten Legion Chronicles

THE SILVER EAGLE

Chapter II: Scaevola

Near Pompeii, winter 53/52 BC

'Mistress?'

Fabiola opened her eyes with a start. Standing behind her was a kind-faced, middle-aged woman in a simple smock and plain leather sandals. She smiled. Docilosa was Fabiola's one true friend and ally, someone she could trust with her life. 'I've asked you not to call me that.'

Docilosa's lips twitched. A former domestic slave, she had received her manumission at the same time as her new mistress. But the habits of a lifetime took a while to discard. 'Yes, Fabiola,' she said carefully.

'What is it?' asked Fabiola, climbing to her feet. Stunningly beautiful, slim and black-haired, she was dressed in a simple but expensive silk and linen robe. Ornate gold and silver jewellery winked from around her neck and arms. 'Docilosa?'

There was a pause.

'Word has come from the north,' said Docilosa. 'From Brutus.'

Joy struck, followed by dread. This was what Fabiola had been asking for: news of her lover. Twice a day, in an alcove off her villa's main courtyard, she prayed at this altar without fail. Now that Jupiter had answered her requests, would it be good news? Fabiola studied Docilosa's face for a clue.

Decimus Brutus was sequestered in Ravenna with Caesar, his general, who was plotting their return to Rome. Conveniently situated between the capital and the frontier with Transalpine Gaul, Ravenna was Caesar's favourite winter abode. There, surrounded by his armies, he could monitor the political situation. Above the River Rubicon, this was allowed. But for a general to cross without relinquishing his military command – thereby entering Italy proper under arms – was an act of high treason. So every winter, Caesar watched and waited. Unhappy, the Senate could do little about it, while Pompey, the only man with the military muscle to oppose Caesar, sat on the fence. The situation changed daily, but one thing felt certain. Trouble was looming.

Fabiola was therefore surprised by Docilosa's news.

'Rebellion has broken out in Transalpine Gaul,' she revealed. 'There's heavy fighting in many areas. Apparently the Roman settlers and merchants in the conquered cities are being massacred.'

Fighting panic at this new threat to Brutus, Fabiola exhaled slowly. Remember what you have escaped, she thought. Things have been far worse than this. At thirteen, Fabiola had been sold as a virgin into an expensive brothel by Gemellus, her cruel former owner. Adding to the horror, Romulus, her brother, had been sold into gladiator school at the same time. Her heart ached at the thought. Nearly four years of enforced prostitution in the Lupanar had followed. *I did not lose hope then.* Fabiola eyed the statue on the altar with reverence. Jupiter delivered me from the life I despised. Rescue had come in the form of Brutus, one of Fabiola's keenest lovers, who bought her from Jovina, the madam of the brothel, for a great deal of money. The impossible is always possible, Fabiola reflected, feeling calmer. Brutus would be safe. 'I thought Caesar had conquered all of Gaul?' she asked.

'So they say,' muttered Docilosa.

'Yet it has seen nothing but unrest,' retorted Fabiola. Aided by Brutus, Rome's most daring general had been stamping out trouble since his bloody campaign had ostensibly ended. 'What is it now?'

'The chieftain Vercingetorix has demanded, and received, a levy from the tribes,' Docilosa replied. 'Tens of thousands of men are flocking to his banner.'

Fabiola frowned. This was not news she wanted to hear. With the majority of his forces stationed in winter quarters just inside Transalpine Gaul, Caesar could be in real trouble. The Gaulish people were fierce warriors who had vigorously resisted the Roman conquest, losing only because of Caesar's extraordinary abilities as a tactician and the legions' superior discipline. If the tribes were truly uniting, an uprising had catastrophic potential.

'The news gets worse,' Docilosa continued. 'Heavy snow has already fallen in the mountains on the border.'

Fabiola's lips tightened. Brutus' most recent message

had talked about coming to visit soon. That would not now happen.

If Caesar couldn't reach his troops in time to quell the rebellion before spring, the trouble would spread far and wide. Vercingetorix had picked his moment carefully, thought Fabiola angrily. If this revolt succeeded, all her well-laid plans would come to nothing. Doubtless thousands would lose their lives in the forthcoming fighting, but she had to ignore that heavy cost. Whatever her desires, those men would still die. A quick victory for Caesar would mean less bloodshed. Fabiola desperately wanted this because then Brutus, his devoted follower, would gain more glory. But it was not just that. Fabiola was ruthlessly focused. If Caesar succeeded, her star would rise too.

She felt a twinge of guilt that her first thought had not been for Brutus' safety. A keen career soldier, he was also extremely courageous. He might be injured, or even killed, in the forthcoming fighting. That would be hard to bear, she reflected, offering up an extra prayer. Although she had never let herself love anyone, Fabiola was genuinely fond of Brutus. He had always been gentle and kind, even when taking her virginity. She smiled. Choosing to lavish her charms on him had been a good decision.

Previously, there had been many such clients, all powerful nobles whose patronage could have guaranteed her progress into the upper echelons of Roman society. Keeping her eyes on that prize, Fabiola had somehow managed to disassociate herself from the degradation of her job. Just as they used Fabiola's body, men were to be taken for whatever she could gain: gold, information or, best of all, influence. From the start, Brutus had been different from most clients, which made sex with him easier. What had finally tipped the balance in his favour was his close relationship with Caesar, a politician who had aroused Fabiola's interest as she eavesdropped on conversations between nobles relaxing in the brothel's baths. The pillow talk that she cajoled from her satiated customers had also been full of promising pointers towards Caesar. Perhaps it was Jupiter who had guided her to become Brutus' mistress, thought Fabiola. While at a feast with Brutus, she had seen a statue of Caesar which reminded her strongly of Romulus. Suspicion had burned in Fabiola's mind since.

Docilosa's next words brought her back to reality. 'The Optimates threw a feast when the news of Vercingetorix' rebellion reached Rome. Pompey Magnus was guest of honour.'

'Gods above,' muttered Fabiola. 'Anything else?' Caesar had enemies everywhere, and particularly in the capital. The triumvirate which ruled the Republic had been reduced by one with the death of Crassus, and since then Pompey had seemed unsure what to do about Caesar's unsurpassed military successes. Which suited Caesar admirably. But now the Optimates, the group of politicians which opposed him, were openly courting Pompey, his sole rival. Caesar could still be the new ruler of Rome – but only if Vercingetorix' uprising did not succeed and if he retained enough support in the Senate. Suddenly Fabiola felt very vulnerable. In the Lupanar, she had been a big fish in a small pond. Outside, in the real world, she was a nobody. If Caesar failed, so did Brutus. And without his backing, what chance had she of succeeding in life? Unless, of course, she prostituted herself with someone else. Fabiola's stomach turned at that idea. Those years in the Lupanar had been enough to last a lifetime.

This called for dramatic measures.

'I must visit the temple on the Capitoline Hill,' Fabiola declared. 'To make an offering and pray that Caesar crushes the rebellion quickly.'

Docilosa hid her surprise. 'The voyage to Rome will take at least a week. More if the seas are rough.'

Fabiola's face was serene. 'In that case, we shall travel by road.'

Now the older woman was shocked. 'We'll end up raped and murdered! The countryside is full of bandits.'

'No more so than the streets of Rome,' Fabiola replied tartly. 'Besides, we can take the three body-guards that Brutus left. They'll be enough protection.' Not as good as Benignus or Vettius, she thought, fondly remembering the Lupanar's huge doormen. Despite their devotion to Fabiola, they had been too valuable for Jovina to sell as well. Returning to the capital might allow her to investigate that possibility again. The tough pair would be very useful.

'What will Brutus say when he finds out?'

'He'll understand,' answered Fabiola brightly. 'I'm doing it for him.'

Docilosa sighed. She would not win this argument. And with few diversions other than the baths or covered market in Pompeii, life had become very mundane in the almost empty villa. Rome would provide some excitement — it always did. 'When do you wish to leave?'

'Tomorrow. Send word to the port so that the captain can ready *Ajax*. He'll know in the morning if the weather is good enough to sail.' Upon his arrival in the north, Brutus had immediately sent back his treasured liburnian to lie at his lover's disposal. Powered by one hundred slaves working a single bank of oars, the short, low-slung ship was the fastest type of vessel the Romans could build. *Ajax* had been lying idle at the dock in Pompeii and Fabiola had not foreseen needing its services until the following spring. Now, things had changed.

Docilosa bowed and withdrew, leaving her mistress to brood.

Visiting the temple would also afford Fabiola another opportunity to ask Jupiter who had raped their mother. Velvinna had only mentioned it in passing, but for obvious reasons, she had not forgotten. Discovering her father's identity was Fabiola's driving purpose in life. And once she knew, revenge would be hers.

At any price.

Taking charge of the rundown *latifundium* when Brutus left had greatly intimidated Fabiola. But it provided her with satisfaction too. Being mistress of the large estate surrounding the villa was tangible proof of her revenge on Gemellus, who had originally owned it. And so she had thrown herself into the job from the start. An initial tour of the house proved that, as in his residence in Rome, Gemellus' tastes were crude and garish. It had given her great pleasure to have every single opulent bedroom, banqueting hall and office redecorated. The merchant's many statues of Priapus had been smashed, their massive erect members reminding Fabiola too much of the suffering that she had witnessed Gemellus inflict on her mother. The thick layer of dust covering the mosaic floors was swept away; the fountains unclogged and cleared of dead leaves. Even the neglected plants in the courtyards had been replaced. Best of all, the walls of the heated bathing area had been repainted with bright images of the gods, mythological sea creatures and fish. One of Fabiola's most powerful memories of her first day in the Lupanar was seeing such pictures in its baths. She had determined to have the same luxuriant surroundings herself one day. Now it was a reality.

Yet it was hard not to feel guilty, she thought later that day. While she lacked for nothing, Romulus was probably dead. Tears pricked the corners of Fabiola's eyes. While in the brothel, she had left no stone unturned in her efforts to find him. Incredibly, after more than a year, she had discovered that her twin was still alive. In the savagery of the gladiatorial arena, Jupiter had protected him. The further revelation that Romulus had enrolled in Crassus' legions could not dampen Fabiola's spirits, but then disaster struck. A few months before, the devastating news of Carrhae had reached Rome. At one stroke, Fabiola lost virtually all hope. To survive one horror only to end up in a doomed army seemed cruel beyond belief. Eager to help, Brutus had done his best to find out more, but the news was all bad. The defeat was one of the worst ever suffered by the Republic, with huge numbers of men lost. Certainly Romulus was not among the remnants of the legion that had escaped with the legate Cassius Longinus. Plenty of cash had been spread amongst the veterans of the Eighth, to no avail. Fabiola sighed. Her twin's sun-bleached bones were probably still littering the sand where he had fallen. Either that or he was gone to the ends of the earth – to some god-forsaken place called Margiana, where the Parthians had sent their ten thousand prisoners.

No one had ever returned from there.

Rare tears rolled down Fabiola's cheeks. While the slightest chance remained of seeing Romulus again, she would not despair totally, but now stubbornness was taking over from faith. Jupiter *Optimus Maximus*, hear me, she thought miserably. Let my brother still be alive – somehow. Determined not to lose control of her emotions, Fabiola dried her eyes and went in search of Corbulo, the aged *vilicus*, or steward, of her *latifundium*. As usual, she found him busy supervising the workers. Never having lived in the countryside, Fabiola knew little about it, or agriculture, so she spent most days in Corbulo's company. The news from Gaul would not change that. The *latifundium* was her responsibility now.

Fabiola knew from Corbulo that the days of citizen farmers working their own fields were disappearing fast, as cheap grain from Sicily and Egypt put them out of business. For more than a generation, farming had been confined to those rich enough to buy up land and work it with slaves. Fortunately for such people, the Republic's war-like tendencies had provided no end of unfortunate souls from all corners of the world to generate them wealth. Gemellus' former estate was no different.

Recently freed, Fabiola hated slavery. At first, being the owner of several hundred people – men, women and children – troubled her. Practically, though, she could do nothing. Freeing the Greeks, Libyans, Gauls and Numidians would achieve little other than bankrupting her new property. She resolved instead to consolidate her position as Brutus' lover, cultivate noble friends if possible and try to discover her father's identity. Perhaps in the future, with help from Romulus, she would be able to do more. Fabiola remembered how her twin brother had idolised Spartacus, the Thracian gladiator whose slave rebellion had shaken Rome to its core only a generation before.

That thought brought a smile to Fabiola's face as she reached the large yard behind the villa. Here, the slaves' miserable, damp living quarters were a stark comparison to the solidly built storage areas. Something would have to be done about their situation, she decided. There were also stables, a two-storey mill and numerous stone sheds. These last were built on brick stilts to allow continuous airflow underneath and to prevent rodent access. Some were filled to the ceiling with harvested grain and oats, while others contained the estate's rich variety of produce. Resin-sealed jars of olive oil stood in well-balanced stacks. There were tubs of *garum*, a popular and strongly flavoured fish paste, sitting beside barrels of salted mullet and clay vessels full of olives. Ready to be used over the winter, apples, quinces and pears were packed neatly in rows on beds of straw. Muddy bulbs of garlic were arranged in small pyramids. Dried hams hung from the rafters beside bunches of carrots, chicory and herbs: sage, fennel, mint and thyme.

Wine, one of the premium products, was prepared and stored in special cellars in yet another building. Firstly fermented in *dolia*, huge pitch-lined jars that were partially buried in the ground, the juice from the crushed grapes was then sealed in and left to age. Only the best vintages were decanted to amphorae and moved to the main house, where they were laid in a special depository in the roof space over one of the main hearths.

Fabiola was fond of checking each of the stores herself, still amazed that the food belonged to her. As a child, hunger had ruled her life. Now, she had enough to eat for a lifetime. The irony was not lost on her and she made sure that her slaves' diet was adequate. Most landowners barely gave their slaves enough to live on, let alone survive beyond early middle age. She might not be setting them free, yet Fabiola was determined to be a humane mistress. The use of force might occasionally be necessary to ensure obedience, but not often.

The main labour for the year – sowing, tending and harvesting crops – was almost over. Today though, the yard was a hive of activity. Corbulo was stalking up and down, shouting orders. Fabiola saw men re-forging broken ploughs and repairing worn leather harness for the oxen. Alongside them, women and children emptied carts of the late ripening vegetables such as onions, beet and the famous Pompeian cabbage. Others worked in groups on the wool which had been shorn from the sheep during the summer. Now it was being combed out and washed, before being spun.

Corbulo bowed when he saw her. 'Mistress.'

Fabiola inclined her head gravely, careful to maintain an air of unaccustomed command.

His brown hair shot with grey, the round-faced, stooped figure would scarcely attract a second glance. His clothes were nondescript. Only his long-handled whip and the lucky silver amulet dangling from a thong round his neck showed he was no mere agricultural slave. Seized as a child on the North African coast, Corbulo had lived his life since on the *latifundium*.

Having a youthful woman as his owner seemed to trouble the old *vilicus* little. Brutus had made it perfectly clear that in his absence, Fabiola was the mistress of the household. Corbulo was delighted just to have someone to tell him what to do to stop the estate falling into rack and ruin, as it had been for years.

'What are you doing?'

'Supervising this lot, Mistress,' said Corbulo, indicating the nearby slaves. 'Always plenty of routine jobs to keep them busy.'

Fabiola was intrigued by daily life on the *latifundium*. She could not imagine her former master feeling the same way. 'Did Gemellus have any real interest in this place?'

'When he first bought it, yes,' Corbulo answered. 'Used to come down here every few months.'

Fabiola concealed her surprise.

'He brought in the new olive trees from Greece and had the fish pools constructed,' the *vilicus* revealed. 'Even picked which hillsides to grow the vines on.'

Fabiola disliked the thought of her former master having a creative side. He had only ever shown brutality at the house in Rome where she and Romulus had grown up. 'What happened then?' she asked.

There was a shrug. 'His businesses started to do badly. It started with goods from Egypt. I can still remember hearing the news.' Corbulo's lined face grew anguished. 'Twelve ships sank on the way here from Egypt. Can you believe that, Mistress?'

Fabiola sighed expressively, showing her apparent empathy. In reality she was trying to understand how a man such as Corbulo could care if his master's fortunes took a turn for the worse. She had been delighted when Brutus revealed the circumstances that had led to Gemellus' sale of the *latifundium*. Yet it was inevitable for slaves to identify with their owners in some way, she supposed. Fabiola could recall how proud Romulus had been about safely bringing back a note from Crassus' to Gemellus' house, dodging the moneylenders' men who were always lounging opposite the front door. Yet her twin had hated Gemellus as much as she did. Even those with no freedom had some pride in their lives. So she should not judge Corbulo on that alone. Although he had worked for Gemellus for over twenty years, the *vilicus* had thus far proved loyal, reliable and hardworking.

Almost on cue, Corbulo barked at a male slave who was sharpening a scythe with slow, indifferent strokes. 'Put a proper edge on that, fool!' He tapped the whip hanging from his belt. 'Or you'll feel this across your back.'

Hastily the slave bent over the curved iron blade, running an oilstone back and forth along its entire length.

Fabiola smiled approvingly. While not a brutal man, Corbulo wasn't scared of using force either. It was a good sign that the threat was enough. 'I thought his fortune was huge,' she said, probing for more information.

'It was.' Corbulo sighed. 'But the gods turned their faces away. Soon, everything the master did turned to dust. He began to borrow money, with no means of repaying it.'

She could remember the heavies waiting outside Gemellus' *domus* day and night and the rumours in the kitchen where the slaves gathered to gossip. 'Brutus mentioned a venture with animals for the arena being the final straw.'

Corbulo nodded reluctantly. 'Yes, Mistress. It should have made Gemellus a king's ransom. He had a third share in a *bestiarius'* expedition to capture wild beasts in southern Egypt.'

Fabiola felt a pang of nostalgia: her brother had often pretended to be a *bestiarius*. Grief quickly dissolved her happiness. Instead, Romulus had become a gladiator. Yet no emotion showed on her face. The Lupanar had endowed her with the ability to conceal her feelings from everyone, even Brutus.

Suddenly an old memory surfaced. Not long before they were sold, she and Romulus had overheard Gemellus and his bookkeeper having a conversation. It had concerned the capture of animals for the circus, a venture with the potential for huge profit. The twins had been shocked that the merchant could not afford the initial outlay. As poor household slaves, his wealth always seemed immeasurable. 'That should have cleared his debts,' she said calmly.

'Except the vessels sank,' Corbulo announced. 'Again.'

'All of them?'

'Every last one,' replied the *vilicus* grimly. 'A freak storm.'

Fabiola gasped. 'Bad luck indeed.'

'It was more than that. The soothsayers said Neptune himself was angry.' Corbulo swore violently, then his face coloured as he remembered whom he was speaking to. 'Sorry, Mistress,' he muttered.

Fabiola abruptly decided to show her authority in front of the slaves. It was something she had seen Brutus do on a regular basis, ensuring that he was feared as well as respected. 'Remember who I am!' she snapped.

Corbulo bowed his neck and waited to be punished. Perhaps his new young mistress was no different to Gemellus.

In fact Fabiola had heard far worse in the Lupanar, but Corbulo had no knowledge of that. She was still learning to give orders, so his response gave her confidence. 'Continue,' Fabiola said in a more gentle tone.

The *vilicus* bobbed his head in gratitude. 'Gemellus was never one for prophecies, but there was one he mentioned just before those ships were lost.'

Her lip curled. 'Haruspices tell nothing but lies.' Hoping for a sign of release from their awful existence, many girls in the brothel spent large amounts of their meagre savings on readings from soothsayers. Fabiola had seen precious few predictions borne out. Those that had come true had been of minor significance, strengthening her determination to rely on no one but herself. And on the god Jupiter, who had finally answered her prayer for freedom.

'Indeed, Mistress,' Corbulo agreed. 'Gemellus said the same himself. But this one was not made by one of the usual shysters hanging around the great temple. It came from a stranger with a *gladius*, who only agreed to do a reading on sufferance.' There was a deliberate pause. 'And virtually all of it came true.'

Her curiosity was aroused. Soothsayers did not carry weapons. 'Explain,' she ordered.

'He predicted that Crassus would leave Rome and never return.'

Fabiola's eyes widened. It had been common knowledge that the third member of the triumvirate wanted military success to win public approval. Crassus' choice of the governorship of Syria had been little more than an opportunity to invade Parthia. Yet few could have predicted that his trip abroad would be his last – except a genuine soothsayer. Someone who therefore might have knowledge of Romulus. 'What else did he say?' she hissed.

The *vilicus* swallowed. 'That a storm at sea would sink the ships, drowning the animals.'

'Is that all?'

Corbulo's eyes flickered from side to side. 'There was one other thing,' he admitted nervously. 'Gemellus only mentioned it once, the last time I saw him.'

Fabiola pounced like a hawk on its prey. 'What was it?'

'The haruspex told him that one day a man would knock on his door.'

She tensed. *Romulus?*

'He seemed haunted by the thought,' Corbulo finished.

'Not a gladiator?'

'No, Mistress.'

Her spirits plunged.

'A soldier.'

And rose again from the depths.

Confused by her interest, Corbulo glanced at her for approval.

The *vilicus* got a perfunctory smile instead. Fabiola would give away nothing.

Not a gladiator, she thought triumphantly. A soldier, which is what her brother had become after fleeing Rome. Gemellus knew how much Romulus hated him: the prospect of seeing him again one day would have been terrifying. Now the journey to the temple of Jupiter had two important purposes. If she could find this mysterious soothsayer, she might be able to discover if Romulus was alive. It was a wild hope, but Fabiola had learned never to give up.

Dogged faith, and the desire for revenge, was what had kept her alive.

A deep baying sound suddenly rose from beyond the courtyard walls. It was a noise that Fabiola had heard occasionally since arriving in Pompeii, but always at a distance. As it grew louder, she could see fear growing in her slaves' faces. 'What's that?'

'Dogs. And *fugitivarii*, Mistress.' Seeing her blank response, Corbulo explained. 'Bounty hunters. They'll be after a runaway.'

Fabiola's pulse increased, but she did not panic. I am free, she thought firmly. Nobody is pursuing me.

Searching for the sound's source, they walked a little way out into the large, open fields which surrounded the villa. Stone walls, bare trees and low hedges separated each from its neighbour. This was flat, fertile land, most of it fallow at this time of year. Two weeks earlier, the soil had been tilled, leaving it to breathe before it was planted with seeds in the spring. Only the winter wheat remained, small green shoots poking a hand span from the earth.

Normally, Fabiola liked to stand and take it all in. At this time of year the landscape was stark, but she loved the noisy jackdaws flying to their nesting spots, the crisp air, the absence of people. Rome's streets were always thronged; inside the busy Lupanar had been little different. The *latifundium* had come to mean seclusion from the brutal realities of the world.

Until this.

Corbulo spotted the movement first. 'There!' He pointed.

Between the gaps in a hedge some two hundred paces away, Fabiola spotted a running figure. Corbulo had been correct. It was a young man, wearing little more than rags. A slave. Clearly exhausted, with his lower body covered in a thick layer of mud, his face was a picture of desperation.

'He probably tried to give them the slip by hiding in the river,' announced the *vilicus*.

Fabiola had taken pleasant walks along the waterway that separated her property from the estate belonging to her nearest neighbour. It would never seem the same again.

Corbulo grimaced. 'It never works. The *fugitivarii*

always check under the banks with long poles. If that doesn't work, the dogs will catch their scent.'

Fabiola could not take her eyes off the fugitive, who was casting terrified glances over his shoulder as he ran. 'Why is he being hunted?' she asked dully, knowing the answer.

'Because he ran away,' Corbulo replied. 'And a slave is his master's property.'

Fabiola was intimately acquainted with this cruel reality. It was the same reason that had allowed Gemellus to repeatedly rape her mother. To sell her and Romulus. To execute Juba, the giant Nubian who had trained her brother to use a sword. Owners had the ultimate power over their slaves: that of life and death. Starkly reinforcing this, in the Roman legal system, the pride of the Republic, there was no retribution for the torture or killing of a slave.

A pack of large dogs burst from the cover of the nearest grove, their noses alternately sniffing the ground and the air for their quarry's scent.

Fabiola heard the young man wail with terror. It was an awful sound.

She and Corbulo watched in silence.

A group of heavily armed men emerged from the trees, urging the hounds on with shouts and whistles. Cheers went up as they caught sight of the slave, whose energy looked almost spent.

'Where's he from?'

The *vilicus* shrugged. 'Who knows? The fool could have been running for days,' he said. 'He's young and strong. I've known the chase take more than a week.' Corbulo looked almost sympathetic. 'But those bastards never give up, and a man can't run for ever on an empty belly.'

Fabiola sighed. Nobody would give food or help to a fugitive. Why would they? Rome was a state based on foundations of war and slavery. Its citizens had no reason to aid those who had fled captivity. Brutal punishments, terrible living conditions and a poor diet concerned them not at all. Of course, not every slave was treated this badly, but they were still the beating pulse of the Republic, the labour which built its magnificent buildings, toiled in its workshops and grew its foodstuffs. Rome needed its slaves. There was little that other slaves could do either, Fabiola thought bitterly. The punishment for helping an escapee was death. Who wanted to die by crucifixion?

The drama was about to reach its climax. Having staggered to within fifty paces of them, the young man fell to his knees in the damp earth. He raised his arms in silent supplication and Fabiola had to close her eyes. Coming between a runaway and the men legally sent to catch him would not be a good idea. Without risking a lawsuit from the slave's owner, there was nothing she could do anyway.

Then the pack reached him.

Screams filled the air as the trained dogs began to savage the fugitive like a child's doll. Fabiola watched in horror. She thanked the gods a few moments later when the lead huntsman whipped them off. Gradually the rest of the *fugitivarii* arrived, more than a dozen tough-looking types clad in dull colours and armed with bows, spears and swords. From under their wool cloaks, the dull glimmer of mail could be made out. They gathered around, laughing at the deep bite wounds on the slave's arms and legs. This was part of their sport.

Fabiola held herself back. What could she do?

Engrossed with their capture, the *fugitivarii* seemed oblivious to their audience. Their brindle dogs had flopped down close by, red tongues hanging from wide, powerful jaws. Similar animals roamed around Fabiola's villa at night, used as protection against bandits and criminals. These heavily muscled creatures looked even more vicious.

Encircled now, the slave had rolled into a foetal position. He was moaning softly and only crying out when struck by his captors. Then something changed. The nearest thug finally noticed Fabiola and Corbulo. Seeing her rich clothing and jewellery, he did not speak, but muttered a few words to the stocky man in charge. Rather than respond, though, the figure delivered a huge kick to the slave's chest.

A muffled scream reached them.

Fabiola stared in horror. The blow had been enough to break ribs. 'Leave him alone,' she shouted. 'He's badly injured!'

Beside her, Corbulo coughed uneasily.

An opening appeared in the circle, hard, unforgiving faces turning towards the stunning woman and her *vilicus*. As they took in her beauty, leers distorted their features and lewd suggestions were made, albeit in whispers. The rich were still people to be respected.

Fabiola ignored the comments; Corbulo glared.

Bizarrely, the slave was then allowed to get to his feet. One of the *fugitivarii* drew his sword and poked him with its tip. Away from them, and towards Fabiola. Confused, the young slave did not move. Another sharp prod followed, prompting a sob. But he took the hint, and stumbled towards the villa. Laughs of derision met his efforts, and a number of the thugs threw clods of earth at him. His pace increased.

'What are they doing?' asked Fabiola in dread.

'They're playing with him. And us. Time to go inside, Mistress,' Corbulo muttered, his face a pale shade of grey. 'Before things get out of hand.'

Fabiola's feet were rooted to the spot.

The slave came closer. As well as the dog bites that covered his body, his torso and arms were a red ruin. Through an old, flittered tunic, oozing wounds were visible, crisscrossing his skin front and back in an ugly latticework. The marks of a whip, they were evidence of a brutal master. Was this why he had fled? The fugitive was young, Fabiola guessed, no more than fifteen. A boy. Sweat and tears had streaked the dirt on his face, which was pinched and hungry. And full of terror.

'Mistress!' Corbulo's voice was insistent. 'It's not safe.'

Fabiola could not take her eyes off the runaway, who did not dare to look at her.

In a trance, he shuffled past them, towards the courtyard. Like a mouse injured by a cat, he would not go far.

At last the *fugitivarii* began to move, and Fabiola's stomach twisted. She glanced around, but none of her bodyguards were in sight. Until now, there had rarely been a need for their presence and they spent much of their time around the fire in the kitchen, telling dirty jokes. Even the slaves who were in the yard had not appeared.

Corbulo's fear had grown so great that he actually took hold of her sleeve.

An urgent desire to help gripped Fabiola, and she turned to face the approaching men. Although fearful too, she was not about to scurry back inside her property to avoid these lowlifes.

Silently, malevolently, they drew closer.

'Who's in charge here?' Fabiola cried, holding her hands together to stop them trembling.

'That'd be me, lady. Scaevola, chief *fugitivarius*,' drawled the leader with an insolent half-bow. A squat, powerful figure with short brown hair and deep-set eyes, he wore a legionary's chain mail shirt that covered him from neck to mid-thigh. A *gladius* in an ornate sheath and a dagger hung from his belt. Thick silver wrist bands adorned his wrists, announcing his status. Hunting escaped slaves was clearly profitable work. 'Can I be of assistance?'

The offer came across as it was meant. Rude. Full of innuendo. It was met with sniggers of delight from the others.

Acutely aware of how powerless she was, Fabiola drew herself up to her full height. 'Explain what you are doing on my land.'

'Your land?' His eyes narrowed. 'Where's Gemellus then? You his latest piece of ass?'

This time his men laughed out loud.

Fabiola gave him an icy stare. 'That fat degenerate no longer owns this estate. I am the mistress now, and you will answer me!'

Scaevola looked surprised. 'I hadn't heard,' he admitted. 'We've been in the north for months. The pickings are good up there. Plenty of tribal scum fleeing Gaul.'

'What a pity you returned.'

'We just follow the work,' replied the *fugitivarius*. 'Been chasing this specimen for three days, isn't that right, boys? But no one escapes old Scaevola and his crew!'

'Does it amuse you to torture the slaves you catch?' asked Fabiola acidly.

Scaevola smiled, revealing sharp teeth. 'Keeps the lads here happy,' he answered. 'And me.'

His men chortled.

Fabiola gave him a withering look.

'The dirt bag would have more reason to scream if it wasn't so damn cold,' Scaevola confided amiably. 'I need a good fire to heat my iron! But that can be done later, back at the camp.'

Now Fabiola was filled with rage. She knew exactly what Scaevola was talking about. One of the commonest punishments was to brand escapees on the forehead with the letter 'F', for *fugitivus*. It was a savage warning to other slaves. If another attempt was made, crucifixion was likely. It explained why most slaves accepted their lot. Not me, Fabiola thought fiercely. Not Romulus.

'Be gone!' She pointed back the way they had come. 'Now!'

'Who's going to make me, lady?' Scaevola sneered, jerking his head at Corbulo. 'This old fool?'

At once his men laid hands on their weapons.

The *vilicus* went pale. 'Mistress!' he hissed. 'We must return to the villa!'

Fabiola took a deep breath, calming herself. Her decision to confront Scaevola had been made, and other than a humiliating climb-down, she had little choice other than to continue. 'I am the lover of Decimus Brutus,' she announced in a loud, clear voice. 'Do you know who that is, you sewer rat?'

Scaevola's face became a cold, calculating mask.

'One of Julius Caesar's most important men,' she continued proudly, rubbing it in. 'A senior army officer.' Fabiola glared at the *fugitivarii*, daring any to meet her stony gaze. None would, except Scaevola. 'If anything happens to me, he would go to Hades to find the scum responsible.'

For a moment, Fabiola's words seemed to have worked. She turned to go.

'The whore of one of Caesar's lapdogs, eh?' Scaevola drawled.

Fabiola's cheeks burned, but she had no chance to respond.

'There are people in Rome who pay good money to see Caesar's supporters . . .' Scaevola smiled, making his words more chilling, '. . . removed from the equation.'

His men's interest picked up instantly.

Fabiola's heart lurched. There had been rumours in Pompeii recently about the brutal murders of a number of Caesar's less wealthy allies. Men who, previously, had had no need for many bodyguards. She had just three.

'Expecting Brutus soon?'

Fabiola had no answer. The first fingers of panic clutched her belly.

'Not to worry.' Scaevola leered at her. 'You'll do. Boys?'

As one, the *fugitivarii* moved forward.

Horrified, Fabiola looked at Corbulo. To his credit, the *vilicus* was not backing away. Gripping his whip in his right fist, he moved to stand protectively in front of her.

Scaevola began to laugh, a deep, unpleasant sound. 'Kill the stupid old bastard,' he ordered. 'But I want the bitch alive and unharmed. She's mine.'

Jupiter, Greatest and Best, thought Fabiola desperately. Once more, I need your help.

Instead, the sound of swords being drawn from their sheaths filled the air.

Squaring his shoulders, Corbulo moved a step forward.

Fabiola's heart filled with pride at his brave, useless action. Then she looked at the thugs and her gorge rose. They were both about to die. No doubt she would be raped first. And she did not even have a weapon to defend herself with.

Just a few steps from Corbulo, the *fugitivarii* stopped and Scaevola's face went purple with rage.

Confused, Fabiola and Corbulo looked at each other. They sensed movement behind them.

Turning her head, Fabiola saw practically every male slave she owned coming towards them at a run. Gripping scythes, hammers, axes, and even planks of wood, there were at least forty of them. Alarmed by the escapee entering the yard, they had spontaneously come to defend their mistress. And yet not one knew how to fight like the *fugitivarii*. A lump formed in Fabiola's throat at the risks these unfortunates would take for her.

Reaching her, the slaves fanned out in a long line.

The thugs looked unhappy. Armed or not, they were vastly outnumbered. And after Spartacus' rebellion twenty years before, everyone knew that slaves could fight.

Fabiola turned to face Scaevola. 'Get off my *latifundium*,' she ordered. 'Now.'

'I'm not leaving without the fugitive,' Scaevola growled. 'Fetch him.'

His head bowed, Corbulo obediently moved a step towards the yard.

'Stop!'

The *vilicus* jerked upright at Fabiola's shouted command.

'You're not having the poor creature,' she said, allowing her fury to take complete hold. 'He stays here.'

Corbulo's face was a picture of shock.

Scaevola's eyebrows shot up. 'What did you say?' he demanded.

'You heard,' snapped Fabiola.

'The son of a whore belongs to a merchant called Sextus Roscius, not you!' the *fugitivarius* roared. 'This is totally illegal.'

'So is physically assaulting a citizen. But that did not trouble you,' responded Fabiola sharply. 'Ask Roscius how much he wants for the boy. I'll have the money sent the very next day.'

Obviously not used to being thwarted or to losing face, Scaevola's fists bunched with rage.

They glared at each other for a heart-stopping moment.

'This is not over,' the *fugitivarius* muttered from between clenched teeth. 'No one, especially a jumped-up little bitch like you, crosses Scaevola without payback. You hear me?'

Fabiola lifted her chin. She did not answer.

'I hope you and your lover have strong locks on your doors,' he warned. From nowhere, a knife appeared in his right hand. 'And plenty of guards. You'll need both.'

His companions laughed unpleasantly, and Fabiola forced herself not to shiver.

Fortified by his mistress's courage, Corbulo made a gesture. The slaves moved forward, their weapons raised.

Scaevola eyed them all with scorn. 'We'll be back,' he said. Gathering his men, he led them back across the muddy field. The dogs trotted at their heels.

The *vilicus* let out a long, slow breath.

Fabiola stood stiff-backed, watching until the *fugitivarii* were out of sight. Inside, she was panicking. What have I done? I should have let him take the boy. But part of her was glad. Whether her decision had been wise, only time would tell.

'Mistress?'

She turned to regard the *vilicus*.

'Scaevola is a very dangerous man.' Corbulo paused. 'And he's on Pompey's payroll.'

Fabiola flashed him a grateful smile, and the old *vilicus* fell wholly under her spell.

'The mangy dog meant what he said too,' he explained.

'His enemies just disappear. These men . . .' He indicated the slaves around them. 'Next time, they won't be enough.'

'I know,' replied Fabiola, wishing that Brutus were by her side.

She had made a real enemy. Journeying to Rome had become an urgent priority.

ALSO BY BEN KANE

The Road to Rome

A Forgotten Legion Chronicle

A voyage of terror and heartache, violence and betrayal.

Betrayal
They have fought for Rome in the Forgotten Legion and been
press-ganged into Caesar's legions in Alexandria, but Romulus,
the ex-gladiator, and Tarquinius, the Etruscan soothsayer, are also
runaway slaves – for which the punishment is crucifixion. Who can
they trust not to betray them on the bloody field of battle?

Conspiracy
Meanwhile in Rome, Romulus's twin sister, Fabiola, faces great
danger. Beloved mistress of Brutus, she is being wooed by his deadly
enemy, Marcus Antonius – and drawn into the conspiracy to murder
Caesar, the man she believes is her hated father.

Murder
As events move remorselessly towards the fateful Ides of March, a
final day of reckoning awaits all three of Ben Kane's great protagonists
on the lawless streets of Rome.

arrow books

THE POWER OF READING